D1192274

Consider Her Ways

Consider Her Ways

Frederick Philip Grove

Introduction by Douglas Spettigue
General Editor: Malcolm Ross

Go to the ant, thou sluggard;
consider her ways, and be wise.

PROVERBS VI, v.6

McClelland and Stewart Limited
New Canadian Library No. 132

CONTENTS

Editor's Introduction

It is necessary to label this as the Editor's Introduction because the text itself has an Introduction—which is also an editor's introduction—but it is a fictional one, ostensibly written by the editor Fred Philgrove, a transparent pseudonym for the author, Frederick Philip Grove. It pretends to introduce the story which follows as though that story had been written—"scented" he would say—by the narrator-ant, Wawa-quee, who passed it on to the author to publish, because of his genuine interest in ants. Though the ploy is fictional, the interest in ants is not. But the author goes far beyond an entomological interest, in this, his last book.

Consider Her Ways was first published in 1947, the year before its author's death, thirty-five years after his appearance in Manitoba in 1912, and twenty-six years after he became a Canadian citizen under the name of Frederick Philip Grove. On grounds of residence and commitment, this is a Canadian book. Perhaps it is also European by virtue of its author's background. Its setting makes it both South and North American. Its subject, Man in Nature, is universal.

Grove is sometimes misleading or contradictory about the genesis of the book, which probably was drafted in the early 1920's and revised at intervals up to 1944. In his autobiography, *In Search of Myself* (1946), he claims to have begun the book as early as 1892, though in fact he was a schoolboy in Hamburg, Germany, at that time. The autobiography also, with more probable accuracy, has him making "abundant notes" for the "Ant-Book" in 1920. In his later letters Grove reports, on a number of occasions, that he is working on his "Ant Book", and these references begin as early as 1927 and continue at least until August 1939. On 25th March 1940 he writes, in a letter to Lorne Pierce:

> Under separate cover I am sending you a Ms. in 4 parts, entitled 'Go to the Ant.'
> This is the Ant-Book so often mentioned on which I have been at work since the fall or early winter of 1919. It has had

even more rewritings than *A Search for America* or the 'Life'; in fact, I believe it is the most laboriously-produced book of mine, the plan of which reaches back to 1892 or 1893.

I had been in hopes of rewriting it once more; but I find that I cannot do anything more with it. Hitler and Mussolini are sufficiently anticipated anyway. And perhaps there is as much laughter in it as I shall ever evoke.

Despite Grove's assertions of early composition, we may say with some confidence that the "Ant Book" was first drafted if not in 1920 then between 1920 and 1924 in the aftermath to the tremendous burst of creative energy that followed the early announcement by McClelland & Stewart that they were prepared to publish his "Seven Drives Over Prairie Trails" at first sight. Grove had written that series of familiar essays during the autumn of 1919, while his wife was away at Normal School in Winnipeg. He read the successive chapters of it to her on her occasional weekends home. It was ready to mail to a publisher by Christmas, and was accepted at once by McClelland and Stewart for publication in the fall of 1920. Excited by this first sign of literary success since he had arrived in Canada, Grove wrote at a feverish pace throughout the spring and summer of that year. In those few months he seems to have begun the first, mammoth draft of *A Search for America*, and may have drafted part of "The White Range Line House" as well as some of the sketches of *The Turn of The Year* before his hopes and health were shattered by word from M & S that they could not after all publish his book; he was free to offer it elsewhere. Although, two years later, McClelland & Stewart did publish *Over Prairie Trails*, Grove could not foresee that eventuality in the fall of 1920, and his reaction was bitter:

In this mood, one of despair, just to be doing something, I sat down to write at last one of of the two books which I had now been planning for thirty years. From the beginning I knew I was spoiling it; just as later I was to spoil *The Master of the Mill*, because a publisher took it upon himself to advance me a considerable part of the possible royalties. In order to write the *Ant Book* in a way which would satisfy me, I had to write it out of an exuberance of triumph, sitting, as it were, on top of the world. As it was, it became harsh and bitter; it became a grumbling protest against the insanity of human institutions; it became a preachment. What it should have been was a laughing comment on all life, which, from moment to moment is always in error; while, through the ages, it slowly creeps up, up, up. It was an axiom with me that human evolution has not yet freed itself from its animal trammels. So far, the book has withstood all endeavour to remedy its fundamental defect; for, as I have said, I was never again to free myself of economic bondage; and with me, too, as someone has said of somebody else, the kind of success I wanted would have acted as a tonic, whereas failure acted as a specific poison.

Though he set it aside during the rest of the decade in which the Marsh and Prairie novels were written, Grove still thought enough of the manuscript to include it with others that he and his brother-in-law stored in a lard tin in a granary in the late 1920's. Nearly thirty-five years later they were found and added to the Grove Collection at the University of Manitoba.

That first draft incorporates the main argument of the book essentially as it was to be published, but has little of the narrative element. In Professor Margaret Stobie's words, "the fiction and the ants soon disappear, except for some awkward footnotes, in a voluminous preachment of over two hundred typed, single-spaced pages." When Grove sent it to Arthur Phelps, who with Watson Kirkconnell constituted at that time the English Department of Wesley College in Winnipeg, Phelps "knocked the conceit out" of him by saying, "A pretty good sermon, that!" —but not publishable as fiction. Grove seems to have taken the lesson to heart; he quotes it in a letter to Kirkconnell in 1927, and that may have been about the time the manuscript was stored away. But when, in 1933, after all the western writings that seemed publishable had appeared, he returned to the Ant Book, he kept the earlier introduction but rewrote the body of the book in the form of the present narrative. It is rather curious that, writing the manuscript of his autobiography in 1938-9, Grove should remember the "preachment" and not the lively characterization, the tensions, the adventure and the humour that raised *Consider Her Ways* above the level of polemics and made it a warmly human book in spite of its load of learning and of commentary. (Of course for modern readers, attuned to scientific and informative writing, that learning is an added value.)

It is true that bitterness is an element in Wawa-quee's story, as there is world-weariness and a certain disillusionment in her personality and position, which, when he is writing his autobiography and casting himself in the role of defeated tragic hero, Grove also sees as tragic. Like him, Wawa-quee is the leader abandoned by all her followers, aged and scarred but bearing the burden of responsibility for mankind to the end. Perhaps this is why those personal elements Dr. Stobie refers to seem to be part of the last quarrels between Wawa-quee and her long-suffering supporter, Bissa-tee.

But Grove may have underrated both his protagonist and his art, because of the mood in which he wrote his autobiography. Both emerge as surprisingly positive, even buoyant, in this last published work. Granted all the suffering, granted age and the weariness of a life overfraught with effort and worry, humiliation and disillusionment, nevertheless Wawa-quee-Grove wins through, and not only wins in the sense of making good her return to her home with the burden of new knowledge she had committed herself to find and to record, but even more in the sense that she upholds against all odds the supremacy of knowledge and imaginative intellect that struggles always towards the light.

Three different influences seem to be implicit in this fiction. The first is scientific. Grove's Introduction identifies a venerable line of scientific sources for the study of myrmecology, beginning with Pliny in the first century A.D. and progressing to Bates, Belt and Wheeler in modern times. Dr. Stobie has drawn attention to the importance of Bates and Belt, both writers on South American ants, as recent sources on whom Grove draws. He makes specific acknowledgement of their assistance. My *Frederick Philip Grove* (1969) stresses the debt to Wheeler, which Grove also acknowledges. Among other references, he quotes Wheeler's definition of instinct and even introduces him transparently as "the Wheeler", the indefatigable entomologist who travels about by bicycle to study ants, and makes himself a nuisance and a menace to the Atta expedition in Grove's narrative. W. M. Wheeler's *Ants: Their Structure, Development and Behavior*, first published in 1910, provided the model for Grove's draft, initially entitled "Man: His Habits, Social Organization and Outlook." It is Grove's dependence on Wheeler that positively identifies the drafting of his book as having taken place after 1913, as it was the 1913 edition of Wheeler that Grove owned and used.

These authors—Wheeler, Bates, Belt and others—provided Grove with his extensive information about the details of ant life. From *Over Prairie Trails* onwards, Grove's writings demonstrate his attraction to scientific fact. He is not content simply to observe natural phenomena, such as fog; in that book he records his experiments with it—what happens if you move a mass in fog? Does fog touch objects or is there a vapour gap between them? He is not content to observe a wolf, he must make friends with it, dropping bits of food as it comes to anticipate his weekly appearances. Dr. Stobie records an incident reported by one of Grove's former pupils from Haskett:

> The boys had found a nest of snakes . . . and they started to kill them. And before I knew what's happening, Mr. Grove stands right in the middle of that nest and he says, "Before you kill another snake, you kill me!" . . . And those boys—they didn't kill another snake.

Perhaps Dr. Stobie is right, that Grove's nature-leanings were theoretical, based on Rousseauistic theories of education and his reading of Thoreau and Burroughs. Perhaps there was an element of guilt and nostalgia in them, as is the case with so many people today whose cultural roots are rural but whose upbringing, like Grove's, has been urban. Whatever the cause, though, there is no denying the strength of Grove's commitment to the outdoors. From the time he appeared in Canada in 1912 Grove never again lived in a city, but for one dreary year in Ottawa.

The second influence is sociological, or better, philosophical: Grove's view of man not only in North America but in the world. And here we should be aware of the pattern provided by an overview of Grove's fiction, and particularly of his protagonists. His first two novels, published in Germany early in the century, depicted young women, either making their way alone in the world or contesting with their parents for the right to self-realization. The battle of the generations begins early in Grove's writings, the young people being frustrated by their parents and defeated by poverty or narrow circumstances, the parents in their turn inevitably defeated by time and life and the internal conflicts that in Grove's view make every psyche a battle-ground.

In his Canadian fiction Grove represents substantially the same struggles, though the emphasis shifts more towards the defeat of older protagonists. His *Settlers of the Marsh* shows the initial successes of a young pioneer turning to ashes, though he attains a kind of wisdom in middle age. *Fruits of the Earth* and *Our Daily Bread* similarly show the rise and fall of the patriarchal fathers, and although *Two Generations* is a "pleasant" book from the point of view of its young protagonists, still their success depends on their father's defeat.

In the course of these books Grove shows the pioneering era in North America succeeded by decades of prosperous farming that in turn are replaced by an industrial age that becomes its own nemesis, destroying the society that fostered it. This process too, in *The Master of the Mill*, he represents in terms of the battle between the generations, but when the scale is as large as modern industrial monopolies, everyone is a loser. In that book Grove speculates on the story of man as an apparently endless cycle of evolution and devolution, a treadmill of the ages from which some undefined triumph of the human intellect might rescue him into the stability of a better life on earth. But not even this slender hope is held by the aged, dying protagonist whose puzzled reminiscences make up the story. He knows only that he has been a helpless participant in an evolutionary process he dimly comes to understand but never could control.

To this extent, *Consider Her Ways* is a more positive book than many of its predecessors. Whereas Grove's earlier protagonists had hoped to exercise their superior wills and been defeated, had hoped to be enlightened masters and had wakened to find themselves slaves gaining at best a disillusioned wisdom, in this last published fiction of Grove's, Wawa-quee's will-power, intellect and leadership enable her at least to complete the quest she was committed to, however real her losses. She is the last of Grove's aged and weary titans, but for her, unlike the others, the losing battle with time, with nature and with one's own kind is compensated for by the contribution to rational understanding of the nature of things.

The structure of *Consider Her Ways* is geographical. The five sections of the book—The Isthmus, The Mountain, The Slope, The Plain, and The Seaboard correspond to the five geographical divisions of the expedition. The journey begins almost immediately—on page 13—and ends with the last sentence of the last section: "Five months later I arrived at home." Apart from the 23-page Introduction by the ostensible editor, the brief Author's Note and the even briefer descriptive Appendix, the whole book consists of the "Narrative of an Expedition from the Tropics into the Northern Regions of the Continent . . . compiled by Wawa-quee, R.S.F.O." The expedition is scientific, its aim to gather enough information "for us to arrange the whole fauna of the globe . . . in the form of a ladder leading up to our own kind." The leaders of the expedition, under the direction of Wawa-quee, are therefore mostly scientists, but what follows is Wawa-quee's "popular" account rather than a scientific report.

The reader who smiles at the pretension—forgetting the first pretence, that it is an ant speaking—that the ant race "stands at the very apex of creation" is reminded of course that this is the usual human conceit: "we" stand at the apex of creation, and Grove humorously suggests that the same assumption would obtain no matter who or what "race" was making the report. Inevitably the emphasis falls on ants and man rather than on other forms, "for we found that, the farther we left our home country behind, the less dominant were ants on earth; and the more distinctly was their place taken by that curious mammal called man."

So this is a "study"—a satire—on the "curious mammal called man," as he would appear if, without prior knowledge, he were studied from an ant's point of view. With a scornful sideglance at scientific posturing, Grove pronounces that whatever the ant could not understand about man, he would ascribe to "instinct," using that term as Grove suggests human scientists do to "explain" activities incomprehensible to our limited and partial vision. There would also be humorous misinterpretations, as in the ants' designation of the removal of clothing as "moulting," with elaborations on the apparent social functions of clothing and the daring hypothesis that "man moults at will."

At times this mock-epic journey becomes almost allegory as the author exercises his ingenuity in making his metaphorical identifications "fit" more and more specifically. The two notable instances are the description of the "repletes" kept by the Myrmecocyst ants (II, vi) and that of the slave-keeping ants, who rushed in myriads to their deaths at the summons of the "perfume of royal favour" defined in human terms as "money;" and "the little Dorymyrmex Pyramicus which builds its tiny nest on the slope of the Pogonomyrmex mound and subsists by waylaying and robbing, in numbers, single members of the host species ... as they return home laden with booty ... " The reader will see a resemblance between these efficient little parasites and the Clarks of *The Master of the Mill*. The elaborate description of the "authors" shows Grove attempting to combine his social purpose with the vast store of myrmecological data his sources provided him with:

> Now authors were held in great esteem in the commonwealth; that is to say, they were ostentatiously honoured and secretly despised as unnecessary and unproductive members of society.
> . . .
>
>   All those who wished to become authors were first of all required to fast for a full year, or for a quarter of their lives, many of them dying during this period of their training. Next they were ... exposed to all sorts of practical jokes, expressions of contempt, and an utter isolation: only critics or minims having access to them. The purpose of this ... was to sweeten their tempers; for no ant that did not have a sweet temper could possibly be successful as an author. . . .

Again we find Grove cynical about the motives, as well as of the public reception, of authors, but not about the importance of their function: "To keep the common inheritance sweet and fresh, and to protect it from any contamination." One notices, appropriately, in this and other sections, echoes of the classics

Grove would have approved of in this sense—Swift and More of course, but Homer and Vergil as well. This is meant to be a quest, in the epic tradition, full of adventure and marvels but also of social and racial significance.

Wawa-quee observes that only "a thread of narrative remains" in the report of the expedition. For the reader, much more than a thread is here, thanks to Grove's success both in particularizing the terrain and the fauna encountered, and in individualizing the ants. Moreover, Wawa-quee underrates the narrative suspense created and maintained by the presence of a traitor among the leaders of the expedition. She is Assa-ree, commander of the army that she plans to use to further her own ambitions. Without her the expedition cannot succeed, but constant vigilance—and a secret weapon—are essential if her meditated treachery is to be thwarted. Here as elsewhere Grove makes no secret of his opinion of the military.

Only two of the leaders remain with Wawa-quee when at last she reaches New York City. They hibernate in the public Library, where Azte-ca becomes a who-dun-it fan and eventually exposes them all to danger by crawling on to readers of mystery stories in order to share their reading. The result is a clean-up, with insecticides, that proves fatal to Azte-ca. Only Bissa-tee and Wawa-quee escape and begin the incredible journey back to Venezuela. Aging, exhausted, discouraged, the two companions find their nerve failing; they begin to blame and secretly to suspect each other. When this last companion dies, Wawa-quee struggles on alone to preserve the record of the scientific discoveries the expedition represents.

Many of Grove's protagonists are depicted late in life when their heroic quests are behind them, their material goals achieved, their success turned to ashes in their mouths. In *Our Daily Bread, Fruits of the Earth, Two Generations* and *The Master of the Mill* the wearied titans see all their achievements undone by their children who turn against them—the battle between the generations is a battle that never ends. *Consider Her Ways* is exceptional in that there is virtually no younger generation to contend with. Like *Over Prairie Trails* it shows the hero battling nature and even the limitations of the species itself and transcending those limitations through the joint power of the intelligence and the will. In *Consider Her Ways* the dangers and obstacles are multiplied many times—hostile ants, storm and flood, drought and bitter cold, destructive machines and natural predators—but not the battle between the sexes and the generations. With Assa-ree's single exception, these thousands are all incomplete females, worker ants. Some of the fun comes about from Grove's playing on the fact of their all being females.

For some readers, perhaps, the sheer quantity of information is a barrier to full enjoyment of the story. But we should remember that this is not a novel but an "anatomy" or encylopedic satire; all the learning, from the details of ant anatomy to the characteristics of cacti, is part both of the function of the form and of the fun. When we call this a satire, we mean that we expect to find its author making fun of human institutions, pet ideas and foibles and pretensions. One favorite target of satirists always has been the pretension to learning and wisdom on the part of fallible man. We recall Swift scoffing at the mad scientists of Laputa, and the conclusion, by the Brobdingnagian king, that man is a race of "little odious vermin." As a young man in Europe, Grove had translated Swift into German.

Here, man's presumption that he is the pinnacle and ultimate end of evolution is one obvious target, for Grove's ants assume the same exalted role for themselves. They have noticed some traces of what might be considered reason in mankind, but closer observation verifies that nothing in human behaviour suggests anything approaching the intelligence of ants. After all, how do we know that we are more intelligent than all other creatures? The answer, as Grove points out, is that we do not know; we base all judgments on our own standards of measurement, assuming that there are no others.

Moreover, Grove has his philosopher-ants conclude that the traces of reason discernible in human behaviour are vestiges rather than prefigurations. At one time, the ants conclude, man stood at a crossroads of social development comparable to that of the ants themselves. But where the ants advanced, man degenerated. This view is based on the study of types of social organization based in turn on economic systems. There are three elementary types, the hunting, the pastoral and the agricultural. The first leads to industrial capitalism and slavery; the second is unstable; the third, the way of the ants, allows the accumulation of food supplies and hence of security and leisure that in turn encourage the cultivation of the intellect rather than of property. Man, taking the way of the accumulation of property and wealth, preys upon his own kind. The worker becomes the slave of the capitalists and, as *The Master of the Mill* shows, the capitalists themselves become the slaves of the system they have created.

For Grove, man is not a creature separable from the rest of nature. He is part of the organic processes that make up what we call evolution. Because it is a process, it can never stand still. Hence no species or race or culture or ideology can claim to be at the top of it—or not for long.

The form of a structure erected on a broad base and sloping to an apex—the pyramid shape—is as old as mountains, or anthills, or as temples or houses. In almost all his writings Grove is house-conscious, building-conscious. His pioneers and prosperous farmers seek to realize some urge within themselves that can only be expressed as a great edifice. When Sam Clark shows his father the first tiers of the great monolith that is to be the almost godlike mill, he exclaims, "There stands your little soul". And so it is in Grove, from the pioneer shack to the automated mill or the alleged "castle" of his fanciful boyhood. But always Grove's ironic glance at human pretension gives the lie to illusion. Fittingly, his last such structure brings his aspiring heroes back to dust, as it were—in an ant hill.

Douglas Spettigue
Queen's University

AUTHOR'S NOTE

Certain human myrmecologists to whom the present book was submitted in manuscript — the editor wishing to make sure of his facts, from the human point of view — suggested that, among ants, the suspicion would arise that definite individuals had served as models for the characters of the story.

As a matter of fact, they have — to the ant. The publication is sponsored by an ant, namely, Wawa-quee, who, for reasons unknown to the editor, wished mankind to become acquainted with her work. Authors are notoriously vain.

If the editor's private opinion is asked for, he can only say that, while he believes the picture of antdom given in these pages to be essentially true to fact, and while he can vouch for the veracity of the introduction, he suspects the remaining five chapters to be the product of the ant's imagination and, therefore, pure fiction.

Pronunciation of names

In transcribing names the Pacific International Convention's rules have been followed: all vowels have the Spanish values; all consonants the German. Thus e = English $\bar{a}$; a = English ah; w = English v; qu = English kw. A mute h is used to lengthen vowel sounds.

A brief description of the city and the mode of life of Atta Gigantea will be found in the appendix.

Here I will give a list of the chief characters of the book:

WAWA-QUEE (pronounce *Vahvah-quay*), organizer, leader and commander-in-chief of the expedition.

BISSA-TEE (pronounce *Bissa-tay*), zoologist-in-chief.

ANNA-ZEE (pronounce *Anna-zay*), botanist-in-chief and renowned philosopher.

LEMMA-NEE (pronounce *Lemma-nay*), geographer-in-chief and most intimate friend of Wawa-quee.

ADVER-TEE (pronounce *Adver-tay*), expert in communication.

AZTE-CA (pronounce *Aztay-cah*), chief signaller and recorder.

ASSA-REE (pronounce *Assah-ray*), military commander-in-chief of the escort of the expedition.

MINNA-CA (pronounce *Minnah-cah*), commander-in-chief of Pogonomyrmex armies.

Names ending in 'ee' indicate that their bearers belong to the highest nobility; if translation were aimed at, the syllable would have to be rendered by 'Lord'.

Names ending in 'a' indicate that their bearers belong to the second rank of the aristocracy, as in English the title 'Sir' would indicate a member of the lesser nobility or gentry.

All characters are, of course, directly transcribed from life.

F. P. G.

INTRODUCTION

IT HAS long been a question interesting both to the zoologist and the psychologist how to interpret the social life of certain members of the order Hymenoptera. In fact, scholastics and ethologists have fought some of their most memorable battles over this problem. On one side stood those who regarded instinct as a mere mechanism of unconscious and hereditary impulses; on the other, those who saw in it something closely approaching to plastic intelligence. In other words, according as the human-race conceit of the investigator was strongly or weakly developed, the behaviour of these insects, and especially of the ants, was placed either in contrast or in comparison with the behaviour of man.

The present book, I believe, will settle that question. The Formicarian author, whether writing of her own congeners or, as she occasionally does, of us humans, reveals a world of which, I venture to say, few men have ever dreamt.

But let me explain how the book came into my hands.

For decades I had been an amateur myrmecologist; myrmecology had been my hobby. My study of ants went back to a time when the science was just developing into something like a systematic survey; and, I being by training a classicist, it had taken its starting-point from such ancient observations as those of Pliny and Aristotle. In more recent times, footing on Latreille's and Mueller's investigations, men like Forel, Huber,

Emery, and, quite lately, Wheeler had in the light of
the evolutionary theory attacked the various problems
presented by the mass of known fact; and while adding
considerably to the foundations, both by observation in
the field and by dissection under the microscope, they
gave their special attention to the task of ethologic
interpretation. Guided by the conclusions they had
arrived at, I improved what opportunities I had of
observing such species as were locally represented where
I lived. Yet, until I met with the works of Bates and
Belt, my interest remained casual. These two authors,
who were not myrmecologists, properly speaking, and
who, perhaps for that very reason, kept the wider con-
nections of the subject more clearly in view, aroused
in me, through the records of their observations, the
desire to see a little more for myself; and since, while
I remained at home, the demands on my time were
always manifold, I made up my mind, a few decades ago,
to devote a prolonged holiday to the purpose of hunting
down one or two colonies of the leaf-cutter ant of inter-
tropical America. I intentionally restricted the scope
of my investigation to a single genus; nor had I, so far,
any idea of furthering science; I merely wished to
satisfy my own curiosity.

My choice of locality fell on Venezuela; and, during
an otherwise uneventful passage from Cuba to La
Guaira, I had the good fortune of falling in with an
American planter naturalized in that country and living
on the very edge of the tropical forest in the eastern part
of the coastal plateau where he grew sugar-cane and
coffee. On hearing of my plans he very hospitably placed
his house at my disposal; and although I knew that

Spanish-Americans will do so without dreaming of the
possibility that they might be taken at their word, I
thought it safe — he hailing by birth from Illinois — to
accept his invitation as being meant sincerely. After
landing at La Guaira, I accompanied him first to
Caracas and then into the interior.

Since my purpose is not to write a book of general
travel in the tropics but simply to explain how this book
came into being, I will not expatiate upon the scenery
or the flora and fauna of the country which many an
abler writer has depicted for the curious reader. Suffice
it to say that, arrived at my friend's plantation, I at
once settled down to a monotonous routine. Daily I rose
at five in the morning, before sun-up, and an hour later
went to the margin of the jungle where I soon located
three colonies of the species Atta Gigantea. About eleven
I returned to the plantation and, after partaking of a
refreshment prepared by my bachelor-host's Chinese
servant, lay down in my hammock on the large, shady
veranda which had been assigned to me as my part of
the spacious house. At four o'clock, when the westering
sun began to beat down less scorchingly, and when the
often violent showers of the early post-prandial hours
had somewhat cooled the air, I returned to my ant-hill
to watch.

Often nothing worth recording happened for many
days. Yet even uneventful hours served to establish a
certain relationship between the ants and myself — a
relationship which led to most extraordinary developments.

I had arranged a not uncomfortable seat by cutting
the arm-thick stems of two hanging lianas close to the

ground and twisting their ends together so as to form a sort of swing, out of reach of possible inroads of ants and other terrestrial insects.

Close by my aerial seat, a foot or so to the left — I faced south — led one of the beaten tracks of the colony which I had singled out as the largest. The main part of the hill which measured thirty feet in diameter and which consisted of the coalesced crater-entrances, each two inches across, to the subterranean burrows was a few yards to the south and to the right or west of myself. A second colony was established a hundred yards beyond the first; a third, as many rods to the south-east. My detailed observations remained restricted to the nearest one.

I always took a book along to read while I was perched on my seat; for, since things extraordinary happened rarely, it would otherwise have been tedious. I soon developed the power of subconsciously keeping an eye on the ants; not, of course, on individual members of the colony, but on their masses. Any unusual commotion at once focused my attention; and, laying down my book, I could concentrate on whatever happened.

I shall try to sketch the routine activities of these ants as they would have gone on had I not been present or had my presence been ignored.

The crowded craters of the hill always presented the spectacle of numberless multitudes of ants entering and issuing forth. There was no confusion; everything proceeded methodically; and continually order evolved out of a seeming chaos. The ants dispersed on the various paths radiating in all directions from the burrow. On the track which passed at my feet and which was worn to a marvellous smoothness, much more smoothly than human work could have made it, three currents could be distinguished. The total width of the path being about twenty inches, the central ten inches were covered by a dense stream of ants returning to the colony; each individual carried in its jaws, projecting perpendicularly upward and backward, a small, circular leaf-disk which gave its bearer the appearance of a medium-sized butterfly sitting with its wings folded up. These ants, however, were not sitting still. Each disk was nearly an inch in diameter while the ant carrying it was somewhat over half an inch in length. One author has compared the procession to Birnam wood advancing up the hill to Dunsinane. On both sides of this returning column there was a counter-current of out-going ants each about five inches wide; these ants, of course, went empty-handed or rather empty-jawed.

By and by I came to know that, besides the main entrances in those crater-like depressions in the mound, the colony had many other exits or approaches which rose slantwise from the subterranean cavities and opened to the surface at considerable distances from the hill, some as far as fifteen or twenty yards away. These were never used by the ants attending to the routine work. Such as I discovered I examined from day to day; and I found them sometimes open, sometimes closed. They served as ventilators to regulate the temperature in the brood chambers, besides affording exits and entrances to those who, for the moment, were not engaged in the routine work. In case of emergency, of course, all openings would have been used; but no such case came under my observation.

These ants do not by any means feed on the leaves which they cut. As Belt conjectured and Mueller proved, they use them as the substratum on which they grow their real food, a minute fungus which is carefully cultivated and forced under optimal conditions of temperature, moisture and illumination, or rather lack of illumination.

Whenever I followed the worker column, I found that they were operating at various and sometimes considerable distances from the colony. They would come to a point under a young tree or bush where the ground was strewn with the circular cuttings. Each ant picked up a disk and instantly fell into line in the central, returning column.

In the top of the tree, each leaf was tenanted by a worker who, holding on with her hind-feet as a sort of pivot, was slowly swinging around, making a circular cut with her scissor-jaws. When this cut was nearly completed, the ant still standing on the disk, the fore-feet of the little worker took hold of the remainder of the leaf; and when the last connection was severed, the disk fluttered to the ground, the ant dexterously swung up on the blade and at once proceeded to make a new cutting. No leaf was left while enough of the blade remained to yield another disk of regulation size.

It would seem that such habits must be exceedingly destructive to the forest; but I found no evidence that it was. When I first came, the ants were working at a distance of sixty yards east of the colony. I instantly concluded that they preferred certain kinds of trees and went so far afield because their supply close to the hill was exhausted. But it was not so. Plenty of trees of the same species were to be found between the burrow and the scene of their cutting activities; and not one of them was dead. Even in our north, of course, a tree robbed of its foliage in early summer — by hail, let me say — will put forth a second crop, though a less abundant one; and if this growth remains undisturbed, the tree will recover. In the tropics, I reasoned, where the demarcations of the seasons are largely obliterated, such a process of recuperation would be possible at any time provided the tree is not at once despoiled again: perhaps, then, these ants did not return to the same tree till it had had time to make good the loss sustained? If this could be proved, it would go far to settle any doubt as to the truly agricultural principle on which they work; they would not be "mining" the forest but utilizing its surplus energies; just as man utilizes, without — in theory — impairing, the fertility of the soil.

A single fact seemed to stand in the way of this explanation. The human population which has had ample experience with these ants is emphatic in the assertion that it is useless to plant vegetables and fruit-trees; sooner or later these ants will find them; and they will despoil them again and again, till plants and trees are killed. That the ants might consciously discriminate against the plantations of man never suggested itself to me till the fact was sprung on me as a complete surprise when at last I entered into direct communication with them. Amazing as it is, these astonishing little creatures discourage the intrusion of man into the tropical forest with definite intention and purpose. They do not approve of man.

I never dug into the burrows of the colony. I felt

I had no right to destroy their elaborate works just
because I had the physical power to do so; and that, I
believe, was one of the reasons why I was singled out for
the mission with which I am entrusted.

But in order to give the human reader an adequate
idea of the material side of the life of these ants, I shall
quote the results of such investigations of others as confirmed my own conclusions. My chief authorities are
Bates, Belt, Sumichrast, and Mueller.

If the weather is propitious, the leaf-cuttings are
carried right into the upper chambers of the burrow.
If, on the contrary, a shower has wetted them, they are
dumped outside and left to dry. In the upper chambers,
other workers, so-called mediæ who on account of their
smaller size are better adapted for work in the crowded
galleries, take charge of the leaves and cut them into
microscopically small shreds which they work up into
a loose, spongy mass. In this condition still smaller
mediæ take them into the garden-chambers and suspend
them from their vaulted roofs to serve as the soil for
the growth of the fungus on which they feed. Their
charge now passes from the mediæ to the minimæ whom
their minuteness (they are less than an eighth of an inch
in length, a thirty-secondth in width) enables to pass
freely through their interstices; and theirs is the task
of weeding and cultivating. All these activities are
supervised by the maximæ who are sometimes erroneous-
ly called soldiers. Their chief characteristic consists in
the relatively enormous size of their heads which contain
brains of a corresponding development. This brain, I
believe to be relatively the largest single organ of any
living being known. The work of feeding and caring for

the broods falls on the so-called callows or immature workers; while the purely sexual functions of reproduction, at least dimorphic reproduction, are the exclusive domain of the short-lived male and the long-lived perfect female or queen.

In order to round off this sketch, I add a brief outline of the history of a colony.

At a given time of year the young males and queens raised in the colony issue for their marriage flight. No queen mates with a male of her own colony. In every formicary hundreds of physiologically perfect individuals of both sexes are raised. The time for this marriage flight is carefully determined by the maxims; and, strange to say, it is, within narrow limits, the same for all colonies of a given district; so that, for a day or so, the air swarms with winged ants, many of them, and those the most vigorous ones, flying at great heights; while the vast majority perishes in the streams and pools of the country.

The fertilized queen — one fertilization fills the seminal receptacle for the life of the queen — at once locates the spot where she desires to found her colony. She excavates a short gallery and, at its end a small spherical chamber. Having done this, she closes the entrance through which she is never again to pass unless extraordinary disasters befall her colony. Next she dealates herself; i.e., she gnaws off her wings. This is necessary in order to bring about, within her tissues, those structural changes which enable her to feed her first brood — as mammals do — on the secretions of her body. At the same time she deposits in the small chamber a little ball of the fungus hyphæ or roots which she has brought from the parent nest, thus providing for the food of her future broods. Meanwhile her ovaries are maturing, and she begins to lay eggs. The hyphæ she manures with her anal secretions; and when the first brood hatches, she feeds them with the metabolized tissues of her hypertrophied organism. She herself can go without food for months at a stretch. Her first offspring consists exclusively of minims. They at once open the gallery; some of them continue the work of excavation, some issue forth and start to cut leaves. Since even their work, small as their number is, yields a surplus, the fungus-garden soon expands. The next brood is reared by these minims and fed with fungi; its members show the first differentiation in size; and the division of labour begins. The queen never works again: she lays eggs instead. In a year or two the colony exhibits all the forms which constitute the complete social organism, a large formicary of this species having been ascertained to harbour, in its eighth year, slightly under a hundred thousand individuals.

A good deal of controversial literature has been written to account for the seemingly automatic functioning of the ant-state. How does the queen know what to do? How do the first minims learn to go out and to cut leaves? On the whole, instinct has been held to explain it all. It is interesting to see, in the pages that follow, how much of man's activities ants ascribe to instinct. Instinct is a convenient word without real meaning which, for that very reason, serves admirably to veil the ignorance of those who use it. There can be no doubt any longer that, as with us, not instinct, but tradition and education furnish the true explanation of the facts:

that much this book settles beyond question. The queen
is elaborately prepared for her life-work while she still
lives in the parent colony; and she, in turn, teaches the
first minims. Instinct is supposed to function automat-
ically and, by its very definition, to be infallible. [1] But
any observer can verify the fact that ants make mistakes
which they rectify. Belt has observed, and I can confirm
the statement, that young workers will cut and bring to
the burrow disks of the blades of grass which are unsuitable for the growth of the fungi. "Aberration of
instinct!" cry the scholastics, explaining one meaning-
less term by another. If they would go to the trouble
of watching, they would see that the very ants that made
the mistake are forced to remove the grass and will
never again bring it into the burrow.

Having thus introduced my human readers to their
formicarian brethren, I resume my narrative. What
I have so far described as the routine of these ants is
simply what I should have seen had I myself been
invisible or unscentable. As a matter of fact, however,
my presence created right from the start a sensation.

When, on the first day, I approached somewhat
closely, I could not but notice a certain degree of confusion in the lines on the path. There was a momentary
delay in their progress, especially in the outgoing
columns which spread in width; and this congestion

---

[1] This is Wheeler's definition: "An instinct is a more or less
complicated activity manifested by an organism which is acting,
first, as a whole rather than as a part; second, as the representative
of a species rather than as an individual; third, without previous
experience; and fourth, with an end or purpose of which it has no
knowledge."

was speedily propagated back to the burrow. The
central, returning column, too, was retarded but after
a second resumed its progress at an accelerated pace.
More important, however, than either of these disturbances was the fact that, long before those who were
passing me when I appeared could possibly have reached
the burrow, a number of huge ants, measuring at least
an inch in length, exclusive of antennae and legs, and
endowed with enormous triangular heads, apex down
and base up, appeared in the openings of the formicary.

For a moment they lingered, surveying the scene;
and I was much impressed with their air of deliberation,
while their geniculated antennæ worked precisely like
groping hands held up in the air. Although I was eight
feet from the burrow, I saw distinctly the so-called
stemmata or median eyes with which their heads were
equipped in addition to the compound lateral bundles
of ommatidia. These stemmata gave the giant ants a
peculiar look, as though they wore spectacles; and that
bestowed upon them an oddly intelligent air. I was
reminded of Belt's remark, " The steady, observant way
in which they stalk about and their great size compared
with the others always impressed me with the idea that
in their bulky heads lay the brains that directed the
community in its various duties. " This impression was
strengthened when they came stalking up to the scene
of the disturbance. There can be no doubt but that the
news of my approach had spread with telegraphic speed,
ahead of the returning column. For the fraction of a
second these big ants gave their attention exclusively to
me; but somehow they must have inferred that my inten-

tions were not hostile; for in less than half a minute after their arrival order was restored in the triple procession: the routine work went on as before.

The maxims, however, did not at once return to the hill. They lingered and seemed to go into conference, touching each other with their antennæ, now at the head, now at the thorax, and even at various points of the abdominal segments.

My readers must figure themselves as being just within the margin of a tropical forest, its giant trees hung with the festoons of immense lianas. Travellers are emphatic in describing the interior of these forests as the gloomiest place on earth. On a quiet day, such as this was, a stealthy silence broods over the moist atmosphere and in the impenetrable shade of the lofty foliage, becoming all the more oppressive when it has occasionally been pierced by the unmelodious scream of an invisible bird. Nothing is so suggestive of panic and unreasoning fear as the thought of being lost, alone, in this vast cradle of terrestrial life.

That day, this feeling was intensified by the weird, incomprehensible scrutiny of these ants. Without analysing my feelings, without even being conscious of the background of hearsay knowledge from which they arose, I felt, almost as a physical presence, the fact that nowhere does life prey on life as ruthlessly as in these woods where fierce cats and serpents live on mammals, spiders on birds, and numberless insects on all things quick and dead. The extreme beauty of detail in the vegetation did not avail: I was in the grip of primitive disquietudes; I was being surveyed and appraised by alien eyes connected with an intelligence beyond my mental grasp.

I did what I had come to do quickly, almost nervously: I prepared the seat from which I intended to make my observations; and then I returned to the estancia, unable to subdue my shivers. A few hours of rest restored my equilibrium; and I laughed at the confusion into which I had been thrown by my first encounter with these ants.

When, next day, I resumed my post, I had a book along. This expedient proved successful; for it was several weeks before I felt again unbalanced. Meanwhile I watched while reading. A careless observer would henceforth not have noticed anything beyond the routine of the carrier columns. But I made it a point not to be careless. Whenever I mounted guard, two changes took place. One of the giant ants made her appearance at a point in the flank of the columns next to my seat. There she stalked up and down, up and down, in a stately, watchful way, over a distance of from twelve to twenty inches. Only once did I prove to myself that she had a definite function. Intrigued by her eternal vigilance, I made, on arrival, straight for the path as though to cross it. Instantly, the maxim having just appeared, the column broke, leaving a clear space where my foot would have descended. The movements were so minutely concerted that there could be no doubt of their being executed in pursuance of an order issued. When a half minute had gone by without my repeating the threat, the column re-formed with the same precision. The second change consisted in the appearance of another maxim on top of the wide, flat mound formed by the coalesced entrance craters. This ant stationed herself so as to be almost hidden in one of the slanting galleries, with nothing but her large triangular head protruding. I was reminded of a sniper in a trench or bomb-hole. She stayed as long as I stayed, never once moving or changing her position.

Thus weeks went by; and since nothing new ever happened, I began to concentrate more and more on my reading. The monotonous routine began to have a beneficial effect on my nerves; yet it seemed that, apart from this, nothing further could be gained by prolonging my stay. As I have said, I did not care to pursue my studies by destroying their city; others had done so before; the purposes of science had been served; and though this particular species, Atta Gigantea, had, to my knowledge, never been investigated in detail, I had no doubt that the burrow and the organization of the community varied in no appreciable degree from those on which authors had written.

In spite of all that, there was a strange fascination about my work. I was convinced that these thousands upon thousands of ants that filed along the path had come to know me and expected my presence at given times of the day. That the maxims were on the look-out for me, was evident; they appeared the moment I entered the forest. A bond of sympathy established itself between myself and the ants; exactly as a commuting clerk in a human city learns to expect certain faces in the train which conveys him from the suburb where he lives to the urban block where he works; till he would miss the face of an individual otherwise unknown to him should that individual fail to appear. I even conjectured long before I knew it to be a fact that one set of workers filed past in the morning, and a different set in the afternoon. It was not an actual observation; the only thing which might have suggested the thought was the sight of workers of all sizes issuing from certain side galleries and moving about in an aimless way, apparently for no other purpose than that of recreation; for, though they seemed busy enough as they scampered about, I never saw them do any work.

Gradually, too, the character of the surveillance under which I was kept underwent a change. At all times eyes were focused on me, critically and appraisingly. But while, in the beginning, that surveillance had been hostile, it had become expectant and purposeful. I cannot say how this shading-off in their attitude was conveyed to me, unless I were to ascribe it to a sort of transference of thought. If anything fits me peculiarly for observational work, it is an infinite patience with life in all its forms. Something like a tacit understanding arose between myself and these ants; I began to look forward to my hours in the forest as one looks forward to hours of congenial company.

Then, one day, a series of extraordinary events opened up. I used to sit tailor-fasion in the loop of the two lianas which formed my seat, my back leaning against one of the pliant stems, my book resting on one knee.

One day, soon after I had settled down, I suddenly saw, on casually looking up, that, along the liana in front of me, one of those giant ants or maxims was coming down from above. I cannot tell whether this was the first time she had appeared there; but it was the first time that I became aware of her. She must have climbed the trunk of the tree, gone out on the branch, and descended along the hanging trunk of the climber. When she arrived at the level of my face, she stopped; and, fastening herself with her four hind-feet to the scaly bark of the liana, she lifted her thorax and head so as to look straight at me, and then she began to wave her antennæ in the most regular, steady, and purposeful manner. For a few moments I remained motionless; then I slowly raised my hand. Instantly she dropped to the ground whence, in her stately and deliberate way, she returned to the burrow.

The following day she reappeared as soon as I had taken my seat. Again she stopped at the level of my face and began to wave her antennæ. This time I did not offer to disturb her. I knew that the bite of the powerful jaws of these maxims is amply capable of drawing blood; but I was not afraid. As a matter of fact, violence seemed to be the last thing she was bent on. For many minutes she sat there, waving her antennæ eighteen inches from my face. More than anything else it was her persistence which held me motionless. The hand in which I grasped my book had sunk down, my knees were spread.

Thus I sat for more than an hour. Involuntarily, my attention had become centred on the black, polished stemmata or median eyes in her head. Their glint and glitter seemed so human. With all the intensity of which I was capable I wished to understand what this ant was about; but her shining eyes and the unceasing motions of her antennæ slowly had a confusing effect.

I was so absorbed that I lost track of my surroundings; till, with a violent start, I became aware of the presence of a second ant. This second ant had climbed up on the open pages of my book where she was standing on all her six feet. She, too, was waving her antennæ; and her eyes glittered with the same intent purpose as those of her sister. As I said, when I became aware of this second ant, I gave a violent start; and as I did so, both dropped to the ground.

I was bewildered and puzzled as I returned to the plantation. Something uncanny had unbalanced me. Without explaining it to myself, I felt as though I were in the power of these ants. I half regretted ever having taken an interest in any such insects. I played with the idea of returning at once to the saner world of our North-American cities. At the same time I was convinced that I should do nothing of the kind; that, on the contrary, I should return to the ants next day: I knew I had " to see this thing through ".

Still, all night long I dreamed of gigantic ants, ants the size of elephants, besetting my path in the forest and standing about, holding me at bay with their huge, trunk-like, waving antennæ.

A sort of obsession took hold of me. I read of nothing but ants; I thought of nothing else; I talked of them; I dreamed of them. I could no longer close my eyes without at once seeing myself in the gloomy shades of a tropical forest, surrounded by ants of mammoth size that lorded it over me. And what happened next was not calculated to rid me of that obsession.

Two days later I was hardly seated at my post when the maxim appeared on the hanging trunk of the liana; and this time she was followed by two others who also engaged in the frantic and incomprehensible waving of antennæ. I kept on the look-out for the one that had climbed up on my book; but she did not come. Instead, two whole rows formed on the ground, to both sides of my seat, all waving their antennæ and focusing their eyes on mine. A shiver ran down my spine; but I did not stir; and thus half an hour went by.

Something was happening to me. A numbness invaded my limbs; I tried to turn my eyes and could not. I knew that the routine work of the carrier columns was going on all the time; but I did not know how I knew. My mind, however, was singularly free and mobile; and this gave me a queer sensation: much as a paralytic may contrast his mental agility with his muscular rigidity. For my body was invaded, like a separate entity, by a purely physical sense of drowsiness. I made a violent effort to rouse myself; in vain.

And suddenly I was aware of the fact that that other ant had again swung up on my book. By a sort of second sight, for I knew I had not moved my eyes, I saw her sitting there, waving her antennæ.

Meanwhile my eyes remained focused upon the group of three ants in front of my face. They formed a short isosceles triangle with its apex down; all three were clinging to the bark of the liana with four hind-feet, holding the front-feet stretched out, downward, as though in the effort to counteract the violent upward twist of their thorax which supported the triangular head with its waving antennæ and glistening eyes.

I must have fallen into a state next to actual sleep or anæsthesia. My eyes were open. Moments of clear but vacant consciousness were obliterated by lapses of an absolute mental void.

After one of these lapses I suddenly realized that the ants had left me. This jarred my mental faculties back into functioning; and I was once more capable of a normal exertion of the will. I tried to swing my feet to the ground; but my movements, resembling those of a man whose limbs have "gone to sleep", were very awkward. I fell with a dull thud, bruising my head against the roots of the tree.

The violent impact roused me, and I got to my feet staggering. My head ached; and without further thought I turned north, into the path leading to the estancia.

My headache became worse; and, forcibly banishing all thought of what had happened, I lay down in my hammock, and was soon asleep. For once I dreamed neither of ants nor anything else; I lay like one dead; and it was with some difficulty that my host roused me for the evening meal. I did not say a word of my adventure; I was determined first to find its key.

On awaking I had had a very peculiar sensation. I had not seemed to be I.

Just what that portended I could not say as yet; but I felt that is was momentous. I can imagine a doctor feeling like that when he has gone into an area stricken with pestilence. He watches himself for symptoms, alert at all times to apply to himself the remedies which he has been administering to others. Even while he is in perfect health, he keeps watching for signs of his being invaded by the disease.

All sorts of inconsequential thoughts floated through my mind that night. I wondered whether the ants who — of that I had no doubt — were responsible for my condition felt as restless as I did myself; whether this thing meant as much to them as it did to me. There was no answer, of course. I pursued the questions only in order to let the preoccupation with side-issues veil the tremendous significance of the facts of the case. By some mesmeric action I, my individuality, had been sucked up or down into an alien mass-consciousness which communed with me through channels other than those of the senses. The moment I surrendered myself, my consciousness was that, not of my former self, but that of ants, and of no individual ant, so far; but of all antdom, or at least of the community of these particular ants. I felt as though I were on the verge of a revelation.

"You did not sleep well last night?" my host asked next morning.

"No," I replied. "The fact is I am on the point of an important discovery in entomology."

"Glad to hear you are successful," he congratulated.

How inadequate it all seemed! As soon as I could decently do so, I left him and hurried into the forest.

I had hardly sat down in my seat when I saw the first of my new friends coming down the liana. Today her movements lacked that ceremonial, circumspect, and mysterious air; they were businesslike and matter-of-fact. Other maxims were all about, on the ground. The individual on the liana gave some sort of signal to her companions, but what this signal consisted in I could not have said. Instantly a second ant swung up on the page of my book. Whether this was the same ant that had been there before I did not know; I presumed so. Now I had my first close look at this individual.

At once I knew her to be an ant of mark. She was hairier than the others, though her hairs were much broken and worn in places. Since I knew that the hairs of ants are improperly so-called, their function being, not that of protection, but that of exceedingly delicate sense-organs of odour and touch, I recognized in her a more finely-organized being, brainier than her companions. I also had the impression of extreme old age; her armour was deeply scored and abraded; and though it may not have been a colour impression at all, there was about her that which suggested greyness — and weariness, that weariness which goes with great wisdom and a wide experience in the ways of the world. Henceforth I should have recognized this ant among thousands of swarming individuals of her caste.

This venerable dean among ants, then, set to work waving her antennæ.

For a moment I was absorbed in watching her procedure. With head lowered, she raised first one then the other of these delicate organs and swung them down again; and slowly, as I watched these manœuvres, I became aware that the movements were not straight up and down either, but modulated and embellished, as it were, by a thousand different vibratory oscillations of varying amplitudes which had at first remained unnoticed.

Almost immediately following that observation, a peculiar sensation invaded me. I felt my own consciousness slipping. There was an intermediate stage, resembling that of a person who is being put under the influence of an anæsthetic: the stage when he is still aware of what is being done to him but already finds it impossible to defend himself against the influence invading him; he tries to lift his hand in protest and thinks he is succeeding; but in reality his body has already given in. At that stage I was still seeing, still watching the ant; but already she was drawing my consciousness into her own; and with her consciousness her purpose had become my own.

That purpose was to convey to me an experience, the contents of a whole life. Just how this experience and this life became my own, I cannot tell, of course; nor how long this state of mesmeric transposition of personality may have lasted. To me it seemed to extend over years and years; in reality it was probably comprised within minutes or even seconds. For, when, on awaking from this trance, I staggered to my feet, I saw that the minute hand of my watch seemed hardly to have moved at all.

I went "home"; that is, back to the estancia; but while doing so, I knew that I was not yet I. I walked and acted like a human being; but my mind was that of the ant; I had lived her life; and her memory was mine. I could look back upon all she had gone through; and it devolved upon me to put down a record of what, by some miracle, had been communicated to, or infused into, my consciousness.

I cannot, therefore, claim that what follows is my work. It is the work of Wawa-quee, the ant; and it must be read in that sense. I merely set it down, under compulsion.

Perhaps I should add that I went back to the formicary once or twice. I never again saw my friend; but the activities of the tribe went on undisturbed as though nothing had ever happened to interrupt their placid flow.

F.P.G.

CHAPTER ONE

The Isthmus

CONTAINING adventures with hostile leaf-cutting ants; man; his great water-beetle; and three armies of legionary ants.

I

AS IS WELL KNOWN to all Gigantean Attas, it has ever been one of the glorious traditions of our dynasty that each queen succeeding to the throne should, at least once in her reign, equip and send out, for the furtherance of knowledge, an expedition into distant parts of the world. In the past, such expeditions had consisted of from half a dozen to a score of ants who, as a rule, had gone south, east, or west. Their aim had invariably been that of geographical, geological, meteorological, botanical, and zoological exploration; and the result is known as consisting in the illustrious body of science contained and digested in the scented records traced on the sacred trees east of our city.

These records contain the natural history of our country. In the past, it had been found that each acquisition of knowledge opened up new provinces of ignorance. Each expedition that returned home, great as was the store of new knowledge acquired, had brought in its train new problems for investigation. For a long time, then, the object of a further expedition had defined itself by the very achievement of the one completed. Yet, when the last, undertaken a score of years ago, had returned, the problem defining itself had seemed to be of such a magnitude as to defy even the courage and enterprise of ants. This had been in the reign of Her Glorious Majesty's predecessor Orrha-wee CLXV.

When our present sovereign had entered upon the fourth year of her reign without sending out, in pursuance of that august custom, a new expedition, it was generally assumed that the apparent neglect was due either to a profound conviction that further knowledge was beyond our reach or to the suspicion that a greater interval of time was needed to digest the results so far attained.

It remained a profound secret from the multitude that Her Majesty, from the very beginning of her reign, far from being discouraged by the problem which had defined itself as the result of previous expeditions, had, on the contrary, conceived the plan of surpassing all her predecessors by the scope of her project. In preparation she had secretly, though in consultation with a few leading thinkers, sent out certain individuals and even groups to reconnoitre the country to the north which, so far, had been considered as presenting insurmountable difficulties to our advance. Her Majesty had honoured me by directing that all findings of these investigators were to be reported to myself; and that I should receive and store up these findings and ponder them till I had found ways and means to despatch an expedition into those terrestrial regions of this continent which lie north and west of the Great Narrows. In all my conferences with Her Majesty it struck me that she never enjoined upon me to ponder *whether* such an expedition would be possible; the problem was simply *when and in what manner* it would be advisable to launch it.

Her Majesty never doubted, never hesitated about the aim; but she was willing to bide her time. Her faith in the powers of the formicarian mind was nothing less than an inspiration; and when, in the fourth year, I outlined to Her Majesty a plan which, I never doubted, would be rejected, on account of the hazards which it involved and the uncertainty of its success, she embraced it with the greatest enthusiasm; and, a little to my discomfiture, she conferred upon me unheard-of powers, appointing me to lead that expedition myself and to take immediate steps to launch it into the unknown.

Now I had the honour of being of the exact age of Her Majesty; and I shrank from the weight of the responsibility. This will be readily understood: an Atta queen is, at four years, a young ant; but a mere maxim has, at the same age, in all formicarian probability, entered upon the declining quarter of her life. I pointed this out to Her Majesty; but she insisted, calling my attention to the fact that a great task had before this enabled ants of my caste to live beyond their traditionally allotted term of life. She was pleased to use many flattering expressions in explaining to me just why I was to act as her deputy, referring to my previous record as an investigator and organizer, and ultimately hinting that, in her opinion, the success of the whole unheard-of enterprise depended on my devotion to Her service; and perhaps I may add that at last she modified her request, changing it from a command into a prayer. At that I could no longer refuse.

Let me define the purpose of the expedition. To use Her Majesty's own terms, it was to complete such a survey of all antdom as to enable us to trace the evolution of the nation Atta from the humblest beginnings of all ants and to make it possible for us to arrange the whole fauna of the globe, or of such portions of it as could be explored, in the form of a ladder leading up to our own kind. This involved a cataloguing and a classification of all forms of life to be found on the continent; a tremendous task.

Let me skip an interval of eight years and speak of the present.

The results of the expedition which ultimately set out and which, with one exception, namely, myself, perished in the course of its work, have been set down in detail on 813 scent-trees surrounding our city. This having been done, it pleased Her Majesty to ask me to compose a popular account of the whole undertaking, to serve as an introduction to the detailed study of special subjects; and the present narrative is the result of my compliance with Her request. The sequence of events and investigations observed is not strictly chronological; and occasionally a record is introduced in an order the very reverse of chronological; for the present aim of Her Majesty is systemic rather than historical. It is to present the main results in such a way that they can be grasped as a whole. Still, a thread of narrative remains; for we found that, the farther we left our home country behind, the less dominant were ants on earth; and the more distinctly was their place taken by that curious mammal called man. More than that; as we proceeded north and left one climatic province after another behind, we found ever new genera and species of ants assuming the leading part in the control of the country; and, as the curious will scent, they offer, in their succession, a definite scale of development. It will become abundantly clear that our own race stands at the very apex of creation as far as that creation is completed today.

II

As I have said, it pleased Her Majesty to give me discretionary powers for the organization of the expedition. I immediately secured the co-operation of five leaders in their respective fields. At first I was tempted to reserve at least one department to myself; but I feel convinced that it was wiser not to do so.

I secured " their co-operation "; for I realized that, though the powers conferred upon me were sufficient to command their services, it would have been inadvisable to use these powers. We were going to be absent for a space of years; we were going to be exposed to dangers from all sorts of sources; we were going to meet with unheard-of hardships and difficulties: unless we were bound to each other by the bonds of mutual esteem, loyalty, and even love, no exertion of authority would have sufficed to keep us together; and had we ever

separated into smaller groups, we should have been
doomed to extinction.

Each of these leaders was in turn to secure her own
staff, being free to choose, from the vast bodies of ants
learned or skilled in their respective fields, whomever
they thought fittest for the work and best able to adapt
themselves to the peculiar conditions and problems that
were bound to arise in an enterprise of so vast a scope.

To myself I reserved no other privilege than that
of convening the plenary meetings for the deliberation
of such problems as concerned more than one group
and of acting the part of a central clearing-house of
ideas and a depositary of their findings.

In this way I brought into being five bodies, each
consisting of from twenty-five to thirty-five individuals
and aggregating 162 maxims. The leader of each group
occupied with regard to its remaining members the
same position which I occupied with regard to the whole
body; and they were at liberty to group themselves into
smaller bodies for the discussion of special problems.
One of these groups consisted of geographers, one of
botanists, one of zoologists, one of experts in communication, and finally one of expert scenters skilled
in reducing the findings of any body into the briefest
and most pregnant scent-form. The task of keeping the
meteorological records was handed over to members of
group four.

These, then, represented, apart from one other
individual and myself, the brains of the expedition and
its High Command.

This other individual was the far-famed Assa-ree,
our general-in-chief, who was to be independent of the

scientists, experts, and artists and responsible to myself alone. She was not told at the time that it had pleased Her Majesty to confer upon me absolute and unconditional vice-regal powers by virtue of which I held her life in my jaws. I will confess that, much as I shall have to praise her undoubted genius in the field, her unequalled courage in the face of an enemy, and her unheard-of ability to organize and to control large bodies of ants, she had one grievous fault which I feared as much as a source of evil as I appreciated its potentiality for good: she was ambitious; she was impatient of control and illy brooked any intervention between herself and Her Majesty. Since, at a later stage, tremendous issues forced me to make use of my powers and since she, as a consequence, did not return, I must enter into some detail.

There had been rumours that she was herself a "throw-back" — an individual not entirely normal and exhibiting characteristics which aligned her with certain ancestral types of retarded development. There had been talk that, though she had never had wings, she had encroached upon the royal prerogative of laying eggs — parthenogenetically produced — from which viable offspring had been raised by our callows who never suspected that these eggs were illegitimate. What lent these rumours an air of verisimilitude was the fact that, from season to season, our broods were found to contain numbers of "throw-backs" resembling an ancestral type of fighting ants more closely than true Attas. There had finally been rumours that treasonable thoughts were no strangers to Assa-ree's heart; that she aspired to the crown; or to a position, below the crown, of all but absolute power; and that, if she failed in her ambitions, she would not hesitate, should occasion offer, to desert her own nation and to join that nation's enemies. I had never credited these rumours; and, I am glad to say, they had never reached the antennæ of Her Majesty. There was, however, in our recent military history, one circumstance which made me suspect the nature of her powers; and that was the ease with which, on the occasion of the last invasion of our territories by an enormous army of Eciton Predator, she succeeded in side-tracking that army, so that we were never even troubled with their raids. It was rumoured that she had singly entered the hostile army and issued orders as coming from their own supreme command. But whatever her powers might be, I held to the fact that she had used them for the salvation of our people.

Yet, when I approached her on the present occasion, I could not rid myself of the impression that there was about her the faintest aura of a fecal odour such as is well-known to surround all Ecitons; and that was the reason why I solicited and obtained from Her Majesty the special power over life and death to which I have referred and which was given to me in the form of very small pellets of the three great royal perfumes: the perfume of Supreme Command, the perfume of favour, and the perfume of death.

When I first approached Assa-ree with my request for her co-operation in the interest of the expedition, I was, for the fraction of a second, conscious of an intensification of that fecal odour. But my disquietude was allayed by the readiness with which she embraced the plan. This was the more gratifying to me as, without some sort of military escort, the expedition could not have started. Her first demand, on the other hand, made me suspicious again. She asked for absolute authority, not only in training but even in levying the army. Unless she was given a free hand, she would not undertake the task. Yet, having gone so far, I did not see how I could refuse. In some mysterious way the conviction came to me that, unless I indulged her, I should make myself the means of driving her into open revolt; and I was too profoundly penetrated with the teachings of our penologists not to feel that her extraordinary gifts might be led into channels where they would work as readily for the good of our nation as, under different circumstances, they might work for its evil. Her next demand could, after this, no longer be denied: she asked for permission to secede from our city: she urged that a fighting body, drilled and organized, and mentally reoriented in such a way as to make them obey her own single will rather than the call of the community as such, would prove a serious source of disturbance within a commonwealth where voluntary devotion to the common weal was the central principle from which freedom flowed. In what she added she seemed to me to be playing with fire, though she tempered her plea with a peculiar ironical humour which was bending back upon herself. Her argument was that, among Attas, military gifts were necessarily associated with a retarded mentality, capable of holding on to only one idea at a time; we were fortunate, she scented, in having no small numbers of such backward members in our midst; for without them we should speedily succumb to a hostile world; so long as these were scattered as individuals among large numbers of fully civilized ants, they might never even be suspected of aberrant instincts; but the moment they were segregated and brought together in solid masses, they would necessarily begin to feel their mettle and become the cause of friction; they might even prove a serious danger to the state.

All which was so reasonable and so self-evident that I agreed in spite of my suspicion that Assa-ree was poking fun at me.

The next question was that of numbers. It so happened that there had just been a census; the total number of Attas, maxims, mediæ, and minims in our city had been found to be 435,313 souls, which number was, of course, subject to slight fluctuations from day to day. Callows were hatched, and old ants died. Now Assa-ree asked for ten thousand; and this estimate was so little above my own estimate of the number necessary, namely, eight thousand, that I conceded it without argument.

But here is the point. When, four months later, Assa-ree reported that her levy was complete and I reviewed the troops in person, I was struck by the fact that the ranks presented an alien aspect and that, above all, most of the officers seemed to have extraordinarily large and curved jaws. Yet I had seen an occasional individual like that in our city; what amazed me was the large number in which, on this occasion, I saw them assembled. But, as Assa-ree and myself walked along the front of the serried ranks of this army, the scent with which I was cheered, though it, too, partook of that fecal quality which I have mentioned, was so enthusiastic that I could not doubt the loyalty of these troops, no matter of what suspicious-looking elements they might be composed. So I suppressed my misgivings, arguing that, if we wanted fighting power in our escort, we had better take it as it offered itself; and that this army had that fighting power, there could be no doubt.

Yet my suspicions were revived once more. Bissa-tee, chief zoologist to Her Majesty and leader of the zoological group of the High Command, expounded it as her theory that even in communities devoted entirely to the arts of peace the birth rate rises when an extra-ordinary enterprise demanding the possible sacrifice of life is planned. She asked for a new census. When it was taken, she triumphed, of course. In spite of the fact that, according to Assa-ree, ten thousand indiv-iduals had been conscripted, the population of the city had risen to 435,328, or fifteen more than there had been before the draft. Even allowing for the correctness of Bissa-tee's theory, this seemed so amazing that I could not account for it.

I will anticipate and state that, years later, just before Assa-ree made her final bid for power, by means of the most detestable treason, I extracted from her an admission, which she made in the form of a boast, that, while she had indeed levied numbers of Attas exhibiting a military atavism (all of them closely related to her; in fact, being her illegitimate offspring), the minutest search for such individuals had failed to produce a levy, among the maxims and mediæ, of more than 2,114 able-bodied ants; the rest of the levy she had made up by winning over, no doubt using her fecal odour for the purpose, stray bodies of Ecitons, of the species Eciton Hamatum, our deadly enemies.

In a way I cannot but rejoice at the fact that neither
I nor anyone else had the slightest knowledge or even
suspicion of the extent of her treason at the time; had
we had such a suspicion, we should never have started
on our expedition; we should, instead, have rushed into
civil war; and who knows what, with such an enemy,
the outcome would have been? Our ignorance of the
facts served the commonwealth in two ways: in the first
place, we led a most dangerous potential enemy away
from our country: more dangerous, in fact, than a purely
Eciton army of ten times its number would have been;
for against such an enemy our usual means of defence
would have availed, whereas this highly trained and
efficient fighting unit knew all about these means of
defence and could have circumvented them, as they
would undoubtedly have done had we, by even the
slightest hesitation, betrayed any knowledge of its true
nature and composition; in the second place, enormous
as were the losses sustained in the course of our march
through a largely hostile continent, the expedition was
led to a successful issue; and the wealth of new knowledge acquired in its course has been made available
for the future, for our nation and all antdom, if only
by the survival of a single individual, namely, myself.

One last word with regard to the army. When I
proposed eight thousand as the number to be levied, I
had in mind that a third or a half of this number should
be composed of Attas intermediate between the fighting
and the carrier types. For in addition to those exclusively levied for purposes of defence and attack we
needed a considerable number of individuals who would

carry a supply of fungus-hyphæ * or roots in their infrabuccal chambers. I anticipated the possibility of meeting with climatic or other conditions which would force us to entrench for weeks or months at a time; and if, in times of unemployment, we had to go without our accustomed food, it might prove an unendurable hardship. I felt certain that we could always secure leaves suitable as a substratum for the cultivation of our fungi; but lack of seed would, in such a case, have been fatal. Besides, I had hit upon the plan of establishing, in favourable localities, hidden fungus-gardens on which we could fall back should hunger or defeat, by whatever enemy, force us into a hurried retreat. I am glad to say that, at least in this particular, the provision made by Assa-ree proved adequate, though it fell far short of what I had expected her to do.

III

The order in which we set out, seven months after we had begun preparations, was as follows. The van, to the number of two or three hundred, was composed of scattered individuals and groups of particularly powerful physique and intrepid spirit. All of them were volunteers, which insured at least that they did not fear but rather relished their task. Immediately behind them came a corps of skilled signallers, specially trained to emit the most pungent and fast-diffusing scents by

---

* See appendix.

which to give warning and information as to what was happening in front.

Then followed a massed body of fighters, commanded from the rear by Assa-ree. These formed a solid front and two solid flanks. Their rear was supposed at all times to form a hollow crescent enclosing that body which I have called the brains of the expedition and in which no particular discipline or marching order was observed. It was followed by another massed body of carriers and fighters who again enclosed the central body with a crescentic arrangement of their forward ranks.

Since the country which we had to traverse before reaching the Great Narrows was well-mapped and known in every detail, we travelled, to begin with, by night. This distance of 95,000,000 common antlengths [1] was covered by forced marches in 150 nights — no mean achievement.

When, after this forward thrust, we made our first stop, we were in a peculiar country of great rocky mountains clothed with verdure and studded with lakes, but exhibiting also more or less barren uplands adorned with only a scanty vegetation of Cecropia and Acacia trees.

So far, provisioning had offered no difficulty. Our march had led past a good many friendly cities of our own kind where arrangements had been made in advance to supply the High Command with shelter and food.

---

[1] A common antlength (length of a media) is ½ inch. 750 miles. E.

The army as such had never entered these cities; for Assa-ree had undertaken to look after her own commissariat; and when I found that she relied entirely on foraging raids, I rested content with this arrangement. It was essential to reduce our demands on hospitably-inclined colonies to a minimum; and even when we found that these fighting hordes of ours reverted very largely to the aboriginal custom of feeding on carrion, I did not object. For no matter how we, the High Command, fared, it was important to conduct matters in such a manner as always to provide amply for the rank and file.

But now we were entering upon terra incognita; and though we met at once with other tribes closely related to ourselves, the Œcodomas, we were, for the first time, to have the experience of finding our overtures tending towards friendly intercourse repulsed.

To our agreeable surprise, Assa-ree had proved herself equal to any emergency; but while we continued our advance, literally fighting our way on all sides, we, the High Command, had at last to go without food for forty or fifty days. And then our whole advance was brought to a stop.

We came to a point where an unbroken chain of Œcodoma cities reached from coast to coast in a north-south direction; more than once we hurled massed bodies of our troops against this chain; nothing was gained. We had to encamp.

I called a council of war to meet at night. I well remember the occasion. We were at an elevation of at least 48,000 antlengths above the sea. All about, we were surrounded by a barren, rocky highland with a broken surface. In front, at a distance of 63,000 ants, rose a forbidding escarpment to a height of 3,600 antlengths; but its crown was covered with a dense forest reaching westward; it was within the margin of that forest that the line of Œcodoma cities barred our way. Almost overhead stood a full moon; and the atmosphere, in the open, was chilly enough to stiffen our joints. But the meeting was held in a recess of perpendicular rocks which retained the heat of the day. To our left, the remainder of our central body had gone to rest in a manner which we had learned from our bitterest enemies, the Eciton Hamatum. This method was as follows: two of the strongest ants attached themselves with their fore-legs to a low branch of a dead acacia. To their hind-legs four were clinging; and so on, till, in the ninth or tenth tier, the flaring curtain thus formed by living bodies reached a width sufficient to fold over from both sides and to enclose a hollow funnel which was filled by the remaining ants in a dense cluster. The army was encamped in a similar manner south of us and out of sight.

When I opened our deliberations, I gave it as my opinion that, at no matter what cost of time or energy, we must establish friendly relations with our cousins, the Œcodomas; and two of the group-leaders, Bissa-tee, the zoologist, and Lemma-nee, the geographer, were inclined to agree with me. But Anna-zee, the botanist, pointed out, not perhaps without a semblance of justice, that it was too late for attempts at conciliation; blood, she said, had flowed on both sides; it could not be wiped out. So I asked her what she had to propose; and she replied sardonically that, once blood had been shed, there was only one remedy and that was to shed more of it. Anna-zee, as we shall see, often had the disconcerting knack of brushing aside what she called self-deceptions. At this very moment I saw Assa-ree stepping into the gap between the walls of our retreat.

By way of greeting she raised her antennæ and then brought them down with a sweeping movement. Both Anna-zee and Bissa-tee spoke to me later in admiration of the physical grace of this great ant-of-war; both remarked upon the proud humility of her bearing. I could not quite understand such a misinterpretation; but, since her greeting was exclusively addressed to me, I being the only ant she had to consult, they did perhaps not have a full opportunity to see her in the same light in which I saw her. I could not overlook the distinct outward swing which she knew how to impart to the movement of her antennæ: it was an unmistakably ironic curve. The scents with which she proposed a way out of our difficulty were respectful enough; yet, to me they seemed to be too exaggerated to be quite sincere. Very briefly, she engaged to induce any colony of Œcodomas to leave their city for our special accommodation, without the use of force. I was on the point of asking her why, if such was in her power, she had not offered to do so before blood had been shed. But my colleagues closed with her offer so enthusiastically that I thought it best to observe a discreet silence.

I must give Assa-ree her due: she was as good as her scent. Next morning we entered a deserted city which contained a wealth of fungus-gardens quite beyond our requirements. The rest of our High Command, even Anna-zee and Bissa-tee, far and away the most eminent of our scholars, accepted this service as a sort of miracle that must not be too closely questioned; and, for the moment, it solved an urgent problem.

But before we moved on, I made it my business to investigate. My motive was neither that of an idle curiosity nor that a desire to spy on Assa-ree. But I considered that the safety of the whole expedition depended on what I am tempted to call my own omniscience with regard to the doings, the wishes, and the thoughts of all its members.

Now, at the very time of entering this marvellously well-built city of the Œcodomas I had been struck by the presence of a faint smell that seemed suspicious. It was not the race-smell of any leaf-cutting ant; nor was it the adventitious nest-smell peculiar to every individual colony. These cannot be mistaken by any experienced contact-odour sense such as I flatter myself to possess. It was an alien smell, hard to identify because of its faintness. It had, apparently, not been questioned by anyone else.

The most minute examination of the main entrance-craters failed to furnish the slightest clue. Then, one day, bent on recreation, I took a turn in the forest; and quite accidentally I came across a wasp on the ground which seemed to be expiring; and instantly I recognized the suspicious smell which here was pungent and pronounced. This unfortunate wasp had been surprised by an army of Eciton Hamatum; had been deprived of her power of motion; had been partially dismembered; and had then, for some mysterious reason, been left behind. I hurried back to our temporary abode and, armed with this clue, soon discovered, in a crevice of one of the side-entrances, a tiny fragment of the abdomen of this very wasp — a fragment so bitten into and almost chewed up by the powerful sickle-jaws of Ecitons as to make it practically unrecognizable.

How Assa-ree had got hold of this fragment I can, of course, not tell; but her scheme now explained itself. These particular Ecitons must be so powerful, and their power so well known that the mere suspicion of their approach was enough to put to flight a whole colony of Œcodomas. This Assa-ree knew; and that was the most disquieting feature of the whole thing. I knew, and I knew that Assa-ree knew, that we could not forever avoid meeting an army of these Ecitons; I anticipated, and I suspected that Assa-ree anticipated, that we should be attacked. If we were, it would be her task to defend us, it was hard to say with what prospect of success: an issue before which the stoutest heart might be permitted to tremble. Yet she could use this fear of the Ecitons to play a joke upon a whole nation of ants closely related to ourselves and, in a manner, upon me and my associates. It was not a thought to allay my secret disquietudes. Above all, I knew from that day on that sooner or later matters must come to an issue between her and me.

To finish this topic by anticipation: a further discovery was in store for me. Assa-ree had driven to flight, not only the one colony of Œcodomas which she had promised she would persuade, by peaceful means, temporarily to abandon their city for our convenience, but the whole line of colonies stretching across the Narrows of the continent. This I discovered in the course of the following days.

One night, the leaders of the High Command being again in conference to discuss the best route to follow from that point, she entered our conclave a second time. The meeting being held in a subterranean chamber, we were in utter darkness, and I could not watch her demeanour in detail. But in her greeting to me, in the course of which she touched first my antennæ, then my thorax and head, I seemed again to detect that exaggeration of deference which could not but conceal her irony. The import of her message was this. Since we should necessarily have to return by the same route, she would like to point out the expediency of keeping this gap open. Lemma-nee, the geographer, was so amazed at the boldness of the proposal that she squirted out, "Can it be done?" Assa-ree brushed the question aside by the slightest motion of her antennæ and repeated her offer in a scent of affected weariness. I resolved to embrace the plan and signified as much. I could feel Assa-ree stiffening: she interpreted my lack of amazement as an affront. Yet her resentment was expressed by nothing but an increase in deference. You wish it, she signified, in scents still more subdued than mine had been, and it is done.

Next morning, when we had left the city, I ascertained, while the ranks were being formed, that she had cunningly concealed a tiny fragment of the same wasp in each of the main entrances of the no less than 103 Œcodoma cities which formed the barrier across the narrowest point of the continent.

IV

I must now reach back in time and resume the narrative at the point where we entered the Œcodoma city.

Not far from the northern end of this barrier across the Narrows and just west of it, stood a city built by man. Although the detailed zoological and ecological study of man was not directly comprised in our instructions, I thought it inadvisable to neglect this opportunity. Man, forming part of that large division of the animal kingdom called the Mammalia, had been studied previously by a number of expeditions, but with inconclusive results. It was known that, by virtue of a number of peculiarities, he occupied a somewhat unique position within that group. It was suspected, on the ground of things reported by trustworthy observers, that his position among mammals might somewhat resemble the position of ants among insects. It had even been suggested that his development, in the past and in certain branches of his kind, had almost reached the same level as ours today; in that case he would represent that most interesting type of a retrograded or degenerate race; and I must confess I was inclined to embrace this view. One daring speculator had even hinted that perhaps man possessed, or at least had possessed, that same imperial gift of reason which is universally held to be the distinguishing mark of ants.

Before I summarize what was previously known of man, I will briefly state what led me to the conclusion that man is a degenerate type. In this I shall, of course, anticipate the results of later investigations. In the first place, it is an axiom among biologists of the first rank that every individual of no matter what species, in its development from the embryonic state to the imaginal, adult, or final state, summarizes the development of the race. If, then, it can be shown that the adult stage, in some essential point, shows a retrogression from the development reached in an immature phase, the only conclusion possible to be drawn is that the adult represents a degenerate type. Now my students will have to take my scent for it that man's instincts approach plastic intelligence in the young; the adult shows no trace of it. For proof of this I must refer to scent-tree number 349. In the second place, I cannot imagine a state of affairs in which, the animal in question having reached the stage where a social life (as distinct from a herd life) becomes possible, as man has, the male is the dominant sex; and it is with man. This is against all reason. Every male is capable of fertilizing many females unless it dies in copula (male man does not); yes, the seminal fluid discharged in a single copulation suffices (at least with us) to fertilize thousands of ovules; even where the male is not restricted to a single copulation (as it is with us), it is the rule that, after having fulfilled its proper function, it serves for such menial offices only as defence or the labour of procuring food, etc. I cannot think of any other animal which has developed to the social stage — distinctly an achievement of the female — and which nevertheless supports its males in a dominant position. I therefore conclude that, in the past, man, too, has lived under matriarchy as we do today. If this conclusion needs further support, that support is furnished by the fact that young human males play at being females, acting as though they had brought forth callows and carrying images of such about in their forelimbs. From this stage, which must necessarily summarize a lost development of the race, they gradually degenerate, even individually, into a pure, arrogant, and ignorant masculinity. This argument seems, to me, to be conclusive.

Now for the summary of our previous knowledge of man.

Even in our own country these destructive animals are to be found sporadically. As is well known, they kill, without provocation or discrimination, all living things, sometimes at sight, sometimes after having enslaved them for a time. The native vegetation on which the rest of creation depends for shelter and food they destroy by fire or otherwise.

On an average they are 70 ants long, 36 ants wide, and 20 ants thick, measuring their length from the top of their heads to the fork of their extraordinarily long hind limbs. Of these limbs, they have four though, as a rule, they use only two for locomotion: a fact characteristic of the contempt in which they hold nature's gifts. The head resembles a hard sphere of bone overlaid with a thin layer of pinkish flesh which, in turn, is covered with a more or less dark-coloured filmy and pliable skin. It is provided with two round, simple eyes excellent for distant, but singularly ill-adapted for minute and accurate vision. Two prodigious skinny excrescences served originally as covers for their ear-passages; but they have long since, through disuse, become worthless for this purpose. A large, fleshy protuberance in the centre of the face is presumed to harbour the vestiges

of a sense of smell, also largely lost by neglect. The
mouth, below, consists of a transverse slit armed with
bony plates for mastication and measuring from six to
eight ants. The most striking proof of a lack of natural
intelligence, or of its loss, is to be found in the fact
that, by millennia-long neglect, man has forfeited the
most important means of communication, orientation,
and fixation of records, namely, the contact-odour
sense. This sense, which we, by intelligent use and careful breeding, have developed to such a remarkable acute-
ness and applied to such sublime purpose, has, with
man, become rudimentary.

Their bodies are not, as ours, protected by a defensive, chitinous ectoskeleton but with soft integuments of varying composition. I shall later speak of
them again. These integuments have, by certain zoologists, been used to support the theory that man as a
species has never yet become fixed; they are of such
extraordinary variety. The latest observations, however,
had led to the daring theory that man moults at will. Of
this, too, we shall treat later on.

To a certain extent man is social in his habits, not
only with regard to his own kind, but also with regard
to certain mammals and birds which, phylogenetically,
stand quite remote from him; as, f.i., dogs, cats, parrots,
chickens, and others. It is significant that all his more
intimate associates are chosen from the lowest of the
great subdivisions of the animal world, the vertebrates.

Such, apart from a few details which the curious
can read up on any standard scent-tree of zoology, was
what was definitely known of man.

Every now and then, however, the assertion is met with, in some more speculative monoscent, that certain acts of man, observed and recorded by careful investigators, argue for at least the traces of a reasoning power. Such-and-such a thing, it has been said, cannot be explained by a mere animal urge or "instinct"; it has to be attributed to more or less conscious deliberation and logical inference; it seemed to prove the existence of a "plastic intelligence" directing a "plastic behaviour". But, if many learned ants have advocated this view, an equal number have scoffed at it. Reason seemed to be such an incomparably precious gift that it was hard to imagine other creatures to be endowed with it, creatures remote from our own race which was by nature destined to rule the world.

Perhaps this is the place for a brief digression. Everybody knows that in most systems of philosophy evolved in the past it is tacitly assumed that reason is one and indivisible, as though, to use a bold metaphor, it had sprung fully armed from the brain of some superant. It is now pretty well acknowledged by most biologists that this theory or assumption is untenable. Even with us, reason is the result of a long and slow assimilation of experience, and it is still in the making. Wherever, therefore, in what follows, the word is used without qualification, it is to be understood as referring simply to the present phase of development among Attas.

Here, then, were a number of problems on which I thought it worth our while to throw as much light as we could. Our present adventure, however, which must

excuse this digression, will be set down without further
comment. The facts speak for themselves.

V

The first notice I received of the presence of man in
these parts came from reports given by Assa-ree; it
consisted in no more than a casual mention of the fact
that a small colony, comprising some 500 individuals,
was located on a bold cliff overjutting the sea.

I commissioned Assa-ree to reconnoitre; and her
second report was more detailed. The colony consisted
of a number of dusky individuals whose integuments
were scanty and bright in colour. They were given to
rapid and incomprehensible chatterings resembling
those of monkeys in our native woods. I had a curious
suspicion that these chatterings might conceivably represent their method of communication; for the widely
attested fact of a social life, with its division of labour,
presupposed some such power. Among these darker men
lived one individual differing markedly from the others,
both in colour of facial skin and in integuments. The
latter Assa-ree described as pure white in colour and
fine in texture, apart from his hind-feet which were
encased in an ectoskeleton of bright brown and of considerable hardness. He — it was a male — must have
occupied a leading position among the rest; for a number of the dusky individuals seemed to wait on him
much as certain adult workers of ours wait on Her
Majesty. His abode consisted of a number of lofty and
spacious chambers one of which contained large cases

of a transparent, rock-like substance filled with glittering, uncanny-looking things of unknown purpose.

These reports inspired me with a desire to see for myself. We knew from former investigations that man's communities are often vastly more numerous; I reasoned, therefore, that this was an opportunity to study him individually, unconfused by numbers.

I had Assa-ree conduct me to the abode of this curious individual. All her observations were confirmed, and at least one was added: among the darker individuals waiting upon him was one who, with regard to the rest (most of them females), occupied a position of intermediate authority. His integuments closely resembled those of the master, consisting of white, fine-textured tissues which covered all but his head, his hands, and his feet; and in one point he was unique: he had two pairs of eyes, one of them being external and consisting of the same transparent, rock-like substance as the mysterious cases of the chamber.

As luck would have it, Assa-ree and I entered this man's abode at a moment when a dusky female came to call on the master. To our amazement, the master, ordering the assistant about in a most peremptory manner, placed the female in a peculiar position in an ingeniously constructed seat and looked into her mouth. From his behaviour I was inclined to think that he was going to osculate or to regurgitate; but suddenly he inserted a claw of his fore-foot into the open mouth of the female and shouted something to his assistant. The latter opened one of the transparent cases and took from it a sinister-looking *piece of apparatus* [2] closely resembling such tongs as certain aquatic members of the Articulata exhibit in our own country. This *piece of apparatus* he handed to the master who brutally thrust it into the mouth of the female, seized with it one of the bony plates used for mastication, and, with a powerful wrench, pulled it out, the female giving a pitiful groan. Profoundly stirred by the suffering of the victim of this brutality, I gave Assa-ree the signal of retreat; and we made our exit.

Returned to our temporary dwelling, I shut myself up in the queen's chamber. I will not dwell on my feelings but merely give the results of my analysis of the facts. He whom I have called the master had clearly enslaved the one whom I have called the assistant, as well as the other members of his clan. It was not a case of co-operation such as exists among ants. What the nature and method of this enslavement might be remained unexplained; in physical power the slave was manifestly superior to his master. But he was of a different variety of the species man; his racial relation to the master was approximately that of ourselves to the Œcodomas, or the reverse. It was hard to say which; for now the one, now the other of these two seemed the less civilized.

---

[2] Whenever dealing with man, Wawa-quee's consciousness became purely visual and was transferred to me in that form. I recognised this "piece of apparatus", of course, as the sort of tongs or forceps used by dentists to extract teeth. Whenever such a case arises in which I understand what the ant does not, I shall, in what follows, use italics. E.

It will perhaps be best simply to relate what happened next and to let the curious draw their own conclusions. I will frankly own that I was little inclined to pursue my studies in this particular abode of man; and I should have left well enough alone had I not been forcibly carried back there.

I made up my mind to take Bissa-tee, the zoologist, into my confidence. As far as Assa-ree was concerned, I had no intention of letting her look too deeply into my thoughts and secrets. I knew her to be at heart impatient of my control; and I knew it to be impossible for her to appreciate my motives. Care for my personal safety was dictated, of course, not by fear for myself, but by my solicitude for the fate of the whole expedition the success of which depended on the preservation of that unity of direction which centred in myself. I have too often shown that death holds no terror for me to have to give a cheap exhibition of courage when discretion is clearly indicated by the circumstances.

Bissa-tee was one of those big, magnificent, and boisterous ants who will rap their thorax with one antenna while they touch yours with the other, and who will breeze in and out of a chamber with a hearty nod; so that everyone mistakes them for commonplace ants and thinks she knows all about them because they seem to carry their heart upon the anterior joint. I knew that all this was mere pretence and that she knew excellently well, as her name, too, signifies, how to keep her own counsel. That was the reason why we were friends.

In order to make sure that we could not be spied upon, I led her far from our temporary abode. I took a north-east path which led close to the wide and open clearing that surrounded the human village.

But I had hardly begun to explain my perplexities when I was interrupted. We found we were not alone in this margin of the forest. The ground shook with the rapid and ponderous tread of some large animal, presumably a mammal. Both Bissa-tee and myself instantly ceased from all motion and stood rigid, every muscle taut. And then, what was my horror when I espied the very assistant of the master man jumping about close by under the trees, bending over and reaching for things on the ground! My first impulse was to hide; but the second impulse was of curiosity. And this second impulse, which I followed, seemed, for the moment, to prove our undoing; for suddenly the man was right upon us.

To our amazement, he reached for us, not with the long, slender toes of his fore-feet, but with a pair of *tongs*. Before I knew what was happening, he had grasped me by my pedicel (of all places to catch an ant: the pedicel!), lifted me and dropped me into a hollow cylinder of the rock-like, transparent substance repeatedly mentioned. Bissa-tee promptly followed me; and, to our horror, we found ourselves confined with a score or two of huge Eciton Hamatum, our worst enemies. The fear of the Eciton is so inbred in us Attas, I presume, that, faced with them, we are capable of exertions which under ordinary circumstances would be beyond our powers. Both Bissa-tee and myself were, a moment later, clinging to the rough paper cover of the cylinder. Ordinarily such a leap of at least fourteen antlengths would have been impossible to any Atta. Yet the imprisoned Ecitons were themselves too bewildered to pay the slightest attention to us.

Meanwhile our bearer was wildly shaking us up and down: apparently he was running in his clumsy human way, using only his hind-feet.

Before we had had time to reflect, he had removed the cover from the cylinder and was shaking us out on a flat white surface of extraordinary smoothness. There, Bissa-tee and myself, together with fifty Ecitons, were instantly rushing about in the wildest confusion. The surface was circular and surrounded by a moat twelve antlengths wide and filled with water. At last I stopped to recover my breath; and as I did so, I looked about. Incredibly, we were in that precise chamber where Assa-ree and I had witnessed the maltreatment of the human female.

Still more incredibly, that same female was lying like one dead stretched out on a raised platform close to the glistening plateau on which we were. Her fore-foot was bared to the upper joint and exhibited a wide, bleeding gash twenty antlengths long and gaping, with its ragged edges separated by at least four antlengths. How such a gash can be produced I have of course no means of telling. But, as I said, red blood was trickling from it.

Perhaps I should explain here what I came to investigate at a much later stage. Man's blood, like that of all mammals, is confined in large, tubular vessels and cannot flow outside of them. If he is wounded and one of these vessels or veins is severed, the blood escapes instead of simply changing its course and flowing around the wound as it does with us; and with its escape life itself ebbs away.

A moment later I saw the master hurrying about; he shouted something to his assistant, and the assistant answered. Again I should, perhaps, anticipate and explain that man produces sounds, not by means of a stridula, but by sending a current of air forcibly over two chord-like membranes concealed in his throat.

The master approached the female, knelt by her side, and laved the wound; the assistant stood by, armed with a *forceps*. By this time curiosity had completely conquered my panic. The Ecitons were still rushing wildly about. No greater proof, I believe, can be found of the superiority of the Atta than the fact that Bissa-tee had coolly selected a point of vantage from which she watched the proceedings; and her I now joined on the bank of the moat.

Having finished the task of laving the wound, the master, by a gesture of his forelimb, gave the assistant a signal; and the latter, bending over the platform, picked up a giant soldier Eciton, applying the *forceps* to her pedicel. I distinctly remember how this individual opened her formidable and menacing sickle-jaws as though to attack her captor. There is one thing to be said for the Eciton: she knows no fear; she is the personification of blind and bold fury; but she is nothing else; she is a mere fighting machine.

As it turned out, this gesture of menace was exactly what the human wanted to produce. With a touch much more gentle than I should have expected him to be capable of, the master took the *forceps* from his assistant; and while, with the extended toes of his free forelimb, he pressed the ragged edges of the gaping wound in the human female's arm together, he approached, with the other, the head of the Eciton. At once the ant buried her jaws, on both sides of the red line, in the human flesh and drew them close together; whereupon the master slipped his soft toes back by two antlengths and returned the *forceps* to his assistant. A second Eciton was picked up; and the proceeding repeated; then a third and a fourth.

Up to this point I had been so fascinated by what was going on that I had no eyes for anything else. Now I cast a fleeting glance at Bissa-tee. To my inexpressible astonishment I saw, behind her, in an attitude of bold and close scrutiny, my ever-present rival Assa-ree. Where did she come from? I feel convinced that, like ourselves, she had been caught by mere chance; but, when questioned, later on, she had the effrontery to assert, though her boldness was disguised under an air of almost apologetic modesty, that she had intentionally allowed herself to be captured in order to find out what these Ecitons were wanted for. How she came to be in the very locality which I had sought in order to escape her *espionage,* she has never seen fit to explain.

I had not yet completely recovered from what amounted almost to indignation at her presence when Bissa-tee touched me with her antenna. The process of closing the wound had been finished. Twenty-five Ecitons had buried their jaws in the human flesh and were holding the edges of the wound together.

And now comes the most amazing thing of all: a thing so horrible that I can barely bring myself to relate it. The master had risen and was bending over the wounded arm. In one fore-foot he held a new instrument, a pair of scissors, of the same metal as the forceps. With this he severed the heads of the Ecitons from their bodies, allowing the latter to fall to the ground. I nearly swooned. The only thing which preserved me from so ignominious a breakdown was the consciousness that, over Bissa-tee's tense body, Assa-ree's median eye was fastened upon me, with an expression of diabolic curiosity.

A few moments went by during which I was aware of nothing but my own efforts not to give way. But suddenly I saw the master bending over our platform, *forceps* in one, and the hollow cylinder in the other forelimb. He was picking up and re-imprisoning the remaining Ecitons. Before I knew what to do in order to escape, he had picked up Bissa-tee, but to my surprise he flung her to the ground; apparently he did not think her suitable for his purpose. I was just on the point of running blindly when I also felt myself grasped. As he lifted me close to his eye, I saw Assa-ree clearing the moat in a single, magnificent leap. Clearly, fear gave her, too, strength beyond the measure ordinarily bestowed on ants. The next moment I was, like Bissa-tee, flung to the ground.

I hastened to escape through the door; but instantly Bissa-tee was by my side and detained me. I hardly know how I managed to attend to what she was endeavouring to convey to me. " Never before had such an opportunity offered to measure the tenacity of life in Ecitons: since we had forbidden vivisection by law, the only specimens on which she and her colleagues had been able to work had been such as were mutilated in war; and neither she nor anyone else had ever succeeded in getting hold of beheaded specimens the exact hour of whose execution had been known; nor had these specimens ever been free from other mutilations and wounds. These Ecitons, on the other hand, were in magnificent health, apart from the fact that they had lost their heads; and so zoology must claim them, not only in order to determine the protoplasmic vitality of the Eciton body as such, deprived of the intelligent direction of the brain and even of the very possibility of adding to the vital force by feeding it; but also in order to study the distribution of instincts between body and head. Surely, she argued, when the head is removed, activities can be directed only by the dorsal and ventral ganglia. Help me, she added, to drive these decapitated specimens, or at least some of them, to our station where I shall provide an orderly as a guard for each individual; and zoology will owe you an everlasting debt.

I could not help admiring this devotion to science which caused Bissa-tee entirely to forget the danger she was in, for she had stopped me in the very door through which numbers of humans were now passing, lifting and bringing down their huge flat feet; to be caught between them and the rock-like floor would have been equivalent to a cataclysm in nature. Nevertheless, I was impatient with her; clearly, this was the moment to think of our own safety first of all.

But at that juncture Assa-ree appeared, her attitude marking a peculiar mixture of jaunty nonchalance and solicitude in our service. As though to set an example of reckless disregard of danger, she came through the very centre of the wide exit; and when the assistant

appeared behind her, she even stopped till the latter's
hard and smooth hind-foot was directly above her before,
with a dexterous and elegant twist, she evaded the descending destruction.

The remainder of this adventure is chiefly of interest to specialists; and a detailed report has been
given on scent-tree number 319 to which I must refer
the curious. Here I confine myself to the bald statement
that we succeeded in securing twelve of the decapitated
Ecitons whom Bissa-tee kept confined during the remainder of our stay at the Narrows; when we left, she
took them along under escort. Those whom we did not
thus capture returned to their army, proving thereby
that the homing instinct is independent of the contact-
odour sense; though with this restriction that the individuals captured apparently never discovered that they
were not with an army of their own kind. In fact, when
we set out again, they seemed quite content to travel
with us and even anxious never to stray: travelling was,
of course, the natural mode of their lives. It was sometimes ludicrous to see how they begged for food, palpating us with imaginary antennæ and lifting the
stumps of their necks as though they were opening
shadowy mouths. Never have I seen a more striking
symbol of such systems of philosophy as try to explain
the universe by means of intuition. Anna-zee, our botanist, indulged in inexhaustible mirth at the expense of
these living corpses. They lived for 39 days and kept up
sufficient energy to continue marching to within the last
but one day of their lives. At no time did they betray
signs of conscious suffering — proof conclusive that the

seat of suffering is the brain, and likely the imagination. [3]

VI

The most interesting, not to say alarming feature of this adventure consisted in the proof which it afforded of the fact that there were Ecitons about. It was, of course, one of our tasks to secure what information we could bearing on the life, the habits, and the anatomy of these ants. But, seeing that their observation was fraught with considerable danger, I had made up my mind to leave it over to the end. We could not afford to run the risk of being greatly reduced in number right from the start; and that was the reason why we had so far travelled by night. For Ecitons, though almost blind, hunt in daytime. In view of their at least partial blindness, this could not be explained by conditions of light. In fact, there is one race of Ecitons which is absolutely blind (Eciton Cæcum); and these hunt with the same efficiency, if not a greater one as those endowed with a vestige of sight, and, what is more important, also in daytime. They are almost completely hypogæic; and when they have to cross open rocky stretches where not even a cover of dead leaves is available, they construct superterranean galleries, using a sort of masonry in the construction of which they are highly adept. Since this race of the blind Ecitons is the one which is geo-

---

[3] See also *Tenacity of Life in Ants*, by A.M. Fielde, Scient. Amer., 1893. E.

graphically most widely distributed, it can readily be inferred, as Bissa-tee pointed out, that the whole trend of evolution, within that genus, must be in the direction of blindness: for some reason or other blindness favours, instead of handicapping, them in the struggle for existence. The fact, then, that Ecitons hunt in daytime must be explained by conditions of temperature rather; and this led me to a further conjecture. Our geographers had already reported that, though our progress in a south-north direction had so far been small, the whole trend of the Narrows being westward, there had already been a slight lowering of the mean temperature, perceptible only to trained observers and by the most delicate physiological tests. The spread between the temperatures at noon and midnight had also increased. This led me to think that, since sooner or later our route would bend more and more to the north, this lowering of the mean temperature would become more and more pronounced. If, then, the difference between day and night was even here sufficient to force the Ecitons to go into bivouac at night, it seemed highly probable that, as we proceeded north, the limit of their distribution would be reached as soon as the daytime temperature fell to a low enough level, at least occasionally, to prevent their being abroad: from then on only did I think it safe to travel during the day.

When, therefore, our work at this station was finished and we all had sufficiently recovered from the effects of fatigue and hunger, I set the hour of departure once more for sunset. To omit all detail, we thus marched for another 27 nights. Many minor observations were made by geographers, zoologists, botanists and meteorologists; and these were reported every morning before we went into our cluster camp. When they were of special interest or too long to be committed to memory, Adver-tee was employed to record them on trees marked in some conspicuous way, so that we could pick them up again on our way home. I often admired the skill with which Adver-tee could compress a great deal of meaning into very brief scents.

And then, quite unexpectedly, we met with an extraordinary obstacle: the whole continent was cut in two by water. It was not a river, for the banks were straight and perpendicular, unmistakably artificial, and of smooth stone. As we found later, it was a work constructed by man: an engineering feat not unworthy of ants. For the moment, however, we did not know that; or I should at once have concluded that no doubt ways and means had been provided for crossing this canal. As it was, there was nothing to do but to go into quarters. This was the first place where we resolved to excavate a cache or burrow in which to plant our own fungi. In this, our chief difficulty arose, of course, from the fact, which I had foreseen, that, we having no minims along to weed and cultivate the plantations, the latter were at once overrun with great masses of unsuitable and even poisonous fungi; and this necessitated burrows of a size quite out of proportion to our numbers. Before our present necessities were relieved by the accident to be related, the new hill had reached the following dimensions: superficial diameter 768 antlengths, depth 380 antlengths; number of chambers averaging 60 antlengths in one and 20 in another direction, 94.

Meanwhile large adventitious bodies of locally represented ants were pressed into service by Assa-ree whose methods I did not care to enquire into; the end was welcome even if the means were not. For it was clear that this great obstacle could be overcome only by a daring feat of our own: we had resolved to fill in this canal or, failing in this, to throw a dam across it. For a whole moon an ever-increasing multitude (they must in the end have amounted to many hundreds of thousands) was employed in rolling pellets of clay over the edge of the embankment. Two shifts of workers prepared the pellets; and two relays were employed in dumping them, so that the work went forward without intermission, day and night. We soon came to the conclusion that this great task would take us a year and 200 days to accomplish.

And then an almost incredible event solved our difficulties for us. One night it was reported to me that a floating monster carrying many men was coming down from the north. I investigated at once and found this monster to consist of a huge aquatic beetle resembling in more than one way a firefly. Every Atta is, of course, familiar with the purely aerial fireflies of our country; but the size of this monster was almost unbelievable: it measured in length at least 7,000 antlengths.

Now, as this monstrous beetle came floating along, with a humming noise, and as it was on the point of passing our station — where all those of us who were endowed with eye-sight stood aligned on the bank of this enormous ditch — the labour which we had so far expended in the endeavour to dam the canal bore fruit in an entirely unexpected manner: the beetle got caught between the far bank and our talus which by this time reached out into the water to a distance of 350 ant-lengths. The firefly came to with a terrific crash which dislocated the masonry of both banks. The whole floating population of men, borne along by the monster, was knocked off their feet; and even we were overthrown by the impact. [4]

Again I must give Assa-ree her due. Very few minutes had elapsed before she reported to me that she had established a practicable route to the other side. I had to trust her blindly; for obviously, if we were to profit by this extraordinary accident, no time was to be lost. Beings who were able to construct such works as this canal and to tame such insects as this beetle would soon find means to extricate themselves. By one powerful emission of the proper scent I issued the order to assemble and to obey Assa-ree in every point.

It was night; and the task of crossing was dangerous in the extreme. But Assa-ree had provided for everything. Along the whole route, with the exception of a few gaps of which I am going to speak, she had stationed huge, alien ants holding in their jaws small fireflies of the kind familiar to us; and these emitted a pale, greenish light. They had already been employed to carry on the night-work. Now they illumined a narrow, precipitous path through the ruined masonry of the hither bank; and when, ultimately, we reached the far bank,

---

[4] See New York *Daily Mail* of April 16, 1924 for a report of this accident from the human side. The paper ascribes it to a land-slide. E.

they were similarly lined up along its acclivity. Assa-ree was here, there, and everywhere.

Bissa-tee, Anna-zee, Lemma-nee, and myself led the way, Bissa-tee in her intrepid manner ahead of us all. We wound our way down almost to the water's edge, first through a rough and almost impassable gap in the displaced rocks, then over the talus constructed by our gangs. As we approached the water, Assa-ree appeared, enjoining caution. The road abutted above the water at a point where, opposite, a round, circular hole gaped like a trachea in the flank of the beetle. The gap, of perhaps 120 antlengths, was bridged by a yielding and excessively narrow, but tough and resistant sort of cable the histological nature of which we had no time to examine. In itself it would have admitted of no other passage than in single file. But Assa-ree signalled a halt and issued an order. Whereupon several hundred ants poured on to this bridge; these fastened themselves sideways to the yielding fibres and thereby trebled its width. At a further signal from Assa-ree we proceeded, marching four abreast. In the opening of the trachea, Assa-ree was waiting for us.

What we walked over next, inside of the beetle, is beyond my guessing. It was a tremendous task; for we had no light here; but Assa-ree, keeping ahead of us, scented the road. At last we came out on the far side; and it seemed that we had escaped one danger only to succumb to another. Here there was no bridge. We were 200 or 300 antlengths above the water, and the bank was as far away.

Assa-ree, however, ran down the perpendicular flank of the beetle and out on the water. As we discovered when we followed her, she was supported from below by a chain of ants clinging together, six or eight abreast, and submerged in the chilling flood. Never in my life had I touched anything as cold as this water; but for good or evil we were committed; and we struggled on.

Assa-ree left us; nor was there any need for further guidance; the moment we set foot on solid ground, the fireflies lighted us again; and we were soon on top of the bank. It took the greater part of the night for the army to cross; and all the time there was a noisy and mysterious commotion going on among the humans on or within the beetle. When the last of us had landed, the grey of dawn was showing in the east; and still there remained one task: the living float of ants had to be withdrawn from the water; for we could not think of leaving them who had been the means of our accomplishing the crossing to drown in the icy floods of this tremendous cut.

However, this was soon done, and all of them were taken, in the mandibles of our carriers, to a wooded patch west of the canal where the rising sun restored all but one to consciousness and normal life.

Such was the great adventure of the human *canal*.

It came as an anticlimax when our geographers, shortly after, discovered that this cut was, at regular intervals, provided with gates over which we could have crossed without any trouble. At any rate, this discovery settled all my worries with regard to our eventual return.

VII

Thus, for another five months, we proceeded by
night marches. How the army fared I am unable to say;
I did not enquire. As for ourselves, the High Command,
we never ate for weeks and weeks. It was a hardship
which we bore cheerfully for the sake of the cause.

As I have hinted, even our night marches yielded a
rich harvest of observations, geographical, meteorological, botanical and zoological. My conjecture that the
trend of the continent would be more and more north-
ward was soon confirmed; and though the fact might
have admitted of various interpretations, the mean
temperature kept falling. Many circumstances led us
to think that the continent was widening out, and this
was corroborated when, a little later, the whole country
was mapped. Naturally, the farther we were at any
point from the sea, the greater would be the spread
between day and night.

At last we came to a country where the whole
character both of the flora and the fauna underwent a
subtle change. Thus, of 356 nocturnal species of Blattoid
beetles observed in our own country — a group which
had so far varied very little, by the occasional disap-
pearance of this or that species and the addition of a
few others — we were almost suddenly, i.e., within, let
me say, a week's march, able to locate only 41; and the
remainder of the new Blattoid fauna consisted of species
not found before. The close biological connection which,
so far, had existed between our own country and the
region traversed was reduced to a slender thread.

This led me to a new conjecture which I wanted to verify; and so I proclaimed another halt. We were at the northern end of a noble sheet of water from the south end of which a not inconsiderable river flowed roughly eastward. The surface, along the east shore of this lake, was less rugged. It was clothed by magnificent forests containing many trees new to us. Man was more common here, too; but I was inclined to disregard this source of danger. To a lesser extent, another consideration decided me, namely the desirability of recuperating our strength; I knew from experience that a total abstinence from food impaired our mental powers when prolonged beyond six or seven moons. [5]

Now this district abounded with Attiine ants of a variety hitherto unknown to us. I have made bold to name them after myself Atta Wawaqueensis. And these ants had not attacked us. [6]

I, therefore, deputed Azte-ca, head of the department of communications, to make an attempt at establishing friendly relations with them. In this she was entirely successful; and the whole High Command was most hospitably received in a huge city of these ants where we were assigned separate chambers and separate

---

[5] Miss Fielde demonstrated the limit of time during which maxims live without food to be 9 months; though queens, of course, go without food in the natural course of events even longer. E.

[6] It is, of course, impossible for a human myrmecologist to identify this species exactly. The "noble sheet of water" I was at first inclined to identify with the Lake of Nicaragua. But the geographical details given point to a more northern location. Every detail applies to the north end of Fonseca Bay, on the Pacific coast. But Fonseca Bay is salt; and I should expect this important fact to be mentioned by so accurate a recorder as Wawa-quee. E.

fungus-gardens. We had hardly entered our quarters when Her Majesty Angza-alla-antra sent to command my presence; and in a brief interview she insisted on having me with her during our stay, as her personal guest. Though I feared that this honour would in a measure restrict my freedom of movement, I could not very well refuse it; royalty will be served.

Before I say any more about our hosts, I will briefly mention that, as soon as we were established, I despatched Lemma-nee, our leading geographer, with a dozen of her associates, on a survey of this part of the continent; and I will anticipate here by stating that this continent was found to have narrowed again and that, further, a transverse valley forming a climatic barrier was found to stretch right across it, from coast to coast, with a pass crossing the mountains at an elevation of little more than 67,000 antlengths. This confirmed my conjectures completely.

Meanwhile, in the absence of this sub-expedition, we lived comfortably with our hosts, the Wawaqueenses. For the benefit of her subjects Her Majesty asked me in the most flattering manner to deliver a number of scentures on our travels and their scientific results. The reception of these scentures was all that could be expected; but it struck me that those delivered on the more adventurous parts held a greater appeal than those dealing with purely scientific results. This interest in mere narrative, I might say right now, became more and more pronounced as we proceeded north. If I do say it myself, though my own interests are exclusively scientific, I seem to have the gift of carrying away the masses by my scents.

Particularly vivid is my memory of the enormous tension which took hold of the multitudes assembled on the slopes of the mound when I related the adventure with the wounded she-man. From all that vast assembly — when I came to the more dramatic parts — not a scent was to be perceived till I reached the moment of our escape. I must say that, while delivering this scenture, I was standing at the very edge of one of the main entrance craters. When I reached that point, however, I was nearly thrown into a faint by a most powerful scent proceeding from behind and below me. Although the same scent was emitted by the countless thousands ranged in front of me, this particular scent was more concentrated than that of all the others combined. Startled, I half turned; and down there, a few ant-lengths below the surface, I caught sight of Her Majesty Angza-alla-antra who, accompanied by only a few of her favourite maxim attendants, was listening in.

Later on she reproved me for never scenting to her privately in such a fascinating way. I apologized, stating that I had thought she would prefer to be instructed rather than entertained. But she gave me such a scent, combined with a gentle touch of her antennæ, that I could not defend myself against the suspicion that her feelings for me were different from those of mere respect and friendship. This suspicion became a certainty when, soon after, I being alone with her, she hinted to me in the most delicate but somewhat agitated way, her emotions betraying themselves by the trembling of her gaster, that, alas, she was not happy. When I looked up, she added, in a scarcely perceptible scent, that at this moment she had only two regrets. I could nŏt but notice that she wanted to be urged to divulge what they were; and though I felt most uncomfortable, I scented to her that, having honoured me above all ants by going so far in her avowals, I should henceforth live in tortures unless she scented me all. She seemed to languish for a while; but at last she hung her head; and I had the greatest difficulty in catching her next scents which were to this effect: she wished, firstly, that she were not yet dealated; and, secondly, that I were a male. I knew well what, on such an occasion, etiquette prescribes at home; but I trembled lest Wawaqueensic custom differed considerably from our own. Yet I could not remain inactive. I approached her in the humblest way and offered osculation; to my surprise I found it was regurgitation she wanted; and fortunately I could serve her in that, too. Having received it, she seemed on the point of fainting; and she weakly waved her antennæ to intimate her desire to be left alone.

But it is time that I return to the sub-expedition sent out under the command of our geographer-in-chief. This sub-expedition had now been absent for over a month, and, the country swarming with Ecitons, I was beginning to worry about its fate. Lemma-nee was one of those small, inconspicuous maxims whose most prominent characteristic is an excessive modesty. To see her, nobody would have thought her capable of daring or endurance; yet she possessed both these qualities in the highest degree. I knew that, if her task could be carried out at all, she would carry it to a successful issue. But the very nature of that task demanded daylight travel; for angles had to be taken to distant points; base-lines had to be laid off; descriptions of surface conditions had to be secured without travelling over every square-inch of ground. Elevations, it was true, she could secure by means of her living barometers whose protoplasmic flow had previously been ascertained under all sorts of atmospheric conditions. Whatever data could be secured without trigonometric calculations had all along been recorded.

I made up my mind to wait one more half moon and, if we received no news, to send out a relief party in search of her.

This interval having elapsed, I called a council which I invited Assa-ree to attend. Little as I wished to be beholden to her, she had given too many proofs of her resourcefulness for me to leave her out of account.

At this meeting Bissa-tee did most of the scenting. She proposed that the search party should be small and that it must consist of ants whose eye-sight was especially acute. For, she reasoned, the country being infested by Ecitons, scent-rays emitted by Lemma-nee and her party would be interfered with by the fecal odours of these hostile tribes — odours so strong that they would drown out, by night as well as by day, any signals given by Attas. There remained, then, only the sense of sight as a means of search. It implied daylight travelling; and a small party would be better able to escape detection than a large one. In a blundering sort of way which made me quite impatient, she took it upon herself to name those whom she considered best adapted for the work: Assa-ree, herself, and me.

That, of course, settled the question. Her reasoning was acute and correct enough; and the remaining members of the council heaved a scent of relief at being omitted from the list. Assa-ree fixed her central median eye on myself; and I could not even betray the slightest hesitation. I nodded; and the council adjourned.

We got ready at once; and after a touching farewell from Her Majesty we set out on our perilous trip. Details are wearisome. Let it suffice that, for close on to a moon, we travelled criss-cross over the country to the south and south-west of our station without finding sign or trace of Lemma-nee and her party. A hundred times we had hair-breadth escapes from Ecitons. It was a life of unceasing agitation which Bissa-tee seemed to enjoy to her heart's content. But not everybody delights in breathless flight from a powerful enemy. Assa-ree behaved admirably; and when the dangers surrounding us seemed, at the last, to admit of no further escape, it was she who saved our lives, though I almost hated her for it. She was of that type which seems to have all her faculties sharpened by circumstances which deprive others of their power of thought.

This situation in which we finally found ourselves was as follows. In a lofty forest of broad-leaved trees which allowed no ray of sunlight to penetrate their foliage, so that there was no undergrowth, we came head-on in contact with the scouts of an Eciton army. What made this possible was the fact that, throughout this forest, the atmosphere was so heavy with the fecal odour often referred to as to make any intensification imperceptible.

We retreated hastily; but in our flight we were taken between two further armies advancing in such a manner as to converge upon ourselves. There seemed to be no chance of escape; if caught, I knew we should be torn limb from limb and devoured.

Assa-ree had arrived at the same conclusion; but her infernal resourcefulness did not leave her.

She bade us stop; and with one of her amazing jumps she disappeared behind a tree. Less than a second later she reappeared, a large spider in her jaws. This spider, to my momentary disgust, she urged me, in an almost imperious manner, to grasp by her pedicel; and I actually did so. Once more she dis- and re-appeared with a similar spider for Bissa-tee. Then she beckoned us and hastened to the only tree which had a branch growing out from the trunk at the low height of perhaps 150 antlengths. Here she dexterously caught a third spider and then climbed up the trunk and out on the branch, with her capture in her jaws.

I surmised that very likely she knew what she was about, though I had not the slightest idea what it might be.

By this time we could not only scent one of the approaching armies almost below us; we could also hear the twittering of the birds which always follow these armies on their predatory marches; chief among them being the ant-thrush wrongly so-called.

There we sat on the branch in a row, the three of us, watching. The nearer of the threatening armies was coming from our right or from the east; and as we peered out, the other column, approaching from the west, suddenly swerved and disappeared in the undergrowth south of us.

In a very few minutes the nearer army swarmed all around our tree. There were hundreds of thousands of them; the total body was at least 200 antlengths wide and ten times as long; and all these ants were hurrying and scurrying in the utmost excitement and fury. Wherever they advanced, they took immense numbers of insects by surprise: crickets, grasshoppers, centipedes, wood-lice, beetles, spiders, and others. Every tree they passed at once swarmed with smaller columns branching off from the main body. I inferred that even this limb on which we were would not protect us. The insects which they surprised indulged, in their mortal fear — for they well knew their danger — in the most amazing antics. Grasshoppers started a series of desperate leaps, scores of antlengths in height; but every time they touched the ground an Eciton, large or small, fastened dexterously on to one of the great legs and, during the upward spring, secured herself to femur or body. Among these were winged grasshoppers; and as they flew up, the birds hovering over the column as camp-followers rushed forward and caught them in their cruel beaks. The grasshoppers that tried to save themselves by leaping were undone by the very extravagance of their exertions; for they soon tired and, whenever they rested for even a fraction of a second, scores of Ecitons swarmed over them; and in a moment their enormous jumping-legs were severed from their bodies. All these myriad insects were at once torn to pieces and cut into fragments just small enough to be handled by the carriers who rushed them to the rear of the column. Though every single member of the army was moving about at utmost speed, the motion of the army as such was quite unhurried.

At last they arrived at the foot of the tree on which we were. Close to the trunk, but fastened to the branch, hung the huge paper nest of a species of wasps. This nest was promptly invaded; and while the adult wasps hovered about, humming angrily and in deathly fear, the Ecitons ran through all the inner chambers, carrying off the eggs and the larvæ and pupæ and young which they dropped to the ground where they were at once picked up by the carriers. Above the branch there was a bird's nest, in a hole of the trunk where another branch had decayed. It was the nest of a trogon and contained young birds. This nest was invaded next; though the adult bird at first picked off the advancing ants singly, it was soon put to flight; and a minute or so later various-sized fragments of the flesh of the young began to be dropped to the ground from the edge of the hole.

So far, our branch had remained unexplored; but the column which was returning from the bird's nest invaded it at last.

Up to this point, Assa-ree had coolly watched every motion of the ants on the tree. Now she gave a signal and carefully placed the spider she was carrying on the very edge of the branch. Promptly, with all the signs of mortal fear, it attached itself to the bark and, spinning out an extra-strong thread, began to drop. Assa-ree followed her, climbing down the thread which was still sticky and so offered her feet an excellent hold. Needless to say that both Bissa-tee and myself did exactly as she did. The spiders lowered themselves to within thirty antlengths of the ground which was covered by the excited and sanguinary hordes. Assa-ree waited till they had come to a stop; then she descended with a rush; and the poor spiders, mistaking us for Ecitons, in their panic bit off the thread and dropped, to be torn to pieces forthwith. I distinctly saw Assa-ree's antennæ jerking with a chuckle. She considered it the height of a good joke to sacrifice to the thirst for blood of these Ecitons those very spiders which had saved our lives.

At this point my strict veracity forces me to reveal what I should gladly suppress, in spite of the fact that it holds considerable physiological interest. Ever since Her Majesty Angza-alla-antra had revealed her tender feelings for me I had occasionally been visited by a queer sensation in my ovaries. In fact, I had not been quite normal. I must protest, however, that never before, nor ever since, had or have I indulged in treasonable practices. But at this moment of extreme excitement I simply could not help myself. I dropped a parthenogenetic egg into the midst of the Ecitons where, I am glad to be able to say, it was at once devoured. The fact did not escape Assa-ree's cool vigilance; and, to my discomfiture and indignation, she emitted three brief and faint scents, " Oh, oh, oh ! "

The Ecitons were meanwhile much puzzled. In addition to the egg, they had our scent; but, being nearly blind, they failed to see us; and the threads of the spiders escaped the notice of those who were above us on the branch.

We were now in a marvellously favourable position for observation; for we were suspended directly above the army of Ecitons and could see in great detail all that has already been described. One more incident I must record on account of its ludicrous effect. A large harvest-man or false spider had been overtaken by the ravenous hordes. Undoubtedly he had been where we saw him from the beginning. He was a huge fellow, with legs three and four antlengths long. When I first noticed him, he was standing in the very midst of his enemies, each of the eight legs stretched straight up, at right angles to the ground, so that he stood on his very toes, with his body just out of reach of the boldest jumpers among these ants. He was looking down and watching his enemies with the greatest coolness. When an Eciton tried to use one of his legs as a ladder to scale the prize, he carefully lifted it; and sometimes he lifted several of them at a time. Once I saw him painstakingly but precariously balanced on three of his eight legs, the other five being lifted high above the level of his body. [7] Though I have no liking for these harvest-men, I was so pleased with his circumspection and cool-headedness that I was carried away and, in my enthusiasm, emitted a very perceptible scent of applause. I truly believe that I thereby saved his life; for the Ecitons within a radius of 60 or 70 antlengths, catching the scent, were thrown into complete confusion and, for several seconds, forgot all about the harvest-man. In consequence of which he had a welcome chance to rest on all his eight legs. I am glad to say that, when the Ecitons finally moved on, he was still alive.

I am equally glad to say that Lemma-nee, our learned little geographer-in-chief, was found late that very day, her return having been delayed by just such encounters with Ecitons as we had had. The number of

---

[7] See Belt's *Naturalist in Nicaragua*, end of Ch. II, for a similar incident. E.

her party, however, had been reduced from twelve to nine, three of them having been dismembered by our enemies. The detailed report of her adventures was at once scented on the trunk of a large Heliconia tree; and it has since been made accessible to all Attas on scent-tree number 423 to which the curious are referred.

Having thus attained the purpose of our sojourn at this station, we prepared for a further advance, though we viewed the prospect of leaving our kind hosts with regret. Her Majesty Angza-alla-antra was pleased to confer upon me the title of S.I.R., making me a lady of her realm, perhaps hoping that I should thereby be induced to stay. But of course it could not be.

CHAPTER TWO

The Mountains

CONTAINING the story of the joke played by Assa-ree on the Ponerines, a picture of the Parthian battle against Pseudomyrmex, fought for the possession of the Acacia tree; a report of the ants that keep cattle as well as of our falling in with the fire-ants; the tale of our disastrous hibernation in a human building; and an account of the marvellous commonwealth of the Myrmecocysts in the Garden of the Gods.

I

AGAIN WE HAD BEEN TRAVELLING for weeks and weeks, yes, months and months, first at night, then in daytime. The number of our High Command had been sorely reduced from 162, exclusive of Assa-ree, to 129. The army was unimpaired in strength and fighting power; but I suspected even then that this was due to Assa-ree's machinations in recruiting new soldiers as we went. Her facility in ingratiating herself with members of alien races had long since made me think that there was at least some truth in those rumours that had been current with regard to her. Yet I saw no reason to interfere; so far even her possible treasons served the ends of the expedition.

On leaving the Wawaqueenses we had gone straight north. I wished to verify my conjecture regarding the gradual change of temperature incident to the increase in latitude. I also wished to leave the Ecitons behind; and these two things were found to be closely connected: with the fall of the mean temperature the limit of their geographical distribution was soon reached. Consequently we were, for a while, able to lead a comparatively quiet and uneventful life, though the expedition was not, for that reason, bare of results. On the contrary, the scientific interest was enhanced rather than diminished: the farther north we went, the greater became the divergence in climatic conditions and, therefore, in flora and fauna, between our home country and the districts traversed.

Strange to say, of our own great family one nation seemed to be omnipresent though never dominant. These were the Ponerines, scavengers by nature. They are the most primitive ants, prototypes from which, I believe, all others have been developed in the course of untold geologic ages.

In the districts visited, the size of their colonies is insignificant; and their workers are monomorphic though, as would be expected from their entomophagous habits, by no means small. In fact, our own tropical Dinoponera is among the largest of all known ants, the worker measuring no less than two and a half common antlengths, Attiine measure. Another striking characteristic of Ponerine ants consists in the fact that their larvæ spin cocoons in enpuping, a fact which connects them with the lower orders of insects. And lastly, their larvæ are fed with the raw meat of insects, without regurgitation — a most primitive feature.

All Ponerines are endowed with excellent eye-sight; and this led me to conclude that even those that kill their prey and are not true scavengers probably hunt singly instead of in armies. The partial or total blindness of the Eciton is of great advantage to the species, for it forces every individual to remain in close and unbroken contact with the army; and since, politically, they are far enough advanced to be communistic, it ensures food for all. I have observed a small Eciton Predator that was continually distracted from the common task by bright-coloured objects, such as butterflies; and having had her captured, I found on examination that she was abnormal in having well-developed eyes, both stemmata and ommatidia. But Ponerines, especially those that, in addition to being scavengers, are also hunters, are well served by their excellent eye-sight.

All the species which we had an opportunity to observe — and I believe they comprise the fullest list ever catalogued — had certain features in common. Above all, they are savage: they resemble man in so far as they attack whatever moves and lives, either killing it or, if that is beyond their powers, stinging ferociously and injecting poisonous secretions. To us, though, they presented no danger; for, partly on account of the small number contained in each colony, partly on account of their clumsiness and their entire lack of science, they were no match for even small detachments of our army.

In fact, Assa-ree considered them almost beneath her notice.

One point, however, had never been cleared up with regard to even such species as are found in our native woods; and my excellent friend Bissa-tee would not hear of letting an opportunity go by to investigate it. It had been asserted that, though the pupæ are enclosed in cocoons, the adults hatch from the pupa without outside aid; in other words, that midwifery was unknown among Ponerines. If this could be proved by actual observation, it would indeed raise the hypothesis of the primitive nature of these ants to the dignity of an established fact.

Since the pupæ could be observed only within the nests, the undertaking had its difficulties. Bissa-tee, however, who was the moving spirit in this investigation, worked out an excellent plan; and since that plan proved her to share at least part of my suspicions with regard to Assa-ree, I will give it in detail.

She proposed that she, Assa-ree, and myself should once more work together. Her plan was not without its delicate touch of humour. Assa-ree was to capture, or cause to be captured, a large myriapod which was to be killed. All three of us were then to be encased in the fatty tissues from its body. The fat, Bissa-tee asserted, if applied carefully, so as not to leave a single ever so minute part of our armour exposed, would completely absorb our tribal odour and surround us with an aura familiar to these Ponerines. If, then, we could enter a colony of Lobopelta or of Stigmatomma by night and with sufficient care, we should have a good chance of escaping detection. Just why Bissa-tee was so emphatic about having Assa-ree along, she would not tell me; I gave in to her wish because I trusted her implicitly.

Both Stigmatomma and Lobopelta were common in the district; and our choice was entirely one of convenience. The nests of both species are burrows in the ground; their single entrances are surrounded by circular crater-like walls built of sand-grains to a not inconsiderable height. We selected a Stigmatomma nest for our investigation for no other reason than that its slanting gallery was the largest in diameter that we could find. It happened to be the only one into which I thought I could descend without making a noise by hitting my head against its walls; it has already been inferred that my brain is of phenomenal size.

We chose a moonless night for the enterprise. Though we had been informed by our scouts that the Ponerines do not place sentinels at the exits of their nests, we wanted to make sure that at least we were not seen.

Lemma-nee was good enough, before we left our temporary burrow, to verify our disguise. Only when she declared herself satisfied that no ant, however acute her contact-odour sense might be, would suspect us of being anything but ants feeding on myriapods did we venture out.

Our procession to the burrow was in single file, Assa-ree leading and Bissa-tee following. This order was indicated because I found myself unable to pick up the scent laid down by our scouts for our guidance: the myriapod scent seemed to drown out all else. Besides, I wanted Bissa-tee in front of me so that she could, in our descent into the gallery, give me warning of any obstruction against which I might bring up with my head.

We scaled the circular rim with the utmost precaution. Not a sand-grain did we dislodge. Arrived at its crest, Assa-ree descended inside, in a slanting direction, till she reached level ground. Bissa-tee, taking hold, with a hind-foot of hers, of a fore-foot of mine, followed till she made contact with Assa-ree. Thus a living parapet was established to facilitate my descent.

The night was exceedingly dark; and as soon as we had located the entrance, we filed into it. I found it very difficult not to touch the walls with my head; but everything went as well as it could possibly go. Presently we arrived in the first chamber of the burrow, spacious for so small a colony. We palpated the walls in order to find our way. Bissa-tee showed her usual intrepidity by signalling to us to remain motionless while she reconnoitred the galleries opening from this entrance hall.

She returned in a few moments, communicating the result of her exploration by touches of her antennæ. Straight ahead lay the spherical chamber of the queen; to the right of it there was a passage too narrow for us and leading she did not know where; to the left, a wider passage led to the brood chambers of which there were three, one containing eggs, one larvæ, and the third one pupæ. Opposite the latter, she reported, was a niche in the wall large enough to receive us; but it was doubtful whether there would be light enough to observe what we had come to observe. I did not see that we could do anything but proceed to that niche and signified my opinion to that effect.

So far, there had not been the slightest alarm. We had, however, hardly arrived in the niche, when a Stigmatomma worker followed us; apparently she was attracted by our scent. We flattened ourselves against the wall; for detection would have frustrated our whole design.

We were aware of her slow and cautious approach; and I, being the hindmost, was the first to be reached. For several minutes nothing happened except that I felt her palpating me.

Then, suddenly and unexpectedly, I felt a sharp pain in my abdomen, just above my repugnatorial glands. I could, of course, give vent to my feelings neither by scent nor by sound. It was a most embarrassing situation; for the Stigmatomma seemed to have no hostile intentions. For several moments I was at a loss to explain her savage bites; then it dawned upon me that, very naturally, she was mistaking me for a myriapod and thought she had found a banquet. I endured the pain as best I could and did not stir; but I began to fear that she would bite her way into me far enough to find out what misconception hers was. So, in the most cautious way, I brought one antenna forward and, by careful palpation communicated my predicament to Bissa-tee.

Bissa-tee acted at once. Just what she did, I was not aware of at the time; but the fact was that the Stigmatomma ceased from her attack on my vitals. When, later on, I asked Bissa-tee by what means she had prevailed upon this ferocious little savage to leave me alone, she just jerked her antennæ in silent mirth; and every allusion to the matter threw her into fits of merriment. It

was at least a fortnight before she would give me the
slightest hint as to her proceeding. Then she asked me
suggestively whether I was female or not? When I
indignantly replied that I hoped at least I was no male,
she went on to say that she wasn't either; but that she
knew, for all that, how a male would behave if he met a
buxom lass at midnight in a dark lane in the clouds; not
for nothing was she a zoologist; and for at least five
minutes she could not control her amusement. When I,
half angrily, protested that I did not understand, she
became serious. Even we, she intimated — and I could
not but acknowledge the justice of her remark — even
we, Atta maxims, had feelings of a certain kind — well,
in one scent, feelings; and occasionally we laid eggs; at
least she had done so; and so had I; even though it might
be thought treason; and of course, they had been entirely
parthenogenetic. Well, if even we were not free from
such visitations, how much less could a Stigmatomma
be expected to resist temptation — an ant of the very
lowest order, only a single step removed from a proto-
type in which sexual and worker functions must have
been united in every single individual! In fact, she
added, the ovarian tubules of many Ponerine workers
are the same in structure and number as those of their
queens; and some have even a receptaculum seminis.
Thus she had simply taken advantage of her ecological
and phylogenetic knowledge.

To return, however, to our narrative. We waited
through the remainder of the night till day broke, when
we were rewarded by the perception of a faint ray of
light creeping straight down through the entrance gal-

lery into our retreat. We ourselves remained in the dark; but the pupal chamber was dimly lighted.

In front of us lay the Stigmatomma worker on her back, in a convulsion of ecstasy. But she soon rose and hurried into the larval chamber, followed by scores of other ants not one of whom ever noticed us. Every one carried in her jaws pieces of insects of various origin; the scent of their booty effectively preventing them from becoming aware of our myriapod scent. Again and again I saw among them that worker who had inflicted upon me a wound which only now began to smart. In the light of Bissa-tee's revelation, her philoprogenitive zeal is easily understood as a consequence of her nocturnal adventure. Time after time she took food to the larvæ who, as I have mentioned, have not yet evolved the more civilized way of feeding on regurgitation.

Shortly before noon, that day, there was a commotion in the pupal chamber opposite our niche. A number of pupæ were getting ready to emerge. Though they formed an irregular pile, all were oriented in the same way, the anterior pole of each cocoon pointing into the gallery. Whenever a callow was on the point of emerging, the whole pile was shaken by seismic movements; and the anterior pole of the pupa began to describe a circular figure in the air. Next a mandible was thrust through the cocoon; a transverse slit was gnawed half-way around its pole. Then the mass came to rest once more; and after an interval an ant began to struggle out. This is a painful process taking many hours: first appears one antenna, then the other; the fore-legs follow; and at last, after many intervals of rest, unless it has died in the process, the adult crawls out.

No help whatever was given by the adults that were feeding the larvæ: what a contrast to the elaborate care with which our callows are trained in obstetrics! The emerging ants, indeed, stretched out fore-legs and antennæ in gestures of supplication; occasionally they even succeeded in palpating thorax or abdomen of the passing adults. No notice was taken of them. But whenever one of them died in the struggle to free herself, an adult returning from the larval chamber at once removed the cocoon from the pile and carried it away; we saw them later on the refuse pile which was located a few dozen antlengths east of the outer rim of the burrow.

Thus this vexed question was settled once for all; no Atta will henceforth doubt that we must indeed look for the most primitive type of all ants among the Ponerines; very likely they represent the form, or at least a form closely resembling that, in which ants were first created.

It had been my purpose to leave the burrow during the following night in the same manner in which we had entered it. What Bissa-tee and Assa-ree had, somewhat to my later indignation, concocted between them, I did not know at the time. At any rate, our retreat during the night was cut off by the fact that at least a dozen workers came into our gallery and lay down, patiently waiting. They did not attack or molest us; but they barred our exit. I could not imagine what they wanted. I understand it perfectly now, of course. That individual of the previous night had been unable to keep her secret to herself. As Bissa-tee said, we were all ants; and much must be forgiven even to Attas.

When daylight came next morning, I noticed a mysterious activity going on between Bissa-tee and Assa-ree. I questioned Bissa-tee; but all she would tell me was to wait and to follow them when they moved; she could promise me a rare entertainment.

So I waited patiently, absorbed by my observation of the pupæ.

It must have been nearly noon when a sudden rush ran through the formicary. The earth shook with it. All the adults that had been feeding the larvæ passed us as though shot out; and every one carried larva, egg, or pupa in her jaws. When the last of them went by, Assa-ree fell in line behind them; Bissa-tee followed; and I brought up the rear, entirely at a loss how to interpret the commotion. At first I had surmised that the burrow was threatened by an attack from the outside; but surely, all these Stigmatommas would, in that case, have rushed into our gallery to rescue the remaining brood.

It was not till we came to the point where our gallery opened into the great central chamber that I had a hint of the cause of the rout. These ants have a savage enemy in a small mammal, Mus Insectivorus, which is provided with a most offensive smell-gland. How Assa-ree had got hold of it, I do not know and did not care to enquire, but she held a small fragment of this gland between her jaws; and the powerful scent drove the whole colony frantic. She must have had it carefully coated with the adipose tissues of the myriapod which, to me, was scarcely less offensive than what it concealed;

but, of course, neither held any association of terror for me; no mouse would dare to expose itself to the bite of my jaws.

What we saw was ludicrous enough. The pugnacious Ponerines rushed in upon Assa-ree, ready to bite and to sting; but whenever they came close enough to receive the full force of the scent, a sort of insanity came over them. They turned tail and attacked their own sisters with a perfect frenzy of valour. Soon things became interesting. For those who had had only a slight whiff of the perfume exerted themselves to prevent others from rushing in; but, getting a little more of the scent, they threw themselves at Assa-ree. The moment they did so, their reason was gone, and they attacked their own kind. Fortunately for the colony as such, there were still a few of the workers unaffected when the queen emerged from her chamber. This was the first time I saw her; and I was forcibly struck by the fact that she was barely differentiated from the workers: there was nothing about her of the awe-inspiring bulk and the next-to-inability to move on her own power which characterizes and distinguishes our own beloved queen Orrha-wee or even my friend Angza-alla-antra. Nor was she accompanied by any body-guard whatever.

Suddenly I saw her seized by one of the ants who had not yet come near Assa-ree. It was a powerful individual; and I saw her shining sting flashing in and out of its sheath. She seized the queen by her mandibles; and in an instinctive reaction to this grasp, which is very common among the less highly civilized ants, she at once curled her body up over the thorax of her captress who rushed out of the exit.

Altogether there were between two and three hundred of these ants; and of these perhaps fifty escaped, half of them grasping other workers in exactly the same manner in which the individual previously mentioned had grasped the queen. The rest fell in this sororicidal fight. Apart from these corpses that were covering the ground, the formicary was emptied in less time than it takes to tell about the battle.

We had now an opportunity of examining the formicary in detail; but beyond the lay-out already described we found nothing of interest. There were altogether six chambers.

This brief section on the Ponerines will prevent the curious from adopting the common error of assuming that the hunting, the pastoral, and the agricultural ants represent all the stages of development that have led up to our own kind, the Attas. Below and behind the steady growth in civilization outlined there still lies the chaos represented by the Ponerines who live on what they can get and who show the first beginnings of a movement towards civilization only in the fact that they do not live singly. No earlier stage of formicarian evolution is preserved; but there must have been one in the past when even these beginnings of a social life were unknown, every individual hunting and feeding for herself, and fighting for herself when attacked; yes, and succumbing by herself till a few of them had learned the wisdom of uniting their forces.

II

I must now reach back in time; for the adventure with these Ponerines took place after we had left behind the country where we met the first ants which follow an entirely different mode of life.

All pastoral ants use for their food sweet plant secretions, honey, or honey-dew, the latter consisting in the excretions chiefly of aphids, coccids, and Lycænid larvæ.

While such ants as live chiefly on the direct secretions of plants cannot strictly be called pastoral, I suspect, and Bissa-tee agreed with me, that they, as a race, go back to the same phylogenetic type as the honey ants properly speaking; and, that being so, I shall here give a brief account of our adventures with Pseudo-myrmex Fulvescens who live on the so-called bull's-horn thorn, Acacia Sphærocephala, which is found throughout that part of the continent lying north of the Narrows, though not in its forest regions. When, in the following sections, we go north again, we shall discuss the geographical distribution of all these tribes in a more general way.

The bull's-horn thorn is a peculiar structure. The tree does not grow to any great height; and it prefers a dry and grassy, semi-arid habitat. The spines or thorns are always united at their bases and grow in pairs, on trunk and branches alike. When they first appear, they are soft and filled with a sweetish pulp.

The bi-pinnate leaves of this acacia form an excellent substratum for the growth of our fungi; and so, wherever a young tree springs up, the Attiine ants that are numerous in these districts despoil them; and for the first time in the course of our travels we found these ants ruthless with regard to the tree; wherever it was untenanted by the Pseudomyrmex, they cut the leaves again and again till the tree died; on such trees the spines dried up into yellow, harmless prickles. On more than one occasion we excavated temporary burrows for ourselves and stocked them with fungus-gardens grown on shredded acacia-leaf cuttings.

But mostly we found the trees pre-empted by populous colonies of Pseudomyrmex; and when this happened the first time, an elaborate burrow having already been prepared and our need of recuperation being extreme, we resolved to oust these audacious tenants.

The tribe was entirely unknown to us; for neither it nor its host, Acacia Sphærocephala, occurs in the verdant districts of our own country; and so, finding these ants to be very small, less than half an Attiine antlength from head to tip of gaster, we never anticipated any difficulty. I ordered half a dozen of Assa-ree's soldiers to march in and clear the road. To our amazement it was not long before these six lay on the ground underneath the tree, lifeless. Assa-ree, determined not to give way, ordered a detachment of twenty forward. They were repulsed in the same seemingly effortless way. Resistance, however, served only to spur Assa-ree on, and she swore she would put the whole colony to the jaw unless they surrendered. This sentence she requested Azte-ca, chief officer of communications to the expedition, to convey to the defenders of the tree. Azte-ca spent the better part of the day, assisted by a dozen signallers, in an attempt to make them see reason; all she got for her pains was a fierce challenge for us to do our worst; they would defend their stronghold to the last ant. This, to use a vulgar phrase, got even my epinotum up. But, it being near nightfall, we temporarily withdrew.

Next morning Assa-ree had five hundred picked fighters ready, chosen not so much for weight and strength as for agility; not one of them was above the size required for the largest mediæ. When Assa-ree gave the scent of attack, they scaled the tree in a closed phalanx, shoulder to shoulder, jaws forward and opened wide. Within a few minutes, the ground was covered with their corpses; and in another few minutes a miserable remainder, less than a score, cravenly crawled back, defeated. These were in exquisite pain; and when Bissa-tee who, in addition to her function as chief-zoologist to the expedition filled the office of chief medical officer, had examined them, she reported that each of them carried, covering part of the cranium, the severed head of a Pseudomyrmex, with its jaws buried in the chitin and, in several cases, reaching through this armour into the optic ganglia. Bissa-tee at once desired some of her assistants to attend to them; and in course of time all of them recovered though several remained blind, and one was deprived of the use of her left antenna which was pinned back over her head by the head of the Pseudomyrmex. Assa-ree, in her first fury, jumped up and down and threatened to court-martial these cravens for having returned alive. I interposed; and ever after they carried these Pseudomyrmex heads about like trophies; for Bissa-tee decided it would be better not to remove them, the operation (which would have involved the baring of very sensitive nerve-centres) being too delicate to be performed while we were on the march.

But this last attack had taught us a lesson: our enemies had shown us how to defeat them. From the unanimous testimony of the survivors, the Pseudomyrmex cannot use her sting before she has secured a jaw-hold. The bite of the jaws is sufficient to repel any ordinary assault, whether it is made by other ants, wasps, or those huge, browsing cattle which frequent the grassy plains on which this Acacia thrives. The fact remains that they bite first and then sting; and it is the sting which is deadly. This gave Assa-ree her clue.

Two days were used to train the columns that were to make the next attack. A thousand majors were picked and taught to hold between their mandibles, and covering the cranium, a tough and coherent mass of vegetable detritus gathered from the turf. Their jaws they held appressed to their thorax but ready to flash up from below and to sever the heads of the Pseudomyrmex as soon as their mandibles were buried in the detritus.

This method proved successful; and when, on the fourth day, the attack was launched, we cleared the tree of its occupants in less than half an hour.

This done, our mediæ were set to work cutting leaf-disks; and Bissa-tee and myself scaled the tree to explore the stronghold of our late enemies.

The huge bull's-horn thorns were all perforated near the tip, the holes being just wide enough to admit a Pseudomyrmex. We, of course, had to have them enlarged. Every thorn — in this tree they were hard and hollow — contained the nest of a small squad of these ants. In a few we found pear-shaped but minute bodies of a gold-yellow colour and a sweet taste. Obviously, they were stored for food. Next we explored the tree to determine the origin of these bodies and found that they grow on the very tips of the leaflets. [1] They made excellent eating. More than that, each leaf carries, on the midrib or petiole, near its base and on the upper side, a nectary in the form of a small, oblong crater. These numerous nectaries were at the time flowing with honey. Such a tree seemed to present these brave and fiery little ants with a veritable paradise to live in.

I felt almost sorry when Anna-zee, our botanist-in-chief who had meanwhile conducted an independent investigation, made her report at night and presented to us the reverse side of this picture of bliss. It was true, she intimated, in her slow and sardonic way (she was no longer young and afflicted with obesity), nodding her head sideways, with a trick she had, over her left shoulder, that our view of the matter held good for the present; but, she added, we were in the rainy season; and these were all young leaves; unless she was much mistaken, the golden bodies grew on the tips of the leaflets only when the leaves first unfolded; and if removed they did not come on again; that much could even now be inferred from the state of the tips. And surely, even though all these minute bodies were collected and stored for use in the dry season, there would never be enough food to tide so populous a tribe over months and months

---

[1] See Belt, Ch. XII. They are called Beltian bodies. E.

of aridity. Furthermore, the extranuptial nectaries being located on the petiole which would fall with the leaf, this source of food would also vanish in the dry season when all acacias were known to drop their foliage. In fact, Anna-zee went on, instead of this being a striking example of a perfect adaptation on the part of the ant, she could not but come to the conclusion that, on the contrary, it was a striking example of a very imperfect or at least incomplete adaptation. As the dry season came, many, yes, most of the adults were bound to perish from want; and their survival, as a large, prosperous colony, could only be tribal. The eggs, indeed, would survive; but the population of any given year must necessarily be provided by a new generation, with the exception of a few individuals to take care of the broods. As for the thorns, excellent as the shelter was which they provided, they could serve as a source of food only when quite young, for the sweet pulp which they contained at that time was as little renewed as the golden bodies at the tips of the leaflets.

This gave us food for thought; and Azte-ca, who was a bit of a poet, besides being a most ingenious interpreter, remarked upon the sorry plight of all ant-life on earth, in the face of a hostile barrenness of nature.

I cannot leave this account of the Pseudomyrmex without mentioning that our investigation gave Bissa-tee, our impetuous zoologist, the first idea of a great and fruitful theory which, while it was proved to be erroneous in the present instance, explained a good many things later on. Visibly, Bissa-tee hated to accept the cruel inferences drawn by Anna-zee. She wanted to save these Pseudomyrmex in spite of themselves. She suggested that they might survive by going into a summer-sleep, an æstivation, which, by reducing the expenditure of energy almost to zero, would enable them to subsist on surplus tissues built up in the season of plenty. Further observations made this theory untenable in the present case; but when we came to districts where, not summer, but winter is the sterile season, hibernation became a fact of actual observation.

III

Perhaps there are more ants on this globe that live, at least in part, symbiotically or in a state of mutualistic co-operation with certain other beings, such as aphids, coccids, membracids, and fulgorids, or with the caterpillars of Lycænid butterflies or blues than in any other way. Some of them, keeping membracids, are well known in our own country and have been minutely studied in the past. Excellent monoscents are available to the student.

If, then, I shall consider one or two of them once more, there are three reasons for doing so. In the first place, this record is to be a bird's-eye view of the whole of antdom. In the second place, certain ants keeping cattle have reached a degree of civilization second only to our own; and since they do not reach that high level in our own country, they demand particular notice here. In the third place, it has been rumoured that man also keeps cattle; and from that fact it has been inferred by certain bold speculators that he must have reached a social and intellectual stage little below that of certain ants, though not the most highly developed kinds. It will be seen how dangerous it is to pursue external analogies into the realm of ultimate values, and how exceedingly difficult for any investigator, to rid herself of myrmeco-morphic or myrmecocentric fallacies when dealing with the lower animals.

A brief digression is called for. Northern ants are generally of the opinion that, the more inexorably climatic difficulties challenge the ingenuity of ants in their struggle for existence, the greater will be the development of that ingenuity; and that, therefore, the highest level of civilization can be reached only by ants whose every faculty and energy is called into play by the fight for the daily bread. That this is a fallacy will not be denied by anyone who reflects that such an intellectual development, as is called forth by a purely material condition, is also made subservient to a purely material end. The struggle for existence, while it creates, also absorbs intellectual and spiritual powers. I have no doubt that, as the development of these northern races proceeds, they will ultimately produce sporadic individuals gifted with sufficient genius to see life whole; these will set before their races certain ideals; and these ideals will inspire great practical leaders who, at long last, will precipitate a return of all higher ants to the tropics whence life has sprung and where it will find its final setting. One clear proof of the inferior-ity of the northern races is surely furnished by the fact that no such expedition as the present was ever dreamt of by these ants whom we had come to visit; and I can positively say that, to many, it was a revelation as well as an inspiration to see us appear out of infinite space.

But to come to the point. Among ants that keep cattle we must distinguish two or even three groups. There are those that live an arboreal life, those that live a terrestrial life, and those that combine the two.

Again a generalization is indicated here. Speaking by-and-large, of all animals that need the air as a medium to live in, terrestrial species are the most highly favoured. Arboreal insects, f.i., come in contact with hardly anything but their tree; flying insects (and ants have flown in remote antiquity) meet, during a considerable part of their existence, with nothing but the empty air and know of terrestrial things hardly anything but what concerns their stomachs. Whereas on earth, every step taken establishes a contact which presents a problem; the moment repetition enters into these contacts, memory arises; and the development of memory is the first step in the birth of conceptual thought.

Among arboreal ants perhaps none has so far advanced as the genus Cremastogaster; I shall restrict myself to this single genus.

A word about aphids and coccids. Both these insects, otherwise of a low order in the phylogenetic scale, are provided with a sharp proboscis with which they pierce the epidermis of leaves and chlorophyll-bearing stems to suck the newly-elaborated plant-juices which contain three chief ingredients in watery solution: cane sugar, invert sugar, and albumen, all of them almost completely assimilable. Yet, strange to say, these insects imbibe quantities vastly greater than they can use; and they eliminate the unused portion through their anus by squirting it out on the surface of leaf or stem, often throwing it to a considerable distance: a process which at first sight looks exceedingly wasteful. To account for it I will advance a hypothesis which will need further investigation to confirm or refute it. Perhaps these insects assimilate primarily the albuminoids which occur in the plant-juices in minute quantities; in order, therefore, to get enough of these, they must incidentally imbibe relatively enormous quantities of sugar and water in solution. What seems to give this explanation a high degree of verisimilitude is the fact that both aphids and coccids lead an extraordinarily sedentary life which requires only small quantities of energy-food; but all sugars are exclusively energy-foods, readily assimilable by insects which by reason of their active lives require a large proportion of them, such as ants. In these northern latitudes there are few ants who do not at least occasionally partake of them. In fact, only the strictly carnivorous Ponerines and Dorylines (Ecitons) on the one hand and the highly graminivorous and fungus-growing Myrmicines on the other despise them altogether.

When the surplus sap is ejected, it dries on the leaf and forms what is variously called honey-dew, lerp, or manna. Ants that are more or less omnivorous (like man) partake of this source of energy-food only in this form by licking it up.

But ants do not stop there. Our investigations showed that they have learned to extract from this source all it will yield. These aphids and coccids suffer from distension after imbibing; and this suffering can be relieved by a very simple process. If the distended abdomen of these insects is gently stroked, in just the

way in which I have seen man stroke the udder of a
cow, the juice is exuded without explosive action in
the form of a beautiful clear drop; and that is precisely
what all those ants living in a close association with
these insects have learned to do; and then they imbibe
the food directly from the anus. Curiously, I have seen
a peculiarly disreputable-looking human lie down under
a cow and apply his mouth to a teat of her udder while
he stroked it at the same time: a most remarkable case
of convergent development between ants and mammals.

Both aphids and coccids are, by the very reason of
their sedentary habits, exposed to the attacks of numerous enemies. Thus there is the lace-wing larva of
Chrysopa, popularly called the aphis-lion, which is
powerful enough to cope on occasion even with an ant.
There are the Coccinellid beetle, the syrphis fly, certain
small dragon-flies and numerous hymenoptera that live
a more or less parasitic life.

From the attacks of some of these even ants are not
immune; and that fact would seem to handicap the
latter in their defence of these omnipresent insects.
The Cremastogasters whom we investigated domesticate
the aphids and coccids; and to guard them the more
effectively, they build sheds for them in the shelter and
protection of which they can devote all their energies
to the extraction of plant-juices. Cremastogaster Lineol-
ata is particularly versatile in the exploitation of various
materials; if clay is available, she becomes a mason; if
not, she manufactures paper to build her tents with.
Both materials are admirably adapted to the purpose, for
they equalize the temperature — a fact which in these
northern latitudes was particularly important; rain was

rare; and the position of these tents, around the more or less perpendicular stems of plants, with the tip pointed and the base spreading, took care of what precipitation there was. I found a coccid tent constructed by a hairier species, Cremastogaster Pilosa, particularly interesting: it was built of paper, such as wasps make for their nests, and placed around a twig of pitch-pine, in a position which protected it at once from excessive exposure to the summer sun, from rain, and from wind.

But the most advanced type of pastoral life is found among terrestrial species, such as Lasius Umbratus. These excavate their nests about the roots of wormwood and similar plants and go on regular raids to capture root-aphids which they bring into their burrows where they soon become tame.

Aphids are wingless in their early stages but develop wings later on. So I was not at all surprised to witness one day, in company with Bissa-tee, how certain ants dealated the full-grown insects. At first sight it might have looked as though this were done to facilitate the imbibing of the excretions, for the wings projected over the abdomen and interfered with the process of stroking it. But Bissa-tee called my attention to the fact that these imaginal aphids were swollen with eggs: the ants dealate them to prevent them from taking their brood elsewhere. This led us to investigate further; I am glad to be able to say that Lasius collects and stores the eggs of aphids in the fall; and that, as their herds increase in their subterranean chambers, they are ever enlarging the galleries around the roots, so as to facilitate the work of the aphids. As for their eggs, they shift them about and transfer them from chamber to chamber in order to keep them under. optimal conditions of temperature and moisture, just as they move and tend their own eggs.

We made our observations with the utmost care, mostly remaining unnoticed by the ants, whether they were arboreal Cremastogasters or terrestrial Lasius. But occasionally we disturbed these aphidicoles inadvertently, as, f.i., when, by our massive bodies and our great weight, we occasioned a land-slide near the entrance of a Lasius burrow. At once all the aphids within the galleries were seized and, by way of a side-entrance, carried to a place of safety. This furnished clear proof that the ants, though holding the aphids as a sort of communal property, yet consider the interests of their cattle as much as their own. Sometimes the arboreal tents are erected over the herds at considerable distances from the habitations of the ants; the latter protect them against their enemies; and, while some of the species that tend them are not entirely mellivorous and retain carnivorous habits, we never saw an ant kill either aphid or coccid for the purpose of devouring it. Clearly, both classes of insects enter willingly into this mutual association; the aphids do not attempt to escape, except when on the point of oviposition; and when solicited by the ants, they exude the droplets with especial care, so as not to eject them forcibly. I can positively state that this association constitutes a true symbiosis.

IV

We shall now, by way of contrast, briefly examine man's relation to such members of his own subdivision of the animal kingdom, the mammals, as he has been able to induce to enter with him into a relationship remotely resembling that of these ants to the aphids.

We had proceeded so far north that we were occasionally exposed to considerable hardships from the climate; and towards the end of our fourth summer abroad, we were made at last aware of the fact that the differentiation of the two main seasons of the year is progressive.

Even during the summer in which our observations on Cremastogaster and Lasius were made, the days had occasionally been so cool as to interfere with the freedom of our progress. Nevertheless we had, within the season, covered some 38,000,000 antlengths; and all of this distance had been travelled in a more or less northerly direction. Moreover, we were, as our physiological barometers showed, at an altitude of over 120,000 antlengths above the sea.

In spite of these seemingly unfavourable circumstances, human habitations had become more and more frequent. As a rule we had avoided them; we were not anxious to renew such experiences as we had had with that medical man near the Narrows.

But one evening we had a strange adventure with ants. It had been raining heavily; and a little brook which we should otherwise easily have bridged was swollen into a foaming torrent. We were spread out along its southern bank, trying to find some way of crossing it when Bissa-tee who was near me suddenly espied a dark, rounded mass floating down the current. This mass landed, or rather was caught, not far from where we stood, by the projecting trunk of a fallen tree; and there it seemed to disintegrate. It consisted of a large raft of ants held together by their legs which they had hooked into each other; their young, their eggs, larvæ, and pupæ as well as their queen they had been carrying in the centre of this raft; and, loaded with their broods, they were now rapidly filing landward along the tree-trunk. To our surprise we found them to be a tribe of Solenopsis Geminata, the fire-ant, which we thought we had long since left behind. This is a graminivorous ant of medium size which is very common and much dreaded in the warmer parts of the country; and it is well known that they like to build their nests near streams.

When they saw us lined up along the edge of this raging torrent, they seemed to forget their ferocity and to be overcome with wonder. I flatter myself that my own venerable appearance was not without its influence in thus subduing their fiercer instincts. But Bissa-tee deserves no little credit for offering a helping foot to one or two workers who were in danger of falling back, under their burdens, into the water. Fortunately neither Assa-ree nor any of our more unruly escort were near, or a battle would surely have ensued; and by this time we could no longer afford to fight any but strictly defensive battles.

I must admit that it was Bissa-tee's gallant action which suggested my next step. For at this very moment

I saw the aged queen of the colony struggling out of the disintegrating cluster of the raft. I rushed to her side and, shouldering her escort away, offered her my antenna as a support. The whole crowd of Solenopsis cheered by emitting a most unbearable scent and even by stridulation. For that I, with my massive body and head which set me apart as at least an ant of considerable distinction, should extend my antennæ instead of a foot, must indeed have seemed almost too much honour. I had reason to regret this excess of gallantry; for it took Bissa-tee two weeks of careful nursing to repair the injury inflicted on these antennæ by Her Majesty's rough and serrate jaws. However, she, in turn, did me the honour of discarding her other attendants and of gaining the shore leaning heavily on my shoulder. Meanwhile, she was not unconscious of the burden she must have been; for, while awkwardly dragging herself along, she scented to me this challenge, " Now confess, lady-errant, that I am the heaviest and roughest queen in these parts. " Since, at that very moment, we reached a flat stone on the shore, I stepped back, bowed my antennæ to the very ground, and replied, " In the world, madam, in the world! " Which ready repartee completely won us her good will; and so mutually hospitable relations were established for the night. Her Majesty persisted in treating me like a male and an old gallant of hers, although she was at least twice my age; and every utterance was accompanied by that ironical curve of her waving antennæ to which she apparently owed much of her ascendency over her tribe. She was one of those enormous dowager ladies who, while apparently expecting everyone, even her servants, to make

love to her, at the same time laugh, half good-naturedly,
half contemptuously, both at them and themselves. I
have found such behaviour to be either the result of
having received immense satisfactions from life or of
having gone on from disappointment to disappointment;
the latter they are too proud to show; and the feeling
of their own vital superiority is driven inward to fer-
ment into an acid scorn for all their kind.

Both Her Majesty and myself, immediately after
the rescue, gave orders to prepare the clusters for the
night. There were plenty of old, hollow willows about,
to serve as temporary quarters. This measure was partly
indicated by the failing of the light; and partly, I suppose, it was dictated by a desire on both sides to get rid
of subordinate witnesses to the conference between the
High Commands of both parties.

Within an hour or so we were assembled in a hollow
of the ground. The weather had cleared; and a magnificent half-moon stood high in the sky. I had been anxious to secure just such a conference with ants that
knew the country and could advise us; and, since our
next great adventure was to be the direct outcome of
that night's revelations, I must give them in some detail.

Naturally, the proceedings were started by Her
Majesty who asked me to give an account of ourselves.
She knew, she said, we must have come from afar and
no doubt had much to tell that was worth listening to.
I complied; and, having finished, went on to say that I
was chiefly worried at finding man so common in these
parts.

"Why?" she asked, adding that she could not
understand the common prejudice against man. A

number of her counsellors who formed the body-guard
gravely nodded assent; and when I asked her whether
she did not think, no matter what else might be said
for or against man, he was at least highly noxious to
ants, she expressed herself amazed at such a notion.
Not at all, she replied; on the contrary, she considered
him outright beneficial.

As for her reasons, I seemed unable to elicit anything that was conclusive beyond the fact that he har-
bours vermin; this indeed was enlarged upon: he being
a very wasteful animal, the earth around and near his
dwellings is always littered with vegetable and animal
detritus which gives cover and sustenance to such forms
of life as would otherwise find it hard to subsist; and
those are the very ones which are most palatable to
many ants. Even in his crops, she added, which were
almost invariably alien to the climate in which they
are grown and therefore attracted an immense number
of insect-parasites, he provided an inexhaustible supply
of food for his betters. She went so far as to assert that,
if nature had not given man to ants, ants would, at least
in these parts, have had to invent or to breed something
much resembling man in order to subsist in safety.
But, of course, having created ants, the crown and supreme achievement of her work, nature could be trusted
to provide for them; and so she had also created man.

I glanced at Anna-zee who sat in the background,
massive and sardonic; I was half afraid she might give
utterance to her thought; but she considered such
teleological vapourings beneath her notice.

Personally, I was struck by one single thing in all
the queen had said: and that was a brief but pregnant

reference to the climate of " these parts ". We had boldly
pushed into the unknown increasing our altitude as well
as our latitude; I had not the slightest idea of what
might be ahead of us. This anxiety of mine I thought it
now expedient to express without reserve.

Her answer amazed me. Did we not know? In that
case there was only one of two things for us to do. Either
we must turn back at once and try, by forced marches,
to regain a district where existence was possible for
such as ourselves in winter-time; or we must drop our
silly prejudice against man and seek shelter in such
buildings as he erected either for himself or for the
animals with which he associated. For truly, she added,
with a side-glance at my enormous head, even if we
could find a friendly tribe in these parts, no ant excavated burrows with galleries large enough to admit us,
nor deep enough to protect us from the upper cold; not,
at least, south of the Garden of the Gods; and, coming
as we did from the tropics, she presumed we had never
adapted ourselves to a winter sleep. This was, by the
way, the first time I heard the so-called Garden of the
Gods mentioned; and before we all retired for the night,
I took care to make the most detailed enquiries with
regard to this locality. And then this old Solenopsis
queen launched into a description of winter in " these
parts " which I thought truly eloquent and, in its sombre
way, almost poetic.

The sun, she said, would lose his power because he
would never rise to any great height in the heavens. He
would blaze down with a cruel, cold light on what she
called a frozen earth, blindingly white. Bitter winds
would sweep these slopes; water would freeze into a

transparent colourless rock; no rain would fall from the sky; but instead there would be whirling masses of six-pointed slabs of shining ice; and the ground would harden to such an extent that none could burrow and none could hunt. To an ant, she said, the mere touch of that earth was instant death; for she would stiffen and harden and remain in that state till she was beyond recovery; or, if milder weather intervened, it would be so much the worse; for she would freeze and thaw and thaw and freeze till there was no help for her: her shining armour would burst, and she would fall a prey to decay in spring or be picked up by carrion-feeding birds with which the district abounded.

This was terrible news indeed; and we sat silent when she had ended. Every statement of hers had been confirmed by a nod on the part of every one of her council; and on my side Lemma-nee, I could see, despaired of any hope of salvation.

I, however, on whom it devolved to keep up the morale of the expedition, promptly asked for further and detailed information about the dwellings of man; and Her Majesty, signifying that any of her counsellors could supply the information fully as well as herself, rose heavily to leave the circle and to withdraw. I and my companions lowered our antennæ to the ground as she swept out, supported by her attendants; and, in the bright moonlight, I saw her eyes twinkle as she acknowledged our salute.

We now received a most accurate account of the lay-out of a man's dwelling, together with directions how to reach it. The counsellor who gave us this account which I recommended to Lemma-nee's special attention

was one of those over-scrupulous and painstaking individuals who will give no one else credit for a bit of understanding, considering everyone as being in need of as
much detail as they would require themselves; and so,
long before she had finished, both Bissa-tee and I were
sound asleep. In fact, I did not wake till I felt myself
supported and almost carried along to the cluster formed by the lesser members of the High Command in the
hollow of a huge willow tree.

Next morning, our friends of the night before set
out to return to their abode along the upper reaches of
the creek whence the flood had ousted them. We, having
had a good rest, resolved to follow Her Majesty's advice
and, under the command of our geographer-in-chief,
made straight for the farm of man which had been described to us; and there we intended to go into winter
quarters.

V

We arrived in the evening of the third day and
found the compound to consist of a large dwelling in
which the man, his female, and three young were housed;
and behind this dwelling, a little lower down the hill,
but still above the creek which traversed the meadows,
of an enormous building divided into four parts: first
vertically, for, below, there were the quarters of the
animals with which this man associated, and, above, the
huge caves in which he kept his forage crops; second,
horizontally, for cows, horses, and pigs were kept in
separate chambers divided from each other by partitions.

Besides, a large flock of huge birds of the gallinaceous order roamed freely over all chambers.

We had been recommended to take up our abode in the cow department; no other part of the barn, we had been told, would be warm enough. On very cold nights, our advisers had intimated, we might find it expedient to climb up on these huge mammals and to crawl into the thick hair on their backs; the clumsy counsellor had thought it necessary to add that it would be unwise to seek shelter on their bellies since we should be in danger of being crushed when they lay down! To our delight we found in this compartment great store of crushed grain which, though itself unpalatable, yet gave us a convenient medium in which to hollow out a number of caves; and we had reason to congratulate ourselves on a timely discovery of Anna-zee's who, on the third or fourth day, reported to me that, in the great store of dried grasses above us, she had found certain clovers which, shredded or triturated and moistened, would serve as a substratum on which to grow fungi. This news much heartened every member of the High Command.

So far, the days were still fine, though the nights became rapidly colder. We soon made the acquaintance of our unwitting host; and he did not appear to be one of the worst specimens of his kind. Although to us he seemed of course truly enormous, he was, in his own measure, no more than medium-sized. What pleased us was the almost formicarian way of his intercourse with the animals. These were not yet kept in the stable throughout. They were let out in day-time and housed at night, at least horses and cows of which there were four of the former and ten of the latter kind. The pigs still remained altogether outside. Now this man never mistreated the cows and horses which were naturally the first to come under our observation; he spoke kindly to them and patted their rumps, though he invariably shooed the chickens out of his way; but, then, these were exceedingly savage and stupid birds.

What, however, at this stage, delighted me most was his relation to the pigs. A marvellously fine spell of weather intervening, I took to going out a good deal, often accompanied by Bissa-tee or Lemma-nee, the only two members of our command with whom I was really intimate. They, too, seemed to be the only ones affected in the same way as myself by the often stifling atmosphere of the barn.

The pigs were not kept in one of those unspeakable enclosures to which they were confined on other farms which we came to visit, but in a field where they could run and roam at pleasure; and a cleanly, jolly bunch they were, though, of course, they were only mammals. All day long they played and gambolled about, hunting grasses and roots; and we observed that the human young that lived on the place would come out and play and run with the little ones among them, and even fondle them in their arms.

Every evening, at a given hour, their master would appear on the road from the farmyard, carrying on his back a bagful of Indian corn. The pigs were waiting for him in a corner of the field where the gate was; there they assembled, expecting him long before he appeared; when the noise he made in walking or some other sign betrayed his approach, they would rear on their hind-legs, resting their fore-feet on the bars of the gate; and at sight of their beloved master they would squeal and grunt in expectation of their feast. The man would stop and laugh at their antics; and sometimes he would pat one of them or playfully hold out an ear of corn and withdraw it again in jest when one of them snapped at it. This man, I thought, realizes that he is dealing with life like his own; he knows that even in a pig there lives happiness and joy, sorrow and pain, trust and anguish and despondency. They did not fear him; they came and sniffed at his hands and rubbed their backs against his legs. Was he not their benign and gracious master who fed them and who had taught them to rely on him in all their needs?

Only one old sow did I see that never took part in these antics. She had a wistful look in her yellow, slit-like eyes and stood back, grunting angrily whenever this pleasant scene was enacted. She knew; and a little later I, too, was to know.

A few weeks went by; and almost abruptly all that the old Solenopsis queen had foretold of winter was on us. Though the sun might shine, it was impossible for us to be outside even in the middle of the day; and for a while it seemed as though we had undertaken more than we could do. All the animals kept on the place remained in the barn now; and our lives, too, were strictly confined. Strange to say, the master seemed to protect us; but it was a long while before I found out the reason for that. Bissa-tee and myself, however, soon resumed our rambles even though they had to be confined to the inside of our refuge.

Thus, before long, we found the pigs again; they were now kept in a shed at the back of the barn where there was a large enclosure connecting by a low door with a smaller stall and by swing-traps with a second enclosure outside, so that, at all times, they could either crowd together in the stall or enjoy a somewhat greater freedom in the pen or in the open. They did not look so clean any longer; nor were they quite so high-spirited as they had been in the field. But they were well fed and had shelter against the death-on-earth that had swept the country. We often went to look at them, climbing up on a partition that separated pen and stall from a gallery on which they bordered.

Now one frosty morning when we had gone there, the man entered briskly, carrying on his shoulder a weapon made of a heavy steel blade into which a long wooden handle was fixed. This he leaned against the outside of the pen, then he climbed in; and as he did so, I caught a glimpse of that wise old sow which had never betrayed any joy at sight of her master in the field. With a grunt she pushed through the swing-trap into the open. But all the other pigs pressed eagerly forward as if they expected a treat.

He, however, chased all of them out but one; that one he held firmly gripped by an ear and the tail. When all the rest had followed the sow, he pulled the remaining one into the stall and, with his hind-foot, closed its door.

Then he fetched the axe which was clearly unknown to the pig, for, as he returned with it, the poor brute betrayed nothing but an expectant curiosity. He raised the weapon aloft, heel forward; and for a moment he held it thus poised, in estimation of the distance. Then he brought it down with a tremendous, relentless swing, straight on to the centre of the pig's head. The pig did not fall but stood stunned; blood rushed into its eyes; it was completely taken by surprise. An immense, bottomless abhorrence was mingled with the agony of pain; it tried to take a step; but it reeled; and then it seemed to awake to his purpose and tried to escape. But the man had coolly raised his axe again and stood motionless, waiting his chance; and at last, when the pig, in a frenzy of fear, finding the door closed, rushed past him once more, he brought the powerful weapon down on that head a second time. The pig collapsed; its legs went rigid, though still atremble. Life was not yet extinct; but the man plunged a sharp instrument resembling the sickle of an Eciton but much larger into its neck, so that the blood rushed out like a fountain. Life ebbed; the joints relaxed; the brute lay limp.

We, Bissa-tee and myself, fled in horror; and it was weeks before we cared to see any more of man's doings. Surely, man, as an animal endowed with reason, if reason it can be called, is a mere upstart. I would rather call him endowed with a low sort of cunning. His self-styled civilization is a mere film stretched over a horrible ground-mass of savagery. Man is no farther advanced in his own development than Ecitons or Ponerines are in theirs.

Soon after the adventure just related we had a revelation of the means by which Assa-ree kept her army alive in that barn. Incidentally, this revelation explained the conciliatory attitude of the man to ourselves.

I must explain that this man had mysterious means of lighting his barn at night. At regular intervals huge, white, bulb-like fire-flies were fixed to the ceiling. These he could induce at will to emit an almost blinding radiance. It is well known, of course, that our own fire-flies respond to any superficial irritation. No doubt he uses some such means; at any rate, he always touched a certain button in one of the walls when he wanted to bring on the light and when he wanted to extinguish it. Now one night he forgot to touch that button when he left after having milked his cows.

We had long gone to rest when a great noise wakened me. I got up and groped my way into the next chamber excavated in the crushed grain which was tenanted by Bissa-tee, Lemma-nee, and Azte-ca. I gently touched the former two; and they joined me at once. I bade them listen; and when they heard the commotion, they followed me in silence. Cautiously we made our way to the partition dividing our bin from the great central aisle of the barn.

We saw an amazing sight. Assa-ree was marshalling her hordes into a great compact body; and never had they looked quite so unmistakably like an army of Ecitons. What puzzled me most was how she gained her ascendency over these alien ants and what induced them to follow her and to obey her commands. It was all to become clear later on.

At a given signal the whole horde started in the greatest hurry and excitement to climb up the stanchions and partitions and even the rough wall that protected the building against the outside. Everywhere they peered into cracks and crannies, seizing hibernating spiders and cockroaches, pulling flies out of their hiding-places, and sending grasshoppers and crickets, still half torpid, flying into the central aisle where they were torn to pieces.

Suddenly one of these columns started a rat. I must say that these rats were not kept here as part of man's establishment; they were intruders and hated as much by man as by ourselves. This rat was skilfully driven into the thick of the army on the main floor; and apparently it was utterly bewildered and frightened out of its wits.

Had it rushed straight through the crowd, it could have escaped; but instead it came to a stop and tried to turn back. This moment of hesitation proved fatal; for at once several hundred of its tormentors swarmed over it; and though it still struggled, it fell, pouring forth its blood which was eagerly lapped up.

We looked on for another half hour or so; and then the murderous crowd turned away to seek the burrow next to our own. Of the rat, nothing was left but a skeleton picked clean of every vestige of flesh.

I often witnessed such raids after this; for the barn swarmed with rats and mice; and I did not feel that I could interfere. But I was much worried at the thought that this was the army on which we relied for protection. Here we were, the very flower of our intelligentsia, bound on a mission of peace; and for our escort we had, through Assa-ree's treason, a gang of thugs and cut-throats, ready no doubt, on the first provocation, to turn against ourselves!

Besides, the very usefulness of our army to our host led to one of the worst disasters that could befall us.

For this man began to take an interest in us. Without
ever interfering, he watched what we were doing. He
knew by this time where we had nested and was careful
not to disturb our burrows. His very interest, however,
harboured our danger.

The explanation of what follows was at the time no
more than a bold conjecture; but it has been since confirmed. I shall relate it as though we had known all the
time what it meant. There are human scientists who
make us ants the special object of their studies. They
do not know as much about us as we know about them;
but they betray a blundering sort of interest in us. No
doubt our host knew such a one and had told him about
us; for one day, soon after the winter solstice, he appeared in the barn with a stranger who at once began to
observe such of our numbers as happened to be abroad.
He was armed with all sorts of weapons, *forceps*, transparent cylinders, bags, boxes, and *trowels*. What some
of these were for I knew; and I gave the signal for
retreat to the burrow.

He, accompanied by our host, followed us and
closely examined the entrances to the two burrows. I,
hidden in the crater of ours, availed myself of a moment
of inattention to gain a post on the wooden partition
between bin and aisle. To my horror I saw thence how
this stranger — who, by the way, had two pairs of eyes
like the assistant at the Narrows — suddenly wielded
his trowel and dug into the burrow which harboured
our army. Our host, meanwhile, was holding a small
bag of tough tissue open; and the stranger, with a deft
movement, scooped up a fine lot of Ecitons and dumped

them into that bag. Having done this, the two men retired.

In the burrow, there was the utmost confusion. Assa-ree stalked about, surveying the damage done. It was the only time on our way out that I ever saw her excited. She behaved exactly like one of those beheaded Ecitons at the Narrows; she had figuratively, as they literally, lost her head. But this was of short duration; in a few seconds she regained her nonchalant composure and gave the necessary orders to have the burrow repaired. Undoubtedly she knew that her safety as well as ours depended on maintaining order among her unruly hordes.

I gave them time to effect these repairs; and then I ordered a general review of the troops. Assa-ree obeyed sullenly; but she obeyed; and the count revealed that the numbers of the army were now reduced to about half of what they had been four years ago. I cannot say that I was entirely displeased, especially since this last loss had fallen exclusively on the soldiers.

A few more moons went by; the winter came to an end; our host turned his animals out into the meadows; and we began to think of moving on; for I had received scent, through our friends the Solenopsis, of a most remarkable tribe of pastoral ants on the highlands just west of a first range of the stupendous mountain system that we had now to our left; and I wished to have unlimited time for their study. After that, I half intended to turn back, for at this time I felt much discouraged by the climatic difficulties opposing themselves to our enterprise. I little knew that most of our sufferings lay still ahead.

My discouragement was much deepened by the final
adventure at this human farm. So far, we had carefully
avoided any encounter with those ferocious birds that
were kept on the place; and when we at last made our
final exit through wide doors which now remained open
all day, we had carefully ascertained through scouts that
none of them was about. They were all, we were told,
scratching in the newly stirred garden-lot south of the
dwelling.

I allowed our army to precede us; and the whole
body had filed out in safety before I and my 120-odd
assistants followed. Now we had just gained the wide
entrance chamber of the barn which was floored with
a single slab of smooth rock when, from a wooden pocket
fastened to the wall, one of these birds flew down, landing right in our midst. No sooner had it alighted than
it began to pick up, with its hard, horny beak, some of
the most eminent of our scholars. Their surprise was so
great that they did not even try to defend themselves
but allowed that ill-omened bird to swallow them alive.
Thus perished a score of my most indispensable assistants: all but one of our physiological barometers, f.i.;
and a not inconsiderable number of our surveyors and
experts in communication. But I could have done without them if worse had not been in store.

For Lemma-nee, my intimate friend, geographer-
in-chief to the expedition, seeing some of the most important members of her staff attacked, in a generous
impulse went to their assistance. Bissa-tee and myself
did our utmost to restrain her; but she shook us off and
rushed to the scene of carnage.

At once the bird pecked at her; but she buried her pincer-like jaws in its tongue, nearly severing its tip. The bird threw her high up in the air and again pecked at her as she fell to the ground. But once more Lemma-nee was ready. This time she succeeded in stinging the tongue and in injecting a plentiful dose of formic acid. The effect was such that the bird promptly dropped her; and, the tongue swelling prodigiously, it found itself unable to close its beak. It emitted a gurgling sound and stood as though dazed with pain. Lemma-nee, grievously hurt and bleeding from a score of wounds, was just on the point of picking herself up again, when the bird, too, rallied and, though incapacitated to the extent of being unable to use its beak, yet in insensate fury rushed forward and jumped on Lemma-nee with its hard, armoured claws and began to scratch. In less than a second my dear friend and one of the greatest scholars living was reduced to pulp.

What, compared to such a loss, was the death or the capture of a thousand soldiers! I should willingly have parted with the whole army if I could have recalled her to life. It seemed a mere irony of fate that, by her sacrifice, she should have covered the safe retreat of the rest of the High Command, though our number was reduced to 109.

Such was our lamentable exit from this farm of man.

VI

It was late in the spring when those of us who remained reached the highlands of the Garden of the

Gods. This was the fifth summer of our wanderings; and we had now covered a total distance of 400,000,000 common antlengths, Attiine measure.

By a detour we had just avoided passing through a human city where there were remarkable mineral hot-springs which I could have wished to visit, for I was beginning to suffer from rheumatic troubles. We had had to cross a number of rapid and turbulent streams, using various devices for the purpose; sometimes fallen trees had served as bridges; sometimes Assa-ree's soldiers had been ordered into the water to span it; and on one occasion when the latter method failed because there were no longer sufficient numbers left to make a living bridge reaching to the far bank, we had made use of the lesson learned from the Solenopsis and, picking a spot where the current had a diagonal set, we had floated over in a cluster. Every one of these crossings had cost us a few lives; but on the whole our losses had been insignificant.

Thus we had arrived on a wide, elevated table-land surrounded by mountains. Ahead of us stood two masses of bright-red rock towering up to a height of over seven thousand antlengths and forming something like a gate.

This was the landmark which the Solenopsis queen had given me.

We halted, and I gave orders for the army to go into quarters here; for I anticipated an interesting and important investigation; and I was not going to endanger it by having these hordes about, which were becoming panicky and unruly. Naturally, Assa-ree had to remain with them; and to my surprise she submitted without a murmur.

The rest of us, 109, proceeded on our road and soon passed through that gateway of red rock.

Beyond, we entered a rough plain strewn with the strangest masses of red and white sandstone and crossed by fantastic mountainous ridges. Vegetation was scarce on this plain; the rare trees consisted of shin-oaks and a few pines. Over large stretches the ground seemed, at first sight, to consist of wind-blown waves of rock, their backs sloping up gradually, their fronts as abrupt as the face of a comber in the sea when it is on the point of breaking. This illusion of a wind-blown arm of the sea having suddenly been petrified is enhanced by sharp, narrow points of rock projecting over the crests of these waves, as though their spray had also been congealed.

A closer examination, however, revealed that not all of this expanse was solid rock. Especially below the breaking crest of the waves the process of weathering has provided a talus. This soil, if I may call it that, is held together by the long, tough roots of xerophytic plants, besides being itself singularly tenacious. Annazee, our botanist-in-chief, pointed out to me how singularly well-adapted this hard soil was for the construction of the most elaborate burrows.

We spent a number of days exploring the plain, and we had abundant proof that the soil-faces of the rock-waves were used by ants. Everywhere they were pierced, near the crest, by wide craters excavated in the central depression of a flat, cone-shaped mound formed of pebbles. These entrances were fully an antlength in diameter, many of them larger; and they seemed to lead into sloping galleries pointing right under those rocky masses. But never an ant did we see.

We were at an elevation of over 144,000 antlengths; and from that it will be clear that the nights were excessively chilly. The climate is arid; radiation, therefore, is swift at night; and shortly after sunset the temperature used to fall to a point where it was dangerous for any of us to be abroad. Fortunately, we found that, in the deeper crevices, the rock retained enough of the heat of the day to make it possible for us to spend the nights there without burrowing. If at all possible I wished to avoid the latter means of providing shelter, for I had learned so much of the high state of civilization, the learning, and the urbanity of the ants that inhabit these districts that I desired nothing so much as to establish peaceful and friendly relations with them. If we burrowed, I feared we might inadvertently break into and disturb their galleries, thereby prejudicing them in our disfavour.

One night, however, hearing a slight noise, Bissatee, now the only one of my friends with whom I was intimate, ascended the naked rock at the back of a wave and was promptly numbed. When, within several hours, she did not return, I tried to follow her but found it impossible to do so, on account of the piercing cold. She was found next morning, frozen stiff; and when, having been brought in, she thawed, she was for a long while unable to move or to answer my solicitous enquiries; but ultimately she recovered though she remained for ever after subject to excruciating headaches.

Bissa-tee reported that, soon after she had been reduced to a semi-comatose state, but before she had lost consciousness altogether, she had been visited by a number of ants of no great size; but beyond that she could give no details. From which we drew the conclusion that our unknown friends were strictly nocturnal.

In this conclusion we were confirmed a few nights later when a stray ant from one of the formicaries unexpectedly entered our conclave, for it so happened that we were in conference. Azte-ca was nearest to her at the moment. Much amazed to scent us so unexpectedly, she stopped short in her hurried walk. Azte-ca is in her way a genius; we shall hear more of her singular gifts by and by. But she is frivolous and given to sometimes indecorous joking; though this time this propensity of hers served us well enough.

I am sure she was as much surprised as the rest of us; but she recovered herself instantly, bowed, and signalled in a most ceremonious way, " This is a conspiracy; and the only way of avoiding danger is to join it. " I saw the antennæ of the stranger jerking and knew at once that our difficulty was solved. Make an enemy laugh and prepare for peace negotiations, says the proverb. Azte-ca had used ambiguous scents, such as an ant is apt to use when she is not sure of being understood. Incidentally she had danced her shoulders as if in clownish merriment. The stranger saw through her artifice and was pleased. She answered promptly, " I shall; but only with Her Majesty's permission. " We all knew, of course, that she meant the queen of her colony; but she managed to impart to this sentence an air of ambiguity by fixing her exceedingly minute ocelli on myself, giving me at the same time the salute royal. I bowed and signified that we desired nothing better. She withdrew, and we waited patiently.

In a short time she returned, accompanied by half a dozen majors who conveyed an invitation from Her Majesty Allas-ta, queen of the Myrmecocysts, for our leaders to follow them into the presence. When I referred to the cold, they assured us that we should be well taken care of and guided through the warmest crevices of the rocks.

We fell in line behind them, five of us: myself, Anna-zee, Bissa-tee, Azte-ca, and Adver-tee; and in a few minutes we entered the crater of their city. Here we had to delay in order to recover a proper sense of time; for, unaccustomed as we were to the climate, our own physiological processes had been retarded by the chill to such an extent as to make all external events seem to be extraordinarily accelerated. Whatever happened, to us it came as a surprise. So we preferred to re-establish the normal functioning of our perceptions before we went out. Then we were taken down through a wide but short, steeply sloping gallery which, at a distance of perhaps ten antlengths from the entrance broke up into a series of galleries only slightly smaller than the outer one; these, too, sloped steeply and opened into vaulted chambers four antlengths wide, from five to six long, and two high. Overhead they were hung with strange spherical bodies. The floors were marvellously smooth. It was quite warm here; and the air was dry and sweetly scented.

Beyond, we again entered a sloping gallery which again opened into a vaulted chamber. Thus we went on from gallery to chamber and from chamber to gallery till I estimated that we were fully eighty antlengths

below the surface and more than twice as far from the
entrance.

And suddenly we saw a dazzling sight. In a large
chamber at the end of the gallery which we were
threading, surrounded by a strong bodyguard, we beheld
Her Majesty by the light of phosphorescent masses of
vegetable detritus. She was very young, pale yellow
throughout, and of marvellous beauty, looking almost
virgin in her pride of place. I surmised that this was
the first time it was her duty to receive ambassadors
from foreign lands; but she acted her part to perfection. She was all trembling eagerness, restrained only
by the knowledge that she represented her nation. I
could fairly see how near she was to giving way to her
palpitating vitality.

Even as it was, she came to meet us at the entrance
to the audience-chamber and deftly prevented me from
giving her the salute royal by taking my fore-foot, with
a gesture at once intimate and betraying her consciousness of the fact that she was bestowing the highest
honour in her gift. My four companions she allowed to
grasp the earth with their fore-feet and to lift their
hind-feet and abdomens into the perpendicular, as they
had seen the first Myrmecocyst do to me. They were
fortunate indeed in having been able to observe her;
for how else could they have known what was indicated
under the circumstances?

We entered the audience-chamber; and, Her
Majesty seating herself at its upper end, we were
motioned to form a half-circle about her, with myself
in the centre. A decent interval was allowed to elapse
before Her Majesty signified her pleasure. I had already

noticed that her subjects conferred with each other exclusively by touches of their antennæ which largely accounted for the singular purity of the air in these chambers. Scents might have polluted it. All the more did I appreciate it when Her Majesty *scented* her request for information as to who we were and whence we came.

"Unscentable, O queen," I replied at once, using the gentlest and sweetest scents for my answer, "is the sorrow which you command me to renew"; and then, having to that extent acknowledged her courtesy in making use of this method of communication, I abandoned it and proceeded by readily interpretable touches on Bissa-tee's body. Before I was going to tell her who we were and how we had come, I begged to be excused for making so bold as to ask a favour. Her Majesty, already impressed by the adroitness with which I had switched back to touch-language, graciously bade me name it. Whereupon I, not ordinarily given to an empty exchange of civilities, indicated to her my desire to be permitted to face Bissa-tee rather than herself, adding that I should not feel at ease if I had to face her beauty and dazzling splendour while searching for the motions appropriate to convey my meaning. I saw at once that I had not miscalculated in this appeal to ant nature. All perfect females are alike: vanity lurks under their skin. Her antennæ trembled with pleasure as she looked upon my simulated confusion. I even saw her cast a swift glance at one of her counsellors, a particularly duenna-like individual of enormous girth, as she gave the permission I asked for. In half turning towards Bissa-tee, however, I was careful to stop short at a point which still permitted me to give Her Majesty now and then a furtive glance of admiration.

It would be tedious to repeat what I signified; it would involve a repetition of the contents of the preceding scent-trees. If I do say it myself, it was a masterpiece of emotion; [2] and more than once I carried Her Majesty, figuratively speaking, off her feet. Suffice it to say that it was morning before I finished; and that was the usual hour for Her Majesty to retire.

Before she did so, she was pleased to order that ample provision be made for my own accommodation as well as for that of all my companions; and I, in turn, charged Adver-tee with the commission of transferring our whole High Command into our new quarters as soon as the temperature of the plain permitted.

I will merely state that we remained with these new friends of ours for more than a moon and then proceed to an account of their remarkable commonwealth, abandoning all attempt at giving our discoveries and investigations in their chronological order. My information derives from one of Her Majesty's counsellors, a very great dignitary of the realm indeed.

First of all I was informed that the city in which we were was one of the largest of its kind in the district. The old queen had died quite recently; and sixteen years ago, she had, in turn, succeeded her own mother at a time when the colony had already been a prosperous and populous one. Her present Majesty had only very recently been adopted. Thus I estimated the age of this

---

[2] A word, formed by analogy to elocution? E.

colony at roughly forty years, which undoubtedly accounted for its wealth and its quiet functioning.

Considering the small size of the ants (the largest workers were exactly one antlength from head to tip of abdomen; the smallest less than half as long), the extent of the excavations was truly surprising. There were at least a score of chambers; and those hung with the mysterious spherical bodies were magnificent structures, with floors of great smoothness and roughened vaults above; and of these there were six. The whole burrow was excavated in very hard and dry soil; and, as I have already intimated, the connecting galleries were of exceptionally large diameter and perfectly tubular. Most of the chambers were placed below the rock, which insured their complete freedom from moisture. In fact the chief engineering problem these ants set themselves seemed to be that of securing dryness and ventilation. As for the proper regulation of temperature, it was taken care of by the depth of the burrow.

These ants live exclusively on honey. The shin-oaks of the plain are abundantly covered with peculiar galls the size of a large pea; and at a given time of the year, which happened to be the very time when we were there, these galls exude each from ten to twenty droplets of honey which is carefully collected by these ants. In addition, there are numberless herds of coccids and aphids stationed on these oaks as well as pines. The Myrmecocysts do not enclose them in tents; but by treaty each nation secures the exclusive right of tending those that inhabit given trees and plants.

Now this supply is seasonal: it is excessively abundant in early spring, but soon dwindles as the summer advances and the dry time of the year begins; in winter it gives out altogether.

This is the point where the mystery of the spherical bodies came in for solution; these spherical bodies are the abdomens of the so-called repletes; and the whole economy of the state revolves around them.

Certain workers are, from early youth, trained to imbibe an over-supply of the honeyed liquids. All of them are volunteers; though certain physiological adaptations must be present if a callow is to be eligible; of that, more in a moment. The peculiar difficulty of the problem will be grasped more readily if I first describe an adult replete.

At first sight she looks simply like a spherical ball three quarters of an antlength or more in diameter. On looking more closely, I found that to one pole of this ball there is appended a perfectly normal thorax and head three eighths of an antlength long, provided with all the ordinary appendages of the adult, legs, antennæ, etc. The sphere, in other words, is the distended abdomen of a living adult. This distension is truly enormous: the ordinary armour-plates which, in a normal ant, cover the segments of the abdomen, joined by an articulate membrane, are spaced over the surface of this sphere at intervals of more than an eighth of an antlength, nowhere touching each other, and looking like little isolated hairy ridges that do not reach anywhere around the sphere even in a direction at right angles to its axis. The articulate membranes are stretched to the bursting point and to a degree of thinness which makes them transparent. All abdominal organs except the ingluvies or pro-stomach are pressed flat against the outer skin, so that these repletes are unable to feed in the usual way. It is that ingluvies which is filled with the sweet liquid.

The repletes never leave the burrow: they are filled by the ordinary workers who bring in the honey, themselves slightly distended after each forage trip. These regurgitate, and the slack repletes imbibe the honey from their mouths; it takes many scores of such feedings before a replete is filled. When that stage is reached, three or four of the maxims who do not themselves go out to forage hoist her up so that she can take hold with her fore-feet of the roughened roof of her cave. There, she can move about with a freedom which, in so bulky a body, is truly amazing. In case of emergency, during an invasion, let me say, she can even drag herself about on the ground with considerable agility; but she is unable to lift herself back to the roof. I had thought that perhaps the surprising width and height of the galleries is meant to facilitate their exit should flight become necessary; but Bissa-tee assigned another reason for this apparently wasteful way of building: she pointed out that the honey, when collected by the workers, is sterile and remained so till imbibed by the repletes. Only when stored in their abdomens, through which it exudes to a degree that keeps the outer skin of the sphere moist, is it liable to foster the growth of moulds on the bodies of the repletes. It was, therefore, she argued, of the utmost importance to keep the air in these caves dry and in motion; and my guide, when questioned, while perhaps from mere courtesy admitting the justice of my own conjecture, confirmed that of Bissa-tee as being the chief object they had in view.

Of these repletes I counted no less than sixty in a single chamber, all hanging motionless side by side; and in the total there must have been nearly four hundred in the various chambers though, of course, not all of them were filled at the time. Those that were not presented a truly hideous spectacle, their abdomens hanging slack and imparting to them an air of weird old age and ugly decay.

An enquiry from my guide brought the information that even from their ingluvies these authors [3] can absorb, directly into the blood, sufficient nutriment to keep them alive. They feed others; but they do not eat themselves except when they are slack. When the dry season comes and foraging stops, one or two of these authors are taken down from the roof by the maxims and stationed in the chamber of the queen where, till they are emptied, they form part of her body-guard. Every one of the authors covets this honour. Her Majesty imbibes from their mouths what she needs. [4] Similarly, one or two are taken down daily for the workers who, however, are strictly rationed.

All these authors, with very few exceptions, were of uniform size; they were majors or maxims. But there were a few mediæ and even minims. When I remarked upon this to my guide, she explained with a humorous

---

[3] I hesitate about leaving this word; but there is no doubt about it. From this point on the manuscript ceases to call them repletes and substitutes the above word; it occurs a score of times. E.

[4] Considering the name of "authors", I am surprised that Wawa-quee does not call these privileged repletes "Poets Laureate". E.

trembling of her antennæ that these were prodigies who had " had the call ".

Since this expression puzzled me, she deigned to give me a few details. When, among the maxim callows, enquiry was made in order to find volunteers to replace those authors that had succumbed to old age or other infirmities, the first thing that was done with those coming forward was to subject them to a very rigorous medical examination. There were always some who showed abnormal developments of their alimentary tract: a flattening of the true stomach or a shortening of their intestines. Only such were admitted to training. It was a strange fact, our guide went on, that nearly every volunteer who seemed really anxious to become an author showed some such abnormality. The two things seemed to go together: the spiritual call and the physiological, or, perhaps, more correctly, the pathological structure. Should an ant, as rarely happened, profess to have the call (which, our guide explained a little cynically, really means the devouring ambition) to become an author without being physically abnormal, she was never admitted to the course of training; and in that case the call had, as a rule, a knack of disappearing. Now authors were held in great esteem in the commonwealth; that is to say, they were ostentatiously honoured and secretly despised as unnecessary and unproductive members of society; yet it was the custom of inscribing their names on a roll of honour and thus conferring upon them a sort of immortality, after death; and sometimes it happened that a media or a minim whose ordinary function in life it would have been to climb about among the authors and to keep them clean and sanitary, picking off specks of dust and spores of fungi and moulds which might alight on their moist abdominal spheres — it sometimes happened that such so-called critics professed to have had the call and at the same time showed such physical irregularities as would have entitled a major or a maxim to the full course of training. In that case she was, without any such training, admitted to the rank of an author; but her name was never inscribed on the roll of honour; it was allowed to die with her.

All this filled me with a sense of wonder; and I expressed the wish to be further informed about the details of this course of training. My guide very kindly condescended to enlighten me.

All those who wished to become authors were first of all required to fast for a full year, or for a quarter of their lives, many of them dying during this period of their training. Next they were, for a period of from two to three moons, exposed to all sorts of practical jokes, expressions of contempt, and an utter isolation: only critics or minims having access to them. The purpose of this, our guide said, was to sweeten their tempers; for no ant that did not have a sweet temper could possibly be successful as an author; every violent impulse, every bitter thought would spoil the contents of their ingluvies for public consumption; and that in spite of the fact that they were at all times exposed to peculiar provocations; for the honour given them freely when they were dead was withheld from them during life; and they had to be at the beck and call of even the humblest of their fellow ants who, no matter how excellent the honey they furnished might be, thought themselves entitled to nag

at the food they received; and that in the exactly inverse
ratio of their qualifications as judges. Only when they
had stood this test were they admitted to a final course
of scentures. Our guide told us that more than once it
had been her privilege to deliver these scentures to such
as aspired to the career of authors; in fact, she said,
that was the very reason why Her Majesty had detailed
her for this service as our guide. In these scentures it
had been her duty, for a period of a moon, to tell these
callows (for the training was administered at a low
age) daily what was ahead of them: that for month
after month, and for year after year they would have
to remain suspended above the common herd, unable to
take part in their pleasures and diversions except as
lookers-on; debarred from all friendly and intimate
intercourse, forbidden even to converse with their fel-
low-authors among whom there might be one infected
with bitterness and apt to impart this disability to her
neighbours; for their task — to keep the common inheritance sweet and fresh, and to protect it from any contamination — demanded the most absolute concentra-
tion of every mental and physical faculty on the state
of their abdomen; they must cease to exist as individuals and live exclusively for the common weal.

All which amazed us much; and we looked with a
new interest on these authors that were hanging from
the roof of their circumscribed world.

A last question remained: did many of those who
volunteered for this exacting service drop out, deterred
by the rigours of the course of training? Quite a few,
our guide replied, quite a few; those who do are commonly honoured among the ants of their time; for they

plainly value what the others value, namely, the pleasures of the belly, above immortal fame. As a rule they
went on storing honey in small quantities, but in a
dilute though highly palatable form which was neither
highly nutritious nor capable of being preserved for
any length of time; and since their honey, unless re-
plenished, is soon exhausted, they are not required to
remain suspended above the crowd with which, on the
contrary, they mingle freely in all their diversions.
Many, however, adhere to their purpose, lured by that
fame conferred upon them after death by the inscention
of their names upon the roll of honour.

I do not know of anything that we met with in the
whole course of our travels which deserved greater
admiration than the selfless devotion of these authors
who persist in devoting their lives to an unattainable
ideal, in the face of going without the common pleasures
of life.

By the time we had received all this information
and thoroughly investigated the whole economy of this
tribe, the dry season had begun; and I judged it expedient to set out again, this time towards the east
where, I had no doubt, new and amazing adventures
were waiting for us. Her Majesty honoured me by giving
me a night-long parting audience; and still further by
dismissing all her train from her presence.

I knew that something like a declaration was expected from me; and so I had provided myself with a
number of love-poems, both of scent and motion; all
these were composed by Adver-tee, with material furnished her by Azte-ca. Her Majesty graciously intimated
that she grasped my meaning; but, as I could readily

understand, that she did not and could not share my feelings. I assured her that, indeed, I did understand; and that, for the rest of my life, I should be the happier for having known her. She took it all at its face value and felt tremendously flattered.

The morning after this audience, we took our leave.

CHAPTER THREE

The Slope

CONTAINING the amazing adventure with the Wheeler; the story of our battle with the harvesting ants and its happy ending; the report given by Bissa-tee of her stay as a captive in the burrow of the Wheeler; the confirmation of my suspicions with regard to Assa-ree's treason; the amazing spectacle of millions of ants committing suicide; and the great debate between Bissa-tee and Anna-zee as to the value of science.

I

A ND NOW BEGAN that disastrous march to the east on which we started 4,243 strong and the end of which saw only three of us surviving.

Right at the start we were faced with terrible difficulties: it proved much harder to descend the mountains than it had been to ascend them. Not a day went by without casualties; and as soon as we reached the more level country to the east, it is hardly too much to say that for weeks and months we fought one single battle till we reached the Atlantic seaboard. Sometimes we

fought both in the van and the rear while struggling
forward at the top of our speed; sometimes we went into
trenches and defended ourselves as best we could; for
the smaller ants that inhabit these northern regions are
excessively fierce and barbarous, even though, in a material sense, they are far advanced; and man or his
slaves proved even more destructive than ants. In those
latitudes, man was gifted with a peculiar, restless energy
which kept him active at fever heat; and he occurs in
such numbers as to make his presence a problem to be
reckoned with at every step.

The very first day confronted us with the three
chief dangers we had to face in the course of this march
which soon assumed all the characteristics of a retreat
and which ended as a rout. Sadly depleted as were our
ranks from the start, we still presented a proud body
full of energy and the lust for adventure — a body, I
flattered myself, which any power would hesitate to
attack. I anticipated difficulties; and I had already
expressed myself to the effect that henceforth we should
have to consider ourselves as soldiers first and as ants
of science only afterwards; but I had not even anticipated what awaited us on our first day.

We were in high spirits when, having crossed a
small river which barred our way, we saw ahead of us,
on a sloping mountainside, a man who was riding on a
curious machine consisting of two revolving wheels one
of which was capable of being turned sideways. This
man, strange to say, we were destined to meet with more
than once; and so I shall give him a name and call him
the Wheeler.

At sight of him, seized by forebodings, I called a halt. Unfortunately, our scouts were too far advanced for immediate and effective control; and the Wheeler, who was looking right and left, must have caught sight of one of them who had lost touch with the columns following her. He alighted; and, having done something at his wheel which, at this distance, I could not observe in detail, straightened up, armed with a bag, a forceps, and a trowel, and looking singularly like that other man who had scooped up so many hundreds of our soldiers in the human barn.

Instantly I was alert; and a moment later Bissa-tee signified to me that she, too, had recognized him. It was, indeed, the myrmecologist.

But for the moment it did not look as though he were bent on booty. Apparently he was stooping over the scout, leaving her alone. She reported later that she lay motionless under his scrutiny, shamming death. From her he proceeded a few steps in our direction. I am afraid I made a tactical mistake; for we were still separated from those scouts by a distance of at least a hundred antlengths; and had we remained motionless, we might have escaped detection. In fact, such was plainly Assa-ree's plan; for she gave the signal to lie low. But I had already gathered all the scent material needed for a general order and could no longer retain it. So my overruling command welled forth, half in spite of myself: Seek cover. It was instantly obeyed; and instantly the motion attracted the Wheeler's attention. Three or four steps of his brought him into our midst; and he bent down to raise, with his forceps, every leaf of every one of the sparse xerophytic plants that covered the ground. Nothing else could be done: we all shammed death. He opened a little bag and, with his forceps, picked up a score of us, slowly and deliberately, scanning each as he did so through his double eyes. He actually picked me up, too; but he dropped me again, preferring to put Bissa-tee into his bag. Since I had no longer any doubt that he was collecting ants for the purpose of study, it was a source of mortification to me that he should choose Bissa-tee as a specimen instead of myself. But, as I have said, Bissa-tee was physically a rather splendid ant, big and active; I had nothing to recommend me but my brain.

Next, this human myrmecologist did something which I did not understand at the time but which I can explain now. He took out a note-book and, with an instrument called a pencil, jotted down notes about the observations he had made. For we found that man's memory is poorly developed; he could never have kept a record like the present one without such aids; and as, for direct communication, he relies exclusively on his voice and his ear, so, for indirect communication, he relies on his very imperfect sense of sight, making visible marks on paper which he knows how to produce. Next, to my utter amazement, he unhooked his outer pair of eyes, put them into a shell resembling a very large pupal case, and slipped them into a fold of his integuments.

And then he was gone from among us. Remounting his double wheel, he turned about.

I was much disconcerted, for I never expected to see Bissa-tee again; but, freed from the menace of the human presence, I at once asked for a report of the missing. It was found that the Wheeler had picked up twelve soldiers and eight scholars of whom, fortunately, Bissa-tee was the only leader.

What was to be done? I gave orders to re-form the ranks and to proceed. I might say that by this time the whole body of the army was massed in front, a formation indicated by the reduction in our numbers.

We were still descending the now gently sloping mountainside, having been on the march again for another three or four hours, when a confusion in front was slowly propagated backward. None of us knew what was going on there; and I was most indignant at not having instantly received a telescent report. Assa-ree, who had lately become exceedingly independent, asserted afterwards that such a report had been given at once but, for unknown reasons, had failed to reach the rear.

The whole column had come to a stop before I knew that anything was amiss. I was anxious not to be delayed; for, though we had been descending all day, and though it was now midsummer, we were still at too great an elevation to be quite safe from the cold. A most vexatious delay held us up. Since Lemma-nee's death in the battle with the chicken I had, in addition to my other functions, assumed that of geographer-in-chief to the expedition, for unfortunately Lemma-nee, in picking her associates, had aimed more at completeness in her subordinate staff than at the qualities of leadership which would be needed in case of accident to herself. So I consulted our only remaining physiological barometer which registered a low atmospheric pressure; from which fact, in conjunction with other indications, I drew the conclusion that the night was going to be overcast and probably warm.

I had hardly done so when a messenger arrived from Assa-ree. This messenger, instead of simply giving her report and quietly awaiting my orders, thought fit to indulge in the most impertinent scents, asking what was the matter with the High Command that there were no orders forthcoming? Were we all asleep that we left the vanguard to perish without support, without sense or purpose?

Such insubordination I could not overlook, and my whole staff agreed with me. Somehow we were all in a state of tension; everyone felt by this time that we had entered upon the most trying part of our enterprise. At the isthmus, surrounded by numberless vagrant hordes of Ecitons, we had never felt thus: our morale had been excellent, our discipline beyond reproach; and the spirit with which our troops had faced danger and certain death had often called forth my admiration. Even this very morning, as I have intimated, we had been in excellent fettle. And now? What worried me most was the question to what extent the behaviour of this messenger might reflect the attitude of Assa-ree.

I moved my right antenna the slightest bit; and I am glad to say that Azte-ca, who was nearest to the offender, understood me instantly. With one leap she was on the offender's back, bearing her down by sheer weight and clasping her neck between her jaws. Thus she waited for my verdict. I lowered my antennæ; the culprit's head was severed; and her body was given over to the soldiery in front. It was not a lovely sight to see them tear it to shreds which were promptly devoured.

Necessary as was this act of discipline, it still further delayed matters, for no report was forthcoming. I despatched Adver-tee, the recorder, to summon Assa-ree.

Adver-tee hurried away. In less than five minutes she was back, dejected and in consternation. The vanguard, she reported, was in touch with a formidable hostile army consisting of many tens of thousands of a small, unknown ant. Assa-ree was in command; and she had absolutely and disrespectfully refused to obey the summons.

Was this mutiny? I gave orders not to stir and moved forward myself, through the lines of my dismayed staff and through the very centre of the army, the soldiers opening a lane for me. But this they did in a sullen way; and here and there I noticed disrespectful scents that were being emitted as I passed. So far, I chose to disregard them.

I found matters as Adver-tee had reported. The ants with which the vanguard was engaged were quite unknown to me; and at this juncture Bissa-tee's absence was particularly regrettable. Assa-ree was in the very front line; some five hundred of our fiercest fighters were with her. In front of them, the ground was strewn with corpses; but ninety-five per cent of them belonged to the enemy. They were small but savage little creatures; and as their ranks were mown down by our sickle-jawed soldiers, wave after wave of new troops of theirs came up to the slaughter.

Fortunately, night was at hand. I waited patiently; and in less than an hour I noticed an abatement in the fury with which the enemy attacked. Gaining a slight hill, I could soon observe backward, concentrating movements in their ranks; they left only just enough troops in the fighting lines to cover their retreat. Now the extraordinary powers which I had received from Her Majesty Orrha-wee before setting out from home had been given in the shape of pellets of the royal perfumes which I carried in my infrabuccal chamber. I carefully selected one of them, the perfume of supreme command, and rolled it forward between labrum and tongue. I left it exposed to the air for just one hundredth of a second and then gave my summons; the effect was instantaneous and complete. Assa-ree shrugged her shoulders, dropped her antennæ, and turned to follow me.

I had half intended to expose, in the midst of the army, the perfume of instant death, most formidable of the powers conferred upon me by Her Majesty, just to set an example among the mutinous hordes and to show them that, the moment I wanted to, I could make them drop like flies before a poisonous breath; but when I saw what an effect Assa-ree's appearance produced in the ranks as she meekly followed in my wake, I thought it wiser to refrain. The whole incident convinced me once more, if further proof was needed, that sooner or later things would come to an issue between me and Assa-ree; but I was not unmindful of the fact that it lay in the interests of the expedition to postpone the evil moment as long as possible, for, though willy-nilly, we were still advancing. The battle we fought was nothing less than a defensive one.

We reached the point where my staff was assembled; and as if by mutual consent they arranged themselves in a half circle to receive us. The open diameter of this half circle was formed by the rear-guard of the army; and in its centre lay the head of the decapitated messenger, still moving convulsively its antennæ and eyes.

It looked like a carefully prepared arrangement; and it suited my purpose. I led Assa-ree to a point just behind that head and bade her stay there. I myself took up a position in the midst of my staff, facing Assa-ree. After an impressive pause I scented my plea, addressing my associates as a court martial.

"What," I asked, "is the penalty for wilfully disobeying Her Majesty's Supreme Command in peace and war?" "Death," came the unanimous verdict in a lugubrious scent. "You have heard the sentence," I addressed the prisoner. "Do you know any reason why it should not be pronounced?" And I touched the pellet of the perfume of death with my labrum — a motion which did not escape Assa-ree.

She blackened; but her sullen defiance was not yet broken; I do not think she knew what the perfume was which I held there. For a few minutes she hesitated, deliberating perhaps whether or not to treat my indictment with silent contempt. But she, too, knew that the time was not ripe for an open breach. My own unconditional followers were still too numerous.

Within a few seconds she stirred. "High Commander," thus ran her plea, "I did refuse obedience; but to whom? I was much provoked. I had long been in the fore-front of battle and was wounded. The stings and bites I had received were smarting; dust and grit had

entered all my wounds. I had been holding the enemy
with nothing but my vanguard; for I did not care to
engage the rest of the army without your consent. Give
that consent at this late hour, and I shall sweep resist
ance away. I sent a messenger to ask for an order; she
did not return. Your orderly appeared at a critical
moment; I know the ant you sent: an idle scenter who,
even at that moment, could not forget that her strongest
point was sweetness and seductiveness of scent. In the
very act of giving your summons, she saw fit to brush a
speck of dust from her antenna with her strigil and to
polish up her fifth abdominal segment with a hind-foot.
I felt overcome with anger and answered sullenly, I
suppose. And who could blame me? I am a fighter, un
endowed with the gift of meek ingratiation. But scents
emitted under such circumstances signify nothing. I
have done and leave the rest to you. "

Now I could not deny a certain justice to that plea
Adver-tee was somewhat of a fop; and perhaps it had
been a mistake to send her. To execute at the present
moment a sentence of death, with the only two of my
staff missing who had been intimate with me, would
have been injudicious; I was not yet prepared to dis
pense with the army; and only Assa-ree could hold it
in subjugation. The very fact that she had condescended
to plead amounted to an apology, given in the presence
of my whole staff and the rear-guard of the army. Her
services had more than once enabled the expedition to
do its work; and while, under the present circumstances
it was peculiarly distressing that she should have been
unable or unwilling — it was hard to tell which — to
avoid an armed conflict, I saw at once that, should I

prove impossible to appease the enemy, there was only one way of getting past, namely, by a wheeling movement which would take us around the hostile formicary while a continuous battle was being fought on a slanting front. Such a battle could not be fought without Assaree.

So I allowed an appropriate interval to elapse and then raised my right antenna into the perpendicular, in sign of suspended sentence. I was conscious of a feeling of relief all around. Assa-ree stood motionless for a while. Then, with a profound salute, so exaggerated as to make me doubt her sincerity, she turned away.

But the thing was done. I gave orders to encamp for the night.

II

We were not yet settled when, to my immense surprise and relief, Bissa-tee appeared in our midst. She was in a state of terrific excitement. One might have expected that excitement to proceed from exaltation or exultation; but it did not: it was simply the result of extreme exhaustion and depression.

All the members of the staff rushed over to her and recoiled; they had meant to overwhelm her with congratulations. But she waved them aside. She never stopped till she had reached me; and I was profoundly moved at the sight of her: her eyes were glazed her antennæ ragged; she staggered; and the moment she reached me, she rolled over at my feet.

I had her attended to at once; all her wounds were thoroughly licked; her antennæ and her legs were straightened out and rubbed.

But the most terrifying thing about her was that she exhaled a disabling smell which made everyone who came near her feel faint. She was soaked in poison. From her whole body a gas exuded; most distressingly from her tracheæ, especially those on the meso- and metathoracic segments; for the latter, ordinarily closed in Myrmicine adults, had opened under the influence of the poison which was readily absorbed by the adipose tissues and which considerably reduced even my weight by liquefying my fat which oozed away into the ground. A physiological analysis which I ordered at once to be made proved it to be a highly complex hydrocarbon.

Fortunately my weather forecast had proved correct; the sky was clouded, and the atmosphere damp and warm. This was especially welcome because Bissa-tee's unexpected return and the nursing she required interrupted the preparations for encampment. I anticipated days of delay.

Night had fallen when Bissa-tee stirred again. By this time the exhalations from her body had become fainter. In the dim, diffused light of a hidden moon I saw her slowly move her antennæ and, thinking that she was groping for me, I stepped into the path of her movements. She at once signified to me that she wished me to come close and to dismiss all those attending upon her. I did so; and with extreme exertion, slowly, and in fits and starts, she told her tale.

First of all she enumerated our associates who had been picked up with her; to add that everyone of them was dead. The Wheeler was indeed a myrmecologist. At his abode in the human city he kept whole tribes of ants in captivity, confined in artificial nests of *glass*. He had dropped a dozen or more of her fellow-captives into these nests, one at a time, and reaching for a new nest whenever he picked up a new Atta. Meanwhile, Bissa-tee had been confined in a large cylinder whence she had been able to look on at the proceedings. In each and every case the ant thus dropped into an alien nest had at once been torn to pieces. Bissa-tee had fully expected to share the same fate; but, strange to say, she had escaped it. When only she was left, the Wheeler had fetched a flat wooden case smelling strongly of certain oils found in the earth. To her horror, she had seen, in this case, innumerable ants of all descriptions, dead, and pierced by steel spears four ants long which were stuck into the floor of the case: it had been a sight to make her blood curdle.

He had picked Bissa-tee up with a forceps and compared her with these specimens. Having done so with one case, he had fetched another; and thus he had been occupied for hours without any result. Every now and then he had consulted huge tomes similar in shape (though much larger) to the note-book in which he had jotted down observations at the time of her capture. These Bissa-tee described at great length, for she did not know that I had already seen this human device; nor did I interrupt her; I feared to distract her and to break the thread of her terrible tale. At last, putting her back into the glass cylinder, he had foolishly tried to tempt her with all sorts of food: honey, starch, fragments of insects, etc. Failing in this, he had picked her

up again and, placing three small sticks on a piece of
white paper, in the position of three radii of a circle,
he had inverted over them a bell-glass and slipped her
under it. For a while longer he had sat and looked at
her. But ultimately he had taken up a small wad of cotton and dipped it into a liquid contained in a stoppered
glass; this he had inserted under the bell imprisoning
her. From it the poison had come with which she had
been impregnated on her arrival among us. It was grue-
some to listen as she went on: how she had first fainted,
then partly recovered; and henceforth, for an hour or
so, crouched low, feeling and watching the process as
this poison slowly entered her body, dissolving in and
spreading through her tissues. By this time the Wheeler
had left her.

At last she had made up her mind to escape or
perish in the attempt. But she was weakened; for the
rough and inconsiderate handling to which she had been
exposed had bruised and abraded her in many delicate
parts; and for a long while she had been unsuccessful
in all her attempts. Yet she had realized that she must
not rest.

And then a great thought had struck her: if she
succeeded in removing one of the wooden sticks, the
glass would tilt over on that side; and perhaps she
would be able to upset it. She had gone to work at once;
and to her great joy she had found the task comparatively easy. Yet, in her weakened state, overcome as
she was every now and then by the fumes, she had taken
an unconscionable time to accomplish it. She had seemed
to be working for hours and hours, pushing and pulling;
and when the stick had at last come out, it had cost her

two metatarsal joints of her right middle foot on which the glass had come down. This had been particularly unfortunate, for she had counted on getting to the other side of the bell glass before the momentum of its tilting movement had been arrested. As it was, the glass retained only a slight trembling motion when she got there. Nevertheless, she had succeeded in inserting her antennæ under its rim and, having done so, had tried to follow them up with the points of her jaws. But she had selected a position too close to one of the two remaining sticks; her jaws had been too thick to pass smoothly through the crack between glass and paper; the glass began to slip away from her. She realized her mistake at once and tried again in the exact centre between the sticks. She met with better success, the crack being wider here. For a long while, however, all she could do was to synchronize her successive heaves rhythmically with the vibrations of the glass, thereby increasing them and gradually they became sufficient to make the glass rock on the paper, till it actually left the support of the sticks, though it fell back upon them after each jump. Under ordinary circumstances, unweakened by the poison, she would now have been able to knock the glass over altogether; but of that she despaired. At last she had watched her opportunity and swung out as the rim on her side was ascending; and she was just fast enough to reach freedom before it came down again.

She had now allowed herself to drop from the edge of the platform on which all this had taken place; and she had soon reached the open. But there was no scented trail which she might have followed. Yet, a gust of wind having swept away some of the fumes impregnat ing her body, she had, in a moment of sudden lucidity, seen a way out of her difficulty: she had thought of the wheel. Near the human dwelling, all tracks had, of course, been utterly confused; but she had travelled on at random, away from the dwelling, for a matter of a thousand antlengths or so; and then she had circled the hominary. This had taken an hour or longer; but at last she had hit upon the smooth track of those wheels. This track had been paved with an infinitesimally thin but continuous film of rubber on the sandy surface of a human road. She had simply followed it to its end; and there, to her indescribable satisfaction, she had picked up our trail crossing that of the wheel.

Thus ran her tale, delivered throughout in a scent of horror and almost despondency which was hard to reconcile with Bissa-tee's buoyant and unconquerable temper.

It was several minutes before I could answer; for that horror and despondency affected me profoundly. I have said that, on this first day of our eastward march, we were to experience the three great dangers that were to dog us throughout the remainder of the summer; and if we had, so far, been confronted with only two of them, namely the incomprehensible animosity of these northern ants and mutiny within our own ranks, here was the third, the danger from man. In addition to man's innate hostility to all forms of life other than his own, there was this particular inducement for him to treat us with a special savagery in that ants of our kind were unknown in this country and therefore attracted his attention and aroused his curiosity.

But I could not afford to indulge in gloomy reflections; there were immediate problems to be solved; I needed Bissa-tee's help.

For another minute or so I stroked her antennæ affectionately, to convey to her some little fraction of what I felt. Then, pulling myself together, I told her by a single scent that we, too, had had our troubles during the day. To my relief, Bissa-tee was at once alert. "Ants?" she asked. And, by a few quick motions, I gave her a summary of the day's doings.

For a second she pondered. Then she scented succinctly, "A prisoner." I did not at once understand; and she elucidated. "We must know who they are. Ask for volunteers to go on a raid and bring in a prisoner. We may have to dig ourselves in before morning. Don't lose a moment."

My first impulse was to rush to the quarters of the army. But better counsel came like an inspiration. I went, instead, to the place where our colleagues were still assembled in great excitement over Bissa-tee's return. There, I issued a proclamation on which I pride myself to this day: "Ants wanted for dangerous service, without reward."

Every single one pressed forward.

My mind was busy. It was plainly a case of taking the enemy by surprise. Surprise demanded silence and secrecy. The utter calm of the night would almost certainly be disturbed if any large number were sent. Three would have to be the limit. I gave the order to line up in parade order; and I walked along the line, touching every ant with my antennæ, for purposes of recognition. By the time I had reached the far end, I called Anna-zee,

Azte-ca, and Adver-tee to the front. Turning to Anna-zee, I signified to her my desire that she should pick from her associates a young ant, nimble and alert, for this service; for she herself was getting old, and her ever-increasing obesity disqualified her in any case. She returned with a singularly powerful and agile individual and assured me that I could place the most absolute trust in her discretion and ability.

I outlined my plan. They were to approach the hostile formicary in the most careful manner; all the rest of us would meanwhile move to a point half-way between our army and the hill; there, having halted, we should all stridulate so as at once to alarm the enemy, drawing forth her scouts, and to cover any noise our raiders might inadvertently make in their approach. Having picked a scout, they were to seize her and to bring her in, giving the scent of purpose achieved as a signal for our retreat behind the lines.

The enthusiasm with which my instructions were received gave me heart. The three selected for the service were fretting at every delay. Yet I restrained them. It seemed imperative that they should not be rash. I gave orders for them to remain with the rest of us till we had reached a certain point between the lines. The night was utterly dark now; the clouds overhead had thickened till every trace even of starlight was excluded. We fell into marching order and circled the army. Two or three times we were challenged by Assa-ree's scouts; but, giving them the scent of the day, we moved on without halting; in about half an hour we reached as favourable a station as we could wish.

All those who were to remain with me — there were less than a hundred now — began to stridulate; and this was the signal for our three raiders to advance. I will insert a continuous narrative here, as though I had been with them; in reality it is pieced together from their reports.

The hill of the unknown ants was straight east of us. Anna-zee's assistant was to approach it in a straight line; the other two from the north-east and the south-east respectively.

All over the mound, as our raiders approached, the scent of the enemy was distinctly perceptible; yet none of our ants had met with anyone when they reached the summit of the hill.

Meanwhile, the chorus of our stridulation was distinctly audible there; and the enemy must have been aware of it. It seemed unthinkable that they should have posted no sentinels. Besides, our raiders had also failed to locate an entrance crater. The whole ground under them — the hill was a hundred antlengths high and covered a circular area with a diameter of at least 240 antlengths — trembled and vibrated with activity. It was a certainty, then, that the enemy was expecting trouble. But where was the entrance? Had it been closed in expectation of just such a raid?

They resolved to circle the mound in a downward spiral: this took over an hour, for the slope was gentle, and they went *en échelon,* Azte-ca leading and in touch with the upper trail which they had made on their previous circuit. To their surprise they had descended two-thirds of the slope before they became unexpectedly aware of the immediate proximity of numbers of the enemy just below them. They halted to take their bearings. By careful observation they arrived at the conclusion that the single entrance to the enormous hill was located excentrically, on the flank, within a score of antlengths from the base; and this entrance was swarming with ants who were in the greatest excitement; in fact, their excitement was such as almost to invite an immediate attack.

It served our purposes particularly well that their whole attention was centred on the plain below. Our raiders were actually within jumping distance and yet remained unperceived.

In the meantime, we were stridulating in a manner which amounted to actual hard work. Fortunately, Assa-ree had moved to the front of our army; and while she was left in entire ignorance of our intentions, she was still sufficiently subdued to hold her hordes back when, among the scents which reached her in confusion, she isolated my body-scent. As we were getting fatigued, however, I began to worry over the delay. Should it be necessary for us to entrench ourselves, we should need time; and this thought made me anxious.

Having communicated with each other and agreed upon a plan, our raiders at last made a sudden rush; and then they retreated at once to the top of the mound. Each of them had secured a maxim. Azte-ca had been least lucky in the grasp with which she secured her prisoner; for, on being seized, the latter had promptly doubled up and stung her severely in the thorax, injecting what amounted to a fatal dose of some albuminous poison. So far, however, she held on and actually succeeded in bringing her prisoner to the rear.

It was Adver-tee who gave the signal of success; and we promptly ceased from stridulating. In returning to the rear of the army, I scented instructions to Assaree to refrain from all hostilities and to await further orders. In case of need she was to retreat.

To our amazement, we came ourselves in touch with the enemy's scouts as we were circling south and west. It was only for a second; and the scouts withdrew at once; but it was a warning to be on the alert.

Within half an hour, we had rejoined Bissa-tee whom we found much improved though still very weak. We waited patiently for the return of our raiders. When, at last, Adver-tee entered our conclave, she was without Azte-ca and the nimble botanist; but she brought her prisoner; and, having surrendered her to one of her associates, she reported that she had left Azte-ca, overcome by the poison of a sting, in the care of the third raider, half-way from the strange formicarium, whence she proposed a number of carriers should bring her and the other two prisoners in.

Meanwhile, Bissa-tee betrayed considerable excitement. She carefully circled Adver-tee's prisoner, limping in a way painful to behold. When she turned to me, her first utterance was one of sorrow; she lamented the fact that our contact with this tribe, which she called Pogonomyrmex Occidentalis, should have been a hostile one. She assured me that they belonged to the great harvesting ants, most interesting and civilized in their habits, though formidable as foes. If Azte-ca had received a full dose of the poison, she added, we should be delayed for days and days, unless indeed we were able to carry her while on the march.

She had barely finished her report when the detachment of carriers which I had sent came in with Azte-ca and the botanist, not to forget their two prisoners. Azte-ca was, indeed, in a deplorable condition; and I was struck with amazement at sight of the comparatively great size and the fierce and proud bearing of the prisoner she had taken.

Scarcely had Bissa-tee seen the latter when, in spite of her debilitated condition, she gave a jump; and, bowing her still bleeding antennæ before the stranger, in a most amusing and yet respectful manner, half ironically, half triumphantly, gave her the salute due only to a commander.

" Here, " she scented exultantly, turning to me, " we have, as a hostage, Her Majesty's deputy-commander-in-chief of all the Pogonomyrmex forces; her capture has cost us heavily, namely, the certain death of our friend Adver-tee, unless we can induce Her Excellency to furnish us with the antidote — which, by the way, I believe we shall be able to do. But even if not, we have paid no more than this capture is worth. "

At these scents Minna-ca, to give her her name as I came to know it, gave a furious spring as though to attack Bissa-tee in spite of her wounds and to end her life there and then. But she was in good jaws; and all she could do was to protrude her sting sheath from which the gleaming weapon flashed forth ineffectually.

At this juncture I saw fit to interpose and to express, in conciliatory scents, my regret, as that of the supreme commander of the Attiine forces, that matters had come to this pass between a peaceful delegation of scientists and a highly disciplined and civilized tribe of ants of whom we had heard so much. This was an empty compliment; for apart from rumours and uncertain tales that had reached us, we knew nothing of these Pogonomyrmex. Even Bissa-tee admitted later on that her whole speech had been based on a bold guess which she herself had been surprised to see confirmed by the behaviour of Minna-ca. I was still at a loss to explain her knowledge of this name; but when I expressed my perplexity, Bissa-tee merely laughed as was her way when she had scored a point. " Wa, be nimble, " she said, " Wa, be quick! " And suddenly it dawned upon me that undoubtedly the first prisoner, brought in by Adver-tee, had, unnoticed by myself, but astutely marked by Bissa-tee, saluted her with the salute due to a commander-in-chief. I could never induce Bissa-tee to admit as much, however; she merely repeated that nursery rhyme when I alluded to the subject.

Now Minna-ca was quite intelligent enough to see that in spite of our small numbers we were a formidable enemy; perhaps she even divined that we had weapons which we had not yet used. Whether my remarks flattered her or not, I do not know; but her attitude became more conciliatory. The rest was a mere matter of negotiation.

Within half an hour a truce had been concluded for the day. Our army was to withdraw to the west; and Minna-ca was to send one of the lesser ants that had been captured to her own city and to enjoin upon her soldiers to refrain from all hostilities. She herself was to remain as a hostage; and she agreed to furnish us with an antidote against the poison injected into Azte-ca.

Perhaps these were severe terms; but we had to make use of the situation as it had shaped itself. Already a plan was forming in my mind whereby we might achieve the higher ends of science.

The terms of the truce were adhered to on both sides; and, seeing that quiet prevailed on the front of yesterday's battle, I more than once took occasion to engage Minna-ca in a brief exchange of courtesies in order to enlighten her with regard to the aims of our expedition. When she began to grasp its scope, she became interested; and in the afternoon she began to ask a few questions. These referred chiefly to the climatic and topographical details observed in our march to the north, and to astronomical questions such as why we considered the earth to be a sphere; how we explained the alternation of day and night; what brought about the seasons and the inequalities of day and night, in summer as well as in winter; whether we considered the inclination of the axis of the earth to be 66½ degrees from the plane of its orbit or 23½ degrees from the perpendicular to it; and how we accounted for the fact that below the surface there was a region of almost invariable temperature in the ground. But she also asked about the civic organization of our state: whether it was communistic or anarchistic; whether our queens were adopted or whether we insured the continuity of our dynasty by adelphogamy.

The way in which she listened to my answers convinced me that she was mostly speaking with her tongue in her cheek. Compared with her own compatriots, she considered us as mere conceited barbarians; as I have invariably found that every nation, except that endowed with the highest degree of culture, thinks itself superior to all others.

When, however, I broached to her the plan that had formed in my mind, she gave it the most favourable consideration. This plan was that we should exchange hostages; and that, when this exchange was effected, we, the Attas, should be permitted to send a delegation into their city for purposes of study.

Within a few hours this was arranged for. I had the impression that Minna-ca could not imagine any better means of insuring our good will than to let us see the perfect appointments prevailing in her city. The only minor captive remaining was accordingly released to submit my proposals to the assembly of maxims. The number to be exchanged was fixed at four; and the exchange was speedily effected.

I, therefore, accompanied by Anna-zee, Adver-tee, and Assa-ree repaired to neutral ground. Assa-ree I took along because only thus could I make sure that there would be no further mischief. Azte-ca and Bissa-tee had perforce to remain behind.

Arrived at the place agreed upon, we were met by a delegation of maxims from the so far hostile city. Both delegations, I should add, were escorted by a force sufficient to guard against treachery.

Within a few minutes we came to the entrance which was situated on the southern slope of the mound. Our reception was cool but respectful; and I quickly convinced myself that there was nothing to fear. Our escort undoubtedly considered that the life of Minna-ca and her three fellow-hostages was worth any number of dead Attas; and the agreement was that, should any-

thing happen to any one of us, she should be the first
to be put to the jaw. Only once, in the course of our
visit, did I see a sting flash; and, one of our escort bending an antenna towards the offender, the motion was
immediately changed into a military salute.

As for the city, a brief summary of what we saw
must suffice; for details the student is referred to scent-
tree number 703 in which, as nearly as possible, considering that Adver-tee was dead, her minute report has
been embodied.

The whole mound was surrounded by a disk of earth
360 antlengths in diameter cleared of every trace of
vegetation; beyond it, to the east, lay the kitchen-
middens or refuse piles. The mound itself was most
carefully constructed of small pebbles brought from the
subterranean chambers, of which there were about a
thousand. The matter excavated had invariably been
piled up north of the entrance where it was in turn at
once riddled with excavations; in fact, the higher we
penetrated within the mound, the greater was the proportion of excavated space to solid masonry; and the
lower we went down, the farther from each other were
the chambers spaced. From the whole arrangement I
could readily reconstruct, in my imagination, the history
of the colony. Like those of most ants, it must have
taken its inception from a single and unattended queen
who, having excavated a tiny chamber and piled the
matter removed in a fan-shaped mound north of the
entrance, at once proceeded to rear her first brood of
minims.

A large majority of these chambers was filled, or
partly filled, with the carefully husked and cleaned

grains of grasses, especially towards the top of the mound. Since these grains had often, after heavy rains, to be brought to the surface in order to be dried, and in order that those that had sprouted might be removed, this seemed a very sensible arrangement; whereas the brood chambers were located at a depth which insured a minimum of change in temperature. Individually, these lower chambers were hard to ventilate; but their more scattered position and the great steepness of the connecting galleries prevented any serious vitiation of the air. In fact, though, as compared with the burrow of the Myrmecocysts, this mound seemed close and crowded, there prevailed a degree of neatness and even elegance which did not fail to impress me.

As for the ants themselves, I was struck with the great size and weight of the hammerlike heads of certain individuals. These, I was told were the crushers whose chief duty it was to comminute the hard grains for consumption by larvæ, callows, and minims. Each fragment of starchy matter was, before being fed to a larva, coated with saliva; and thereby the starch was, at least partly, changed into sugar and made more readily digestible. The workers were, however, not highly polymorphic.

We did not see a sign of Her Majesty. I made a discreet enquiry and was promptly told that Her Majesty was upset by yesterday's losses and had gone into mourning.

So, when our circuit was completed, we were politely ushered back to the entrance; and we took the hint. Our guides had observed the most scrupulous courtesy; but it had remained untempered by any cordiality. We had, indeed, been invited to partake of the crushed seeds; they were tendered, however, not as the offerings of hospitality, but solely for the sake of acquainting us with their strictly vegetarian diet.

We returned in solemn procession to our starting-point where we were met by a detachment of our own ants surrounding the four Pogonomyrmex hostages which included Minna-ca.

There remained a last formality: that of ratifying the terms of our retreat. Minna-ca insisted on our leaving within seven days. I had been in hopes that we should not be exposed to such a demand; but, after having sent a messenger to enquire from Bissa-tee and Azte-ca whether they thought seven days sufficient for their recovery and having received an answer in the affirmative, I agreed. This messenger I sent chiefly in order to save my face; I did not want it to appear as though I embraced Minna-ca's terms too readily.

III

As a matter of fact, we held a general review on the fourth day and departed within the next twenty-four hours. We still went straight east; and for a number of days we passed one Pogonomyrmex colony after the other. There was constant battle; wherever we appeared, we were attacked; and this warfare of attrition did not cease till we were beyond the range of these ants. Whenever we came within 2,400 antlengths of any clearing of theirs, we were in contact with their scouts; and at last we established a regular routine in getting past. We trained a shock-troop of some 500 picked fighters who met the attacking column and, gradually swinging to the right or the left, as the case might be, so as to cover our flank, they kept the enemy engaged while we marched past; when we had done so, they defended our rear till we were disengaged. No doubt the records of these numerous colonies boast to this day of an unbroken series of victories over an invading army of giants.

It goes without saying that such actions could not be fought without losses; and while they were comparatively slight on our side, they counted more heavily against us than those a hundred times as large counted against our enemies. The worst of it was that we soon came to the point where we had to leave our wounded behind. At first we made an attempt to carry them with us; but we found that we were unconscionably delayed by them and that the efficiency of our army was seriously impaired by such a burden. Assa-ree claimed that our wounded were the direct cause of further losses; for, if we marched unencumbered, we passed each hostile colony in half the time; and our losses were directly proportional to the time required for doing so. Still another consideration had to be urged in favour of the unantly expedient of abandoning our casualties to the untender mercies of our enemies: only about half of them recovered ultimately. Only too often did we find that we had carried an ant along for four or five days in order to have her die anyway at the last. I even found that, in Assa-ree's ranks, there were those who found themselves unable, in spite of all warnings, to resist the temptation of cannibalism; and all those who partook of these ghoulish feasts were promptly taken ill themselves, some of them with fatal results. I was in despair. Expediency demanded that I should do what no Atta had ever done before; and I was to do it on the motion of Assa-ree! The whole expedition had now entered a phase in which we could consider nothing but the ultimate aim: not to let the ever increasing sum of our findings perish with ourselves.

Desperate counsel came to me sometimes, at night. I knew it was the opinion of Bissa-tee, Anna-zee, Azteca, and many others that we could increase our chances by getting rid of the army and advancing henceforth by stealth. They admitted that, without the army, we could never have done what we had succeeded in doing; they even suspected that, without it, we might find it next to impossible to get home again. Yet they did not shrink from the conclusion that, for the present, our chances of survival would be increased if we could make ourselves less conspicuous. Occasionally I was almost inclined to reason as they did, especially when one of my own associates fell a victim to the sting of a Pogonomyrmex. We thus lost our last two physiological thermometers and the only remaining barometer. All three had to be abandoned; for here is another point: we could no longer claim privileges over the rank and file; differences between privates and officers were wiped out. I could neither detail carriers for the service of conveying members of the High Command nor delay our incessant battles by allowing those among ourselves who volunteered to carry their own associates; in either case I should have precipitated a mutiny in the ranks.

Yet, for a handful of us to sneak away and to leave the rest to their fates — no, I could not yet do that.

And then, one night, I received an entirely unexpected revelation which added tremendously to the burden of care which I was bearing already. We had somehow managed to evade two hostile armies; and every ant in the army as well as in the High Command was completely fagged. I had been in hopes that I might still give the order to entrench; for we were in the centre of an area which served as a no-ant's-land for three equidistant Pogonomyrmex colonies, all of them ready, at the first provocation, to fall on us or on each other. But Assa-ree declared that she dared not give any such order before the troops had had some rest. " Very well, " I replied, " form clusters. " Fortunately we had a few dead gum-trees in sight; and preparations were instantly made. I was, during a last tour of inspection, forcibly struck with the slenderness of the army cluster suspended from the small branch of a tree. Our own cluster was outright minute.

I was turning to the latter in order to insert myself in its very centre when I was accosted by an ant from Assa-ree's staff. She touched my abdomen and then crouched down in deep grass. At first I thought she was wounded; but her next touch conveyed to me a desire to have private communication with me on a vital matter. She was a powerful ant; and I hesitated: she came from Assa-ree's immediate entourage, and there might be treachery afoot. Yet I liked her way: she seemed to be worried but frank. I allowed her to take the lead and to guide me to a secluded point within the cleared disk around one of the Pogonomyrmex mounds.

I suppose she chose this location because it enabled us to see all about us: no spy could have approached unperceived.

Treachery was afoot indeed. This was what Assaree's aide communicated to me.

All our findings, geographical, geologic, climatic zoological, and botanical, had been carefully watched by Assa-ree and records of them entrusted to certain ants in her suite; among ourselves, they were severally entrusted to certain ants, besides being communicated to myself who, by reason of my enormous memory, was best fitted to act as a depositary and a check on the separate mnemonic prodigies which formed Adver-tee's group of associates.

This was amazing news. Assa-ree had no scientific training; nor, of course, had any member of her staff They were unable to grasp the import of our findings except in a popular recast. Any check record would have been welcome; but the value of these records kept by Assa-ree was necessarily impaired by the fact that they were made by ants who knew nothing of what they were supposed to record. Whole contexts were almost sure to be entangled and subverted.

But above all, what was the purpose?

My informant hesitated; and what she signified next made me inclined to place an absolute trust in her Much of what she had to say was conjectural, she admitted; but it was based on facts observed. Thus, one day, Assa-ree's body-servant being indisposed, she, my informant, had been detailed, much to her indignation to supply that functionary's service. Knowing Assa-ree's ungovernable temper — a characteristic I was unac quainted with, never having served under her in an inferior capacity — she had complied without protest; and, while absolute certainty in such a matter could be arrived at only by a medical examination, yet she would be willing to stake her life on the assertion that Assa-ree was fertilized.

This was a tremendous blow. I saw it all in a flash. It explained so many things that I accepted it at once as true. It had been rumoured at home that Assa-ree laid eggs. It was no uncommon thing for a worker to lay an occasional egg; the fact was treated as a misfortune rather than as a crime, though repeated lapses were looked at askance. But among Attas, as among most other ants, parthenogenetic eggs produce males only; and, if Assa-ree had laid parthenogenetic eggs habitually, it must have resulted in a preponderance of males over females in our colony; it had not done so; in fact, the approximate equality of the numbers of males and females in the perfect castes of our colony had been the cardinal fact in my disregarding and discrediting all those rumours. If it was true that Assa-ree was impregnated, the fact furnished a new and different explanation.

And then came another still more staggering revelation. My informant, having given me time to digest what she had told me, went on as though there had been no pause. In spite of the fact that Assa-ree had, at the time, not partaken of any food whatever for more than twenty days, there had been a distinct fecal odour about the tip of her gaster.

I could only stammer, " What do you mean to imply? " But of course I knew well enough before she

told me. That fecal odour could have proceeded only
from her receptaculum seminis. Horrible as it was in
its implications, the inference could not be escaped. The
implications were not only horrible in the extreme; they
were so far-reaching that I reeled with their impact.

The first of them was, of course, that Assa-ree herself, though she had certainly never had wings, had
been fertilized by an Eciton; all her offspring, therefore, were crosses between Atta and Eciton; and that
accounted for many things: for their easy fraternization
with pure-bred Ecitons; for their ferocity and their
strange appearance; for the ease with which they had
lived on the land as we went; for their fanatical attach-
ment to their leader.

But would an Eciton male have paired with Assa-ree
at the time of her criminal romance if she had herself
been undoubtedly Atta? If not, there must have been, a
generation ago, an older Pseudogyne or false female
among our mothers and foster-mothers; and a third
before that; and so on, back into the past, ad infinitum:
a terrible thought! Unless, indeed, this whole series of
crimes was initiated, at a comparatively recent time,
by some freak of nature? But that was unlikely; for all
biological experience shows that variation takes place
in a divergent, not a convergent line. The whole thing
was bewildering in the extreme.

And what about the future? Assa-ree, knowing that
she was fertilized and, therefore, able to produce offspring of all three castes, male, female, and worker,
was securing to herself the results of this expedition
which constituted the greatest undertaking ever vent-
ured upon by ants. With what aim in view? There could

be only a single one. She harboured treasonable thoughts: she was going to return to our home; and she was going to court popularity there by making it appear as though she and not we were the ones through whose devotion, enterprise, and initiative the findings of our scholars had been obtained and preserved. But in order to reap all that glory for herself, she would have to dispose of us, the true explorers. What could be easier? She had the army: she would turn the army against us; and in all normal probability we were lost, one and all. Then, what? She would lead the remainder of her forces home in triumph; and, patiently waiting her time, she would ultimately reap even the crown or, alternatively, bring the crown under her domination. She would pass herself off as a perfect dealated queen; and there would be the end of our glorious nation. She might even attempt a *coup d'état,* deposing or beheading our Gracious Queen, Her Majesty Orrha-wee. Nothing would be beyond her reach.

But, it may be asked, why should she go on protecting us? Clearly, for one single reason. Without us all further exploration would cease. Every day new discoveries were being made, new territory was described; for that she needed us; without us she could do one thing only, fight her way home. Neither she nor any of her associates could do our work: the only record she could have accumulated would have been of a military exploit: and she knew, of course, that Attas lay little stress on military fame. No doubt she meant to keep us till we had reaped the full harvest and then to sacrifice us to her ambitions.

In this she had overlooked one single point, namely, that, as the highest of the powers conferred upon me, I held that little pellet of the royal perfume of death in my infrabuccal chamber; and Assa-ree, not being a perfect female, was unable to produce either it or that other perfume which annuls the former's action.

A second point was in my favour: I was forewarned and therefore forearmed: and Assa-ree did not know it; at least not yet. But henceforth continual watchfulness and suspicion must be the order of the day; never again could I approach Assa-ree without being prepared to lay her low at a moment's notice; and, what was worse, never again could I allow myself to be cradled in sleep without having someone stand guard over me and mine.

I pondered this. The thought struck me that this officer who was apparently pure Atta might join us and that she and I might take turns in this duty. It would not do. Such a course would betray my knowledge to Assa-ree who was bound to notice what I had done. I could not even allow this officer to return to the army. Just how much she knew of what her revelations implied I could not tell; but, unless she realized at least part of their import, she would hardly have come to me in this way. In other words, she was essentially a traitress; she must know that she had delivered over her supreme commander into my jaws. This was a terrible dilemma. If safety there was for me and mine, it was owing to her; but it was achieved through treason. Without that treason we might at any moment have been murdered. Yet treason begets treason. Treason is not a casual act of misdemeanour. Treason is the outcome of a treasonable disposition; and a treasonable disposition deserved death. But, though her death was indicated, I resolved to make her happy before she had to die.

Slowly I brought forward, in my infrabuccal chamber, between labrum and tongue, the pellet of royal favour which, when inhaled after the royal perfume of death, overrules it; but, when inhaled before it, merely makes the latter painless in its effect but is itself overruled by it. I saw the officer who shall remain nameless faint with ecstasy; and then, as I allowed the pellet of royal favour to slip back and brought forward the pellet of instant death, I saw her rear on her hind-feet as though in greeting; and then she was blotted to the ground. Peace be with her soul!

IV

We remained at this station for three days. Even I needed the rest. I was now in my ninth year; and, while Her Majesty's prediction that my life would be prolonged by the greatness of my task had undoubtedly come true, yet I was beginning to feel the effect of extreme old age. I am happy to be able to say that it did not impair the powers of my mind; but the incessant marches of the last forty days told on my bodily strength; and the constant worry had superinduced a severe insomnia.

In order to ensure that my rest remained unbroken, I issued orders that nobody should leave camp. I took Bissa-tee and Azte-ca partly into my confidence, telling them that I feared mutiny in the army; and henceforth

both faithfully shared my vigils. I have mentioned that
our cluster was fastened to the lowest branch of a dead
gum-tree; and every night we took turns in mounting
guard on that branch.

Now the third night Bissa-tee who had had the
second watch, did not, when I came to relieve her, go to
rest in the centre of the cluster but remained with me
on the branch. I at once surmised that she had something to communicate.

The night was absolutely calm; and the lower atmosphere was laden with moisture. On such nights all
scents seem intensified: the perfume pervading the air
dissolves in the minute droplets of water afloat and
saturates them. Bissa-tee was facing the point where I
had had my interview with Assa-ree's disaffected officer;
and suddenly she raised her antennæ rigidly up into the
darkness above. I did the same and perceived a peculiar
though very faint odour coming from that quarter. It
was a scent of death and decay, uncanny, alarming. It
was not carried by any motion of the air; it was itself
dead and motionless. Whatever was decaying there was
exhaling an aura that expanded about its point of origin
like a huge atmospheric hemisphere; but, this aura
being heavier than air, it flattened out in this utter
calm and reached our post by gravity.

My first thought was, of course, of the officer who
had dropped there; but a little reflection caused me to
dismiss it; to create an aura pervading such a distance
an ant of the size of a horse would have been needed. I
was profoundly disquieted; and so was Bissa-tee. She
had made no motion, had emitted no scent. We stood
there for half an hour or longer, as though the prolong-

ation or repetition of our perception could have furnished a clue.

At last I lowered my antennæ and turned to descend the tree. Bissa-tee followed me; but, as we passed the cluster of our associates, she touched me to signify her wish that I should wait for her. She entered the cluster and, in a few minutes, returned with one of her subordinates who at once began to lick me from head to sting-sheath, coating my whole exoskeleton with her saliva which I recognized as being aseptic. Having finished with me, she did the same for Bissa-tee who at last desired her to go back to sleep. I felt grateful to Bissa-tee for taking this precaution dictated by her solicitude.

When we reached the ground and began to proceed in the direction of the smell, it became speedily intensified and so distasteful that, under any other circumstances, I should have turned back. Soon we distinguished the germs of pestilence floating about in the air, greatly enjoying themselves in the warmth of the night; for it was now midsummer. Some of them were charming little things, iridescent in the faintest colours of the rainbow. The wisdom of the precaution taken by Bissa-tee became apparent now; for many of these germs began to alight, in frolicsome and elastic springs, on our armour, especially in the neighbourhood of our mouth-parts and our tracheæ. Every one was instantly killed by the protective coating we had received.

At last, through an ever-thickening cloud of these germs, we approached the scene of my interview with the officer; and an appalling sight met our eyes, for by this time there was the faintest trace of light in the east.

In front of us lay an enormous heap of dead ants,
all of the hostile species. It was piled just inside the
cleared disk surrounding the mound of the nearest
colony. There were hundreds of thousands of them, piled
to the height of a hundred antlengths; and all were
stark-dead. It was a scene to shake the stoutest heart.
Far in the east the grey of dawn stood in a sky of
featureless cloud; a sloping plain stretched away to meet
it, without a tree, without a shrub, without even a tall
weed, featureless like the sky which it seemed to reflect.
It looked like chaos before the creation; or like some
scene from the end of the world, such as our poets sing
of, when life has just become extinct on earth. We
shivered.

And then we turned back. Bissa-tee, the unconquerable, was conquered. " We must flee, " she scented as we
went. " This is the end of all life on earth; at least of
all ant-life. An epidemic is sweeping the world. " And
then, having turned for a last look, she stood arrested
again.

I had been following my own thoughts; but when
she stood still, I, too, stopped and looked back. And now
we saw something which seemed for the moment still
more appalling. We had swerved a little to the west of
our former path; and so a corner of the pile came in
sight which had before been hidden from our eyes.

There, from a neighbouring formicary, a long line
of living ants was coming through the low-growing and
spreading plants. On and on they came, hurrying, scurrying, helter-skelter, all pressing forward toward that
pile of destruction. Those that reached it, promptly began to scale its flanks, hastening upward and spreading

out and then falling dead and forming a new layer over the old ones.

This was so amazing that for some time I could not tear myself away; and when I did so at last, I moved over still farther to the west. Thence I saw a second line of ants coming from the east, behaving exactly like the first; and then a third and a fourth line; they were coming from all directions; and all of them climbed the pile of death and fell dead themselves, most of them remaining where they fell, though a few of them rolled down the slope and widened the base.

The light was getting stronger with every moment; and the germs which in the previous dimness had been phosphorescent and easily visible began to pale; but when I held my eyes focused a little in front of the pile, I could still see them. They formed a dense cloud covering the pile like a hood. Since they thrive in darkness, they were all trying to enter the interstices between the dead ants; but the temptation to feast was too great; and they are peculiarly organized in such a way that they coil up in contact with a surface from which they absorb food through the skin. This is quite mechanical; and as the food is absorbed, their bodies swell out at the point of contact; but, in order to distribute the absorbed liquid, they straighten out with a sudden jerk which, by reason of their exceeding lightness, sends them flying up again. It was, therefore, a long while before I could see any diminution in the size of the cloud. But very slowly it contracted.

It was time for us to depart; orders had been given to be ready for marching at sun-up.

Bissa-tee signified her desire to take one of the dead ants along for analysis and dissection; but I, knowing how the destruction had been wrought, interposed my absolute veto.

At our tree nothing was stirring yet; and I was glad of it; I thought it best to avoid all unnecessary enquiries. I remounted my post, enjoining the greatest secrecy on Bissa-tee; and I remained on the branch for another half hour before I gave the general alarm.

In that interval I pondered what I had seen. The dead Attiine officer had, in her death, been impregnated, first with the perfume of royal favour, then with the perfume of instant death; and though I had given her only infinitesimal doses of both, they are very tenacious; and I had been able to distinguish both in the faint aura as we had approached the pile. Now the perfume of royal favour is much more volatile than the perfume of death; and it has this further peculiarity that the faintest trace of it, absorbed by an ant, induces that ant to bring into play her power of differential apperception: she will ignore all other scents but this single one; it she will follow no matter where it leads; for it seems to promise power and everlasting satisfaction of all desires; and this satisfaction appears suddenly as a veritable heaven on earth. She has, from that moment on, no other desire than to inhale this money. [1] Nothing will hold her back;

---

[1] This is another case where, in the text, as communicated to me by Wawa-quee, a word appears which seems to have no connection with the context and the provenance of which I am unable to explain. In the previous chapter it was the word "author". I leave these words without trying to account for their presence in the text. E.

no consideration of honour; no love of kind; no sense of
formicarian dignity. Have it she must should it lead
her to death. But the royal perfume of death lingered
more closely about the officer's body; and, as the pile
of its victims grew, it was successively absorbed by the
outer layers at the top.

That was the appalling explanation of what we had
seen.

V

I was fully aware that, in leaving the place, we
should have to use great care not to expose our own
forces to danger from the perfume of royal favour;
though I had already concluded from Bissa-tee's im-
munity that Pogonomyrmex, perhaps by reason of their
smaller size, perhaps by reason of the more material
bent of their minds, were accessible to the effect of
vastly smaller doses than we were ourselves. We must
leave at once; or we should be caught by the pest; the
urgency of the case admitted of no delay.

Fortunately, a light south wind sprang up before
the day was far advanced. Yet I ordered a south-east
direction to be taken for our line of march; and when
we had gone a matter of some two hundred thousand
antlengths, I sent word to Assa-ree to bend north-west
again, so as to resume our original line of travel.

More than once, I might say, we came upon hurrying columns of Pogonomyrmex, all striving with might
and main to reach that pile of destruction which I was
anxious to leave behind. They had caught the scent and
were doomed. As we advanced and broke through their

lines, they seemed to have lost all their pugnacity; they were not bent upon battle; they were bent on the perfume of royal favour and death. We had to kill not a few in order to force them to give us our way.

All day long, and for a week more, we pursued our march downhill; and from the second day on it was fight, fight, fight once more; though the formicaries seemed to become less populous as we went. Bissa-tee was much interested in this fact and, from it, at last drew a conclusion of comfort which, to our joy, we had shortly an opportunity of verifying as correct. This conclusion was that these ants do not live below a given altitude; for under the increased pressure of the atmosphere they become sluggish.

Having travelled a matter of twelve million antlengths, we were at last freed from this scourge and could breathe freely once more.

No sooner were we assured of this than I called a halt and held a grand review. The result of the census taken was that our army had shrunk by more than a third: there were 2,314 fighters, officers included; and the High Command consisted of 69 scholars. This was terrible news; and it had a depressing effect on most minds.

Even Bissa-tee seemed to be inclined to advise an immediate retreat to the south; but when I reminded her of the old legends that tell of slave-making ants, her enthusiasm was revived. That was what I loved in her: the passion for knowledge made her forget all danger and every suffering past or to come. Never lived a more intrepid spirit.

The plenary meeting of the remainder of our Command was memorable in more ways than one.

In the first place, the scientific results of this march through a hostile country were discussed in great detail (see scent-tree number 567). It must not be thought that the Pogonomyrmex were the only ants, or ants the only object of our study. There were the flora and the fauna, and within the latter the more or less parasitic insect fauna; there were the ecto- and endoparasites symbiotic or synechthrous with Pogonomyrmex, some of them polishing their armours in their endeavour to make a living off their skeletal excretions or the coatings with which they covered each other; some preying upon or within their intestines. Above all, however, there were ants who, in spite of the dominance of Pogonomyrmex were able to eke out a living in the midst of enemies and who would perhaps have been unable to subsist anywhere else. To illustrate, there is the little Dorymyrmex Pyramicus which builds its tiny nest on the slope of the Pogonomyrmex mound and subsists by waylaying and robbing, in numbers, single members of the host species — if it can be so called — as they return home laden with booty; for Pogonomyrmex never hunts in files, as we concluded from the fact that no well-paved highways radiate from their clearings. Why individuals of the more powerful species submit to these hold-ups without invoking the revenge of the whole tribe on the robbers was long a secret to us. At last Bissa-tee hit upon the explanation: every single individual so robbed would be careful not to expose herself to the ridicule of the whole tribe by admitting that she had yielded to the compulsion of ants manifestly inferior in size and power.

Probably there were not many Pogonomyrmex in any mound who had not at one time or other been held up successfully; but they would never admit it; on the contrary, they would be all the more emphatic in scoffing at anyone who proclaimed her shame. This conjecture was strikingly confirmed when a Dorymyrmex was caught; the sardonic and contemptuous way in which she referred to her hosts as vain, arrogant, and blundering giants was comical to see; and we, having no tenderness for Pogonomyrmex, released the little thing, not without admiring her psychological insight. In a purely ethnographic sense this encounter was highly interesting because this Dorymyrmex had a distinct race odour almost identical with that of Tapinoma and Formica Incerta, the former a close relative (a Dolichoderine), the latter from a different sub-family, but both occurring over the same area.

We had also made further observations on man; and we had even seen the Wheeler again. The latter, however, did not come near us.

A general survey of ants was arrived at. There could be no doubt that, in our own country, we were the dominant ants; in the next climatic zone to the north, the Ecitons were masters of the situation; and thus we mapped the continent out as far as it had been explored. The eastern plateaux of the mountains were ruled by honey ants; their eastern slopes by the harvesters. This does not mean, as I have already pointed out, that no other ants occurred in these zones; but all ants inhabiting the same zone must, in every aspect of their lives, take into account the dominant ants.

This led to a great discussion between Anna-zee, our botanist who was also a philosopher, and Bissa-tee. But of that anon.

One word about man in this connection. I will admit that I had long feared that ultimately we might reach districts in which man was dominant. But the conclusions arrived at on the present occasion and confirmed later on pointed to the fact that man is nowhere on earth truly dominant except within his cities and his superterranean burrows; and often not even there. While he forces individual ants and individual tribes to adjust themselves to him, yet, on the whole, he must adjust himself to ants. Ants are vastly more adaptable, more plastic than man. Even where man grows crops over large areas of the surface of the globe, ants utilize these crops to a greater extent than man; so that, in a more profound view, man also has been subjected and made serviceable to ants. This is one of the great general and important conclusions arrived at: no matter where you go, into the tropics or into the subarctic zones, wherever life subsists at all, there ants subsist and subdue nature to their ends; the rest of creation pays them toll. To this conclusion about the fundamental dominance of ants as lords of the animal world there is only one single exception: we Attas alone have reached a level of civilization which makes it possible for us to live self-contained lives, respecting, and not interfering with, other forms of animal life unless we are ourselves interfered with. That is the reason why, without any hesitation, we can now assert, as a conclusion backed by science, what, in the past, has perhaps been asserted as a matter of mere national prejudice, namely, that we Attas must ultimately redeem the world from the sin of predacious life. We alone are in full accord with nature's purpose; we alone, as our ancestors would have expressed it, serve the will of God.

Now for a summary of the discussion that took place between Bissa-tee and Anna-zee. I have already said that even Bissa-tee, at the nadir of our fortunes, would have been inclined to advise an immediate return home; and that she had changed her mind when I referred to the ever-accumulating evidence pointing towards a fourth mode of life discovered by ants, namely, that of enslaving other ants or, which means the same thing, of making themselves dependent upon these slaves.

As for Anna-zee, it was at all times difficult to arrive at a precise estimate of her views; she was so given to ironical statement that she often seemed to argue on both sides of the question.

When we were to decide whether to proceed or to return, Bissa-tee spoke convincingly in favour of going on with our task; and since both Azte-ca and Adver-tee fulfilled functions not immediately, but only indirectly bearing on the ultimate aims of the expedition, they were open to conviction. I, therefore, welcomed Bissa-tee's eloquent effort; for it will be remembered that I had deprived myself of my vote and could only act as chairman of our meetings and as a clearing-house of ideas. Once a thing was resolved upon, it was my duty to see to it that it was done; and to this there was only the one exception of a dead-lock in the meeting of department heads, in which case I held the casting vote.

Having listened to Bissa-tee, Anna-zee, in the manner characteristic of her, wagged her huge head over her left shoulder and slowly heaved herself to her feet. Even the privations and hardships of our last desperate march had not availed to reduce her obesity. There are ants who will thrive on next to nothing; and Anna-zee was one of them. Amid a profound silence she began her great argument.

All formicarian endeavour, she scented, was oriented in one of two directions: towards the knowable or the unknowable. In a superficial view it might seem as though, for a reasoning being, there could be no choice: the knowable alone was worthy of her effort. But the mere fact that, throughout the millennia, those who represented perhaps the finest minds among ants had striven towards the unknowable must bid us pause; and when we looked at the present state of our precious inheritance, what did we find? Did not the mass of what was handed down to us in the fields of philosophy, art, poetry, religious thought, etc. vastly outweigh what was handed down to us in the field of science? In fact, what was left of the science of a few millennia ago? Names, that was all; and, perhaps, a few things to laugh at. Venerable names — names revered in spite of the fact that the theories, hypotheses, and so-called discoveries with which they were associated have long since disappeared into the limbo of a forgotten childhood of thought. Did we think it would be different with our findings?

Science asks one question only, she went on: the question " How? " But ant insists on asking that other question " Why? " This latter question has not only never been answered; it has been proved to be unanswerable except by so-called spiritual vapourings which, by any thinking ant, cannot be received with anything but scepticism. The question "How?" on the other hand, can be answered after a fashion by one provisional answer after the other. In a matter of fact, it would seem, certainty is within our reach; the trouble is that certainty on one point answers one limited question only and itself opens up other questions. The achievement of any ant of science is merely the basis for the achievement of another ant of science; from moment to moment it is superseded. In fact, she went on, gathering momentum as she went, since the province of fact, unknown but knowable, is infinite in extent, all that is knowable will never be known; though, in a way, we might be said to approach that end; in another way, however, we may be said to be farther from the goal the nearer we come to it; for everything knowable that becomes known opens up a view into realms of the knowable not yet known which exceed in magnitude all the provinces of the knowable already known by something resembling infinity.

But suppose for a moment this were not so; suppose that, with everything knowable that becomes known, we diminished by exactly that much the realm of the knowable not yet known; and that ultimately we succeeded in changing all knowable things into known things, what should we have gained? Precisely nothing. Man, it is true, from what she had seen of him, might conceivably think himself a gainer; for man does not strive after knowledge for the sake of knowledge; he strives after it for the sake of increasing his power. Ants, who have long since abandoned that aim, seeing clearly that material progress — which means no more and no less than the increase of power for the achievement of material ends — would side-track them in their essential task which was to live this life of theirs fully — ants could never be satisfied with so low an aim; and that for the very reason that they see themselves as thinking, exploring, feeling, and reasoning beings — not as slaves of material ends. What, then, stands at the end of a complete exploration of the knowable world? What, if such an end there is, stands at the end of science? At that end stands neither more nor less than a complete realization of our ignorance. For, since it is ant-nature, since it always has been and will ever remain ant-nature, to ask that question " Why? " we shall merely find ourselves confronted with the whole realm of the unknowable; in other words, the best that science, even on the basis of our assumption, can achieve is the conversion of the vast knowable universe into an unknowable universe.

But, of course, as she had already pointed out, the knowable universe being infinite, this dilemma could never arise. Well, then, ultimate value there is none in science. Meanwhile, is there a relative value? There is; but that value is not increased by increasing knowledge. A single known fact would be sufficient to create that value. For the moment a fact is known, the moment a single how is known, that moment ant-reason hammers at it with the question why; and in that lies its sole and exclusive ultimate value. Ants are constituted in such a way that they must ever try to storm heaven. They are suspended between two worlds: the world of the knowable and the world of the unknowable; and from that very fact arises their transcendent mission which consists in the task of expressing their feelings with regard to a callous universe. To go on adding to the collection of known fact is merely one more way of expending one's life uselessly, not superior, perhaps not even equivalent, to that other way of swinging the hammer "Why?" But, if it had to be one or the other, the gift of expressing her feelings being denied her, she, being old and obese, preferred the latter; and she could swing that hammer sitting in comfort at home.

This, she proceeded, after an impressive pause, might seem strange, as coming from one who had gone so far. But it had always been her opinion that one thing was as good as another; and, while she hoped that we should support her by our vote, she would go on with us if such were our pleasure. It did not matter. She simply found it easier to sit and be fed than to march and go hungry.

She stood with her antennæ trembling sardonically. Then she dropped heavily to the ground, resting her case and spreading out her legs sideways.

Her discourse had made a profound impression on both Azte-câ and Adver-tee. I was vainly searching in my mind for something to counteract that impression when, opportunely, Bissa-tee stirred her long limbs and briefly gave her opinion to the effect that all that was "rank nihilism".

Anna-zee's head shook over her left shoulder, and her antennæ trembled. It was most unusual for her to deliver herself of long speeches; in all my experience she had done so only twice; once on the occasion of our visit to the ant-colonies on Acacia Sphærocephala, and just now. For the former she had made up by a silence of many months, broken only by monosyllabic remarks on the flora of the districts traversed. In the present case, all four of us understood her silence to mean that she considered Bissa-tee a consummate ass; and I could at once see that Adver-tee was sufficiently sensitive to be won back to Anna-zee's side by this attitude of silent contempt.

Azte-ca remained doubtful. In her way she was a genius; she could find ways and means of communicating with ants and other insects and even, as we shall see, with mammals which no one else could find; but essentially she was an ability in the concrete, without brains. Yet she stood too near the throne and the powers that be; the scent nihilism had thoroughly frightened her; and her expression betrayed, when she looked at me, that she was conscious of having very nearly walked into a trap — a fact of which I was glad.

Adver-tee, on the other hand, was won to Anna-zee's side; and in a way I could not but admire her for it. Whoever is familiar with the reaction of sullen resistance which had, at home, greeted advanced and ultra-modern speculations, political as well as scientific, tending in the direction of this scientific nihilism or in that of political anarchism, will at once understand that Bissa-tee could not have said anything more effective in counteracting her opponent's arguments than the thing she had said. At home, the mere suspicion of being in sympathy with such dangerous speculations had been sufficient to ruin an ambitious ant's career. Yet Anna-zee's prestige was such — and since the very beginning of our expedition it had been steadily on the increase among the members of the High Command — that a comparatively young ant like Adver-tee was dazzled by her intellectual powers and foolishly inferred that Anna-zee was a coming ant.

As for me, I was now quite satisfied with the course the argument had taken; I knew what I had to expect. I promptly put the question to the vote, which was evenly divided: a fact which gave me what I wanted, the chance of deciding the issue by my casting vote. With its help it was resolved to proceed as soon as we were sufficiently rested.

CHAPTER FOUR

The Plain

CONTAINING our adventures with slave-making Rubicundas and Polyergus, and the marvellous speculations of Bissa-tee on the same; a report of the single combat between Assa-ree and an Amazon; the supreme disaster of the human road; further evidence of Assa-ree's treasonable practices; the crossing of the great river by means of metallic threads spun by great spiders, the trial and execution of Assa-ree; and my own speculations with regard to the final stage of degeneration perhaps not yet reached by any slave-making ants.

I

IT WAS A STRANGE COINCIDENCE that in course of time we should once more have run across our old human enemy the Wheeler. But one day, a month or so later, there he was again, crossing our very line of march a few thousand antlengths ahead riding on his two wheels. I promptly gave the signal to halt and to lie low.

But he never troubled us; and since we were marching without a vanguard of scouts, we were not perceived,
in spite of the fact that he alighted straight in front, in
the margin of a small copse. Having laid his wheels on
the ground, he picked up a stick of wood and stuck it
into the soil and into certain masses of decaying wood.
Then he bent down and, with his fore-feet, took hold of
a huge flat stone which he upended and allowed to drop
upside down.

At this moment a tremendous wave of sound swept
over us, produced by a second human whom we had so
far not noticed. He was stationed a considerable distance
to the north, in the margin of the same copse; and he
was excitedly shouting to the Wheeler, no doubt sum-
moning him to his assistance; for the latter ran for his
wheels and departed.

We were near enough to getting beyond reach even
should he turn back. So I gave the signal to proceed.

Our path lay a little to the north of the point where
the Wheeler had been halting; and since I had given the
order for a forced march, we soon passed it. Judging
that we were out of danger from the humans, I halted
again; for I was curious to see what the Wheeler had
been doing. I took the precaution, however, of sending
scouts back to watch their movements, with instructions
to give the alarm should they, or either of them, turn
back in our direction. As for the army and the remainder
of the High Command, I gave orders not to break ranks
and to be ready to march at a moment's notice.

Then Bissa-tee and myself made for the point where,
at the foot of a tree, the Wheeler had raised the huge
flat stone. A very short time only had elapsed; and we

were able to witness the last consequences of the
Wheeler's action.

In order not to expose ourselves unnecessarily, we
climbed the north side of the tree to a height of perhaps
seventy antlengths and then circled the trunk.

To our delight, we saw a large, irregular, flat
chamber which had been covered by the stone. In its
centre a cylindrical opening led perpendicularly down
into the soil. A small corner of the chamber was still
filled with naked pupæ and excitedly hurrying workers
of a pale, medium-sized ant of the genus Formica. As I
have said, we were just in time; for the workers promptly seized the remaining pupæ in their jaws and poured
down, with them, into the subterranean galleries.

We were on the point of turning away when, in the
south, a motion caught my eye. I stopped, watching
closely; and within a few moments I became aware of a
widespread disturbance in the sparse, parched grass
covering the soil. Bissa-tee had also seen it.

A minute later it became clear that it arose from
the approach of an army of a larger ant belonging to
the same genus Formica. They were drawn out in an
irregular semicircle south of the uncovered nest, advancing rapidly and excitedly.

When the first scouts reached the uncovered spot,
they stopped, emitting volley after volley of scent signals
which much increased the excitement prevailing behind.
Soon the edge of the uncovered patch was swarming
with ants, many of them clambering over those in front
to get sight or scent of what lay before them. But they
did not invade the chamber. In fact, their hesitation and
the indignation of the ants in the front lines who kept

pressing back while those behind pressed forward was ludicrous to behold. They quarrelled and jostled till the very rear-guard of the army had arrived, and even longer.

At last a huge worker leapt into the chamber and made for the opening to the burrow. But at its edge she suddenly turned tail and scurried back. Her example, however, had brought down three others. These, in a more dignified manner, approached the opening less precipitously; and, having reached its edge, seemed to be peering down, as though trying to explore it without entering. This again went on for several minutes, the hordes on the edge of the clearing meanwhile pushing and jostling each other in the most laughable manner. Those behind called those in front cowards and slackers; but the moment they reached the edge of the chamber themselves, they became cowards and slackers in turn.

Till at last another powerful individual made her way from the rear, over the bodies of those in front. This ant, with a sort of deliberate braggadocio, approached the entrance and actually vanished in it. But in less than a second she came flying out again as though propelled by some superformicarian power. For the whole remainder of the time she stood in a corner, brushing and combing legs and antennæ with her strigils, and working jaws and lips as though anxious to remove whatever had been flung on her.

From then on one ant after the other did exactly as she had done.

Meanwhile orators had begun within the ranks to deliver the most insulting and stinging scents which increased the general confusion; for those wedged in struggled fiercely to pull these demagogues down from their exalted stations on the shoulders of the rest.

Suddenly, after more than half an hour, the whole army surged forward and poured down into the entrance till it seemed as though they must fill every subterranean chamber and gallery to capacity. Yet they remained invisible for fully a quarter of an hour before the first of them re-emerged with a larva in her mouth, setting off for home. After another interval a second ant appeared, carrying a pupa.

Then, to our amazement, the queen of the species attacked made her exit, followed by a solid phalanx of her own workers, all carrying larvæ and pupæ; and these escaped, breaking through the ranks of a cordon which had remained behind, circling the edge of the patch. The ants in this cordon tried to tear these fugitives to pieces; but they, dropping their pupæ and larvæ which were promptly seized by the assailants, offered such a resistance that the robbers were glad to let them escape.

And now began a general flight from the nest. The assailed species left everything behind as they poured out. Arrived at the surface, they still fought on; but they did so only to cover their retreat, leaving many of their number on the field of battle, whereas the assailing species had very few casualties. Fifteen minutes after the commencement of the retreat no ants of the attacked species were left on the premises; and the raiders, laden with larvæ and pupæ, went home in triumph.

Within two hours of our arrival neither assailants nor assailed were to be seen. We secured one each of the corpses of the two species and returned to the army. Both these species were new to science, and Bissa-tee named them very appropriately Formica Rubicunda and Formica Subsericea, the Rubicundas being the assailants.

This raid which we had witnessed opened up a number of problems; and Bissa-tee and myself were discussing them on our way back when one of the scouts returned to report that the humans were approaching rapidly on their wheels. We reached the army in record time.

I gave orders to our forces to dig themselves in. But to my surprise Azte-ca asked for leave of absence. Naturally, I demurred. She insisted; and when I asked for her reasons, she hesitatingly made an amazing announcement. To put it briefly, she proclaimed that *she had found a key to the human language.*

This was so extraordinary a thing that, had I fully grasped its import, I should have been willing to send the whole army and my own associates into certain death, provided that such recklessness had given *me* that key. As it was, I gasped; and Azte-ca spluttered out her tale. Ever since we had met with man, she had carefully noted his sound-symbols; and by tabulating them, she had been able to arrange them in order of frequency — till she had succeeded in interpreting half a dozen of them with a fair degree of certainty. But the great find had come during our stay in the human barn when she had made it a rule to scale the great height of the human shoulder, thus, unperceived herself, going about with the man as he did his work and listening to the ejaculations in which he indulged and to the occasional louder speech

with which he addressed other humans; soon she had
enlarged her vocabulary to a degree which enabled her
to grasp the drift of almost anything he might say. She
had kept this a secret even from me because she had
wished to attain perfection before we reached that part
of the country in which, according to the legends handed down to us, man was more or less dominant.

I was at once dumbfounded and delighted; and so
was Bissa-tee who begged me to let her accompany
Azte-ca. I had only one hesitation. Azte-ca — and I
believe I have said this before — was in her way a
genius; and I did not wish to expose her to any danger.
Yet, when I saw the eagerness and enthusiasm of these
two who, as far as age went, were mere striplings as
compared to myself, I too was infected.

In a flash my mind was made up. I would not only
send them: I was going to go myself. This did not suit
Azte-ca; for the first time I saw her half rebellious; but
a moment later she submitted, stipulating, however,
that I should mount a tree and look on from a distance
only. Stipulating! Under any other circumstances I
should have punished her for daring to prescribe to me.
But in my excitement I overlooked the fact and agreed.
After a last look around, to see that my orders were
being obeyed, I turned, and we departed.

On the way to the point where we expected to find
the humans we ran into the excited multitudes of the
Subsericeas who, however, did not pay the slightest
attention to us; they were far too busy digging a new
nest for themselves under the enormous half-decayed
root of a fallen tree. The humans we found examining
their deserted nest.

We halted at a respectful distance and adopted a waiting attitude. They soon left the Subsericea nest and methodically began to circle it. No doubt they were searching for the Rubicundas, intending to enslave them in turn.

A matter of 5,000 antlengths straight south they came upon their burrow. Azte-ca, as by common consent, assumed command of the situation. She led the way to a tree near the new location and climbed it, signalling me to follow her and Bissa-tee to wait at its base.

When we had reached a convenient height, she motioned to me to remain where I was and herself dropped to the ground. I was mortally afraid that her motions would attract the attention of the humans; but they, too, were preoccupied. I lost sight of my companions and did not see them again for some little time.

It was mere chance that I did so at last. Imagine the daring of these investigators! When I caught sight of them, they were stationed on the concave rims of the boat-shaped integuments covering the crania of the giant marauders. I admit these were excellent points of observation; but, considering that the humans were rapidly moving about, bending down and straightening up, I trembled for their safety.

Meanwhile, the humans were incessantly conversing and laughing; for thus I interpreted the seismic tremblings of their shoulders and the spasmodic withdrawals of their thick lips from their flashing teeth, symptoms occasionally accompanied by rumblings as from distant earthquakes.

Next, one of the two, the Wheeler, dug into the Rubicunda nest with a huge instrument consisting of a

flat metallic blade and a wooden handle. Azte-ca later
assured me that it was called a " spade " though these
humans did not so call it; they used a different sound
which she tried to imitate and which sounded like
" pelle ". I will not waste time over the matter; we
found later that humans have many different systems
of communication called languages which they can use
interchangeably though the medium used is always the
voice: thus language serves two purposes with them, the
purpose of communication and the purpose of preventing
communication.

The Wheeler having opened the formicary, his companion scooped up a large number of the frightened in-
mates who were wildly trying to escape with their
larvæ and pupæ. But their speed could not compare
with that of these ruthless robbers who, by a single step,
could cover a distance of eighty antlengths.

The whole raid was over in a tenth of the time
which the Rubicunda raid against the Subsericeas had
taken. Laughingly the humans packed up their booty;
and then they gathered their tools, fastened them to
their wheels, mounted the latter, and departed. Where
were my friends?

I was just ascertaining that half of the Rubicunda
nest remained undisturbed when, to my infinite relief,
I saw both Bissa-tee and Azte-ca waiting for me at the
foot of the tree. Their purpose achieved, they had dropped to the ground and escaped. The Rubicundas had been
too dismayed to molest them.

The eyes of my companions glistened with excitement; and since I was very anxious to hear whether
they had observed anything that had escaped my vigil-

ance, I beckoned them to join me on the tree and to
report. Azte-ca briefly stated what I have already told,
adding that, under the circumstances, the progress made
in her knowledge of human speech had been negligible.

But Bissa-tee had secured more information with
regard to the composition of this colony than she could
have secured by any other means in the course of many
days. In this nest there had been at least three Subsericeas for every Rubicunda; and the Subsericeas, the
slaves, had been just as much dismayed by the human
raid as the Rubicundas, and just as anxious to rescue
the broods which had also consisted of the same proportions of the two species. A few adult Subsericeas,
however, had apparently been taken in the recent dulotic
raid; and those, she had been able to observe, had still
retained the alien nest-odour. Not even the general
disaster of the human irruption had sufficed to overcome the hostility of the worker mob to this foreign
body in the commonwealth. She had seen Subsericea
and Rubicunda workers laden with eggs and larvæ
dropping their burdens to decapitate in passing these
alien adults who had been brought in, perhaps by mistake, perhaps by callows not yet sufficiently versed in
the tactics of the Rubicundas. For the adult Subsericeas
that had the nest-odour of the formicary were treated
as equals by the Rubicundas and even seemed to applaud
them and to rejoice in the success of the recent raid
which must have added hundreds of eggs and larvæ to
the common stock. What interested me most was that
Bissa-tee, in one or two cases, had actually observed
Rubicundas in the act of devouring Subsericea larvæ;
for this fact explained to me the origin of these mixed

colonies: it was hunger that sent the robbers on their raids; the keeping of slaves was more or less incidental.

Another interesting point was that among the slaves there were a few individuals of a third species (Neoclara) which shows that the militant Rubicunda does not, when driven by hunger, restrict herself to a single species of victims. But, once adopted or raised in the nest, the slaves are accepted on an equal footing with the broods of the host. The raiding army, however, had consisted exclusively of Rubicundas.

Those were the results of our observations. Before I leave this subject of the Rubicundas, however, I will add that we met with them every now and then for many weeks, and that once we had the singular experience of being the object of one of their raids.

On that occasion, Bissa-tee presumed so far as to issue a general order without consulting me. We were entrenched in a temporary formicary and had made a futile attempt at raising fungi on leaf-shreds of the corn plant cultivated by man. Bissa-tee's order was to lie low and to offer no resistance. I did not think it advisable to insist on a reckoning with her for this breach of discipline; for, as it turned out, I could not have given a better order myself. The Rubicundas swarmed all through our chambers, expressed their disgust at our abortive fungus gardens and their admiration at our size; but, finding neither eggs nor larvæ or pupæ, left us unmolested and departed to search for more suitable victims.

In this I am anticipating; for by that time we were already in contact with another type of ant which saw

to it that, throughout the remainder of this march to
the east, we did not forget them.

II

We did not remain in as continuous a contact with
this new ant of the genus Polyergus (the species varied
with the locality) as we had been, let me say, with the
Ecitons of the isthmus or the Pogonomyrmex of the
slopes; we met them only occasionally; but when we did,
we had to admit that, as far as sheer courage and
military brilliance were concerned, Pogonomyrmex and
Ecitons had been mere amateurs and bunglers. Both
Ecitons and Pogonomyrmex had been formidable chiefly
through their numbers; but the colonies of Polyergus
were not populous. Neither was their sting as formidable as that of Pogonomyrmex; nor their jaws as large
as those of Eciton. They were perhaps the most beautiful terrestrial creatures whom it was our fate to meet
with in the whole course of our expedition. They were
wine-coloured; or, when two-coloured, the gaster was
black and the rest of the body a delicate mauve-red; or,
towards the Atlantic seaboard, the reverse. As for their
stature, the first species we met, which Bissa-tee called
Polyergus Breviceps, were stockily-built, and their legs
were short; but as we advanced and met with the two-
coloured species, their stature underwent a corresponding change, becoming slenderer, longer-legged, and more
elegant, till, in Polyergus Lucidus, the largest of them
all, we had to acknowledge that, owing to the delicate
proportions of their slim and shining bodies, their long,

gracefully articulated legs, and their brilliant colouring, we seemed to see the ideal of earthly beauty. Strange to say, among these, the male was the greatest marvel, for the colour-scheme of the body was almost miraculously enhanced by the fact that their wings were pure white.

But what made them such formidable enemies? Their morale.

When we had our first meeting with them, we were approaching that great river which divides the northern continent into two unequal halves; and we were travelling through an almost level country densely populated and cultivated by man.

The season was that marvellous one in which the year seems to come to a halt. The heat of the summer sun still seems to linger in soil, rock, and water. Yet a certain crispness of the atmosphere calls for brisk exercise and the exertion of all physical powers. At the precise moment of the meeting we had been on the march for eight or nine hours; but we hardly felt any fatigue; the dry and clear air made us forget such hardships as we had had to endure.

The order of our march was the usual one, with a few scouts in front, spread out in fan-shaped lines, and the shrunken body of the army following in massed formation, with the High Command bringing up the rear. The army, I should say, marched in a loose column, sixteen abreast.

Suddenly report after report came in from our scouts, of the approach of a small body of red ants from the south, at right angles to the direction of our march.

Anxious to avoid hostilities, yet impressed with the necessity of being prepared for anything, I gave orders to execute a flank movement, thereby doubling the width of our column. Our soldiers, I am afraid, were itching for a fight: the movement was carried out with beautiful precision. We never stopped or even slowed our march.

Assa-ree repeated my orders in a precise, almost nonchalant way which showed that she was in no way flustered or alarmed. Her attitude was exactly what I should have wished; it was well calculated to make a potential enemy inclined to negotiate rather than to fight.

The Polyergus came straight on, led by some four or five maxims who, however, were constantly changing.

Assa-ree now speeded up our march in such a way as to let the clash, if clash there was to be, take place between the van of the approaching enemy and the strongest part of our own body where our ranks now marched thirty-two abreast.

Both she and I had climbed the stems of some tall weeds so that we could communicate with each other across the whole hostile army; for by this time a conflict seemed unavoidable. I gave the signal to halt and to face the enemy.

The Polyergus came on in a dense, massed formation of twenty-five ranks twelve abreast; they strained eagerly forward as though unaware of our presence.

And there was no battle. The Polyergus kept straight on, barely delayed. With their short, sickle-shaped mandibles they put our soldiers to the jaw as though they were defenceless callows of some peaceful kind; or as though they sabred their way through so many dead masses of vegetable debris.

And then, having passed through our ranks without a casualty on their side, they disappeared to the north.

We could only gasp. Yet I must say that we were as yet hardly aware of what had happened; the whole encounter, if such it can be called, had not taken more than ten or twelve seconds. Where, half a minute ago, the flower of our veteran forces had stood, straining for battle, there was nothing but an expanse of sparse, cropped grass strewn with writhing bodies in the agony of death.

Disconsolately I climbed down and advanced to the scene of the disaster where I met Assa-ree. For the second time since the beginning of the expedition she, too, was prostrated with dismay and grief. Every one of our soldiers who had been in the line of the Polyergus march had head or thorax pierced; and either brains or ganglia were trailing in the dust. There were 384 casualties, forming a lane twelve antlengths wide through the centre of our army; and every one of these casualties was a total loss; but the worst consequence of this disaster, as I realized at once, was the effect it was bound to have on the morale of the dwindling remainder of our troops.

What with the occasional small losses which we had had of late, our total number was now reduced to less than 1,800. Two or three more encounters like this, and where was our chance of survival? How were we going to cross that great river which I was firmly convinced we should shortly reach? Yet, of course, it would never have done to let anyone in army or Command suspect how this disaster discouraged me. I gave orders for our medical officers to examine the wounded and to save as many lives as they could. We were delayed for an hour or so, till Bissa-tee, rejoining me, reported that nothing could be done.

I had the ranks re-formed; and we proceeded; it seemed imperative to get away from the place.

On the march, Bissa-tee kept close by my side. For a while she observed silence; but at last she began to communicate to me the thoughts which had been set in motion by this encounter.

The tribe of Polyergus, she signified, belonged to the slave-making ants. That column which had just marched through our lines was bound on a dulotic raid. From the numbers of other ants available in the district it seemed likely that their slaves were the same as those of the Rubicundas. No ant, indeed, had been as commonly met with during the last few weeks as the peaceful and comparatively uninteresting Subsericea. Whenever and wherever we had met them, they had invariably been occupying newly excavated nests; and rarely had there been many callows; which seemed to point to the fact that their formicaries had recently and frequently been raided for their broods. Subsericeas, then, were the most likely slaves.

What sort of life did the masters live? Bissa-tee reasoned thus: a military endowment so brilliant, so irresistible, cannot but be compensated for by the lack of endowment in other directions; it implied generation upon generation of tradition and a lifelong training besides. This, then, was the picture she painted for me.

In the nests which swarm with Subsericea slaves — probably there are six or seven slaves to every master — these amazons of the jaw lead an idle life doing nothing.

Their mouth-parts are such as to disable them from taking nourishment by themselves except perhaps a little liquid food on which they stumble by chance. Left to themselves, even with an abundance of food available within easy reach, they would starve to death. Most of their time in the intervals between raids is taken up by their begging food from their slaves who regurgitate freely to them; or by their submitting to the complex processes of the toilette which is also performed by the slaves who never tire of combing their antennæ and legs and of polishing and coating the highly chitinized and exceedingly hard plates of their armour. Thus these hero-masters lounge about, abject in their behaviour to the slaves, or treating them with the haughty disdain of a superior race; but constantly degenerating in all the faculties demanded for the ordinary functions of life and developing at the same time in that one direction of military exploit and enterprise.

The time comes when the whole colony, masters and slaves, face starvation unless a raid is made. Since the very continuance of the colony is dependent on the raising of pillaged pupæ and of the eggs laid in the nest by the Polyergus queen (who, Bissa-tee conjectured, is probably not much larger than the soldiers), it would never do for them to feed on uninjured pupæ of the slave-species; and the broods of the master-species are of course sacrosanct.

Ultimately, the masters must sally forth for a raid. Meanwhile, individual scouts have been scouring the neighbourhood, travelling singly; the results of their explorations have been communicated and discussed in great detail by all the soldiers. Their plans are made in advance: everybody knows exactly what is to be done.

One afternoon they start out. There is no hesitation. The location of the Subsericea nest or the nest of any other species to be plundered is exactly known. If, when they arrive, everything is found to be as it was signalized, they never stop but pour in at once. According as they do or do not meet with resistance, they plunder or fight. A colony of the slave-species that has never been plundered before is apt to oppose itself to the proceedings; but those who are familiar with the results sure to follow submit, bent only on escaping alive without irritating the raiders into violence.

On returning home, the masters are greeted by their slaves who admire their prowess and take their booty from their jaws. Carefully they sort out the larvæ and such pupæ as are injured by the hard, denticulate mandibles of the robber-barons. The uninjured pupæ are stacked in the brood-chambers; the others placed in the coolest parts of the burrow where they are likely to remain longest alive.

In the meantime, the Polyergus soldiers are impatiently tramping about, stamping the floor of the chambers and loudly demanding to be fed. The slaves pay little attention to them till their task of sorting and storing is done. But at last they hurriedly fill their ingluvies; and, having done so, they hasten to placate, by regurgitation, their masters who by that time are threatening to put every slave to the jaw unless their appetites are stilled at once.

The larvæ and the worst-injured pupæ are eaten first; the less badly injured pupæ are left for later; and often the slaves hide from their masters large numbers of them which promise partial recovery; for the inclement seasons of the late fall, before hibernation begins, and of the early spring have to be provided for by storing living food.

Often, Bissa-tee continued her imaginative sketch, the lust of battle overtakes the Polyergus, especially the younger ones, long before such food as has to be consumed at once is exhausted. In that case the slaves restrain their masters in their military ardour; and often, among the old, the reverse happens: the slaves have to urge them to go on a raid long before they like to do so. Who, then, exclaimed Bissa-tee, is master, who slave?

Worse may happen. The free Subsericeas have observed a Polyergus scout exploring their locality. They hold a council; and as a result of their deliberations they decamp. When the Polyergus arrive, there are no slaves to be carried off; they have had their pains for nothing.

Perhaps they have been in the neighbourhood for a year. Every colony of the slave-species is aware of their presence; every one of them migrates. No matter how eager, brave, and brilliant the raiders are, there is no booty, there are no slaves to be found; from raid after raid they come home empty-jawed. Perhaps, when they can find no more nests of their proper slave-species, they try the expedient of bringing in booty from the nests of a new species. But their slaves are partial to their own kind. They tear all the pupæ of these alien species to pieces; and the masters find themselves threatened with the extinction of their slaves. Perhaps, however, an ever-increasing proportion of a new slave-species is raised by the old. In that case, in the course of a few years, a new slave-population takes the place of the old, thus postponing but not eliminating the evil day; for the perhaps once numerous formicaries of the new slave-species also decrease in number; and ultimately they disappear. And then the evil day has come indeed; the masters must follow their slaves, perhaps invading the territory of a rival colony of their own kind with which they will henceforth be at war till either they or their rivals are exterminated.

Truly, Bissa-tee added in conclusion and with a deep sigh, the life of the capitalist[1] is no bed of roses.

III

Now the strange thing about these speculations of Bissa-tee was that they were so strikingly confirmed in the near future; in order not to weary by repetition, I shall content myself with this mere statement, omitting the incidents which brought that confirmation.

When we proceeded, we did so in a state of extreme nervousness; and henceforth we had almost daily proof of a disintegration of the fighting spirit in our army. I tried to close my eyes to a good deal of what was going on; but much of it was forced upon my attention.

---

[1] This is the third time that a word occurs in the text which seems to be not only without precedent but without justification. But again I leave it because it is unmistakably there. E.

Thus, one day when we had halted for a rest, I saw a small group of our soldiers who had organized a game outside of the lines of our bivouac taking flight from a single Polyergus scout, thus leaving us completely exposed on that side. This scout, therefore, came boldly into our midst. I happened to be on the outskirts of our encampment; and so I promptly summoned Assa-ree and told her what I had witnessed. Whereupon she flew into a towering rage which, I thought at first, would turn against myself. But suddenly she gave the general alarm; and the whole remainder of the army boiled up as it were out of the ground. She had just begun to stalk along the lines in order to find those who had offended when the Polyergus scout appeared boldly in front of these very lines behind Assa-ree's back. I gave her a warning; and she veered about.

A moment later she and the scout had closed in single combat. I was inclined to give Assa-ree credit for the noblest motives in thus exposing herself to the gravest danger. Who knows but that she thought of what might not have happened to us if this scout had returned to her tribe? That, however, did not worry me. It was late in the afternoon; and it was unlikely that an attack would be made at once. Besides, why should they attack us? As far as I knew we had no brood with us. But Assa-ree might well have overlooked these two facts. I was still far from having fathomed the whole of her treachery.

The fight which followed furnished a sight worth seeing, indeed. Never had I seen anything as ludicrous as the surprise of that Polyergus scout when she found

herself suddenly rough-handled. I believe these slave-
makers have no enemies at all capable of preying upon
them; and it was this element of surprise which gave
Assa-ree her first tremendous advantage. In her initial
whirl-wind attack she succeeded in tearing one antenna
and one middle leg from her adversary's body; but even
in doing so she realized her own danger. The Polyergus
was so quick that Assa-ree's superior length and power
of jaw and even her much greater weight were a handicap rather than an advantage. The Polyergus scout got
to her flank whence she could ward off the bite of her
aggressor; she might even have fastened on to her in a
death-grapple in which the greater hardness of her jaws
would have been of immense benefit to her. But again
Assa-ree adopted the exactly suitable tactics: she sprang
free and did not return to the attack for several seconds.
This gave the Polyergus time to realize her wounds
which, by this time, had no doubt begun to smart.

The moment Assa-ree had left her, the scout began
a series of motions which to all lookers-on seemed utterly laughable.

Apparently she did not grasp the fact that her left
antenna was gone; but she must have been conscious of
the pain produced by the fact; for she promptly lifted
her left front-leg which was provided with a pectinated
strigil and tried to comb the smart off the missing antenna. But the moment she lifted the front-leg, she remained unsupported, on that side, except by her hind-
leg; and so she tumbled over on her shoulder. She right-
ed herself with the help of the fore-leg and tried the

same manœuvre again, with the same result. [2] Clearly the fact that both antenna and middle-leg on that side were gone was beyond her grasp; nothing of the kind had ever happened to her before. Again and again the same sequence of motions was repeated; and unmistakably, in the course of these futile endeavours, the fighting spirit oozed out of her. She seemed to forget that she was in the presence of the enemy, and bent only on brushing away whatever irritated that missing antenna of hers: the very mishap occurring when she lifted her left front-leg prevented her from realizing or ascertaining that that antenna was no longer there.

Meanwhile, we all stood about, our antennæ trembling with mirth, all except Assa-ree who patiently bided her time. When at last the Polyergus scout, in utter dejection, turned away to go home, thinking no doubt to resume her attempts with more success there, her tormentor was suddenly on her again, moving like a tornado. This time she straddled her victim from behind; and in less than a hundredth of a second she had clasped her neck between her jaws. It was all over, of course. On the highly chitinized armour of head or thorax she could not have made the slightest impression with her jaws which, powerful though they were, were not hard enough even to scratch that armour; but she could easily sever the articulate membranes; and when she sprang free again, the scout's head lay on the ground, its jaws opening and shutting convulsively.

---

[2] See Wheeler, *Ants*, 1913, page 484, for a similar description. Was "the Wheeler" an unobserved observer of this scene? E.

For a moment we lost sight of Assa-ree. Bissa-tee was now running around the amazon's headless body, closely observing it as it moved off in a sort of high-legged, indignant prance.

When I saw what was happening — undoubtedly she was returning to her formicary — I gave a quick warning to Bissa-tee. Would not the return of a headless amazon set all sisters upon our trail? But Bissa-tee waved a reassuring answer. The trail had not yet been scented; and while this scout could find her way home in a purely instinctive manner, she would, without a brain, be unable to find her way back to our quarters; and in her present state she was unlikely to scent the route.

When I turned away, I saw Assa-ree once more stalking along the lines of our army; she was entirely unhurt; and soon she had singled out all those who had run from the Polyergus scout. There were six of them; and she aligned them in front of the ranks. Then, before I had time to interfere in their behalf, she gave the order to tear them to pieces. As, somewhat later, when everything had once more assumed the peaceful air of a bivouac, I pondered this proceeding of hers, I came to the conclusion that perhaps it had been a wise one. Coming immediately after her own demonstration of the fact that these amazons were not invincible, the punishment of deserters in the face of an enemy was bound to raise the morale of the army; and it did seem to have that effect; for there was a new spirit in the camp that night. Everywhere, till sun-down, groups were standing or lounging about, discussing the duel and appreciatively recalling every detail of Assa-ree's tactics.

But this revival of morale was destined to be of short duration.

Next morning we came to a strange structure which could not be natural. We spent several hours in exploring it before I gave the order to cross. We had, of course, many times come upon roads made by man; but never upon one like this. We had at first concluded that this, too, must be a human road; it had the same crosswise dimensions, and it showed signs of having been scored lengthwise in the same manner in which other human roads had been scored, either by such wheels as we had seen used by the Wheeler and his companion, or by the iron-shod wheels of certain gigantic wooden platforms which man uses to convey burdens on. The material with which the scorings on this road had been produced was the same as that observed by Bissa-tee in escaping from her human captor a few months ago. But the scorings themselves were much wider; and there were four bands of them. Besides, the surface of the road was not of earth but of a substance which must have been liquid when applied. The two or three chemists who were still with us pronounced it to be a tarry secretion of some unknown animal, probably, Bissa-tee added, an animal enslaved by man.

But there seemed to be no profit in delaying over an unsolvable problem. Reluctantly I gave the order to cross.

Now we were hardly well on the road when a most terrifying thing happened. The road began to heave under us like a living thing; and from a distance, coming from the north, there swept over us an ever-increasing noise, compounded of a strident swish and a pulsating thunder. I did not know how far our army had advanced. I did not even know where my own associates were; for when we arrived at this strange structure, we had scattered considerably; and after I had given the order to cross, I had myself been delayed by a call of nature. As soon as these terrible portents manifested themselves, I therefore gave the counter-signal to return to the west side of the road. This order, however, was already being interfered with by a powerful current of air rushing along the road and spreading out fan-wise to the south. A moment later a weird and gigantic shape, glittering like a newly polished beetle but many million times as large and rushing along at an inconceivable speed, loomed up from our left. The speed was such that I hesitate over a comparison that suggested itself: the speed of a meteorite such as have been known to fall out of the heavens to the earth.

This monster, whatever it was, animal or heavenly body, was barely upon us when it was gone again, to the south; and the whole series of portents: the increasing heavings, the wind, the pulsations, and the strident swish went through a series of mutations in an opposite sense, decreasing instead of increasing. As for the wind, nothing will give so adequate an idea of its force as the statement that, at the moment of the monster's passing, I — who am no light-weight and who, even in a hurricane, am held down to the ground by my head — that even I, I say, was whirled off my feet, lifted high into the air, and turned round and round, being carried along for seven or eight hundred antlengths, before I fell down again, in the middle of the road, rolling over and over many times.

I was stunned; but as soon as I recovered I started back to the scene of the disaster. Already I was painting to myself what must have happened; for the terror of the thing had completely unnerved me; and I was prepared for the worst. Nevertheless I must confess that this time my imagination proved entirely inadequate to the facts.

A not inconsiderable part of the remainder of our army had been killed; but I saw at a glance that the High Command had fared worse. With a feeling of utter nausea I turned away and emitted the scent of rally. I trembled at what I might see.

The first ant I saw was Assa-ree; she was as much unnerved as I. Perhaps the word unnerved is rather mild: we felt annihilated; both of us could hardly stand; we trembled from head to foot. Yet Assa-ree had only yesterday vanquished the amazon in single combat!

Behind her, out of still whirling dust, emerged Bissa-tee and Azte-ca; and these three, besides myself, were all that were left of the High Command!

Gradually a few hundred soldiers straggled in, all of them bewildered, many wounded, a few disabled to the point where they could barely move their limbs. I had to hold on to myself in order not to surrender to the same sort of despair as Assa-ree. To give those who survived something to do and thereby time to get over their first shock, I ordered a count to be taken. Only 1,204 soldiers and four officers answered the roll-call. I was still hoping that others would straggle in; but in that hope I was disappointed.

The only one of us who kept her head was Bissa-tee. Having assured herself that, apart from contusions and abrasions, I was unhurt, she went off by herself to investigate.

Since I had to readjust all our plans to the altered circumstances, I gave orders to prepare a small burrow. Somehow I felt that we could not immediately leave the scene of this disaster; and since we had to be prepared for similar monsters rushing along the road, I thought it imperative that we should have a retreat which offered safety.

While these preparations were going on, the soldiers, still preparing, from force of habit, a separate burrow for me and my two associates, I pondered the situation. For that purpose I sought refuge behind a grassy dry ditch flanking the tarry expanse; and there I was joined, after a while, by Bissa-tee.

If, at the rally after the disaster, she had still preserved a measure of her jaunty air, it was now gone. She was profoundly serious. For a moment she remained motionless; then, as though despairing of her ability to give me an adequate idea of what she wished to convey, she touched me with her right antenna on the third abdominal segment, thereby indicating her desire that I should follow her.

We went out on the road; and Bissa-tee began to explain to me just how things had happened. The monster had been moving on four wheels; this she had observed with the greatest distinctness; there was no possibility of a mistake. The army had been in a position half-way beyond and half-way this side of the far pair of wheels; so that the most central part of it had been crushed. But the High Command had been exactly in the path of the near pair of wheels. That was the reason

why the disaster had taken such a terrible toll of ourselves. But she wanted to show me certain details, she
added; she despaired of conveying to me in any other
way the extent and the pathos of the catastrophe.

I followed half unwillingly; and a moment later
she was pointing out what indeed was calculated to
make the stoutest heart tremble.

Sixty-six great scholars, every one a leader in her
field, and collectively perhaps the greatest and most
amazing aggregate of learning that had ever been seen
assembled on earth, were reduced to a greasy smear on
a highway! The futility of it all! The utter senseless-
ness! And, as though still further to emphasize the
inanity of all antly endeavour, Bissa-tee led me forward
to show me one such smear spread in front of the others,
detached and isolated from the rest. Here, a single ant
had been caught in the act of trying to escape: the
smear was enormous in size, measuring at least eight
antlengths in width and thirty in length. It was still
possible to distinguish the various parts of the body.
To both sides the legs were flattened out; and the artic-
ulations between femur and tibia and between tibia and
tarsus were still recognizable. In front of the head, the
antennæ stretched away, a quarter of an antlength wide
and six antlengths long, still showing the geniculate
joints. I marvelled at the size of the smear, wondering
whose remains these might be. Once more Bissa-tee
touched me; and then she scented a name. This, then,
was what was left of Anna-zee, that storehouse of botanical knowledge, that fountain of searching philosophy,
that greatest of all sceptics! If such was her end, what,
then, was the use of all antly striving? What the mean-

ing of the thirst for knowledge and achievement which
had burnt in that obese body with the brightest aspir-
ations on this globe? How much more easily could we
not have spared a hundred soldiers, nay, every last one
that remained! I vowed that, should I ever return to
our own blessed country where such monsters did not
exist, I would myself scent her name on the tree of
honour — a vow which, I am glad to be able to say, I
have kept. And to that vow I added another: I had now
become the sole depositary of all the results of her investigations and speculations on subjects botanical:
these I would carefully rehearse to myself from time to
time; and, in the exceedingly improbable event of my
safe return, I would devote a separate scent-tree to her
findings and her often highly ingenious theories, so as to
preserve them for posterity.

Immersed in such thoughts and glowing with a
sombre flame of sadness, I was on the point of turning
back when Bissa-tee asked me once more to follow her.
This time she led me to the front of the huge smear
which now represented the flower of what had been the
central squadrons of our army. Here, too, flattened
smaller smears were detached from the main one; and
these had a peculiar circular shape which puzzled me
much. Within each of these circular smears there was
the flattened image of an ant that had been crushed in
a peculiar position: with her legs folded and appressed
to the body, as though she had tried to withdraw into
the smallest possible space.

I could not, or perhaps I should say, I dared not
explain this sight to myself, till Bissa-tee cruelly form-
ulated this sentence: "The pupæ which the carriers

released as they were caught and which, therefore, had rolled ahead of them!" The pupæ! There was indeed no other explanation of these marks. And their carriers — such is the philoprogenitiveness of ants — had still thought of saving them, when they themselves had perhaps already begun to be crushed by the monster! Perhaps they had even tried to give them an accelerated sideways motion as they rolled from their jaws. But the destruction had been too swift.

I did not, at the time, grasp the full significance of this discovery; nor did Bissa-tee. We simply concluded that parts of the army, taught by the Rubicundas and the Polyergus, had gone on raids to provision themselves with portable food. Little as yet did I fathom the whole depth of Assa-ree's treason; entrusted as she was with our protection, she had been plotting our utter overthrow.

I signified to Bissa-tee my desire that she keep our discoveries strictly to herself, so as not to lower the morale of the survivors still more; and she agreed mournfully, adding that she, at least, would go on with her task as though nothing had happened.

IV

We remained at this station for only a single day; and then, though in our state of physical and emotional exhaustion a longer rest would have been most welcome, I gave orders to proceed, impelled to do so chiefly by the fact that every now and then one of those roaring monsters passed along the road, now going north, now south; and every time our soldiers were thrown into a panic, till I came to the conclusion that my first duty was to distract their thoughts from the disaster that had overtaken us. Assa-ree soon recovered from her despair and grew even more jaunty than she had been before, the obsequious deference with which she treated me assuming a still more ironical shading. Plainly, a reckoning with her was approaching; but I must wait till we had crossed that great river which we had so long been expecting to find.

For close to a moon we went on by forced marches, and sometimes, when the weather was warm, we prolonged our forward struggle far into the night.

Three things kept me from brooding too much on our misfortunes. In the first place, Azte-ca seemed now to be attracted to me in a closer friendship; she showed much solicitude for my comfort and conversed more freely with me. She admitted that, in the past, her ambition to find the key to the human language had stood in the way of any intimacy between her and the rest of us; but she had realized, she said, that without our help and sympathy she was not likely to work her problems out to an entirely successful issue. She asked for my advice and sometimes for my assistance. Whenever we spent the night near a human habitation, she visited it, discussing with me ways and means and telling me of the progress she was making. Her chief difficulty arose from the very loudness of man's voice which prevented her from distinguishing its modulations. I advised her to coat her ear-drums with many successive applications of saliva till she was deaf to sounds of ordinary intensity; and when she did this, she made the most amazing progress.

In the second place, I had been much struck with what we had seen of our slave-making sisters; and this formed the subject of endless discussions between myself and Bissa-tee. There were two problems involved. Firstly that of the line of development through which this mode of life had arisen among ants; and in the solution of this problem Bissa-tee showed once more her profound penetration and unrivalled ingenuity. Again I must refer the student to the special scent-trees, numbers 734 and 735, in which I have given the details of her reasoning. While Bissa-tee acknowledged that of the three great modes of life, the hunting, pastoral, and agricultural modes, the latter was the highest, making possible a degree of security which cannot be attained through any other, yet it contained already the germs of degeneration, evolution splitting up from that point on: one line leading to the mode of life adopted by ourselves, the Attas, who devote the energy liberated from the struggle for existence entirely to the pursuit of intellectual aims; the other line leading on to the mode of life chosen by the slave-makers, through a corruption of the instincts making for security of the material life into instincts demanding the accumulation of property; which accumulation led back to a military life, for it demanded the adoption of methods, first of defence, and then of aggression. Secondly there was the problem of the ultimate phase of this line of development; and this was the one in which I took a special interest myself.

In the third place, there was the problem of these tarry roads which became more and more common as we went east. We had no further losses from this cause; for now that we knew about the monsters travelling along these roads we soon learned to avoid them. Whenever we reached such a structure, a scout was sent to its centre; and if the slightest vibration was perceptible, we waited; if not, we proceeded at a run. Bissa-tee's conjecture that the animals travelling along these roads were enslaved by man was soon confirmed. They enclose huge hollow spaces, produced probably, similarly to the air-spaces in the bodies of our queens, by the atrophy of certain muscular tissues; and into these hollow spaces men insert themselves when they travel; time and again we had occasion to observe them. As for the origin of the roads themselves, that problem was also solved in entire accordance with the theories advanced by our lamented chemists. One day we actually saw a huge animal of an entirely different and new shape crawling along such a road; and it was, near the anal end, provided with an enormous serictery from which a score or more of thick strands of the tarry substance were spun out; these, on reaching the ground in a viscously liquid state, promptly spread out sideways and coalesced, producing a smooth surface which slowly hardened. As, in a spatial sense, everything about these animals is colossal, so, in a temporal sense, the hardening of this substance took an enormous length of time. We had to make a vast detour in order not to be entangled in the sticky mass.

Nothing else needs to be added with regard to this part of our march except that, on the twenty-seventh day after the great disaster, we suddenly found ourselves on the muddy banks of the great river which we had so long expected to encounter.

V

Naturally, this river being one of the most stupendous obstacles to our progress, we settled down to explore it and to find ways and means of crossing. It was so wide that we could barely see its far shores; and its channel was divided by many islands all of which seemed to be massive and wooded at their upper extremities, whereas, at their lower ends, they trailed out into long shallows and sand-banks. The current was sluggish enough and would have permitted us to cross by means of a living bridge if we had had the ant-power to make one. As it was, we had to concentrate from the beginning on other methods of accomplishing the task.

All sorts of ways were proposed: to form a raft and trust to the current, taking boldly to the water in a mass; to use spiders floating, at this time of year, on their webs, anchoring one strand of such a web on the hither bank and forcing the spider to keep on spinning by following her and frightening her into ever more frantic efforts; to roll logs into the river and again, bestriding them, trust to the current. In all which methods we were, in the last resort, depending on a favourable wind.

Two of them were actually tried. Assa-ree caught spiders and sent them on their aerial voyage. She had the brilliant idea of releasing a score of them at the same time, from the outermost tips of the branches of willow trees growing on our bank, and entangling their threads into a stout cable upheld by the floating power of twenty webs at once. She then launched out behind them. But, the threads being anchored, progress depended entirely on the spinning power of the spiders; and it was exhausted long before the first island was reached. Then they came to a stop, suspended over the water; and, the wind failing, Assa-ree slowly sank down into the muddy flood where she must have perished had not our workers pulled her out by hauling the cable in. A few days later, when she had recovered, she set out on a large chip of wood but found that, weighted down by its load, it did not offer the wind a sufficient hold and was too much deflected downstream. To her discomfiture, she landed ignominiously on a sand-spit of the hither bank.

Thus, in the face of this huge expanse of water, we were delayed from day to day and at last began to think that we should have to acknowledge defeat.

Meanwhile, Azte-ca was not idle and kept going about from one human habitation to the other. She reported strange things. There were black men living here; and paler humans of all shadings of colour between white and black; and it was during this forced delay that she made her next great discovery: she succeeded in deciphering human records inscribed on paper with black fluids.

We were just beginning to suffer from the effects of idleness among the remainder of our troops, while the leaders were exploring the neighbourhood, when one night Azte-ca returned from a two-days' absence in a state almost of exaltation but so utterly exhausted that she could barely move her antennæ. Yet she managed to convey to us the idea that our problem was solved. Having grasped as much, both Bissa-tee and myself urged her to rest and postpone further communications to the next day.

In the morning, then, she scented to us that she had found a line of most peculiar structures crossing the river — structures which were joined to each other by metallic threads apparently spun by enormous spiders. On the basis of the proportion obtaining between the thickness of an ordinary spider's web and these metallic threads, she had calculated the size of these spiders as being many times that of a horse, the latter being the largest animal hitherto encountered. She had not seen these spiders, but — such was her obsession by this time — she had no doubt that they, too, were enslaved by man; for the more she saw of the latter, the more she stood in awe of his powers.

Bissa-tee and I were of course very curious to see this marvel: a spider's web consisting of native copper instead of a glutinous carbo-hydrate; but we were also alarmed at Azte-ca's report. Yet we were willing to attempt almost anything in order to get away from where we were; it was one of the least favourable stations we had ever been at; for the ground was so saturated with moisture that we could not possibly have wintered here, and that terrible winter season was rapidly approaching now. Something had to be done at once.

So, early next morning, we prepared for another march; and at noon we arrived at the spot signalized by Azte-ca. We found the strange structure to consist of white steel; and it resembled a huge, four-legged harvest-man or false spider standing on the tips of its toes. Azte-ca at once climbed up on one of its legs; and, seeing her so sure of herself, a number of us followed. I venture to say that the height to which we climbed was not less than a thousand antlengths; and there, to a framework of nervures, still of steel, we found fastened large mushroom-shaped bodies of *glass* around which these copper cables were wound. To the west, they stretched away as far as we could see, dipping ultimately below the horizon; to the east, they reached all the way across the river, looping from island to island at a dizzy height above the waters.

There we stood, Azte-ca, Bissa-tee, and myself; and behind and below us the whole army — what was left of it —- came clambering up, with Assa-ree at the head. Assa-ree looked at me with such a Satanic glance, half ferocious, half grinning; and she had the three of us so absolutely in her power there that I did not see what else I could do. I started ahead post-haste and began to cross the river via these aerial threads. As for the copper, it was strong enough to support any number of us; but I could not rid myself of the idea that this was not a spun thread at all: I had a vague feeling that there was something going on inside that thread; or that in some mysterious way it was alive. This feeling became stronger as we advanced, I leading, with Bissa-tee behind me; for the thread began to vibrate and to hum in the most frightening manner so that we had at last the greatest difficulty in holding on. This difficulty was enormously increased when, after an hour or so, a violent wind began to blow from the south. Below us, the river raised angrily foaming waves; and in order not to be swept off, we now crawled forward in the shelter afforded by the thread on its north side. On and on we went; and the thread, under the ever-rising sun, became intensely hot, till it scorched our feet.

On and on we went, hour after hour; and then, just as the weather took an ugly turn, we reached the next steel support where I called a halt. The wind had blown up huge domed clouds which now obscured the sun. Convoluted thunderheads pushed north straight overhead, their inner chambers lighted up by fitful winkings. A hush had fallen over the landscape; and then, suddenly, like a Polyergus let loose, a flash of lightning leapt, passing close by us; and the universe shook with the vicious bark of the thunder. The afternoon light assumed a lurid shade.

Below us there was the first of a series of islands; and I gave the signal for a quick descent. Long before we reached solid ground, the rain fell in torrents; and we had the greatest difficulty in resisting its wash.

I, Bissa-tee, and Azte-ca had barely touched ground when the world about us exploded. Behind us, the earth leapt up around one of the legs of the steel support; Assa-ree was catapulted forward over our heads; all about, it seemed to hail ants; and even the pebbles of the beach on which we were, danced. Lashed by the wind and the rain we stood blinded, unable to realize what was happening. The water, though pouring down from above, seemed simultaneously to spout up from every pore of the ground, such was the violence of its rebound. Within a few seconds rivulets were scoring the soil into the pattern of miniature mountains and valleys; and we could only stand and hold on.

This lasted for half an hour before the fury of the storm abated. Then, the rain slowly subsiding into a warm, steaming drizzle, we had a chance to breathe once more. But another half hour went by before we were in a state to investigate.

When we did so, we found that almost one half of the remainder of our army had been killed. That ghastly flash of lightning had struck the support of the copper threads; it had fused the quartz pebbles at the foot of the leg over which we had been descending; and the intense heat had not only killed, it had shrivelled up five hundred of our soldiers; Assa-ree and the rest had saved themselves by a desperate leap.

By this time night was falling; and all we could do, surrounded as we were by water, was to make for such shelter as some straggling bushes afforded on the crest of the beach. It turned cold after the storm; and though we little knew what was ahead of us, we did not remember ever having passed so miserable a night. I personally do not think I could have survived had not Bissa-tee and Azte-ca insisted on covering me with their bodies.

But there was no way out of it: when morning came, we had to go on. Again we climbed up to one of those copper threads and proceeded. It was a cold raw day; there was little wind; but the sky remained overcast.

All day we struggled along; and if yesterday the heat of the thread had caused discomfort, today the cold caused misery. On and on we went, hour after hour, passing island after island below; and yet, when night fell, we were still far from the goal. Owing to the intense cold which invaded our bodies from contact with the metal, our progress became slower and slower. We could not stop to rest, for that would have meant certain death; we could never have held on; we should have fallen into the icy flood below where we should have been swallowed by the fishes which we had had ample opportunity to observe.

If it had not been for this cold, we should have finished this trip about midnight; as it was, we travelled on well into the next day; and when at last the task was accomplished and we descended to the ground, there was not one of us who would have wished to go on. Everyone, on the other hand, would have taken food of almost any description, be it ever so nauseating.

Yet there was one thought which sustained at least the three of us: we had accomplished an almost super-formicarian task. Who could, after this, say that there are things from which formicarian ingenuity and form-icarian enterprise must shrink? Who, that Attas could ever be daunted?

As for food, the small remnant of our army was plentifully provided: in the course of the wind-storm the river had disgorged innumerable fishes, large and small; and we knew that our soldiers did not despise such fare. What Assa-ree did, I do not know; but she recovered in a remarkably short time. Bissa-tee, Azte-ca, and myself managed to find some enormous fungi growing like shelves on dead trees; but we consumed barely enough to restore our strength, they were so unpalatable. If I looked in any way like Bissa-tee, I must have been a sorry sight.

So we three were not anxious to make a long stay; and on the third morning I issued the order to proceed. I had half expected trouble; but all went smoothly. It is true, there was in the bearing of the soldiers a subtle something resembling insolence; but there was no outright mutiny. I was prepared for anything; for I had now also come to the conclusion that the army was henceforth an encumbrance; but for the moment it was probably best to wait and see.

I began to despair of the very possibility of reaching the Atlantic seaboard this fall, the sixth since our departure from home. Five years were the average lifetime of all but the queen among Attas; and I was now twice that age. Even Bissa-tee and Azte-ca began to show their years; and the only member of the High Command who looked as young as ever was Assa-ree. The trip home, I reflected, would take two years; I felt that I still had it in me to live through such a term; but I also felt that I could not leave our geographical exploration of the continent unfinished. Another year... It was almost more than I could face with equanimity; and if anything happened to Bissa-tee and Azte-ca?

The burden of responsibility seemed almost too great to be borne; and Bissa-tee felt and sympathized with me. Only Azte-ca was blindly pushing on: she was now entirely preoccupied with man and his works. She was haunted by the insane idea that man had perhaps surpassed even Attas in the development of his mental powers; and she was bound to find out. I wished to indulge her, if only for the purpose of convincing her of her error.

But, after another month or so of ceaseless struggle, fate took a hand and decided all our questions.

VI

I had at last given in and accepted the fact that we had to remain in this northern country for another year. The season was beginning to be too inclement to proceed when we came upon a location which seemed favourable for wintering.

Perhaps I should mention that every now and then we had, of late, met with friendly tribes of minute ants who lived a very precarious life within human habitations; and occasionally we found among them some who, to our amazement, had travelled widely and seen much of the world. They laughed at us when they heard that we were marching; they never did. From their descriptions we concluded at first that they made use of those monstrous animals which we had seen on the tarry roads; but it seemed there were still other ways and means of utilizing human contrivance. These little ants told us of what they called space-machines. At any rate, the stories which reached us mostly through Azte-ca had given me hope that perhaps we should winter in a human city; for we heard much of a huge hominary built around certain inlets of the eastern sea; and what we were told about this hominary made me think that it must be a place very different from the human farm. But it so happened, much to our ultimate advantage as it turned out, that we were caught by a wintry spell at a point far removed from any human habitation.

We arranged for what we thought would be our winter quarters. A small but deep formicary was excavated in a steep hillside protected by a fringe of trees. It held only one chamber for Bissa-tee, Azte-ca, and myself; and in addition there were four fungus-gardens. Fortunately, there were still a score or so of carriers left, preserving pellets of fungus-hyphæ in their infrabuccal chambers; and fortunately, too, there were, in that fringe of trees, a few Gleditschias which supplied us, in their leaves, with a substratum suitable for growing them. At the depth at which our gardens lay the ground was still warm enough to ensure a growth sufficient for our needs. A second, larger formicary was dug for the remainder of the army, considerably lower down that hillside; and it was stocked with the wingless bodies of grasshoppers and crickets paralysed by the sting of wasps; for this hillside was a favourite haunt of these insects.

When we had been living here for some ten or twelve days, fretting but resigned, the weather changed again, and a spell of marvellous mellowness succeeded the wintry winds of the last fortnight. All our ants, accustomed now, for more than five years, to a wandering life, became restless again; and it was quite a task to keep single small groups from straying off by themselves.

But not in our formicaries only did life revive; the whole hillside swarmed again with insects and finally with ants.

I was naturally reluctant, now we had resigned ourselves, to sacrifice the preparations for wintering which had been made, especially since fungus-hyphæ

were beginning to be scarce. Nor could we know jus
how long this summery weather would last. Alread
we saw, in the leafy domes of the trees below us, indi
ations of a new colour to come: that colour which i
these latitudes precedes the fall of the foliage. But on
afternoon, the air being exceptionally warm, a series o
events began which settled my troubles once for all.

A large army of Polyergus overran our formicary
Bissa-tee, Azte-ca, and myself were lazily basking in th
sun near the entrance to our little burrow when Bissa
tee gave the alarm. We dived down into our chambe
above the fungus-gardens; and Bissa-tee closed it
entrance with her head. Hundreds of these dreaded an
murderous amazons swarmed in and out of our burrow
not one seemed to suspect our hiding-place, for they
brushed past without stopping, never even touching
Bissa-tee's head; and then they left us. A hurried invest
igation showed that they had done only inconsiderable
damage to our gardens. They had torn the leaf-sponges
open; but they had not carried them off nor sprayed
them with their poisonous excretions. They were after
eggs and pupæ, Bissa-tee concluded laconically; and
with that she led the way to the open.

The Polyergus were just swarming into the second
formicary; and we saw some of the fiercer of our
soldiers, led by Assa-ree, engaged in a desperate battle
against the raiders who, however, had come in such
numbers that Assa-ree's defence barely delayed them.

As we appeared at the opening of our gallery, we
were just in time to witness the whole proceeding. It
was only a very few moments before the first of those
who had entered returned. We had expected to see them

carrying fragments of those orthoptera that had been stored as winter-food for the soldiers; but to our amazement they carried nothing of the kind. They carried eggs. Eggs? Eggs. And these eggs were of a shape and size which no ant native to these parts could have produced. There were only two nations known to us that could have produced them: Atta Gigantea and Eciton Hamatum; and we soon saw that there were hundreds and thousands of them; for the Polyergus who, by the way, were fiercer and more elegant, both in colouring and build, than any we had so far seen, promptly carried these eggs away and then returned for more. The coming and going lasted for half an hour.

In the meantime, east of the entrance, the battle was waging. Assa-ree performed marvels of valour; but her small band of helpers was rapidly dwindling; the Polyergus had distinctly the upper jaw; the merest touch of the tips of their mandibles pierced the armour of our soldiers; and soon the hillside was strewn with their corpses; before the raid was over, there were hundreds of them to the enemy's scores. It seemed that only Assa-ree had both the science and the strength to slay her assailants.

Bissa-tee was immensely puzzled; more so than I; for I had never told her what, months ago, had been revealed to me by the officer on the Pogonomyrmex disk. Yet it was Bissa-tee who connected this sight of the eggs with another puzzling discovery which we had made together. "The pupæ!" she scented suddenly. "What pupæ?" I asked absent-mindedly. "On the first tarroad," she replied. "Don't you remember?"

I remembered indeed. With a sickening feeling I realized the whole depth of Assa-ree's treason; and I could barely refrain from sending at once absolute and final execution down that hillside. In fact, I took several steps forward but was held back by my companions. They were right, of course. No matter how treasonable Assa-ree's conduct had been, her condign punishment must wait till the last Polyergus had departed. Nor did we have long to wait; and as soon as I was sure that no living enemy remained on the premises, I summoned my two companions to accompany me.

Assa-ree had disappeared into the crater of her burrow, exhibiting all the signs of bewilderment and despair. We took our stand on the north side of the entrance, forty antlengths above the upper lip. Azteca and Bissa-tee were visibly nervous; to re-assure them, I divulged for the first time the great secret that I was carrying a pellet of the royal perfume of instant death which I held ready to use at any moment; and then I gave the great scent of summons.

I had expected mutiny and revolt; but Assa-ree promptly obeyed, raising her head within the hollow of the entrance. Her enquiry, however, as to what was wanted was sullen and defiant. She did not care what happened to her.

Holding the pellet ready between labrum and tongue, I launched forth into what, I flatter myself, was one of the greatest pieces of forensic eloquence ever delivered by an Atta. I regretted even then the untimely loss of Adver-tee who alone would have been able to record it in full for the instruction and delight of future ages. As it is, I can give only the barest abstract.

I went back to Assa-ree's early life in the formicary at home and summarized the rumours that had been current about her; and next I mentioned the circumstances which had seemed suspicious to me during the early years of our expedition. All this, I told her, I had disregarded because her unrivalled courage and resourcefulness had seemed to outweigh whatever might be said against her. But, I went on, since she was now facing the most solemn moment of her life, I asked her to answer my questions with absolute truthfulness: were the soldiers with whom she had started out without exception true Attas?

She darkened; and then, true to her nature, she answered boldly, " They were Ecitons. "

" And the recruits enrolled at the isthmus? "

" Ecitons. "

The frankness, I went on, with which she had answered these questions did honour to her soldierly character. I next referred to her methods of foraging which were unworthy of any Atta; but I conceded that they had been most convenient for the expedition and therefore should not serve as the basis of an indictment. I was coming, I said, to the more important points. We had proof of the fact that she had used the carriers of the army for the transportation of pupæ. Where had they come from?

They were carried, she evaded, in order to maintain the morale of the troops. Was it not well-known to me that ants of a less exalted kind than ours were ever willing to fight in defence of their broods?

That, too, I supposed, was the reason why she had this day been detected in harbouring thousands of eggs in her burrow?

It was. Though incidentally they were meant to recruit the army in spring.

Would she tell me, I asked at last, whence these eggs and pupæ had come?

At that she saw she had marched straight into a trap. Yet she recovered her composure in a moment. She issued entirely from the crater and now stood in full view. I divined her purpose: she was giving the few of her most trusted soldiers who remained a chance to come close to the lip of the crater; I saw a dozen claws reaching up to its edge; they were ready to mow us down with their flashing jaws. Then she raised herself proudly and answered, "I am an ergatogyne."

At this Bissa-tee moved. I knew her favourite theory that all the types transitional between the three chief castes, the male, the female, and the ergate or worker, were pathological; and no doubt she was on the point of signifying as much when I restrained her.

Was it, or was it not, a fact, I went on, that she was not so much an ergatogyne as an abortive queen?

"I have never been winged," she said.

I did not know; but I professed myself profoundly interested. At any rate I did know that her eggs produced all normal castes and thence concluded that she was fertilized?

What if she was?

It explained her ambitions, I replied. What could be her purpose in carrying with her recorders who were in possession of all the important results of the expedition?

She had thought fit to make sure that these results, secured chiefly through the protection she had given us, should not perish if we perished.

And she had felt sure that we were going to perish, had she not?

To this she did not condescend to reply; but I saw her move her antennæ so as to verify the fact that her followers were ready.

I should now, I went on, summarize my indictment by revealing to her those plans which she thought were entirely hidden from me. In the first place, she was not a true Atta herself but a hybrid. In the second place, she was fertilized by an Eciton male wherever she might have encountered him. In the third place she aspired to the throne or to a position within the monarchy which could enable her to hold even the crown in subjection. The former two points, while less terrible things had among Attas before this been thought deserving a sentence of death, did not dishonour her personal character; but the latter constituted treason. If she aspired to the throne, why, then, it might be asked, had she come on this expedition? That, too, I was prepared to explain. She had admitted that she was an ergatogyne; and I was willing to prove that she was fertilized. Physiologically, therefore, she was able to assume all the functions of a queen; and, interpreting many puzzling and suspicious circumstances observed in the past by the light shed upon them by recent discoveries, I was prepared to show that she had exercised these functions even before we had left the maternal formicary; for the car-

riers taken from that formicary for the army had been
her daughters. But she knew that no Attiine nation
would ever consent to be ruled by an ant not a true
queen unless that aspirant had claims to glory and
distinction eclipsing the exaltation of royal birth. These
claims she had meant to establish by first aiding our
explorations and then depriving us and even our
memories of their results. For she must not think for
a moment that I was ignorant of the fate she reserved
for ourselves. Yet, what I had resolved upon was not the
outcome of self-regarding fear: it was what the danger
of the state at home demanded. As a matter of fact, I
wound up in a stinging peroration, the thought of that
state being ruled by an ergatogyne could be borne; but
in my opinion she was not an ergatogyne but a gynæcoid. [3]

At this Assa-ree could no longer contain herself;
it appeared to her a fortuitous insult; and in that rage
which can deprive even an ant of her self-control, she
issued the scent of attack. Her few adherents surged
up through the opening behind her. She herself advanced, flashing her scissor jaws; but I was ready.

I, too, advanced, so as not to expose Bissa-tee and
Azte-ca to any side-thrust of the deadly perfume which
was already sending its murderous rays straight ahead.

A moment later, just before she came within reach
of me, Assa-ree reared up in the typical attitude of one

---

[3] An ergatogyne is produced by the physiological degradation
of a queen; a gynæcoid by the excess development of a worker or
ergate. The expression means, therefore, that Assa-ree had risen
from the ranks. Apparently, among ants, too, genius ranks below
birth. E.

stricken by Her Majesty's most potent perfume; and as she did so, those following her also stood up on their hind-feet and then broke down. More and more ants followed them, and all went to instant death. Knowing as I did from former experience how persistent the perfume and its effect must be, I at once retreated, giving my two associates the signal to follow me promptly.

We climbed up the hillside to the crater of our burrow and thence looked back. There were still a few ants issuing from the lower formicary; and every single one shared the fate of her leader till the whole remainder of the army had perished. Not one was left of that proud body which more than five years ago had started out except Bissa-tee, Azte-ca, and myself.

What I had done had been done under the dictates of state-craft. I venture to say that no ruling caste among ants or any other order of animals would have hesitated doing the same. Yet, somehow, when it was done, the world seemed empty.

We retired to our chamber underground; and there Bissa-tee relieved her mind of all her misgivings.

What, she asked, if in future we should need a formicary? Our jaws were not adapted for digging. What if we were attacked? Azte-ca, it was true, was still nimble enough to defend herself. But we?

I did not answer at once. These and similar questions had occurred to me, too. But such perplexities could not outweigh the danger in which we were so long as Assa-ree lived.

Azte-ca was not interested in such things. She accepted what I had done because it was done and could

not be undone in any case. Why waste time on it, then?
She was impatient to be gone; and her impatience helped
Bissa-tee and myself to get over the first shock of so
radical a change in the conditions under which the
future must be lived. It was for that very reason that
I did not at once give her the permission which she
asked for. She fidgeted about in evident embarrassment.
For a little while Bissa-tee and I enjoyed this game;
we even asked her certain questions; but her answers
were confused and so much at cross purposes that we
had to laugh; and when she had thus helped us to overcome the constraint laid upon us by the solemnity of the
occasion, I turned to her at last, signifying that she
might be off to her beloved humans. And she shot out
of our formicary in such a precipitous way that Bissa-
tee and I were highly amused. She did not return for
two full days.

I went out to make sure that the perfume of death
could not be blown our way; in a dead calm it would
travel downhill, of course, since it was heavier than air.
There was no wind.

When Bissa-tee and I were alone in our chamber
at last, we settled down to a freer and less worried rest
than we had had for many a month; and my good friend
let herself go and rumbled along in the most comfortable way, speculating on what had happened.

"I admire you," she said; "but on what grounds
do you justify your verdict?"

"On the grounds of necessity."

She asscented. "What is justice? Take this case.
Treason? Assa-ree could not help herself. She was what
she was. You called her a hybrid; and I believe you were

right. Could she help that? Is the accident of birth to be made the basis of moral condemnation? I have my doubts about her being a gynæcoid, by the way. I don't believe that any excess development of the ergate will ever enable her to become capable of fertilization except in the lowest orders of ants, the Ponerines perhaps, in which the differentiation of castes has not yet reached any high degree. But even if she was an ergatogyne, she was unique in Attiine experience. Ergatogynes, too, occur as a regular thing only with ants of the lower orders. Be that as it may; she could not help herself. If she was an ergatogyne, it was certainly her fate to seek fertilization; and I defy any perfect female to remain a virgin when she is courted by an expert male. The very hybridity of her sexual union would in my view rather excuse her than aggravate what you called her crime. If her union had been adelphogamous, she must have done the courting herself."

Little as I was inclined to argue the point — for I was surrendering to the comfortable feeling of being for once out of danger — I could not refrain from throwing in, "It may have been adelphogamous at that; she was half Eciton herself."

"So you say," Bissa-tee went on; "so you say; and perhaps you are right. But that does not solve the problem either; it merely removes the difficulty further back in time. I still disagree; I can still not acknowledge that what you have done is justice."

"Justice? I do not call it justice. I call it expediency; it was she or we, that is all."

"Quite," Bissa-tee agreed. "If you put it on that basis, there is nothing else to be said. But a higher being, if such there is, might question whether she or we had more right to survive."

I was nearly asleep by this time; but I still managed to murmur, "My dear Bissa-tee, justice is ńot a question of right but of might."

"Ah," Bissa-tee asscented. "Now you are scenting something. And..."

That was the last I perceived, for I was sound asleep; and though even in my dreams I remained conscious that Bissa-tee had been thoroughly aroused and was holding forth at the top of her scent-glands, I did not grasp any longer what it was she was propounding; nor did I want to. For the moment I felt as though I did not have a care in the world.

VII

I must now, very briefly, unfold certain speculations of mine; for I wish to wind up what is known and inferred about slave-making ants before I proceed to the strangest of all our adventures, namely, our life among men of a city.

By the comparison of Pogonomyrmex Occidentalis, Formica Rubicunda, and the various tribes of Polyergus I seemed to have arrived at a very definite though incomplete line of development. Perhaps I should, instead of Pogonomyrmex Occidentalis, have mentioned Dorymyrmex Pyramicus, for the latter species is really the one in which the slave-making instincts take their inception. These little ants live, as I have mentioned, in burrows placed within the cleared disks or even on the flank of the mound erected by Pogonomyrmex; and they provide their sustenance by relieving single harvesters of the booty they are bringing in. If we consider this as the beginning of slavery, its origin is clearly to be looked for in piracy.

Now true slavery may be of two kinds, but one of them is practically unknown among ants, whereas man has both. One of these two kinds is characterized chiefly by the loss of personal freedom on the part of the slave. The slave-maker uses her superior powers to force the slaves to perform tasks which are uncongenial and irksome to herself; and the slave, confined to such tasks, works unwillingly and must be restrained from the full use of her powers. This type of slavery is very common among men. The other kind cloaks a relation which is originally similar under the form of symbiosis; and it is not as dangerous and degrading, in the long run, to the slave as to the master; for it produces, in the latter, a physiological degeneration which makes it actually impossible for the master to live apart from her slaves; the slaves acquiesce, for any sort of symbiosis is apt to produce a state of mind to which this symbiosis appears as the natural order. The masters, on the other hand, develop powers which, though valueless for the purpose of sustaining life, yet enable them to render certain apparent services to the slaves, f.i., to defend them against their enemies.

While, therefore, in the case of the Rubicunda, the keeping of slaves seems to be the by-product of simple piracy, the Polyergus ant represents the perfect phase of a slave-keeping state. The masters are no longer able to attend to the simplest tasks of their lives: they cannot even eat by themselves. Even the power of finding food which is readily available seems to be lost. They can live on honey; but we had seen them, crazed with hunger, swarming all over a hive of bees; and they did not notice that all they needed to do was to lick the honey up. That, physiologically, they were able to do so was proved by the fact that one of these valiant fighters happened to slip, head foremost, into a honey cell; and, the food thus having been accidentally brought into contact with her tongue, she promptly gorged herself. Much less are they able to excavate their formicaries. Their mandibles are hard and brittle and, as we had reason to know, eminently adapted for piercing the armour of an enemy; but they were utterly unfit for the ruder task of struggling with rock and soil. This fact makes them dependent on alien races even in the establishment of their formicaries. For, while the Rubicundas could simply invade an alien nest and put queen and workers to the jaw in order to raise the broods they found, no Polyergus could possibly raise larvæ and thus train a band of slaves for herself. There is only one procedure open to the young Polyergus queen when she invades the nest of her slave-species. It is well known that, when such an intruding queen succeeds in establishing herself on the back of the queen of the invaded nest, the workers will leave her alone. Thus she has time, while tolerated, to acquire the nest-odour; and as soon as she has done so, she can devote all her energies to the congenial task of sawing off her protectress' head; and when this task is completed, she takes the place of that unfortuante potentate. Figuratively, the same procedure is adopted in many of the organizations of man, especially the political ones; and though we never witnessed the thing among Polyergus ants, we may well draw a conclusion from analogy. From the beginning the Polyergus queen is dependent on the good will of her slaves who raise the broods, first of their own, then of the alien kind. Still, as the Polyergus colony becomes established in a Fusca or Pallidefulva nest, it assumes its own proper functions; it brings in the broods of other colonies, partly for food, partly for the purpose of preserving the race of the slaves.

This leaves the development incomplete; and since our observations on ants were at this point to come to an end, owing to the extraordinary events to be related in the following chapter, speculation must take the place of observation; and again that speculation with regard to ants is confirmed by certain things of which we were informed as being prevalent among men, especially among their royal families and what they call their plutocracy.

I must anticipate. When at last we were able to decipher man's records, we found in them reports of man's observations on ants which would go far towards confirming my own conclusions were it not for one single thing, namely, that, in these human records, assertions are made which it is impossible for an ant gifted with reason and critical faculties to accept — a fact which would seem to discredit all his so-called science. These observations on slave-making ants purported to have been made in a far country across the seas to the east. Since in this ocean islands are known to exist, this subterfuge might still have passed if, in certain other human records, geographical ones, distances and dimensions had not been given. Thus this country which they call Europe was said to be over 3,000 miles from our own continent, across the sea — or about four hundred million antlengths — a distance which certainly no terrestrial mammal can swim. But what is much more important, the orbit of the earth around the sun and the path it describes in its swing around the moon postulate an entirely smooth surface on the far side of the globe, such as can be furnished only by an unbroken hydro-hemisphere. From what knowledge I gained of human nature, my conjecture is that this so-called continent of Europe, and two or three other continents as well, is simply an invention of a human caste, the merchants, who claim that certain goods they "sell" — or exchange for other goods — are brought from these far countries overseas — goods which are in reality, of course, produced right at home — in order to enhance their value. This explanation is in such close accord with human nature that, to any ant acquainted with man as we became acquainted with him, it would carry *prima-facie* conviction even if man's assertions were not flatly contradicted by the unanimous conclusions of our formicarian geographers and astronomers. The fact, therefore, that my speculations about the final evolution of slave-making ants is confirmed by man constitutes the one circumstance which makes me hesitate in affirming their unconditional conclusiveness.

But I must propound them, nevertheless, in order not to leave the present chapter incomplete in a purely scientific sense.

The most striking thing about any race of slave-making ants is undoubtedly to be looked for in the methods employed in order to found a colony. The slave-making queen grafts herself, as it were, on an already existing colony of the slaves. Only then does she proceed to lay eggs from which the three castes of her own kind are produced. Her own workers or soldiers, as far as the ordinary functions of life are concerned, are from the beginning entirely dependent on the slaves with this one exception that, as the colony grows, they forage for them. Now let this slave species be of an aggressive kind easily able to support itself, and the slave-making workers or soldiers can obviously be dispensed with. But it is an axiom universally accepted by biological science that organs which are not needed first become rudimentary and finally disappear; and this holds good not only for the individual organism but for the social organism as well. Applying this principle to the compound colony of slaves and masters, we can draw only one conclusion, namely, that the slave-making workers or soldiers will disappear; and finally a state of affairs will be reached in which the progeny of the slave-making queen will consist exclusively of perfect males and females who exist for one purpose only, i.e., the propagation of their own caste and who, in every other function of life, are entirely dependent upon their slaves. But, since the generations of the slaves are never renewed, neither by natural propagation nor by capture, the end of any colony that adopts the slave-making queen is, from that moment on, in sight. According to man, this state of affairs is actually reached in mythical Europe by certain species which he calls Anergates or workerless ants. It is not without interest for our knowledge of man that, in these fictions, he is just sagacious enough to postulate an exceedingly small size for the males and females of these Anergates; but not sufficiently so to arrive, from analogy, at the exactly opposite result. I suppose the reasoning, if such it can be called, on which he bases his own conclusion is as follows. Since the slave or host species of such degenerate slave-makers must be able to look after their own provisioning, they are apt to be of greater size than the slave-makers; and especially their males and queens are larger, the latter being perhaps even so-called macrogynes or giants. If that is the case, there is a momentary advantage to them in the adoption of these parasitic queens who are supposed to be minute and therefore require less feeding; and the slaves are of a sufficiently low mentality to be unable to forecast their own racial extinction as a result of their policy; for we must not forget that, in order to explain this hypothetic state of affairs, man must postulate that the queen of the slaves be killed by her own workers, the slave-making queen or parasite being, on his own premises, unequal to such a task.

Man himself, at least if we may trust his own records to that extent, which would be doubtful if they remained unconfirmed by our conclusions, has castes which live thus parasitically; but these parasites, contrary to what he postulates with regard to ants, are enormous in size and over-developed to the point where their organs become useless to them, not from atrophy but from hypertrophy. Needless for me to do my students' thinking for them; they will, from that, be able to draw the proper inference. With this hint, then, I will abandon this speculative glance into the realms of the unobserved.

CHAPTER FIVE

The Seaboard

CONTAINING the marvellous story of our trip, in a space-machine, to the human city by the sea; the unheard-of hardships suffered in reaching the hominary where we wintered; a report of the life which we lived there and the studies which we pursued; the no less marvellous story of our return to southern latitudes; a summary of what we found out about man; and a brief account of my own final dash home.

I

I WAS FREED OF THE DANGER of Assa-ree's proximity; but I still had much to worry me; and I fully realized that whatever we might undertake henceforth would be in the nature not only of a dangerous but a desperate enterprise; and Bissa-tee shared that conviction.

We were both in this frame of mind when, early on the third morning after her departure, Azte-ca returned in a state of complete physical exhaustion. I was on the point of administering to her a minimal dose of the perfume of royal favour in order to put her to sleep; for it seemed to me that she needed nothing so badly as a complete rest. She, on the other hand, would not hear of anything of the kind; she urged us in the most insistent way to load up with fungus-hyphæ and to follow her. The greatest of all our adventures, she scented, was ahead of us, provided we did not delay. We wanted to ask questions but she waved them aside. There would be time for all that. Just now action was needed.

She set both example and pace. She completely despoiled one of our fungus-gardens, tearing it apart and selecting the innermost and tenderest hyphæ which she rolled into a ball. This ball she pressed and pressed, turning it over and over, till it was small and compact enough to be pushed, with our help, into her infrabuccal chamber. This done, she at once proceeded to despoil a second fungus-garden for Bissa-tee who entered into the spirit of the thing with gusto. A dozen times Bissa-tee and myself judged that the ball was large enough; but she insisted in her vivid and dramatic way that a zoologist could swallow and carry a larger one. I will anticipate and state right here that, though we succeeded in inserting the ball as it was when she declared herself satisfied into Bissa-tee's infrabuccal chamber, it remained there to the day of her death which, strange to say, was caused by starvation while food aplenty was stored below her mouth whence it could not be removed without a surgical operation, so tightly was it wedged in. Next, Azte-ca wanted to roll a third ball for myself; but I pointed out to her that my infrabuccal chamber was already filled with the three perfume pellets. Hers being a single-track mind, this put her quite out of counten-

ance for the moment; and, becoming conscious of her
extreme fatigue, she squatted down, doubling her legs
under her body.

But this lapse lasted only for moments. She rose
again and turned to me, asking me to surrender the
leadership to her for the space of seven days. "If you
do," she added, "I undertake to place you in a human
habitation where you will not be offended with any of
the cruder aspects of human life and where we all shall
be comfortable throughout the winter. As far as I can
see, mine is the only plan that can save our lives."

I glanced at Bissa-tee who, by this time, was catching the infection of excitement from Azte-ca. She winked
at me; and I consented.

Whereupon Azte-ca promptly led the way. We travelled all day. Fortunately, the mild weather still held
though I seemed to discern the signs of a coming change.
Most of our day's progress was in the margin of an
ordinary human road which, from the ever-increasing
traffic we concluded to be one leading to some human
centre. Towards evening, however, having covered some
700,000 antlengths, Azte-ca, now reduced to a state in
which her motions were purely automatic, signalled to
us to remain behind and to wait till she returned.

It was many hours before we saw her again; Orion
had risen in the east; and the night was far advanced
though by no means dark, for the moon shone brightly,
and the sky was dusted over with stars. Altogether,
Bissa-tee and myself enjoyed the interval, for the
weather was fine.

Azte-ca was not alone when she returned; with her
were four small, very pretty ants whose bright, shining

eyes scanned us curiously. They were tremendously
impressed with our size; yet they were too well-bred to
stare at us; and it amused me to watch them as they
tried to examine us without appearing to do so. Meanwhile, Azte-ca told us that these friends of hers had come
from a human city millions of antlengths to the east, in
fact, the chief human city of the continent; and they
had done so by utilizing what they called a human
invention to which they were willing to introduce us.
This was the first time that we met with this scent
"invention" as applied to human beings. We ants seek
for discoveries rather than inventions; but it is characteristic of human perversity to prefer to invent things:
I have already intimated that they invent whole continents. However, both Bissa-tee and myself signalized our
willingness to be saved further marching; but, we added,
even though the whole of the human world might be
entirely imaginary, we did not care to be turned into
human inventions ourselves; for we had work to do, and
we meant to do it. One of our new little friends assured
us that, while there might be discomforts, there would
be no danger of our disappearing; just as an ant had, at
one time, invented a time-machine, so man had invented
a space-machine. You entered a large chamber; you were
shaken a bit; and when you left the chamber, you
were somewhere else.

All this sounded so absurd that both Bissa-tee and
I laughed; but Azte-ca was almost offended; perhaps
she feared we might at the eleventh hour refuse to follow
her leadership. We raised no difficulty, however; we
were only too curious ourselves.

We asked our little friends, great admirers of man, to lead the way; and for the rest of the night we struggled along, using our legs. But towards morning we arrived in a human town where all was still quiet; and having crossed a not inconsiderable part of it, we reached a wide open space traversed by pairs of steel-bands from eight to ten antlengths high. At the east end of this open space stood a number of huge, rectangular, wooden parallelepipeda on wheels which in turn rested on the steel-bands mentioned. As we made for them, we discovered that they were hollow and thence concluded that they were structures similar to the aphid tents of the pastoral ants. I will confess that, when I saw them, I was profoundly sceptical as to the truth of what our little friends had told us about them. They might be built by humans; in fact, they probably were; but as to their being space-machines in the sense in which our venerable Etsch-Dschie had, as Azte-ca had put it, invented the time-machine, I could not yet believe it: I remembered too well the endless discussions as to whether that time-machine had been real or imaginary.

However, from the open door of one of these chambers a twisted cable was hanging down; and our friends promptly climbed it, we following in their wake. The inside was not a pleasant place; it was covered with a litter of debris, like a many-years-old kitchen midden of harvesting ants. Azte-ca gave a single glance around and, looking at one of the little ants for confirmation that this was the place, promptly went to sleep in a corner. Bissa-tee and myself, seeing that our little friends were about to depart, took a courteous leave from them, thanked them for having gone to the trouble, and, a moment later, were left alone.

We waited for hours and hours before anything happened; then suddenly a great shouting arose outside, unmistakably human; and a few minutes later the enormous doors were shut. Another half hour went by before, with a rumble like that of an earthquake and a great puffing like that of a snorting mammal, but a million times as loud, something passed outside. We saw nothing, but I must report that Bissa-tee trembled. Suddenly we were both violently thrown off our feet; and Azte-ca rolled over half a dozen times without awaking. Then a strident whistling noise; and the whole structure came to life with a series of deafening clankings. From now on and for several days during which we lost track of the passage of time, that chamber did not again come to rest except for short periods occurring at irregular intervals of several hours. The floor of our chamber vibrated and leapt in the most amazing way, in all three directions at once, forward and backward, right and left, and upward and downward; so that we kept rolling and pitching about till we were sick. What made it worse was that these motions were every now and then complicated by adventitious jumps of a quite unimaginable violence. We came to the conclusion that the chamber must be alive after all and that it was trying to escape from its fetters.

Azte-ca slept for three days before she awoke. Meanwhile, we had more than once tried to escape but without success. Smaller ants could have squeezed through various cracks around the door; but we were fairly caught; and from the moment on when Azte-ca woke up, she restrained us from our endeavours, assuring us that all we were going through was perfectly normal. I replied that, no matter how general insanity might be among humans, it could never be called normal so long as there remained a single sane ant in the world.

As I said, we lost track of the passage of time; and when, after what seemed an eternity, that chamber came to rest without starting again while we were in it, we all three went to sleep from utter exhaustion; and I have no means of telling how long we slept. This sleep was finally disturbed by a sensation of intense cold; and after another half day or so we were roused by a most terrific noise accompanied by a renewed trembling of the floor; simultaneously an icy draught swept over us; and wet flakes of snow settled all about and even on our backs. I was at once convinced, from the quality of the air, that we were at the seaboard if not actually on the sea.

I was on the point of issuing a command when Azteca anticipated me, insisting that she was in charge. We left the chamber by dropping down from the edge of its floor where the door had been; it was wonderful to have the solid earth underfoot again; but the air was like a threat of death; and the ground was covered with a mixture of liquid and frozen water which chilled our limbs to the flesh.

It was night; and all about were amazing sights. We were on a sort of jetty thrown out into the water and scored with two double bands of steel on one of which rested the chamber from which we had come, with many similar chambers in front and behind. The deep gurgling water to both sides of the jetty was in perpetual motion and, to the east, reflected a high half moon. To the west, whence the wind came, no stars were visible, for the sky was obscured by low-hanging clouds. Straight ahead of the jetty, on the far side of the inlet, for such we concluded it to be, from the fact that the fine spray which dashed up on the jetty was salt, there loomed thousands of hominaries, all shining with lights similar to those we had seen in the human barn, only much brighter. What amazed us most, however, was the fact that the water of the inlet was alive with scores of firefly beetles of a size undreamt of in our latitudes; some of them must have been fully 2,400 antlengths long; and all of them carried more than one light, red and green as well as white. Altogether it was a sight as of some scene in the dim, geologic past.

The air was vibrating with noise: whistling noises and human cries lifted themselves against a background of a low, rumbling humming. When one of these enormous fireflies swept by close to the jetty, I could distinctly see how it moved; it had a tail under water which it kept twisting around, with a sound as of churning: alligators lashing the water produce such a sound.

All this we observed in a space of time so short that it seemed as though we had not stopped at all. For, in the first place, Azte-ca, acting as if she were perfectly familiar with these sights, summoned us to follow her; and in the second place, we could not stand still, from fear of being congealed by the cold.

We followed our temporary leader; and she turned south. Here, human beings were running along the jetty, carrying fireflies in their forefeet, encased in *glass* spheres. We paid no attention to them but struggled on in Azte-ca's wake, dodging snow-flakes as we went, and splashing through pools of ice-cold water. On and on, for hours and hours.

And then we came to a wide road leading west, flanked on both sides by enormous dark and sinister-looking structures and dimly lighted by occasional fire-flies perched on poles. The centre of this road was crowded with such animals on wheels as we had already met on the tar roads in the west. Both sides of this thoroughfare were raised by about ten antlengths above the centre; and on these sides human beings were hurrying east or west in great numbers. We had considerable trouble in finding a safe path close to the buildings on our side. Azte-ca never stopped, but hurried on as if she knew exactly what she was about.

It was turning colder all the time, the temperature at last falling almost to the freezing point; the clouds had now hidden the moon; and snow and sleet were whirling through the air, carried by a dark wind. Our progress became slower and slower, though our extreme exertions counteracted to a certain extent the chilling effect of the cold.

On and on, for hours and hours.

Then Azte-ca, still leading, turned north. Bissa-tee and myself hardly knew any longer where we were or what we were doing; we struggled forward as in a trance. Azte-ca was now darting this way and that, dodging the crushing feet of humans who paid no attention to us; and suddenly we became aware that we were right on top of one of those enormous beetles which we had seen shooting about over the water with their red and green lights. It was an extremely smelly place, the atmosphere being laden with the scent of human sweat and the exhalations of the beetle itself. Azte-ca, following the apparently minute and accurate directions she had received from our small friends, now invaded, without a moment's hesitation, the inner anatomy of the monster on which we were. Soon we were out of the weather; the air was warmer; in fact, we seemed to change from one extreme to the other. We were amazed at the amount of mineral matter to be found within the bodies of these beetles: the floors of the inner cavities were of iron; and when, a few minutes later, we found ourselves actually within its gaster, we saw that even its intestines were metallic; everywhere this iron and steel and copper was coated with an oily secretion; and from it radiated the monster's body-heat.

Then there was a terrific snorting; the vitals of the beetle began to move in the most unexpected way, hissing and screeching; and the floor on which we stood, keeping out of sight as much as we could, began to tremble and to vibrate, just as the floor of the space-machine had done, though not to the same extent. We became aware that we were moving; and we soon arrived at the conclusion that we were crossing the inlet. In addition to ourselves, the monster carried hundreds of humans.

The passage across the water took over a quarter of an hour; and then, with a bump and a terrific noise of churning, we came to against a jetty similar to the one at which we had first left the space-machine.

Here my memory gives out. I still seem to hear the noise of innumerable human feet shuffling about, and to see ourselves, after a long time of renewed effort, hurrying along at the bottom of a canyon 2,000 antlengths deep, struggling, struggling. Daylight came, dim and dismal; and then night came again; but it brought no rest.

Once more, in this compound hominary, we came out into a new sort of canyon where there were not only thousands of human feet shuffling along, but in the centre of which space-machines were gliding on steel bands; these, however, were brilliantly lighted; and they stopped here and there to take on and to discharge human passengers. Man, as we found out by and by, is obsessed with the idea that continual motion is bliss. But we were too tired to watch; and it seemed as though forever after we should have to follow Azte-ca's crazy lead.

Once more day came and once more night fell; and still we were struggling along; but it was not dark; the walls of the canyon through which we proceeded were pierced on both sides with enormous hollows from which light flooded out as by magic into the central space. The thundering noise of the space-machines and the purring and hooting of the land-beetles which were darting about on every hand fairly stunned us and made us indifferent and insensible. There was barely any abatement in the numbers of humans crowding along on their mysterious errands. No doubt some purpose propelled them all; but what that purpose was seemed to transcend formicarian understanding.

And then day came for the third time since our landing. We were committed to a ceaseless wandering through a world gone insane. We were still hurrying on at the foot of the structures occupying the south side of the canyon, now over solid snow that began to accumulate there, and in a never-ending, blind monotony of endeavour which seemed to deprive us of reason and sense. But Azte-ca led; and we followed; to stop would have been to invite certain death.

Then that certain death seemed to swoop down on me anyway. I remember it had just struck me as strange that we were not being observed: here we were, three scholars of great repute, come to explore this human city; and the humans did not even seem to be aware of our presence. I should have thanked my stars for their callousness! For suddenly I *was* observed. A human hurrying along, with his head bent low, saw me and stopped. He stopped and, deliberately lifting his near hind-foot, he brought it down on top of me in order to crush me out of existence! I had just time to scent a warning to the other two while I was furiously digging myself into the snow before the enormous flat sole of that foot descended. I succeeded to the point where its pressure was largely taken up and absorbed by the snow to both sides; but exhausted as I was and no longer as nimble as I had been in my youth, I was not quite fast enough; and so I felt my carapace crack and nearly swooned. I don't know how I know; but that man's name was Ayr; and I want to hand at least his appellation over to the everlasting condemnation of antkind. Fortunately he was too stupid to understand that his fell purpose was not achieved; and so he went on at once. I was badly hurt: several of the dorsal plates of my thorax were cracked; but I had buried my head deep down in the snow; and Bissa-tee, who made a quick preliminary examination, pronounced my wounds to be serious but not mortal. In front, Azte-ca was clamouring for us to follow her, assuring us that before long we should have a chance to rest; and so I dragged myself forward again, racked with pain, but triumphant nevertheless at the thought that I had saved my brain from destruction.

It was some time after noon that day when Azte-ca turned at right angles. In thinking this adventure over, without actually remembering the details, I have come to the conclusion that we must, in the course of our wanderings, have crossed many side-roads; and whenever we did, we must have been in the gravest danger of being crushed to death. But our danger had no doubt been slight compared with the risks we had to run now; for as we traversed this main artery of human traffic, thundering space-machines and humming beetles surrounded us on every foot. I can only say that more than once we were separated; and I, being the oldest and heaviest, was always in the rear. Somehow or other I never failed to pick up Bissa-tee's scent again, even after I had, on one occasion, crouched down with a space-machine thundering along right over my head and flashes of lightning breaking right and left. It was an incredible experience.

But at last we arrived in a sort of forest cleared of underbrush, just east of the canyon. This forest was traversed by a number of human roads or paths; and on these we saw human males and females hurrying up to a great structure ahead of us or issuing from it. This, as we were to find out, was Azte-ca's destination, and it consisted of an enormous hominary containing human

records. We were destined to spend two whole winters
there.

In the forest we stopped, and Bissa-tee examined
me once more. Then, having conferred with Azte-ca, she
gave it as her opinion that I stood a fair chance of
getting to the end of our journey. I myself was not so
sure of it, for my wounds had by this time become
chilled; and in this forest the snow lay deep; but I was
determined to go on or perish: there was no choice; we
could not remain where we were.

It was late in the afternoon when, singly, we made
our way into the hominary, for each of us had to wait
till a human entered or issued, we being unable to move
the enormous doors.

The moment we were inside, we had one relief: it
was warm there; but the edges of my wounds had been
frozen; and as they thawed, I fainted. From that
moment on I cannot tell what happened further. [1]

II

When I recovered my consciousness, I was alone,
surrounded by twilight, though, throughout the outer
reaches of the structure in which I was, broad daylight
flooded the air. I had some trouble in remembering; too
much had happened. But as my memory returned, I saw

---

[1] Perhaps it will help the human reader's comprehension if
I state that the above description as well as what follows, barring
minor inaccuracies, fits the approach and lay-out of the Public
Library of New York City.

myself, or rather the three of us, struggling again through snow and sleet and rain, the human road roaring with noise and traffic; and I felt sorry for myself.

I tried to move but could not. Where was I? Though I recalled that I must be in that great hominary where the humans of this city kept their records, I had not the slightest idea of what was immediately surrounding me. To the right, a rough earthen wall rose to a dizzy height; to the left, there were peculiar columnar structures fifteen antlengths high, terminating in an uneven line above; these exhaled the smell of paper made of wood and of cotton fabrics mixed with that of fish glue and oil — a mixture I had never smelt before.

There was no light near me; but as my glance followed the right-hand wall upward, it lost itself in a sea of sunlight above, barred with black lines of shadow. Again I tried to move and failed in the attempt. My wounds, which I now remembered again, did not smart while I lay still; but at every motion a pain as of tightening ligatures encircled my thorax, so intense that I winced and henceforth was content to remain motionless. Thus I lay for hours.

Then, to my infinite joy, I scented Bissa-tee approaching along the broken upper edge of the columnar structures to my left. I even saw her peering down at me. But she did not yet come. In my weakened and helpless state, this precipitated me into the depths of despair. I feared I was completely abandoned; I was left there to die alone; for, unless I was surrounded by the care of helpful friends, I could see nothing ahead of me but a miserable end.

However, presently Bissa-tee returned.

I must here express my profound and sincere sorrow at Bissa-tee's untimely death of which we shall hear in due course; not only because by that death she was deprived of the full harvest of renown and glory which was her due on account of her great discoveries and achievements in zoology; but also because the example of her unrivalled tact as a medical ant was lost to ant-kind. Her surgical and medicinal knowledge and skill, I have no doubt, can be equalled by others, remarkable though they were; but the subtle gradations of her bedside manner were unique. It was her theory that a patient must above all heal herself; and that a doctor could help most by putting her into the humour which was appropriate to her condition. Thus when rest and relaxation were indicated, she could be so tenderly and sorrowfully sympathetic that her patient simply surrendered herself to her ministrations, just as a callow surrenders herself to her nurse-ant; and when a cheerful fighting spirit was needed, she would beat her thorax and rumble along in a loud, boisterous way which made you laugh and desire to get up at once in order to have a playful bout with her. Between these two extremes she had an infinite number of gradations so subtly adapted to the condition of the patient that I am inclined to assert her mere occasional presence had a curative effect even on my wounds, however slight or serious they may have been.

On the present occasion she was all soothing drowsiness. In sweet, soporific scents she assured me that I was doing famously; but I must not yet try to satisfy my curiosity; I must lie quite still; with proper

treatment and nourishing food I should, in a very few
days, be exploring again for myself.

At the scent of "nourishing food" I realized with
something like a pang just how hungry I was; for I
had not eaten since, led by our tiny friends, we had left
our station in the middle-west of the continent. So, when
Bissa-tee gently raised my head and regurgitated food
for me, it seemed the most natural thing for her to do
— as though the mere fact of her having anything to
regurgitate were not an almost miraculous circumstance. And what she had was fungi; it is true they were
not the species cultivated at home; in fact, as I found
out, they were properly moulds and not fungi at all;
but Bissa-tee administered them with such a matter-of-
course air that I swallowed them readily, in spite of a
slightly bitter taste which I ascribed to medicinal ingredients. Meanwhile she kept up a constant, murmur-
ing stream of scents, conveying to me the information
that, for the time being, all our troubles were at an end:
man was providing for us, not only shelter and heat,
but excellent food as well.

If it was her purpose to put me quietly to sleep
again, she succeded completely; as, after having partaken of this food, I became drowsy, her manner changed
to one of absolute somnolence; as though, like some
goddess of sleep, she were pouring hypnotics into my
antennæ.

I believe I slept for many days; for, when I awoke
at last, my wounds were nearly healed; and Bissa-tee
had completely changed her behaviour. This time she
was present at the moment of my awaking; and she
was engaged in dissolving those tight bands about my

thorax by applying saliva to them. No sooner did she notice that I was emerging from my long sleep than she began to scent to me in the most inspiriting way that, as soon as she had finished removing my bandages, I might go and find out where I was.

Only then did it strike me as curious that, while I had a subconscious memory of the frequent visits of Bissa-tee during my long illness, I had not once, in all that time, been visited by Azte-ca. I promptly enquired after her; and Bissa-tee shook with laughter. It took her quite a while to recover from her mirth; but when she did, she told me that Azte-ca was indeed lost to the world: she had succeeded in deciphering the human records and had now no time for anything else. She was positively reckless, Bissa-tee added; she was transscenting some of her more amazing discoveries at a point to which she, Bissa-tee, could lead me if I so desired. Her recklessness consisted in pursuing her studies day and night, often under the very noses and eyes of man; and she devoted no more than an indispensable minimum of time to rest and sleep. She frankly admitted, Bissa-tee added, that she exposed herself to constant danger; but she had gone insane with her curiosity; and she averred that, since her discoveries were scented on the wall of the building, her death did not matter, so long as she could pursue her studies, as she called them, to the end.

My impatience became such that I could hardly wait till Bissa-tee had finished her task before I asked her to show me these scent-fields — for such she called them — of Azte-ca's. Accordingly, as soon as we could, we set out for the place which was excellently chosen, for to the left, there being a gap in the obscuring co-

lumnar structures, a warm current of air ascended along
the wall. These walls curved upwards from all sides to
a circular opening which was crowned by a vaulted
dome admitting a flood of light from above. As far as
I could survey it, the whole chamber resembled, on a
gigantic scale, those which we build for our fungus-
gardens. No doubt some man had seen the latter and
brought home the art; for man is the most imitative of
all animals.

Incidentally, I discovered on this first trip of exploration the source of the food which Bissa-tee had
administered to me. I must, however, not forget to
mention that she had also informed me of the nature of
the columnar structures which I had noticed to my left.
They were what, in a scent new to me, she called books
or human records; and in describing them as a collective
unit she used another scent unknown to me — a scent
which I will render by our own scent literature. Now
all this human literature was mouldy; and, as I walked
along behind my physician and nurse, I could not refrain
here and there from nibbling at these moulds which had
the exact taste of Bissa-tee's regurgitation. When, on
the present occasion, she saw me, she laughed. " Bitter? "
she asked; and when I agreed, she added, " Queer stuff;
no doubt the bitterness is imparted by the contents.
It's wholesome food; but, if I'm any judge, it must be
poison for man. You won't see many healthy and normal
specimens here, such as we've seen in the fields and the
streets; those that come here, somehow look like worms
to me; if it were not flattering them, I'd call them book-
worms. I hope no real bookworm will scent me, though. "
And again she laughed in her boisterous way, shaking

from head to gaster as she went on, "They'd have made good food for our lamented friend Assa-ree and her hordes."

I thought her almost frivolous; it had been tacitly understood between us that Assa-ree was not to be mentioned.

But to come to our records. I was soon absorbed in what Azte-ca had recorded: it formed amazing scenting.

First of all, in an introduction of her own, she explained the physical nature of human records. Man had a limited number of visual symbols standing for sounds. These sound-symbols were arranged in groups called words; and words were arranged in lines; and groups of lines in pages. These pages were imprinted on sheets of paper made by chewing wood — a manufacture familiar to us from certain tribes of our own kind as well as from wasps. These sheets of paper, both sides of which were used, were then fastened together in bunches of from one to three hundred and formed a book. The only way in which an ant, even when she had deciphered this cumbersome system of symbols, could read human records was to run along line after line and to look at symbol after symbol, carefully fitting them together into an auditional perception; and, next, to fit the auditional perceptions together into a conceptual context. By way of an admiring foot-note, Azte-ca added that man had taken great pains to guard against these records being used by the uninitiated; for, she explained, the same symbol or group of symbols is often used for very different sounds; and many symbols are carefully imprinted between others without having any sound-value whatever: a perversity which, to me, seemed to render the whole system worthless. I was inclined to think that Azte-ca was simply mistaken in her assumptions; I convinced myself later on that she was right; but I did not agree with her in admiring man for having found a way of making access to his records intellectually very difficult to his fellow-men. Still later I found, from man's own records, that it takes his callows, according to the degree of initiation required, from six to sixteen years to acquire the art of deciphering such records as they may need in the station of life which they wish to occupy. On the other hand, it took me, once I had grasped the complicated principles involved, exactly one hour to learn to read any record of his.

But to continue. When such a book is opened, two consecutive pages are accessible; to make the next two available, a leaf has to be turned. And this, Azte-ca stated, she had learned to do. One considerable difficulty, which I discovered later, Azte-ca failed to mention, namely, that the order in which the primary sound-symbols are printed runs invariably from left to right, instead of alternating from line to line, which means that we, after having run along one line, had to return to our starting-point idle. The labour involved was thereby doubled.

In order to finish this topic before I proceed, I will anticipate here. Azte-ca was indefatigable in her labours and soon became so infatuated with man's perverse ways that she devoured this literature of his seemingly for no other purpose than to transscent it on the walls of the building. Whatever books she found open on the reading tables provided for humans she went through indiscriminately. Bissa-tee, on the other hand, though she learned the art of deciphering, never indulged in its exercise beyond a measure which she prescribed for herself for the purpose of reducing or "slimming" as she called it; like our lamented Anna-zee, she was rapidly becoming obese.

I myself used more discrimination in the choice of books which I read. I soon found that Azte-ca was wasting her time on an enormous amount of what the humans call fiction, i.e., books written on entirely imaginary things; she actually used to get excited about them, especially when they dealt with crime and its detection. It did not take me long to find out that, whenever she came to a record of human science or history, she promptly left it; I only needed to watch her in order to have the very thing which I wanted; it was invariably what she disdained. As for her omnivorous and injudicious reading, I will give one or two figures. During the seventeen moons which we spent in this hominary, she read no less than 6,321 books; which feat involved travelling, afoot and at top speed, a total distance of 1,769,880,000 antlengths or about 13,696 human miles. In all which she had no other aim than to satisfy a vulgar curiosity. I myself, on the other hand, aimed at understanding man's social organization which would decide his position in the phylogenetic scale of evolution.

It goes without saying that in this brief record I cannot even summarize the information gathered. The curious are referred to scent-trees 346 to 389 and 733 to 813 for such a summary. At present I must be content to relate events rather than give the results of investigation and research.

During our stay in this *library* we had, naturally, to adjust our own day to that of the humans. Or perhaps it would be more correct to state that I had to do so; for Bissa-tee stood apart from our labours, learning to decipher the records of man more from a motive of vanity than from that of a thirst for knowledge which is the fountain head of all intellectual achievement; and Azte-ca, in spite of repeated warnings, took such risks as no ant should take.

To speak of her first, I might say that she pursued her reading at almost any time of the day or night. Usually the library began to fill with human readers quite early in the morning; and Azte-ca soon knew a good many of them. That is to say, she knew their tastes in literature and the places where they preferred to sit. There was accommodation for eight hundred human readers. I will briefly tell of the circumstances which first induced her to disregard all danger. On the counter near the door where at night nearly all books that had been used and were required again must be deposited, she had become acquainted with a record which, from what she reported about it, dealt with a peculiarly intricate murder story; and she had just reached the most exciting part of it (for in all this branch of literature man aims chiefly at excitement) when, next morning, the human officers of the library arrived; so far, she had always taken that for a signal to retire; and she did so on this occasion. She watched, however, for she was trembling with excitement; and soon she saw a human female appear and take up this record which she carried to a certain favourite seat of hers. This was exactly what Azte-ca had expected. But within an hour

the human female finished her reading and returned the
book to the counter where she was supplied with another.
Azte-ca had, in the meantime, on one of the shelves
where the books were kept, run the whole round of the
hall, getting herself quite out of breath with hurry. She
hated to lose sight of that precious record. To her
disgust, a human attendant promptly picked it up and
replaced it on one of the shelves. Again Azte-ca ran a
race with this man and, helpless to prevent it, saw what
he did. There it was to stand henceforth, much regretted
by Azte-ca, tightly wedged in between other records. I
believe that, had she lived a thousand years, she would
still have been impatient whenever anyone alluded to
that book; for although she read meanwhile thousands
upon thousands of other books, she could never forget
her being disappointed of this one. She asserted, of
course, that her curiosity was solely concerned with the
question whether man's resolution of the mystery agreed
with her own which she pronounced to be highly ingenious. We often teased her about it. But from that day on
she began to take undue risks. Whenever, henceforth, she
had been unable to finish a book, she made it a point to
linger about the counter where she could not turn the
pages without being detected; and when the human
reader returned for the book, she jumped on to his
flowing outer integuments and climbed up on shoulder
or head of this reader. When he sat down, she remained
and read with him. This was an art which she acquired
by infinite practice: I never did; my eye-sight was no
longer good enough. For man does not run along the
lines when he reads; he merely follows them with his
eyes; and Azte-ca who, as I have repeatedly said, was

a genius in her way, soon learned from him. Many and many a time she was seen, of course, and ruthlessly brushed to the ground by a human fore-foot; but she was not to be discouraged by such slight reverses, not even after she had lost a middle leg by a fall. Ultimately, as we shall see, Azte-ca brought disaster upon herself and came near bringing it upon Bissa-tee and me as well.

I myself read chiefly at night and rested in daytime. The sort of books I read — science, history, philosophy, and the like — were mostly used by privileged human readers of a more or less advanced age who had the right to leave them, piled together, on the tables where they had their seats; and there these books were left undisturbed when at night their readers went home. Such records, which were often of considerable bulk, presented, however, one considerable difficulty, namely, that they were exceedingly hard to open. Almost every night I had to enlist the help of both my associates in order to achieve that feat; and though I did manage to turn the often large and stiff pages by myself, that task, too, required the exertion of every ounce of my strength. I pursued my studies invariably till the first human readers appeared which was an hour or two after the attendants had arrived at the counter.

As for Bissa-tee, I have already said that she took no interest whatever in our pursuits; for two or three hours every morning she indulged in what she called gymnastics, in order to keep her ever growing bulk within manageable limits; after that she undid whatever effect these exercises might have had by roaming all over this hominary in search of the choicest moulds;

she asserted that these varied considerably according to the kind of literature they grew on, being bitter and tasting of medicinal substances when growing on philosophic works; sweet and ethereal, when growing on poetry written by females; and having an outright intoxicating effect when growing on works of so-called theology. Personally, I never could taste the difference.

III

For a long while — in fact, for over a year — life thus went on placidly enough. The moulds growing on this human literature furnished an inexhaustible and nourishing though, to me, slightly unpalatable food; the temperature was almost as equable as in our brood-chambers; and we seemed to be perfectly safe.

Then I had the first terrifying intimation of the fact that our presence had not remained unnoticed. What I am about to relate forms one of the most harassing memories of this period; and it is with some hesitation that I set it down; only a strict regard for truth forces me not to suppress a single feature of the adventure.

I had by this time completely mastered the art of understanding human speech. For this purpose I had my ear-drums coated, just as in the past I had coated those of Azte-ca; but we now used a different substance for the purpose, namely, a liquid · which, on exposure to the air, hardened quickly and which we found in large glasses on the counter by the door; man calls it *mucilage*. These coatings which Bissa-tee applied for me, so deadened the thunder of the human voice that it reached my delicate auditory nerves as from a great distance, resembling the pleasant murmur of a brook.

One night, then — I believe it was in the fourteenth moon of our stay in the library — I had run across a book dealing with ourselves. My students will hardly credit the fact, which is nevertheless quite true: this book was written by our old friend or enemy, the Wheeler. It seems only natural that I should have been sufficiently absorbed to lose track of the passage of time; and suddenly I became aware that I had read on, still turning the pages, till it was broad daylight. Already there were numbers of human readers scattered throughout the great chamber and engaged in their studies. Now the human which had frequented this particular reading platform, in a remote corner of the hall, was a young female which did not, as a rule, make its appearance much before noon. So, glancing about and finding that I was in fair privacy, I made up my mind that it was safe to go on for another hour or so; for I had just reached an account, from the human point of view, of the Attas.

To my dismay, however, the human female appeared shortly, and at the very moment when I was laboriously turning a page. She was a bold sort of callow, not over forty years old; and humans, I suppose, would have called her handsome. Her head was covered by a sort of smooth clypeus; and her neck rolled up in a thick fur resembling that of a fox (I shall have more to say about these singular human integuments in the next section). She was tall, slender, and athletic; and her face showed several coatings of a wax-like substance of two colours, white and red. This coating, Bissa-tee conjectured, was applied by the tongues of males; one day, she asserted, she had, in a recess of the library, distinctly seen a male applying its mouth to the cheek of a female; and, investigating at once, she had, beyond the possibility of a doubt, ascertained the fact that the same substance, also red and white, was coating the lips of the male which promptly protruded its tongue to lick it back into its mouth.

Now I must explain that, from the very moment on when Azte-ca had first deciphered human speech and records, I had cherished the hope of establishing communication with man. This could not be done orally; for man's auditory nerves are far too coarse to perceive the fine and delicate sounds we produce by stridulation. It could be done only by way of his records, and I had already conceived a practicable method.

When, therefore, the human female appeared on this fateful morning, I made up my mind to attempt this great task then and there. Here, I said to myself, is a human being which, by the very nature of its reading, shows that it is interested in ants. What better opportunity could I expect to find?

I dropped the leaf I was on the point of turning and began running along the lines of the page; and whenever I found one of the symbols I needed, I carefully deposited a drop of my black anal secretion below it. I could not believe that she would fail to see it.

Imagine, therefore, my surprise when this female, at sight of me, uttered a low scream and instinctively, at least so it seemed, swept me to the ground by a terrible swoop of her fore-foot. Yet even then I could not conceive of a young female's soul being so devoid of all finer stirrings as to make it instinctively bent on murder. Had she watched for just a minute, she could not have failed to grasp my intention. But what did she do? She ran after me and, raising her hind-foot, tried to bring it down on me, just as the man had done in the street some fourteen moons ago.

It was my good fortune that I did not for a moment lose my presence of mind. Seeing what this human female was about, I remembered an anatomical peculiarity of the female foot as compared with that of the male. The fore-part of the foot consists, on its under side, of a huge, flat expanse which, towards the rear, curves up into a vault behind which there is a columnar heel; this heel is, in the female, much higher than in the male. I have sometimes thought that it would be possible to classify human beings by their heels: the higher it is, the larger the share of the female characteristics, even in males; and the lower it is, the larger the share of the male characteristics, even in females. I believe this would furnish a perfectly sound basis for division. But to return to my story.

Remembering this peculiarity of the foot of the female, I turned on my back when I saw the foot descending upon me. At the exactly right moment I propelled myself upward with an extreme exertion, first raising abdomen and head and then bringing them down with a thump on the smooth stone of the floor, imparting a spring to my whole body. I had to calculate that jump to a nicety; for had I reached sole or heel instead of the arch of the foot, it would have meant certain death. To my relief, however, I found myself, a moment later,

securely clinging to the vaulted roof of that arch; and
then the foot, with a terrific impact, came down on the
floor, nearly dislodging me.

Apparently the human female was half exhausted
by the effort; for she dropped into a sitting posture in
what humans call an arm-chair. This sitting position
was of a kind peculiar to humans which must ever seem
offensive to the modesty of ants. My students can imagine the state of mind I was in. The moment the tension
resolved itself into the feeling of relief, I simply shook
with indignation: a clumsy human female had nearly
annihilated me, the depositary of the most advanced
science of ants!

In relating the remainder of this adventure, however, I cannot but confess to a certain degree of shame.
I, a votary of science, having just, by a special dispen-
sation, escaped from imminent danger, should not have
allowed myself to be carried away by unreasoning anger.
Yet, had I not been so carried away, we should not have
had the warning to which I have referred. Let the
student remember that even science leaves us, in our
lesser moments, mere formicarian beings subject to
passion. For my own justification I can say that I
struggled against the lower impulse which, however,
proved stronger than my more elevated thought.

Slowly and stealthily I left the cave of my refuge
and swung up on top of that foot. There, too, it was
partly covered with the same coriaceous integument as
the sole. I proceeded upward along the tibial reach of
the leg, covered, up to and slightly beyond the genicular
joint, by a different, fibrous integument. Over this I
ran carefully and swiftly, feeling comparatively safe,

for I was here hidden from the female's eye by a series of outer, long, curtain-like coverings. More than once, however, the human female made sudden rubbing movements, leg against leg, as if to brush me off, just as we should try to brush off a particle of dust irritating our legs. Whenever she did so, I stopped, keeping out of the way.

And then I reached a large, bare expanse of soft white skin and stopped. I was standing on the very edge of the fibrous integument covering her tibia. While pausing, I collected in my poison glands as large a quantity of formic acid as I could muster; and, taking hold, with my jaws, of the soft flesh, I injected, in a sudden giddy burst of passion quite unworthy of myself, an enormous dose of the poison.

A scream resounded such as I never hope to hear again. The sound loosened my joints. It was followed by a most violent motion. The human female had, with one single bound, sought the privacy of a niche behind a book-rack; and before I was aware of what was happening, she there lifted up her outer, loose integuments. She must actually have seen me in the act of withdrawing my sting. Fortunately her scream had attracted the attention of a number of males who came running; and as they appeared, the young female for one reason or other dropped those fringe-like integuments. I took a leap, reached the rear edge of these fringes, and jumped to safety on a book-shelf.

Thence I watched and listened. The young female turned to one of the males who seemed to be a man in authority and said, her eyes flashing, " The whole place swarms with ants!" "Yes," replied the male. "We have had complaints before. I shall see to it shortly."

That was our warning; and I did not fail to communicate it to my associates. The incident has been given in such detail chiefly because I suspect it led directly to the catastrophe which was to terminate our stay in the library. But, strange to say, this catastrophe was delayed for several moons, perhaps because we, having had a warning, became much more cautious; till, early in the spring of the second year, the seventh of our absence from home, we became just a little careless again and thereby perhaps precipitated the vengeance of man.

One morning there appeared a whole squad of old human females of a type which we had, so far, seen only singly. They were the charwomen who looked after the cleaning of the floors. Bissa-tee was, at the time, absorbed in her gymnastic exercises which she now performed religiously every morning in order to keep her ever growing corpulency down: she was at the back of that row of books behind which, a year and a half ago, I had regained consciousness. Azte-ca was on the counter near the open door, reading a detective story and, therefore, lost to the world. I was sunning myself on a shelf along the eastern wall. It was a most beautiful day of the early spring.

The moment I saw that squad of old women with their pails, carrying long-handled, loose, fringy things called mops, I felt invaded by a sense of coming disaster. They looked so sinister and determined. Only then did it strike me that no human readers had yet appeared although it was quite late in the day. For a moment I thought this must be one of those periodically recurring days on which the library remained closed. But I also knew that these days came in a regular succession and that none was due. I felt it my duty to investigate at once.

One of the women emptied the fluid in her pail on the floor; and promptly all of them began to swish it about with their mops. By this time I had gained a vantage-point on a window-ledge directly above them.

There I felt suddenly assailed by sickening fumes rising from that liquid which they were mopping about. For the fraction of a second I remained inactive; for the fumes seemed to deprive me of the power of motion; in fact, I came very near to falling off the ledge.

Then, with the sense of a coming disaster intensifying, I made a superformicarian effort and hastened away, towards the place where Bissa-tee was performing her exercises. I was still under the illusion that Azte-ca was on the counter near the door. Unfortunately I chose the outside of the shelf for my hurried run. Had I been on the inside, between books and wall, I could not but have passed the very place where, at that moment, Azte-ca was engaged in recording the contents of her latest story on the wall. Only when I arrived opposite the spot where, an hour or so ago, I had left Bissa-tee, I swung up on the cliff formed by the books; and, a moment later, I espied Bissa-tee who had interrupted her exercises and was now standing rigid, waving her antennæ in a first realization of the coming danger; for the fumes were already faintly perceptible even here. When she saw me, she scented the single word, "Chlorine", and stared at me. I told her what I had observed; and she turned at once, scenting, " Come, " and began to scale the wall. This wall consisted of a rough-cast of aluminious clay. I soon passed Bissa-tee who, by reason of her recently-acquired obesity, was no longer quite as quick as she might have been. But when she reached the dizzy height of the next tier of windows, her scent overtook me, signalling " Stop! " We were here above the fumes; but I feared that, owing to the diffusing power of gases, they would soon reach us. I waited for Bissa-tee who was laboriously following in my wake. She turned at right angles to our previous line of ascent; and, going north, we reached a window-shelf, I being first again; but when Bissa-tee caught me up, she, to my infinite relief, pointed out a small round opening between frame and sash of the window — an opening through which a strong current of fresh air was entering from the outside. This opening was large enough for us to crawl through, a feat which Bissa-tee promptly proposed to perform. It was a feat indeed, for the air pressure against which we should have had to work was enormous. At the very moment, however, at which Bissa-tee was inserting her head into this tunnel, I thought of Azte-ca and held her back.

Having communicated to her my misgivings with re-gard to our associate, I took a flying leap down to the topmost book-shelf where I intended to wait for Bissa-tee. But when she did not come, I looked up and saw her on the very edge of the ledge where she stood, waving to me in great distress that, owing to a fatty degeneration of her heart, she dared not to take the leap. I signalled back to her to wait and hurriedly ran south, in the direction of the counter near the door. Azte-ca was not there. I became frantic with alarm.

I quickly descended to the lower shelf on which we had had our quarters. Here, the fumes were now much thicker; but disregarding all danger I dashed forward at a speed of which I should not have thought myself capable. I had barely reached our abandoned station when I caught sight of Azte-ca on the wall where she had only just become aware of the fumes.

I noticed that these fumes had here already taken sufficient effect to shrivel up the delicate moulds on which we had lived so long. But I did not delay over that; I was bent only on attracting Azte-ca's attention; and I cannot believe that the powerful scents I emitted should have failed to reach her; yet she paid no attention to them.

For a long while Azte-ca had shown symptoms of a peculiar mental aberration. It had become a mania with her to imagine herself in the part of a human being engaged in detecting crime. She had even elaborately constructed methods of committing such crime in a way which would make its detection impossible or at least exceedingly difficult. I am sorry to say that both Bissatee and myself had, in the beginning, encouraged her in this pernicious activity. We took an unreasonable pride in the fact that an ant should prove herself superior in ingenuity to man, a thing we should have treated as a matter of course. For our justification I can only aver that we ceased doing this as soon as we became aware of the effect this preoccupation had upon Azte-ca's practical sense.

This utter lack of practical sense, a consequence of the submersion of her mind in human folly, showed itself disastrously at the present moment. Already half overcome by the fumes, Azte-ca, instead of obeying my summons, precipitated herself from the dizzy height at which she was to the floor beneath. She was alive when she landed; but in her panic she made a dash in a direction exactly opposite to that which she should have taken. A moment later she lay, expiring, in the swirling flood whence our danger arose. It was my sad destiny to see her perish there. One of the old women said in a voice full of unspeakable disgust, "The nahsty crayture!" and squarely planted her foot on the dying ant. Thus perished Azte-ca, one of the most ingenious signallers the world had ever seen. She was crushed to a pulp. To such senseless accidents are we ants exposed on this earth!

I could not help her; I was by that time half overcome myself; and I sought safety in flight.

When I rejoined Bissa-tee, the news I brought almost prostrated her; and if I had not kept my head and propelled her towards the tunnel, she would have stayed behind and perished like Azte-ca. There was not a moment to lose.

The narrowness of the passage came near frustrating our escape. More than once Bissa-tee found her abdomen tightly jammed between its walls. Fortunately I was behind her; and so, after much squeezing and pushing, we arrived outside. When we did, we were so exhausted that we resolved to anchor ourselves as best we could and to stay where we were till we had regained a measure of our strength. During the interval of waiting we vowed to each other that under no circumstances would we allow ourselves to be separated after we had descended to earth. There was much speculation with regard to the direction to follow; for neither of us had paid much attention to this matter when we had arrived a year and a half ago: at that time we had simply followed the lead of our lamented Azte-ca.

We left our eyrie with the fall of night; and when the steep descent was accomplished, we struck east. There was no lack of light and scarcely a diminution of the traffic usual on these human roads; and we found this so harassing that, after a few hours, we were glad, on catching sight of another huge hominary, to be able to escape from it. This hominary which we thus entered by a mere chance turned out to be a sort of aphis-shed or stable for those enormous beasts that pull the human space-machines over the bands of steel provided for their progress. [2]

We remained there for many days, watching and studying; Bissa-tee regained a measure of her former agility and enterprise and spent many hours exploring by herself. Ultimately she brought the news that she had found out when and whence a certain space-machine was going to start for the south-west.

That this south-west of the continent must be our destination was tacitly understood between us. With only the two of us left, we were bound to strike for home at last; and such is the power of hope which dwells

---

[2] In human words, it was a railway station, probably the 42nd Street station in New York. E.

forever in the breast of ants, that from now on we began
to live mentally once more in the great and glorious
formicary in the valley of the Orinoco River. I, for one,
needed only to close my eyes in order to see myself
stretched out luxuriously while half a dozen media
groomed my long-neglected body — a luxury which I
had foregone for so many years. Bissa-tee, too, avowed
that when she slept she dreamt of home; and henceforth,
when we were awake, we both struggled and fought in
order to get there. Already the sufferings and incessant
labours which lay behind us counted for nothing; ahead
of us lay the happy return.

A matter of six or seven days later we arrived, in
a human space-machine, in a city near the mouth of that
very river which we had crossed so long ago by way of
the metal-threads of that mysterious spider which we
had never seen after all. This river we crossed by an
enormous bridge built on the same principle of which we
make use in spanning smaller waters; and after various
vicissitudes of which there is no need to speak in detail
we were launched on our last great march to the south
and west. The difficulties and privations we had to cope
with were worthy to inspire our minstrels and to be
preserved for the memory of posterity as an inspiration
to future generations. Before I record a few details,
however, I must briefly summarize the conclusions we
arrived at with regard to man.

IV

First of all, then, both Bissa-tee and myself verified the remarkable fact that man moults at will, seasonally as well as diurnally. This gift seems at first sight to place him apart from all the rest of nature as one of the luckiest of all created beings. Yet, when we reflect what pangs, let me say, a grasshopper has to endure in order to change his coat three or four times in his life, we may well hesitate in pronouncing him blessed in this fact. We shall soon see that, though man moults at will and is able to adapt himself to all changes of the weather, there is good reason to infer that he does not do so without suffering and pain.

Unfortunately we had, in the earlier part of our stay among men, small opportunity to observe man in his more intimate private life. The nearest we came to such observations was on our last trip in the great space-machine which took us south; for this space-machine was provided with special chambers to which the human passengers retired at night for the purpose of resting. There, then, we saw this curious mammal in a state least protected against the vicissitudes of the climate. The integuments which he wore in daytime were discarded and others were donned, of a kind which would serve but poorly to keep out the cold and to shed rain, sleet, or snow. The process of change from one set to another, which we had a good chance to observe, was essentially similar to that by which a grasshopper moults: man crawled out of the integument to be discarded, often using his limbs to push it forward while he withdrew.

When every one of the successive integuments was removed, the body was found to be covered only by a soft membranaceous skin of a porous texture with a sprinkling of hair here and there and a few chitinous plates distributed over the extremities of his limbs. The hair was rudimentary; not one of them retaining even a trace of the power to serve as a sensilla. The chitinous plates were found exclusively on the upper surfaces of the toes of both fore- and hind-limbs where they serve as a protection to the most sensitive nerve-endings of these members. This, too, is curious in the extreme. For of what use can these sensitive nerve-endings be when they are covered with an insensitive armour? That they are there, was conclusively shown when a man's extreme toe-tips were caught between the frame and the movable part of a heavy door: this man gave evidence of pain by using frightful language, calling upon his god and that god's counterpart to bear him witness that the door had wronged him.

When, on retiring at night, man had thus divested himself of his diurnal integuments, he remained in this naked state for only a minimum of time; and then followed what seemed to be the most startling part of the performance. For, while, no doubt, a new integument is gradually being secreted by the inner skin, he assumed provisionally another integument *by crawling into it*. Similarly in the morning, when the nocturnal integument was discarded, he crawled back into the diurnal ones. What is more, he carried about with him a choice of such integuments, both diurnal and nocturnal: a most amazing thing which would have been entirely incomprehensible to us if we had not in a manner already been prepared for some such discovery.

During our long stay in the hominary of the great human city we had more than once had an opportunity of listening in when two or three human beings, mostly females, indulged in a little relaxed conversation about their integuments. Strange to say, integuments form the chief and most absorbing theme of their thoughts, and they are the chief object of their pride. It was long before we understood this. As far as I could make out, both male and female man produce these integuments in advance and in number, so as to have them on hand. It is exactly as though a grasshopper moulted three or four times in succession without growing in size and, therefore, without outgrowing the discarded moults. He would, then, store these moults, which would be of varying strength and consistency, in a place which he could remember; or he would carry them about, suspended, let me say, in an appropriate leaf-fold from his forefoot; for that is exactly what man does.

The process by which these integuments are produced we had no opportunity to watch; but I heard a good deal of it; enough to give me a fairly accurate idea.

Undoubtedly man produces his integuments in exactly the manner of the grasshopper; namely, as a secretion of his skin. This was strikingly confirmed by a conversation which I overheard in a remote recess of the library where it took place between a young male and a female who were getting ready for their marriage flight. The male reproached the female for never having time for him; and she replied that she had to keep working in order to have integuments to cover her nakedness;

man, by the way, is not satisfied with one plain and clear word for anything; in this case she called her integuments "clothes". Whereupon the male said smilingly, "In the sweat of thy brow shalt thou clothe thyself, eh?" If any ant can put a satisfactory interpretation on these words other than the one suggested, I should like to know it. I visualized that condition of the female. Just like the grasshopper she sat or lay, sweating in anguish as she produced a new integument. Worse than the grasshopper, she had to go on maturing this integument till she could slip it off; for only from that moment on was it of any use to her. Unlike the grasshopper, she could henceforth slip back into it at will. This explanation of the process furnishes at least a working hypothesis, scientifically sound because it explains all the known facts.

Another remarkable feature about these integuments, perhaps the most remarkable of all, is more difficult to explain; and for the present I must content myself with a simple statement of the facts. All man's integuments are mimetic. I presume it to be well known that mimicry occurs among insects wherever a species is either formidable on account of the weapons with which it is provided or unpalatable to its potential enemies. The most striking examples of this human mimicry came under our observation during the two winter seasons spent in the human city. Nearly every human wore an outer integument closely resembling the hairy covering of some other mammal. Bissa-tee identified among them those of the wolf, the fox, the beaver, the squirrel, the sheep, the marten, the mink, and many others. Why man who, in his own cities, can to a certain extent be said to be the dominant animal should mimic, let me say, the rat, in his integuments, is beyond my power to understand. As a matter of fact, Bissa-tee was of the opinion that not man but the small rodents, rats, mice, etc., were dominant there. To me, the relation between man and these rodents seemed to be rather of the nature of a symbiosis. I do not think that man could live without the scavenging service performed by the rodents; in return for which man furnishes them with shelter, warmth, and food.

Be that as it may, Bissa-tee had another remarkable theory which might explain at least some of the facts. She suggested that these integuments were not true integuments at all but trophies; just as some of our soldiers had been wearing the heads of Pseudomyrmex ever since the battle at the isthmus. This theory of Bissa-tee's, highly ingenious as it was, seemed inadequate to me. If, f.i., the integuments mimicking rat skins had been real rat skins worn as trophies, we should occasionally have seen humans who wore only two or three such skins, or five or six; but the integuments in question were always complete. It cannot be presumed that in every battle between humans and rats — and battles do take place — the two species are always represented in the exact proportion of one man to so-and-so-many rats, enough to furnish the former with a complete integument; nor that man should always and invariably be victorious to the extent of killing the exactly right number. Further observation will be needed to decide between these two contending theories; but I venture to say, after mature deliberation, that there is no third way of explaining the facts.

So much for the morphological side of this mooted question.

There is, however, an ecological and even an ethnological side to it; and a very brief summary of our investigations is perhaps needed here to round off the subject. I must say, however, that in this respect our expedition shared the fate of all former expeditions sent out from our own city: it opened up more problems, at least with regard to man, than it answered. In saying this, I am well aware that I am confirming the speculations about the ultimate fate of all scientific enquiry which our lamented botanist-in-chief expounded to us in her disquisition on the knowable and the unknowable worlds.

So far, it has been considered as axiomatic that only insects have reached a point of development where the division of labour attendant upon a social life is reflected in a morphological division into physiological castes. Such castes, it has been held, do not exist in any other subdivision of the animal kingdom, least of all among mammals. Not even the dimorphism of the sexes was, strictly speaking, and apart from the purely sexual functions, reflected in a division of castes. The cow grazes as much as the bull; the she-panther hunts as laboriously as the male. Now the very conditions under which we studied man imposed certain limitations upon our investigations. But enough was seen to place one fact beyond doubt, namely, that man's whole social organization is built up on at least the ideal of a strict division into castes. If I add that much of the certainty with which I can assert this derives from human records, I must beg leave to point out that, in this particular case, the general unreliability of these records does not invalidate our conclusions. They are based, not on what man consciously meant to put down, but on a critical interpretation of what he put into them without being aware of its import.

Thus certain integuments disqualify their bearer for certain occupations. No conclusion could be more certain; and if Azte-ca's promiscuous reading in human fiction had any value whatever, it must be looked for in the confirmation her summaries gave to this theory of mine. When, in a story, a man wishing to perform certain work is debarred from achieving his ambition, because he lacks the proper integuments, that is evidence of the highest importance; and it is trustworthy for the very reason that it is indirect. Nevertheless, if there is such a purely physiological division, it is not yet rigid or fixed; for, strange to say, man can pass from one caste into another, provided he can produce the integuments proper to that caste. At first sight this may seem wholly admirable. I thought of the mediæ and the minims among the Myrmecocysts of the Garden of the Gods, those unfortunates who, while physiologically not adapted for the function of authors, yet thought they had had "the call". But among humans it leads to a state of affairs which, among ants, would never be tolerated. For man's occupations — i.e., among workers — are not considered as of equal value, or, as he would express it, of equal prestige; and this is the incomprehensible thing about it: the more necessary and indispensable a given kind of work is, the more it is despised; and the less necessary and indispensable it is, the more

highly is it rewarded; till absolute idleness and paras-
itism become the coveted goal.

Consequently, man's chief aim in life is to produce
such integuments as confer upon him the admission
into a higher caste, either in fact or in semblance. If
we can trust the conclusions we drew from Azte-ca's
transscentures of human fiction, most of human life is
taken up by a frantic endeavour to produce ever finer
and more respected integuments; most men, and especially females, spend the greater part of their waking
hours in so-called "sweat shops" to produce them; and,
having produced them, they spend the remainder in
flaunting or discussing them. We even met with evidence
tending to show that integuments can be produced by
one individual for another; but what reward can be
offered to induce anyone to do so is beyond my understanding, especially when I reflect that such vicarious
production might enable the producer himself to enter
the higher caste. From what I have said, however, it will
be clear that the very fact of the fluidity of the castes,
instead of being a blessing, is a curse to mankind; it
keeps man enslaved to purely material ends. It was a
surprise to find that, under the circumstances, there
should be any men at all who devoted themselves to
science, art, and other things of the spirit. The difficulty
was partly solved when we found that these are precisely
the ones who despise the pomp of integument; and that,
on the whole, they live the lives of the lowest castes.

One more point I must mention though I cannot
explain it. Man has a way of enslaving his fellow-men
by means of a thing of which we read much — a thing
he calls money and which some have and others have

not. Just what it is, I do not know; and neither, I suspect, does man himself. It is a cruel thing, since its lack condemns to abject slavery or actual want; whereas its possession confers the highest privileges. It has something to do with man's integuments; but just what the connection is I never found out.

Since man has the rudiments of a medical science, I could never understand either why he does not, by certain innocent surgical manipulations, so alter the structure of the brain of all those whom he intends for slaves as to make it impossible for them to covet a higher status. If he gave his medical officers the power to enquire into the financial circumstances (as he calls them) of the parents of a new-born child — man, as I infer from analogy with other mammals, is viviparous — and, if these financial circumstances are found to be such as to predestine the child to a life of slavery, what could be simpler than for this medical officer to make the future man happy in that acquiescence in slavery which will be enforced in any case, but by methods both cruel and inefficient?

The curious will infer from this neglect of simple expedients that man has either not yet risen to any very high degree of civilization; or — which is my own opinion — that he has considerably degenerated from a level previously attained. In this opinion I was confirmed by certain historical records of man which dealt with the past of this continent from the human point of view.

If, then, I were, in conclusion, to give my final idea of man, based on such experience as we had with him, I should say that he is at present a degenerate type; and that, even in a happier past, he has never attained a level of civilization which could in any way be called comparable to our own.

V

Bissa-tee and myself had been struggling along for months and months, going roughly in a south-west direction. So long as we were north of the range of the Ecitons, we travelled in daytime, resting at night in any hollow that offered, mostly in the cracks of the bark of certain trees. We suffered as we had never suffered before, from hunger, from exhaustion, from that depression which I now recognized as arising from the fact that we were alone. This may sound strange; the point is that the responsibility for others and the very magnitude of the task which had so far been ahead of us had, during the first five or six years of the expedition, distracted our thoughts from ourselves. A whole compound organism had been functioning; and we had been part of that organism. It had carried us along. Now that organism had disappeared; the task, apart from reporting our results, had been accomplished or abandoned. Perhaps both of us felt that we were entitled to our rest; both of us resented the fact that we had to go on struggling in order to get home before we could rest; and, worst of all, each of us resented any delay that became necessary, not as a new misfortune opposing us, but as the fault of the other.

Thus, one evening, we came to a stream which, at any earlier date, we should have promptly crossed, for

it was shallow and all but bridged by stones. I was the
first to arrive; and had I been leading any considerable
number of my associates, I should have gone on and
crossed at once. As it was, I waited for my companion;
but during that wait my joints stiffened; for the day's
work that lay behind me had been enormous. By the
time Bissa-tee joined me, I was moving about painfully.
She recommended a rest, speaking sharply, as though
she noticed my condition only now, and with alarm;
there was another hour of daylight left. I, thinking
chiefly of her — for she had lost considerably more
weight than I — acquiesced; I was willing enough not
to exert myself; and I will admit I dropped without
replying. This was bad; I had more than once reflected
upon the desirability, if not the absolute necessity, of
observing the strictest forms of politeness all the more
punctiliously when any discourtesy on my part was apt
to be interpreted as pointing directly against the only
companion I had left. I saw Bissa-tee darkening. But,
instead of feeling compunction on account of my rude-
ness, I resented the interpretation she put upon my
silence. Any over-exertion which is continuously repeated has this demoralizing effect. Half an hour later I felt
suddenly as though it were absolutely necessary to cross
the brook at once; and, gathering every remaining ounce
of my strength, I rose and signified as much. But by
this time Bissa-tee had reached that state of stiffness in
which I had been when she arrived. She groaned as she
rose; seeing which, I scented somewhat impatiently
that we might as well stay for the night. She was obstin-
ate now, and painfully moved on to the ford. From the
way she moved I concluded that she would never be able

to take those desperate leaps from stone to stone which were required. I, using the scent of supreme command, gave the order to postpone the crossing to the next day, impersonally, as though the order were addressed to an army; and simultaneously I turned to search for a hollow suitable to spend the night in. Bissa-tee had hesitated; then, I having meanwhile found a place, she followed me resentfully. Neither of us gave a scent. We did not even wish each other good-night. There being nothing to eat, we dropped and were instantly asleep.

That night it rained; and next morning the brook carried a turbid flood which covered all the stones: for a whole week it was impossible to effect a crossing.

During that week the relationship between Bissa-tee and myself — a relationship which could no longer be that between a commander and an inferior officer — slowly disintegrated. I remember how, the first morning, we both stood on the bank and looked out over the flood. No signal, no scent passed between us. But both of us wept. Had we crossed last night, we should now have been well on the way. But Bissa-tee's attitude conveyed an unmistakable reproach. " I was willing to go on, " it seemed to say. " You prevented me; and now see what has come of it. " I was thinking of the fact that, when I had arrived at the brook, I had had to wait for Bissa-tee; had she not lagged behind, neither of us would have stopped. We turned in silence and began to search for such food as we could find, each for herself. It was little enough, very unpalatable, and not sufficiently nutritious to repair a day's loss of strength.

Thus the time went by; the brook subsided and then swelled once more, as a consequence of another rain.

Every now and then I caught Bissa-tee, now recovered
to a point to which I, being so much older, could not
recover any longer, looking wistfully across the brook
and scanning the horizon; and I knew that she was
blaming me in her heart. How I knew I cannot tell.
Perhaps it is simply ant-nature to judge your fellow by
yourself.

Towards the seventh evening the brook showed once
more signs of subsiding. But then the sky clouded over
again; and though I kept a furtive eye on these clouds
myself, I resented it in Bissa-tee that she, ostentatiously
I thought, climbed a hummock to look about. For a while
I merely looked on, darkening slowly; but at last, when
my anger had reached an explosive pressure, I emitted
a faint scent of rally. I did this only to relieve myself;
I never thought the scent would reach Bissa-tee. But it
did, and she veered around, snarling. I will throw a
scent-screen over the scene that followed. For more than
an hour we indulged in mutual recriminations. Both of
us were partly in the right; and that fact blinded us to
that other fact that we were both wholly in the wrong.
At last we ceased from sheer exhaustion; for, though we
had found little bits of food, tiny moulds and fungi
which, however, caused us severe digestive disturbances,
we were very weak; and at no time did we, up to the
day of Bissa-tee's death, succeed in recuperating to the
full measure of our natural strength.

An hour or so before dark I retired to our temporary
quarters, angry and despondent, but at the same time
longing for comfort and companionship, longing for
Bissa-tee to come and make it up. She did at last; slowly
and shame-facedly she came in; touching me with her

antennæ. Both of us felt stirred to our depths; and we begged forgiveness from each other, blaming fate, blaming the state we were in; feeling sorry for each other, feeling sorry for ourselves.

The amazing thing was that, half an hour later, we had somehow crossed the brook. We spent the night on the far bank; and for a few days all went well; we were most solicitous of each other; carefully we avoided any cause of possible disagreement; we rehearsed to each other the sum of our findings as though we were anxious only to make sure that, no matter what happened to either of us, should one survive, they would not perish.

But under the extreme exertions of our ever-slowing forward-thrust, and under the privations which we had to endure, our mutual solicitude slowly waned again; once more it was each for herself; our communicativeness merged again into a sullen taciturnity; more and more frequently one of us lagged behind while the other ostentatiously pushed forward; the latter blamed the former for delaying progress; the lagging one blamed the other for a lack of consideration. The resentment was borne till it had again reached explosive pressure; and then a quarrel ensued, more violent from time to time and the more demoralizing the less our state of exhaustion permitted us to give vent to our feelings.

Thus matters went from bad to worse; the weaker we grew, the more of our resentment remained unexpressed on each occasion; and what remained unexpressed naturally formed the starting point and nucleus of a new quarrel.

And then we were back in the country of the Ecitons. There, certain findings of ours had been recorded on conspicuously marked trees. Without any express agreement we arranged our marches, which were night marches now, in such a way as to lead us through familiar territory; and as we found that we succeeded beyond our boldest hopes, picking up station after station where, six years ago, we had spent a night or rested for some time, a false semblance of strength returned to us. A great hope beckoned: the hope of finding the friendly formicary of Angza-alla-antra where, we felt sure, we should find rest and food aplenty. This hope united us once more; we struggled on in an almost cheerful spirit. On, on, and on. We conversed again; we even laughed at the idea that, six years ago, we had marched over this same territory, 10,162 strong; and that now we were just two!

On, on, and on. Marching at night; resting in daytime. And then — we were already far into the northern part of the isthmus — I had a terrible revelation. Bissatee, my intimate friend, the companion of all my adventures, was turning traitress!

Though we had struggled on more cheerfully, we had not had anything like a sufficiency of food for months and months. We were mere skeletons; I venture to say that what we now called a night's march would have been little more than an hour's march two years ago. Somehow Bissa-tee had become habituated; mostly we halted because it was I who could not go on. Bissa-tee had often energy enough left to hunt for some sort of food, unsuitable though it might be: Beltian bodies or a little honey or a rare, rare fungus. Whatever she found, I suppose, she meant to share fairly; the fact remained that, whenever she found a supply, she fed on the spot and brought me what was left. How much was needed to support life we had to guess at, for we had long since ceased to feel the pangs of hunger. But it was a fact that Bissa-tee recovered to a certain extent: she was gaining in strength now, if not in weight, while I was still falling off.

At any rate, on the morning on which I made the fateful discovery I had been unable to proceed before the sun rose; and Bissa-tee had rather cheerfully advised me to rest in the crotch of a tree; she herself would go and hunt for food. So far, whenever we had done this, I had promptly gone to sleep; but it so happened that this morning my inability to proceed arose, not so much from excess of fatigue as from a sore foot which pained me badly. So I watched Bissa-tee as she climbed to the ground; and it struck me right then that, the moment she reached the earth, she turned back, not like one who is searching at random, but like one who knows exactly where she is going and what she is after.

Within half an hour she reached a tree north of the resting-place; and she promptly began to run round and round that tree, in an upward spiral, *rescenting a record.* There could be no doubt. The tree was one of those on which, six years ago, we had scented our findings. In my preoccupation with the difficult task of moving I had overlooked it in passing. At once the question flashed through my mind how often a similar thing might not have happened before this, when I had been sound asleep. I watched for Bissa-tee's return; if this was an isolated first occurrence, she would naturally at the first opportunity tell me about it; if she did not, I should have proof that she had done the same thing before and was hiding her purpose from me. Her purpose? There must be a purpose. What was it? There was one explanation, and one only: she counted on returning home *alone* and was making sure that she had all our findings. Why was she counting on returning home alone? Was she predicting an early death for me? From natural causes? Or was she going to make sure that I did not return with her? I was in a state of tremendous excitement. I felt suddenly so tired that I could not have slept; and yet I should have been willing to go to sleep never to rise again. I was weary, weary of life, of everything.

Bissa-tee came back to my resting place and, bringing a small supply of food, wakened me; at least she thought she did. Even then the possibility struck me that she might be administering to me a slow, wasting poison. I did not care. I accepted her regurgitation. I was bound to sound her treason to its utmost depth. For she did not volunteer the slightest hint of her discovery. That secret of the scent-tree she meant to keep to herself. I could have wept.

What can I say? We went on next night, on, on, and on; and the overnext night and every following night, covering less and less ground in every succeeding march; for I did not rest any longer; I watched. Occasionally I saw, late in the night, towards morning, a scent-tree which we had marked on our way out; and intentionally I did not call Bissa-tee's attention to it but proceeded a short distance before I signified my desire to rest for the day. Invariably, as soon as she thought I was asleep, Bissa-tee returned to it and rescented its contents. Never once did she mention the fact to me. But now I waited on my part till, having

returned, she went to sleep and then hurried down to
rescent the tree myself. This in turn exhausted my
strength and retarded our progress. Again several
months went by.

And then, one morning when we climbed a tree to
find a halting-place, I saw the gleam of water ahead:
this was the noble lake at the north end of which we
had enjoyed Angza-alla-antra's hospitality. All thought
of rest was gone, of course. I communicated my discovery
to Bissa-tee; and though the country swarmed with
Ecitons, she did not hesitate a moment. Food, rest, help,
and proper nursing were within our grasp: we must
proceed at once.

In the course of four more hours of a slow, weary
march we arrived at the head of the lake. The Wawaqueensic colony, as both of us remembered with the
utmost distinctness, had been situated a few thousand
antlengths south-east of a rock rising sheer out of the
waters of the lake; and we saw this rock to our left.
Having reached it, we took our bearings with the greatest care; we could not afford to waste a motion. We were
surprised not to have met any Wawaqueenses so far;
for their favourite foraging grounds had been near this
rock. But we reflected that quite likely they had shifted
the scene of their activities to the east or the south.

After a short rest we went on, holding anxiously
to the line on which we had decided. Every three or four
antlengths we had to halt now; for my exhaustion was
extreme; and I could no longer take twenty paces at a
time. And then, directly in the line of our slow advance,
we saw the mound. My heart sank; for no ants were
going out to, or returning from, their labours. Yet we

went silently forward; and at last we reached the first of the main entrance craters on the flat top of the hill.

To our infinite disappointment and grief we found the burrow a perfectly desolate habitation. There were the chambers, it is true; but they were slowly caving in; and there was no sign of a fungus-garden; there was no trace of the once populous tribe that had inhabited it; there was not even a scented record of where they might be found. It would be impossible to describe our sensations after entering this abode: both Bissa-tee and I shed tears.

In our first dismay we simply let ourselves drop to the floor of the last chamber which we had entered in the hope of finding at least a survivor. Neither of us slept; yet sleep, and though it had been a never-ending sleep, would have been the most welcome gift.

But Bissa-tee, who was not nearly as much exhausted as myself, soon began to stir. I did not know what her purpose might be; I did not care. Not without bitterness I thought that, if she was going to hunt for the kind of food on which we had been subsisting, she would most likely return too late to rescue me; but that did not matter, either: I had never withheld from her a single item of our findings; her memory was excellent; and if, perhaps, it did not serve her quite as well as mine did me, at least for the earlier phases of our expedition, she had recently refreshed it by her rescentings of the records left behind. I had now referred everything that happened to us for so long to this one aim only, to take safely home the results of our long and arduous labours, that my own personal fate weighed very light in the balance; and, for the moment at any rate, I only wanted to be left to myself.

Yet, when Bissa-tee returned from her first absence, I accepted regurgitation; but I am afraid I did so in an impatient, ungracious way. Bissa-tee, however, took no notice of it and promptly went out again.

The scanty food which I had imbibed had at least the effect that it put me to sleep; it worked like a powerful soporific. In an indistinct, shadowy way, however, I remained conscious, as though in a dream, of a constant going and coming. When, many hours later, I awoke to a full consciousness of my surroundings, I saw that Bissa-tee had brought in a not inconsiderable quantity of leaf-cuttings which, in one of the garden chambers, she was now engaged in shredding.

I must remind my students of the fact that, before we left our last station in the northern parts of the middle-west of the continent, Azte-ca and Bissa-tee had filled their infrabuccal chambers with large pellets of the hyphæ of our fungus. Azte-ca's pellet had perished with her; but Bissa-tee's, as I mentioned at the time, was so tightly wedged in that we had found it impossible to remove it. We had often tried, of course; for, had we been able to propagate that seed, we should, at least in the south, have had a permanent supply of food; all we should have needed to do was to stop from time to time, to grow our fungi, and, when we moved on again, to take a new pellet of the hyphæ along. But, the pellet having swollen and hardened, we had found it impossible to remove it or even part of it from the chamber; to get it out, a major operation, namely, the removal of the tongue, including the salivary glands, would have been

necessary. Although I am no surgeon, Bissa-tee had
more than once proposed that, under her direction, I
should perform that operation. Three considerations
had kept me from doing so. Firstly, we had no orderlies
left; and they, as is well known, are chosen for the
aseptic properties of their saliva; to perform a major
operation without proper asepsis seemed too risky to
me. Secondly, I feared that the scar-tissue which must
form over the wound would deprive the opening of the
infrabuccal chamber of the elasticity necessary for the
retention of further pellets of hyphæ, so that we should
indeed have had a single supply of the fungi during
our retreat, but no more. Thirdly, we both had our
doubts whether the hyphæ, after having been carried
so long tightly compressed, still retained their viability
the small chance of their doing so did not seem to justify
the risks involved. It was true that, with regard to the
second objection, Bissa-tee had argued that I might
leave the pellets of the three royal perfumes behind and
charge myself with the task of carrying the hyphæ. This
I had been unwilling to do for two reasons. In the first
place, I had still expected I might be in need of these
pellets, at least of one of them. In case of an encounter
with Ecitons, I could, if alone, defeat any number of
enemies by exposing the pellet of the royal perfume of
instant death; for I myself, having carried that other
pellet, of the perfume of royal favour, for so many years
was impregnated with it to such a degree as to be immune from the effects of the mortal perfume; though
any companion of mine would most probably have
shared the fate of the Ecitons. In the second place, I
felt that, if I left them behind, they would cause another

disaster like that worked by the exposure of the body
of that officer who had first given me proof of Assa-ree's
treasonable practices; in fact, the slaughter of all antdom over a considerable area would have borne an even
worse aspect; for the pellet of supreme command would
have deprived the death of hundreds of millions of ants
of its character of suicide; it would have changed it
into murder on my part. For all these reasons I was still
carrying the pellets; and Bissa-tee, the ball of hyphæ.

But when I saw her shredding the leaf-cuttings, I
knew of course that she had made up her mind to induce
or even to force me to perform the operation; and by
this time things had come to such a pass that I did not
see how I could refuse. Dark thoughts accompanied the
recognition of this necessity. Bissa-tee had turned
traitress: if she insisted on having the operation
performed, she was going to do so, not to save me, but
to save herself. She was younger than I was. She stood
a better chance to reach home than I did. On that she
was counting. I could not imagine that her treason
extended to the point where she would actually kill me;
she was not a murderess; but she was not unwilling to
let nature take her course with me after she had done
her utmost to keep me alive long enough to have my help
in carrying the fungi which she could no longer carry
till home was within reach. On the way out it had taken
us a year or longer to reach our present station. We
knew the road now; and no further explorations were
going to cause delay. It would take us perhaps nine,
perhaps only six months to get home. Was I likely to
survive another six months? I thought I was; but per-

haps she did not share that belief; and she was a medical ant.

Such were my thoughts during that day and the three days that followed; for the leaf-shreds had to shrink and to decay before they would support the fungi.

On the fourth morning, having fed me by regurgitation, she approached me with her demand. I consented. Nothing else could be done. She gave me the clearest and minutest directions; and apart from these no communication was exchanged. Then she placed herself in the most favourable position; and in a few minutes I was at work.

The operation was highly successful. When it was finished, I removed the ball of hyphæ and at once tore it apart and placed the best of the roots in contact with the leaf-shreds. Before evening they had begun to grow; but Bissa-tee lay expiring. She had felt sure she would survive; but one of the last things she communicated to me was that, no doubt as a consequence of the utter lack of proper grooming during the last year or two, the wound had turned septic. Then she went on to tell me that she had, of late, often rescented the records which we had left behind on our way out without telling me about it; she had wished, so she averred, to save me all unnecessary trouble; but she wished now to give me a condensed report. This she did. Whether, in this her most solemn hour, she spoke truth or whether she was impelled by an unquiet conscience to give up her secret, I do not know and do not care to surmise. She died by night.

Next morning I had my first meal of fungi. I remained at this station for a full moon. When I set out again, I had discarded two of the three pellets of the royal perfumes and retained only that of instant death; instead of the others I carried a very small ball of fungus hyphæ.

Five months later I arrived at home.

APPENDIX

Note on the habitat and mode of life of Atta Gigantea

As far as is known, the geographical distribution of Atta Gigantea is limited to the interior of central and southern Venezuela and of the northernmost provinces of Brazil where the latter drain into the Orinoco basin.

Atta Gigantea lives in huge, partly hypergean, partly subterranean structures. Most of their older cities number hundreds of thousands of ants. Like all ants they are polymorphic, that is, each tribe is composed of a queen and three castes: the maxims, the mediæ, and the minims. The maxims are the leaders and organizers; the mediæ, the ordinary outdoor workers or leaf-cutters; the minims the indoor workers who attend to the culture of the fungi on which the Attas feed.

Their burrows are many-chambered, the upper ones serving, as it were, as residences; those only slightly below the surface of the ground, as brood-chambers; the deepest, for their fungus-gardens.

Armies of the mediæ, every day, repair to certain acacia trees where they swarm into the foliage to cut circular disks of the leaves which they carry home, to be shredded by the minims and to be inoculated with the hyphæ or spores of the fungus which grows on them. All work is directed and supervised by the maxims.

In their fungus-gardens the leafy substratum forms a huge spongy mass which can be penetrated only by the minute minims who weed and cultivate the fungi and see to it that they remain at a uniform, optimal temperature. To the latter end they open or close perpendicular passages used for no other purpose. Except as a measure of warfare against man no trees but Acacias are ever attacked; and a tree despoiled of its foliage is given time to recuperate before it is attacked again. This fact constitutes the whole race a truly agricultural tribe. As the book proves, their civilization is of the highest order.

THE NEW CANADIAN LIBRARY